A Spoonful of Sugar

A novel

By Amanda Orr

A Spoonful of Sugar is a work of fiction. Names, characters, places and incidents are products of the author's imagination or are used fictitiously. Any resemblance to actual events, locales, or persons, living or dead is entirely coincidental.

Published in the United States by MaGu Publishing.
ISBN-13: 978-0692750216 (MaGu Publishing)
ISBN-10: 0692750215

For permissions: magupublishing@gmail.com

Cover Art by Brett Hyland
Cover Layout and Interior Design by Penoaks Publishing,
http://penoaks.com

For Madeline and Gus

One

Thank God there's a pill for everything. Like the enticingly translucent backlighting of a high-end cosmetics counter, the early light of dawn casts a dim glow on the lineup of capsules neatly perched upon my dresser. Two Advil (for back pain), one B complex (for who knows what . . . memory?), one slender white calcium (bone health), a D vitamin (sunshine in a pill!) and two gag-inducing amber fish gel tabs (I spent extra to get the fermented version, worth the stinky burps, or so they say). I open my mouth and toss them down my gullet, followed by a splash of coffee. *Ahhh*, there we go. One by one, I picture each special little pill giving me a surge of super powers as they slide down my esophagus. I polish off the cup of coffee, take a deep breath and do a few shoulder circles for good measure, just to make sure the medicine goes down.

Now. Where is my body armor? I bought a new pair of Higher Power Spanx® just two days ago, so maybe, just maybe, my smooth buttocks could spread a little Zen and confidence up north.

I root around in my underwear drawer. Searching, digging and clawing my way deeper into the vast pit of granny panties, worn out bras, bleach-stained pajamas and graying athletic socks, but I can't find them. Hot pink packaging, cute front cover design featuring sassily illustrated women who look totally confident and in control: that needs to be me! Where did they go!? I had them, right *here*, less than 48 hours ago. My airway tightens as if one of my supplements has just flipped ninety degrees and is now straddled inside my throat like a two-by-four. My fingers churn through meaningless, useless items of clothing like a hamster burrowing through sawdust. Lacy thongs? *Why?* A strapless bra? Was there ever actually a time where *that* supported these sand bags??? I just need this *one simple thing* and then everything will be okay. A few more frantic moments and *voila!* My hands triumphantly grab hold of the sturdy cardboard, and I exhale loudly in an orgasmic cry of relief.

It's possible I'm putting too much stock in the whole body shaper situation.

I lean against the dresser, take a deep breath and balloon out my cheeks like a puffer fish. What am I supposed to be doing again? 'Leaning in' to my modern challenges of 'having it all,' or should I 'lean back' and just start pill popping and drinking heavily? My mother's generation had it easy: become a teacher, a nurse or stay at home. No trying to rule the world or have it all – which may have resulted in a little too much control of the children, and later in life, living vicariously through your children. Grandma worked hard on the farm and never gave a second thought to baking pies from scratch, hand-sewing Halloween costumes or having a pot roast on the table every Sunday. Did either of my female role models suffer from chronic existential dilemmas around whether or not they were pursuing their passion? No. Their rules were clear. But mine are murky -- the choices are too many, and the unwanted advice from "experts" is everywhere -- and still, I'm not really sure I know what I'm doing. Except for today. I'm going back to work, and I refuse to torment myself by playing out eerily realistic scenarios in my head in which I fuck everything up and come home to one repo man driving the car away and another slapping a foreclosure sticker on our front door. That's not my life, I remind myself, although sometimes it feels as if it would be all too easy to recreate.

I flick on the light inside my tiny closet and survey my 40-year-old body in the full-length mirror behind the door. I'm well-equipped with a few laugh lines around the eyes, a tired but still vibrant sparkle in my eyes, a barely detectable hint of gray around my temples that shimmers when the light hits it at certain angles, and the boobs . . . well, what can I say about the boobs? Not *so* bad considering they've been sucked on for a total of 30 months in the past four years.

I open up the package, step into leg #1 and strain to pull it up to mid-thigh. I stand up, breathe a deep sigh and immediately have a flashback to lying down on my bed at age 16 straining to close the zipper on my Guess jeans. But just as my mind starts to calculate how many more years I have to go squeezing my body into clothing before I give up and start wearing a Mrs. Roper muumuu around the house, I'm distracted by the sight of my thigh in the mirror: the Spanx looks more like a leg tourniquet than a body shaper. Is that even healthy to wear all day, I wonder? Will the extra blood flow rush to my cranium and make me smarter at work, or will it put me at risk for an aneurysm?

I realize now that Spanx are actually for skinny people who simply want to avoid underwear lines, so I ever so briefly consider taking them off, but then I decide against it. The promise of looking svelte-ish in a pencil skirt and heels while parading baby Max through the office is a temptation too great. And in my business, perception is everything.

The last time anyone from the office saw me was six months ago. Bundled up in a maternity raincoat and aubergine rain boots, I waved goodbye as I boarded a waiting ambulance after my water broke suddenly two weeks before my due date. I had never before worn the rain boots to work, but since they had become somewhat of a fashion statement, I decided to use it to my advantage since my pregnant feet were busting out over the edges of most of my regular shoes. I was thankful for the excuse to hide the swollen bricks they had become.

Rain boots, water breaking; a flood of tears. This is the last image my colleagues have of me before my boss, the ever-slippery ad agency owner, Slade, called 911 and shooed me out into the lobby. *"You gotta leave now, Moore. You don't want to be one of those dreadful women they feature on the news who deliver on the I-5."* Oh well, I've got to hand it to him for not bothering me on leave, not even once. The poor man must be pulling his finely coiffed hair out by now.

But my rebranding campaign begins today. If Bill Clinton can shake Monica Lewinsky and Alec Baldwin can shake the fat little piggy voicemail, I can shake a little end of pregnancy fall from grace.

I take a deep breath, lift my right leg and slowly shimmy it into the vice-like contraption (which, for the record, I don't think I would be exaggerating to say that it would even be too tight on baby Max's thunder thighs). I wiggle my hips from side to side to give myself a little momentum, add a few quick hops, suck in my gut as best as I can – and *ohhailmaryfullofgrace*, the torture trap has made it over my hips. *Phew.* A few beads of sweat form at my hairline, but I'm otherwise unscathed.

I look over to see my six-month-old, Max, stirring in his sleep, laying on his back in a pose that looks like he's about to make a snow angel. I should have put him back in his crib after the last feeding, but since Patrick left for his business trip at 3 a.m., there was plenty of room in bed. Nothing disturbs Max after he's been fed - breast milk is like infant Ambien for him. He's been the easiest baby of the three since the day he was born. Sleep, eat, coo; wash, rinse, repeat. Part of me wants to dive into bed with him and gnaw on his thighs for a few minutes, or another few months.

But I can't. I have to keep moving. Gloria Steinem, Betty Friedan, and my Alma Mater, Smith College will be sorely disappointed if I don't kick some serious leadership butt and haul my ass back to the office to claim my seat at the table.

I hop into our bathroom and dab a little rejuvenating serum on my cheeks while trying to avoid touching anything else. Patrick's sink is covered with a bubbly mousse-like film of dried toothpaste spit sprinkled with tiny black hairs from the electric razor -- the debris of several days worth of hasty morning and evening routines. Boxer shorts lie in a heap on the floor, on top of a soaked through diaper that missed the diaper genie, a bloodied band aid draped over it from a scooter accident and a toy fishing pole with a gummy worm dangling from the hook – the entertainment from last night's bath with the kids. "Embrace the mess." Isn't that what Nora Ephron said? But ah, that would be so much easier to do if I had just one nanny to help me embrace it. I dare not imagine the possibilities… a magical, Mary Poppins-like nanny equipped with a carpetbag and a wet vac. Sigh.

I walk over to the shades and gently undo the cord and raise them up two more folds. Morning light gently tiptoes across Max's face. He's blissfully unaware of the adrenaline surging through my body. It's shooting out of me like lightening streaks and I feel like it's the first day of school, not the return to the job I've had for more than a decade. Ending maternity leave shouldn't cause this much anxiety that's for sure.

I brush it off to focus on the things that need to happen in short order before I do "the baby walk" through the office. It was a tradition at the agency, and if you didn't do it, no one believed you were coming back. It said, "look at me, I can do it all– I can have babies and I can come back to work!" Fathers of course did not have to do the baby walk. But even in this day and age, no one trusted a woman to come back, even if you had already done it with babies #1 and/or #2, or rather, *especially* if you had already done it with one and two. Even my own mother, who had three children of her own, doubted me. "Forty and having another baby and going back to work? Maybe you should think about scaling back and let Patrick step up to the plate a bit more," she said… day after day. It took all my self-restraint to not say, how'd that work out for you, Mom? But I didn't. It was mean. And Patrick was different . . . and I was different. I sold Swedish fish and Cokes to the kids at the pool snack bar at 14, cleaned out the fitting rooms at Nordstrom at 16, graduated to the drive through window at McDonalds at 17, and then at 18, I was off to college where I restocked the stacks in the library. I had always shown up and earned my way, and I was going to do the same today. Max's adorable thighs would have to wait.

I hop down the stairs and round the corner into the kitchen. I decide to run outside and grab the paper before I get the girls' breakfast ready. *National Unemployment on the Rise, Boeing Shutters Plant, Seattle Targeted to Play Major Role in Seasonal Affective Disorder Study . . .*

I don't need to read beyond the headlines to know its time to go back to work. I snap back into morning mode, checking email with one hand while whisking eggs with the other.

Oh. No.

Today the headline simply says, "outbreak." Last week it was strep throat and yesterday it was lice. *Ugh.*

I click open the latest missive from Sandi, the director of the Children's Creative Development Center a.k.a. the CCDC, or as I like to refer to our daycare, the CDC.

To: All Parents
From: Sandi Peterson
Date: September 4
Subject: Outbreak (and reminder: early closing today!)

Good morning CCDC parents! Please *don't read the rest of this note if you are enjoying your breakfast. Ready? Ok then. No need to panic, and I'm sorry in advance for the gory details, but I need to tell you that we have two confirmed cases of pinworms in the Dolphin room. Pinworms live in the stool of humans and lay their eggs around the opening of the anus. If your child is waking between 10 p.m. and midnight complaining of an itchy bottom, they may have pinworms. That's the time the little buggers like to come out and lay their eggs. If you suspect a case, you can check stool floating in the toilet to look for the very small thread-like worms. Or an easier way is to have your child kneel in bed after complaining about itching with his/her bottom in the air. Shine a flashlight as you spread the cheeks apart (a helper is useful here) and you'll likely see the little rascals in short order. Asking your child to "push a little" as if they are trying to poop will likely make it all too obvious. One of the many joys of parenthood, I know! ; -) Happy Hunting!*

Oh, and P.S. - A friendly reminder that our staff training begins at 4 p.m. today. In order for us to start on time, please arrive no later than 3:45 p.m. You will be charged $20 per minute for each child here past 4 p.m. Have a great day!!!

Thanks so much Sandi with an "*i*." Could you have given *me* a little more notice?

As I type "pinworms" into Google, I can hear Franny begin to stir. The birds are squawking outside and a muddy hue has begun to fill the kitchen. I make a mental note to replace the light bulbs.

"Mommeee, Mommee . . . Mommeeeeeeeeeeee . . . "

I run upstairs to Franny's room to see her standing up rattling the crib rails. She's ripped off her pajama bottoms and flung the diaper across the room. She sees me and immediately throws her arms out. As soon as I embrace her to lift her up I realize her pajama top is fully soaked through with urine.

Lucy, my sophisticated beyond-her-years four year-old, appears in the doorway with tears galloping down her face. And then, as if on cue, Max lets out a wail. With a wet-bottomed Franny on one hip, a screaming baby on the other, and Lucy frantically tugging on my skirt, I catch a glance of my urine-soaked self in the mirror. This will give a whole new meaning to *eau de toilette* if I show up at the office with this shirt on. If all else fails I can sell stock images of the family online I think. GETTY IMAGES KEYWORD SEARCH: Frazzled Working Mother Circa 2016.

And now, we interrupt this program for an important commercial break.

A Nanny Fantasy, by Anna Moore.
A double-tall latte for me in one hand and a carpetbag full of tricks in the other (the selection of which is always appropriate depending on the exact time and occasion— today, for example, the tote may contain a new roll of adhesive tape for tonight's anus checks, a new outfit for Franny and perhaps an Ativan for me), she arrives at my home in a fashionable, yet functional protective Hazmat suit

designed exclusively for nannies of her skill and stature. She drops the kids off at daycare in her waterproof flying umbrella and picks them up with time to spare, never incurring a late charge.

She's my very own Personal Mary Poppins™.

Not available in stores.

Back to our regularly scheduled program.

Montlake Boulevard is moving at a snail's pace – make that a snail recovering from knee surgery. *Supercaliclusterfuckalicious.* I bang my fist against the steering wheel and roll down the window to air out my nerves. In a mere 14 days, the 35,000 students who attend the University of Washington will add to the congestion, clogging this two-mile stretch even more.

Brrrring. Before I can react, Lucy has unsnapped her seat belt and grabbed my cell phone out of my purse in the front seat.

"Hi Nana, We're going to daycare!" She enthusiastically says before going silent. The silence means my mother is lecturing Lucy, who will then lecture me, about why I need daycare at all, when I have my dear old mum down the road. I dare not say that agreeing to let her watch Max alone is the only leap of faith I can handle right now.

"Give me the phone, Lucy," I say hoping to intercede before Lucy can mention any number of things that will cause my mother to go off on a tangent such as the reason for Patrick's business trip, or why I'm going into work when I have one more week of leave. "The light's green, have you fallen asleep?!?!," I snap at the car in front of me before taking it from her hand. "Not you, Lucy," I whisper.

"Mom, hi there, I'm heading into work, can I call you later?" I say before hitting the mute button so she doesn't hear me honking. Honest to god do these people have anywhere to go?

"Sweetie, remember that song that we used to listen to on the way to school? I was just trying to remember the name of it and I can't. It's on the tip of my tongue."

"*Stardust*, Mom. Is there anything else? You know, I *am* in the car, which means, I'm on my cell phone, and you always tell me not to talk on the phone while I'm driving."

"Oh you shouldn't! I know. Please tell me you won't text and drive. I saw the saddest story today about a ..."

"MOM, you called ME, on my cell phone, remember."

"Ok, I'll call you later, sweetie. I love you, you're the best Mom, sweetie, and you work so hard, remember that. Don't let the traffic upset you. You'll get there."

I'm about to hang up when I remember about the early close. I decide to kill two birds with one stone and give my mother a bit of company and not worry about the threatened fine just in case I take longer at work than planned. But before I can ask, she adds, "Ok, well, I'm going to go take one of those marijuana cookies now. It really does make my eyes feel better you know."

Ok, then. A grandmother high on cookies is not exactly what my kids need today. If I had a nanny, I would have left for work two hours ago, wouldn't have had to shower twice and change clothing, thrice. Six months of breastfeeding must have wiped out my memory of what a fucking nightmare this race in the morning can be.

I look at the clock as I search for parking somewhere in the vicinity of the CCDC. 9:57. Oy. I've been up for three hours, and I already feel the need for a nap.

There's an orange note taped to the glass door with hand-drawn balloons on it when we finally arrive. "What does the note say?" asks Lucy, not looking up. "Does somebody have lice again?"

The regularity with which these girls see certain words has actually made for good phonics lessons. L is for Lice, W is for Worms, V is for

Virus, P is for Projectile; T is for Tummy Bug. I should really come up with my own line of flash cards.

"No," I say, "It's just a note from Miss Sandi – school's closing early today."

Sandi waves to us. "Good morning, ladies!" she says brightly through frosted pink lips. A shimmery white shadow following the full length of her brows gives her an extra awake look today. I spy her feet as she wobbles toward the door. Teetering on three-inch spike heels, Sandi looks more dressed for a cougar cruise than a morning of getting jiggy with a bunch of toddlers.

"Don't forget the late fee today, Anna!" she chirps, waving a finger at me, "I'm sure the girls would rather have that money for haircuts or new fall clothes. Have a great day!"

Maybe a toking grandmother really isn't so bad after all.

Max is poised to charm, sitting up straight and alert as I wheel him out of the elevator bank. The glow from Suite 200 is almost blinding. I pause, take a deep breath and mentally ground myself before grabbing the handle and propelling myself through the heavy glass doors, pushing the stroller towards the boob-high stark white desk. It looked like something out of Star Trek, thanks to Slade's desire for an atmosphere that felt "modern" and "edgy" when he rebranded the agency five years ago. I cautioned him that it might come off as too extreme for some of our more traditional clients, but he wouldn't listen, telling me to stick to client campaigns and leave the interior decorating to him. I still cringe every time I see the blazing yellow YOWZ logo, another one of Slade's brilliant ideas. Yellow to grab attention. Y meant to make the client say yes. O and W for "oh, wow" and z because market research proves that any name with an x or a z sound is memorable for the customer. We used to be McAllister &

Chamberlain. Simple. Understated. Classic. Seattle-friendly. But when then Creative Director Mike Chamberlain left to "pursue other projects" and sold his portion of the company back to his partner, Slade went for a complete overhaul. I knew better than to argue for McAllister & Moore (or even jokingly suggest something nonsensical like "MAM" or "McOore,"). Even though I'd been granted the Creative Director title upon Mike's departure, Slade made it clear that he would never *ever* share ownership of the agency again, "unless the right man came along." He actually said this, loudly, in front of me during a Seattle Ad Club luncheon. I remember rubbing my temples, gulping some ice water and thinking, as I looked up at the conference room chandeliers, that I had just hit the glass ceiling.

I wheel Max over to the side of the reception desk so I can sneak up on Gloria and show off the goods. But she isn't there. Instead there's someone who I can only imagine is striving for a Marilyn Manson-as-receptionist look. I make a note to tell Slade that we're going for "yowz," not "yikes! I pray that Gloria is on vacation and that this woman made a wrong turn looking for the tattoo parlor.

"Are you new?" I ask, tentatively.

She ignores the question and rolls her eyes. "Who are you?" she responds with a curl in her upper lip, which reveals teeth in an unsightly shade of gray.

"Well," I say firmly. "I'm Anna Moore." Surely she's heard of me. "And this is Max." I lean over to brush his hair from his eyes.

Instead of saying "How lovely to meet you," or standing up to shake my hand, or any other gesture that might be appropriate if the boss just showed up at the office, Marilyn says, "And who are you are here to see?"

"I'm here to see my office… I'm the creative director," I say as I grasp the stroller handles and head past her desk and down the hallway.

She's careens her head from behind the reception desk and leans so far over I wonder how she hasn't fallen completely out of her chair. I hear zippers and chains clamoring around the armrests. "You can't go back there without an escort," she scolds. "The creative director is in a meeting now," she shouts at my back.

I halt the stroller to a stop. Maybe there's some sort of logical explanation . . . like she's the daughter of a very important new client, or Slade's new Dominatrix perhaps, and she hasn't heard my name because she's been locked up in the playroom. I wouldn't have this problem if my name were part of the logo, I think. I take a deep breath, turn around and present the friendliest smile I can muster.

"I'm sorry. I didn't catch your name," I say.

"Miranda," she spits out, momentarily sidelined.

"Well, *Miranda*," I say, sweetly but firmly. "I'm sorry that Slade didn't let you know I was coming. But we'll be going to my office now." I march on, feeling her daggers pointing at my back and hearing her pounding digits on the phone. I try to shake the feeling that I need to walk more quickly or duck into a storage closet or something. Sheesh. I WORK HERE I want to shout, not only to Miranda but to remind myself.

The hallway to my office is lined with framed posters of our best work: the home grown coffee company gone global, technology startups that were fostered in the shadow of Amazon and Microsoft, retailers and fashion stars. In the past ten years I've worked on most of these campaigns and the posters remind me of how much I've shaped the agency, and how we have grown from local boutique to an agency on the cusp of national recognition.

I look down at Max, who is slumped down in his seat a bit. I fish a rattle out of my purse and hand it to him. "Here you go, baby."

"Did someone say baby?" I turn around, and Lauren is standing behind me drowning in a stack what looks like bound presentations. Lauren, my dream assistant, the one I can always count on. And I feel at home again. But her mouth is squished into a smile that looks like she's covering a bitter taste. And her eyes look startled. But then she seems to relax just as quickly.

"Anna," she exclaims as her eyes truly light up. "Oh it's so good to see you… I had no idea you were coming." She puts down her papers, and we hug on each other for a few moments and then she kneels down to squeeze Max's cheeks and tickle his tummy, which he loves.

"Well, I figured it was time to dip my toes back into the pool so Monday's not such a rude awakening. You didn't get my message?"

Lauren stands up suddenly, as if she just remembered something left on the stove. "Well, I'm not sure I did honestly. It's been so busy I must have missed it."

She looks down at her stack of presentations, picks them up and hugs them to her chest. "Have you talked to Slade? Does he know you're coming back?"

"I left him a message too, but I'm just going to pop into my office, clear out whatever's accumulated over the past couple months and then go see him," I say. Lauren starts to look behind her as if check with someone, but then just smiles without saying anything. I feel myself getting flush and try to will my body temperature to cool down. I can feel the redness creeping up my neck and face and a beads of sweat searching for escape between my skin and the Spanx. Max is starting to squirm.

"Slade's not here today. He's out on a golfing trip with some new potential client. He says it's a big one, so Monday's probably the best day for a pop in," she says. "But I can tell him you came by? Or do you want to try him on his cell?"

My office is a mere four doors down from where we are standing, but it's now painfully clear that Lauren is encouraging me to head home, to not go those extra steps. *My* Lauren. Lauren who always has my back and always looks out for my best interests is now signaling that I should get out of here. "You know Lauren, it's been a long day for us already, believe it or not, with the accident on I-5 this morning. I'm just going to go sit down and check my mail," I say as I steer the stroller around her. "Plus it will be good for Max to get out of the stroller for a bit."

Rather than wait for her to object, I move full speed ahead and see that the "fish tank" as we call the conference room because of the glass walls, is filled to the brim. It's like a party is going on with everyone on my team. I turn the corner and ram the stroller right into someone.

"Ow, ow, ow, ow!" Clare falls back and rocks back and forth in a little ball, grimacing wildly and clutching his shin. Clarence, or Clare as he likes to be called, is the lead copywriter on my team. He moonlights as an actor in one of Seattle's fringe theater troupes so any encounter with him, even one that doesn't involve physical injury, is usually pretty dramatic. Max giggles and squeals, delighted by the performance.

"Oh gosh, I'm so sorry," I say, leaning over to extend a hand. "Are you okay?"

Clare looks up, and it takes him a moment to register my face from under his long bangs. Still on the floor, he takes his slender fingers and carefully adjusts his hair before responding. "Oh. Hello Anna. What brings you here?"

"I'm back!" I proclaim, squaring my shoulders and looking down at Max, ever proud of my accomplishments. "Time flies when you're lost without your leader, right?" But the joke falls flat.

Clare looks at Max and back up at me with a puzzled look, rubbing his leg.

"Well, I'm officially back on Monday, but I was in the neighborhood so thought I'd stop by." I'm hoping my cheer pulls him up off the floor, so I can scoot inside my office. I smile apologetically. "I didn't think anyone would be in my office so I just charged in. Sorry about that."

I take a step forward and see my desk. It's cluttered with bobble heads, snow globes, stacks of files, and then beyond, multiple photos of Clare and his boyfriend Stu, arm-in-arm, grinning in their matching fleece vests and neatly trimmed beards.

I take a step back and glance at the door. The nameplate says Clarence Hall.

Clare scrambles to his feet and turns to Lauren. "Are these the presentations? Bring them to the conference room so we can start the meeting" he says and he's off without another word.

Dumbfounded, I don't move. Suddenly my fingers hurt, and I look down to see that my knuckles have turned white from clenching the stroller handles.

I look at Lauren, and before I can find the words even to say, 'what the hell is going on,' she jumps in.

"Slade appointed Clare interim creative director when this opportunity came in and asked him to organize the team to get ready for next week. Don't worry," she adds, with a sweet smile that conveys more of an "I'm sorry" expression than "Gotcha, you've been punk'd."

"What's next week?" Steam is going to shoot out of my ears any second.

"Some big pre-meeting with the client in San Francisco. I've got to get to this meeting, but call me this weekend if you want," her words drifting behind her and she heads into the Fish Tank.

I'm about to plot my verbal assault on Slade when my phone starts ringing. I look down. It's Sandi from the CCDC. She's never once called me on my cell phone and has specifically told parents she would only call our mobiles in case of emergency.

I step away from the doorway so I'm out of earshot. "Oh, hi Anna" she says. Her voice is syrupy, yet grave, so I can't place the tone although I can sense her teetering uneasily on her stilettos.

Calls from daycare normally start with the reassuring words, "Everyone's fine so don't worry, but . . . , " but this call does not start that way and I can tell in the first two seconds that something is amiss.

"What happened?" I dive in. "Is everything all right?" I feel my breath shortening.

"Well . . . not exactly," she starts, her voice about to crack. Alarms go off in my head. Shit.

I put my hand up against the wall, bracing myself. My mind immediately goes to my two nightmare scenarios: First, the children have been kidnapped and are being held for ransom— although whenever I panic (which is more often than I'd like to admit) about dropping the kids at a building downtown, Patrick reminds me that neither Bill Gates, nor Jeff Bezos have children, nieces, nephews, or children of their household staff who attend the CCDC so its simply not a target. The second is that one or both of them have toppled head first out of the indoor tree house that I have been lobbying for years to remove. Despite the fact that it's made of fake wood, I swear the thing is rotting, and the children act like little Tarzans swinging in and out of it instead of properly using the flimsy ladder. I visualize my two precious daughters lying lifeless on the floor below the tree house, dead on impact. Instinctively, I clutch my chest.

"I'm really sorry . . . " Sandi stammers, "there's a bit of a situation here . . . I'm calling all parents . . . I don't want anyone to panic but . . . "

Panic?

"I'll need you to pick up Lucy and Franny as soon as possible."

Referring to them in present tense! They are both still alive so my panic goes down a notch while my annoyance goes up.

"What happened exactly?" I say..

"Well, I'd rather not get into it on the phone . . . can you just—"

"Just . . . what?"

"The police are here, and—"

"The POLICE?" I shriek.

"Yes. And the Health Department is . . . "

I don't wait for her to finish. Police? Health Department?

I dash into the conference room, retrieve Max out of Lauren's arms, blurt something about a daycare emergency and run down the hallway, pushing the stroller with one hand, clutching Max under my other arm like a football. The stroller whirs and zigzags along the carpet. Max starts to cry. As I pass my office I give the stroller an extra shove so it spins ahead a few feet ahead of me. I reach my free arm out and rip off Clare's nameplate. I say nothing to Miranda as I rush past her and through the glass doors, but I can see her smug grin out of the corner of my eye as I frantically punch the down button on the elevator.

Sweat is pouring out from along my hairline and my chest is heaving up and down. I don't know if the Spanx will be able to hold it all in.

Two

B.M. (Before Max), Slade was never afraid to call no matter what time of day or night with his ludicrous insights into current clients, hoped-for clients, or anything that he could potentially pass from his plate to mine so he could get back to his main job of schmoozing. His methods were actually to be admired. I had worked with him for seven years and he could still seduce me – strictly in a professional manner of course – with his televangelist meets Oprah style. He could fill me with a sense of urgency and purpose, while also somehow getting me to tackle the lion's share of the work.

Even so, I had never minded taking his calls, because he always took mine. But now he's ignoring me, even my most recent assertive, yet-veering-into-bitchy and inappropriate email.

Patrick is still away wooing potential investors for his company, so I made this decision on my own. Well, that's not entirely true. Lucy and Franny fully supported the decision and helped with the advertising campaign.

"I want her to be pretty," Lucy had said, resting her chin on my shoulder as I crafted the Craigslist nanny ad not long after our narrow escape out of the CCDC. "Like Barbie. Or a Bratz Doll!"

"Don't be sexist girls. You know, the best candidate could be a Manny," I said, pausing to see how that would gel with my Mary Poppins daydream. Maybe Matt Damon meets Jon Stewart meets Hugh Jackman? Days filled with liberal indoctrination followed by some song and dance wrapped up in a nice package for my eyes to rest on at the end of a long day. "Ok, Franster, how about you?" I asked, fingers poised over the keyboard like a concert pianist.

"Hmmm . . . " twirled Franny before pausing on her tiptoes. "I want a faywee pwincess!"

"That's right, with a magical wand and all. Ok, Max? How 'bout you?"

Max blew bubbles and muttered something that sounded like *shujjsh*.

I decided to round out the kids' requests with an ad that could have won a CLIO for its copywriting creativity that included stellar subliminal messaging that relayed that we were a most desirable family to work for. Regardless of whether I liked my job, crafting messages was now a part of my being.

But then, the first response to my ad had me doubting my professional skills.

"I write for my cusin. She is good with child. Does not have computer so I write for her. Please call. What do you pay?"

Perhaps with all my years at daycare I missed the secret memo on where to post nanny ads. Then the second response came in:

"Hi, I love kids! I am free right away, except for the last two weeks in September, Tuesday and Thursday afternoons until May and the entire month of December. What do you pay?

Just as I began revising the ad copy, the third response comes in . . .

"We hope you'll consider our nanny placement service for your childcare needs. Don't trust the care of your children to just anyone. We provide complete background checks, reference checking and CPR training. We guarantee a placement with a loving nanny who will become a part of your family. WeeCare

Nannies requires a small initiation fee and then we can meet with you in person to hear more about the particular needs of your children."

After the first two dismal responses I had actually gone to check out the WeeCare Nannies website but decided that the "small" initiation fee of $5,000 could provide me with a well-deserved spa vacation. And besides, Patrick would put the kibosh on $5,000 faster than I could say nanny cam.

With my fantasy of receiving a response to my Craigslist ad from a Julie Andrews-type nanny fading fast, and my need to get back to work in less than two days, time was of the essence.

So I was ecstatic to receive a fourth, promising response later that night:

Hello, I read your posting and it sounds exactly like what I've been looking for! I'm going to school part-time at UW and my focus is in early childhood education. I am originally from Colombia but have lived in Seattle for the past four years. I would love the opportunity to hear more about you and your children and take care of them!

Sincerely, Maria

Her email handle wasn't anything overtly disturbing like the other ones from gothgoethe@me.com or lonelover@hotmail.com and there weren't any glaring spelling errors or immediate pleas for cash, so I wrote back, "you had me at early childhood education!"

Not my exact words, but I did request an interview for the very next day. Hopeful that my sense of urgency would not dissuade her from meeting me, I thought to myself: If I can't have Julie Andrews, at least I might be able to snag Maria.

Now, just a few blocks away from the Starbucks where I am about to meet my potential nanny-in-waiting, I'm at a loss for words. I had assumed my years of experience interviewing would-be employees at work would translate into an easy Q & A session, but now I'm not so sure. What do I say to this woman?

"Seen any good Red Cross training videos lately?"

"When was the last time you washed your hands?"

"True or false? Talking on your cell phone while feeding a baby is appropriate."

"How familiar are you with pinworm anus checks?"

I had never had anyone watch the children alone besides my mother. Now, with only one traffic light left between me and my potential savior-in-waiting, I make a silent prayer, please let her be perfect.

It's an unusually hot day for the first week of September in Seattle. "Heat wave" is what the newscasters will pronounce on the evening broadcast, which means the temperature has hovered above 80 degrees for two days straight. Tomorrow the rain might set in, or maybe today, but in any case, it could be May before I see the sun again. *Enjoy this*, I tell myself, summer is coming to an end, and so is my maternity leave.

I look down and adjust Max's cap to keep the sun out of his eyes just as I start to see a wince creeping onto his face. I quickly follow up with some deep knee bends, the sure-fire fix to avoiding a red light tantrum. Up, down, up, down, up, down. I sacrifice my comfort and endure my sticky butt flesh hitting the back of my upper thigh with each up and down. At least I'm down two kids thanks to Mom. She took Lucy and Franny for the afternoon so I could attend to my most pressing needs. I can only hope she's not on the cookies today.

Green light. Out of nowhere, the wind picks up, causing me to stumble forward slightly. Strands of dirty hair blow in my eyes and mouth. I charge ahead. So what if I wing it during this interview? I am now more certain than ever that we need this. What was a mere hassle with two kids -- getting them dressed, packing their snacks, lunches and bottles, trailblazing at work, cooking dinner, drawing baths, trimming nails, and reading stories — has grown into a sometimes colossal nightmare with three kids and a traveling husband. And it's all because I've been doing it without the help of a nanny, manny, mother's helper, sitter, or anything else remotely resembling in-home help. What our family desperately needs is a governess. Forget the "do it all" debate! All I need to do is delegate. I should have done this sooner!

The line at Starbucks is out the door. I push my shoulders back and march on. I bypass the line and ease halfway into the glass door when a man grumbles, "The line ends outside Ma'am."

Ma'am? Really? This guy needs a hearty lashing and a lesson on the proper use of the word. It should be forbidden until you can safely assume a woman is in her sixties, and even then, would it kill you to humor her and simply say, "excuse me, Miss?"

And then I see her.

Glossy black hair cascades down her back covering most of a camouflage tank top. Hot pink three-quarter length cargo pants flaunt toned, tanned legs (and what I'm quite certain are Candies circa 1980 four inch cork wedge heels). Dangling down her side is one of those enormous trash bag style purses that young Hollywood starlets carry. Not *exactly* what I imagined as my nanny in shining armor.

As I stand propped up against the door wondering whether to flee or stay, the wind picks up again, sending hats and sunglasses flying onto the sidewalk and clattering against the windows. The line momentarily dissipates and Maria turns around. I have the advantage—I've seen photos of her but she hasn't seen any of me. But when her eyes meet mine, she raises her hand and waves me over without a hint of hesitation.

"Anna!"

I wave back. I must have "desperately seeking nanny" scrawled across my face. Either that or she has magical abilities. "That could come in handy, I think as I push through the crowd to the front of the line.

"Hey! So glad I saw you! Scoot in here," she says, grabbing my arm and literally pulling me in front of her so that I am now facing the cashier. "Good thing you're here. I was about to hop out of line and get back in at the end."

Before I can even say, "Hi," or "Nice to meet you," or "Wow, you look even more lively in person," Maria leans around my shoulder and, flashing an enormous, sparkly smile, says to the barista, "Tazo green tea creme Frappucino, please. Oh, and with a little whipped cream on top please." With her hands planted on my shoulder, she shimmies out from behind me and plants herself firmly in the waiting area by the coffee bar. It's a good ten feet away, and I'm left standing solo in front of the register.

I make a mental note that for Patrick, who hates going to Starbucks because he absolutely cannot stand people who order complicated fussy beverages instead of black coffee, the interview would have started and ended with Maria's order. But for me, the meeting begins with me paying the $9.60 for our drinks.

We collect our coffees and Maria leads me to an outdoor table, teetering slightly on her heels along the way. With her whipped tea in hand, she smiles over her shoulder at me as if we are old college buddies who haven't seen each other in years and have lots to catch up on. Her earnest smile is full and innocent, her eyebrows are raised, and she lifts and squeezes her shoulders as if she's about to pop with some exciting gossip and can't get to me fast enough. But then she sits down and says absolutely nothing. Instead she just dives into her frap and sips coquettishly as her eyeballs move from me to Max and me to Max again.

Maria continues slurping and smiling up at me like a pre-teen with her first Shirley temple. She dislodges herself from the straw long enough to say, "I totally knew it was you when I saw you standing there with Max."

"Hmm, interesting" I reply. It's not really a conversation starter, and I'm ready to dive into the substance. But she goes on.

"I mean, I wasn't completely sure. You look so young and so pretty, so for a minute I thought maybe you were a nanny and not a mom."

Ridiculous. I'm about to tell her that she's completely full of shit and that embellished flattery as an interview tactic will *not* work, well, probably not, when she pauses and says with a completely straight face:

"But you look mostly like you looked on TV, but maybe a little more relaxed today."

"Oh Jesus," I say, and then cup Max's ears after the fact. My eyelids lower in humiliation. I've been caught . . . and by my potential nanny no less. Advantage Maria.

"No, no, you did great," Maria leans in and smiles reassuringly. "For real! I mean, how awful for you that your daycare got shut down, and how nasty how it happened. Yuck."

Agreed. I feel the tendons in my shoulder blades relax one tiny notch. I look down and cradle the base of my iced coffee, turning it around in my fingers. "Thanks," I say. I look up at her and pause, "Can I ask you something though before we move on?"

"Oh, sure, sure," she says, voice full of compassion and concern. I almost trust her.

"Did you actually see me on TV or was it . . . "

"YouTube," she nods. "The extended version."

I throw my hands over my eyes and look down at the ground. "Ugh . . . " I moan. I was hoping that she might have missed this unexpected repeat performance.

"But it's good!" Maria reaches over to touch my shoulder. "Don't you think? I thought those guys did a really nice job mixing it together. I think it's up to almost a million hits by now! Let me check."

Before I can stop her, Maria pulls out her phone, and I hear the familiar beat to "My Daycare is a Shit Box."

My daycare . . . m-m-my d-d-d-aycare . . . m-m-my d-d-d-daycare is a shhhi-i-i-it. M-m-m-my d-d-aycare is a sh-i-i-i-i-t b-b-b-b-b-b-b-b-o-x . . .

My voice is auto tuned over the deep beat of the electronic base. I hold my hand up as if to gesture a time out and furtively look around me to see if anyone is staring at us. I shake my head in a downward spiral as Max begins to kick to the beat of the music.

M-m-m-m-m-y d-d-d-d-d—d-d—d-d-d-d-d-dayyy . . .

The local cable news station was already outside the doors of the CCDC by the time I arrived in a frantic mess to pick up Franny and Lucy. Somebody had obviously tipped them off as to what was going down. Members of the Health Department in full protective gear were busy containing the "contamination site" as police rounded up all of the children on the other side of yellow caution tape. I didn't have all the details of what *exactly* had happened, but I'd seen enough to be freaked. *All* the parents were furious. But the only one "savvy" enough to talk to the media? That would be me. I thought my offhand comment about my daycare being a germy cesspool shit-box was merely an off-the-record rant. Despite considering myself somewhat of a media maven, my emotions got the better of me, and even so, where was I when the FCC began allowing broadcasters to air the word "shit" on television?!?! Apparently the bleep button is now only used for true emergencies like the "C" or "F" word. (Not that I would know after watching PBS kids for years.) In any event, I wasn't at my best. My face was blotchy, my points were all over the place in an incoherent tirade and, worst of all, a roll of fat had pushed its way out of my Spanx, giving me the appearance of having a rack of four boobs, or *quattro* as my college roommate used to say. As of 3 p.m. yesterday, I can now check "YouTube sensation" off my bucket list – and add it to my LinkedIn profile if I so choose.

It was the perfect storm of breastfeeding hormones meets getting mommy-tracked at work combined with Mama Bear, my kids are in danger, rage. If I thought about it, I'd bet Clare was behind this; probably one of his theatre friends also blogs in his spare time. When *Gawker* picked it up, the hits really started accumulating.

My d-d-d-d-d-d-aya-daya-daya-daya-daya. My-d-d-d-d-d-daycare i-i-i-i-i-i-is a s-s-s-s-s-s-s-s-h-h-h-h-h-h-h-it b-b-b-b-b-b-b-b-b-b-b-b-ox.

Maria clicks off her phone. "One million, three hundred thousand and forty-two hits!" she grins. "This is really amazing. Maybe in another few days, you'll be as famous as that woman who laughed maniacally in her Chewbacca mask."

"Yeah, God willing," I smirk, wiping the sweat off my face with a crumpled napkin. "Just in time for me to go back to work on Monday!" Oh shizzle, I'm not sure whether I should have told her that yet or not.

"Anyway," Maria says, putting her phone back inside her bottomless purse, and seemingly not picking up on the work deadline, "thankfully it was you because I just hate when I have to go up to strangers and ask if they are the person whom I'm supposed to meet." Then she flips her hair to one side.

"Oh, have you been interviewing a lot?" I ask, immediately feeling a pang of panic spread through my body over the thought of not being able to lock this down. The weight of the interview suddenly shifts -- almost before it has even started -- from "can this woman do the job?" to "what do I have to do to get her?"

"Oh, yes, well I am, but I actually meant with school," she grins. "You know, meeting with advisors and interviewing for internships and stuff. Then she looks down and takes another long slurp of her Frappucino. "But with you, I just knew. It's like a have this good feeling right away."

I could go for a good feeling myself, I think. Because right now, I'm a little squeamish, like this is a first date and Maria already knows too much about my sordid past.

"So, you mentioned in your email that you have a lot of experience with early childhood education," I say, finally getting down to business.

Max has fallen asleep, and his head is slumped forward over the infant carrier. There's a growing stench from some spit up on his shirt that's just slightly bearable (I'm not sure who smells worse, me or him), so I keep sipping from my iced latte and pull Max's baseball cap down to shield his face from the sun and wind.

"Yes, I've been taking courses in it, and I've done some internships in day care centers for school. So I guess I was looking at it kind of critically from the beginning, but I mean, these children are so young, and the parents are so harried. It's just like a breeding ground for stress, you know?"

Breeding ground? Stress? Nope, don't know anything about that.

I tell Maria about my job at a big time ad agency downtown, how I'm kind of like a female Don Draper, only I don't drink martinis during the day or cheat on my husband. She laughs, flips her hair over the one side, and then the other. She nibbles on her straw, listening attentively. I keep talking. My message is clear: I've got a stellar career, at least I think I do; my kids are beyond adorable; we live in a nice, safe neighborhood; and I still love my husband, although boy did he pick a bad weekend to go away. I restrict the downsides—like the fact that I'm about to lose my shit if I don't hire a nanny five minutes ago—to the fine print. I feel like I'm pitching Maria on my latest advertising campaign. Doesn't she just want to sign on right now to become a part of our family? I've barely asked her any questions. Maybe I'll gather some great info by osmosis.

Maria leans in and lowers her voice. "So anyway, one more thing about these daycares. I have to tell you something . . . " she pauses with the straw held between her glossy lips and scans the other tables to make sure no one else is listening.

"I think you're right to take your kids out," she says, leaning over and shelving her boobs on the café table like a package of hotdog buns. "Your kids should be happy. And *you* should be happy, you know?"

I *should* be happy. I like that.

"So you're free, right away?" I ask, as if I'm kidding but I'm really not. So what if I've just come across as overly eager; I learned much too late that if you want something, you've got to grab it before it's gone.

"Oh, yeah, yeah," she says, straightening up in her chair. "I'm free . . . for sure! I actually just have two classes left, but that's only two nights a week. I'll have my degree by Christmas!"

A fresh, energized, student with a background in early childhood education who can give personalized attention to my kids, and me! Could it be? I thought about my friends with nannies. As much as I may have envied the fact that they had convenience way beyond what I had, over the years I couldn't help but look with a bit of a judgmental eye at their childcare help—every time I saw them they looked tired or were ignoring their stewards and texting as far I as I could tell. I thought my friends seemed to be settling. Could I have done it? Could

I have really found the perfect nanny? Young, smart and enthusiastic and someone who wants to be *my* partner!

All of a sudden my phone starts vibrating across the table, causing heads at nearby tables to turn. When the "She Works Hard for the Money," ringtone blares it can only mean one person. This is Lauren's doing, to ensure that I am never blindsided by a call from the boss. Max stirs but doesn't wake up. Hopefully he'll stay that way. I push myself up off the chair and say to Maria, "This will just take a minute."

Maria nods and reaches down for her purse.

About to hire a nanny for a job that was potentially on the line, this was a welcome interruption from the interview. I'd called Slade at least ten times in past two days, leaving several voicemails of increasing urgency and finally resorted to one long rant in the form of a blistering email. *Now* he calls back, on a Saturday at 2 p.m.

"Hello, Slade," I say, walking a line between nonchalant mom at Starbucks mode and eager to transition back into work mode.

"Moore, what took you so long to answer? You're not letting your reflexes go on leave are you?" I clear my throat but don't answer his question. My body straightens up and my eyes look straight ahead. I take a deep breath, preparing myself for battle. Maria leans over and pulls her trash bag purse onto her lap and begins cleaning it out. I can tell even she knows this is going to be a difficult call, so she doesn't make eye contact with me. I watch as she removes various items from her bag: three different colors of nail polish, two lipsticks, an enormous key chain, a notebook and a compact umbrella sporting some sort of psychedelic bird pattern. She sees me eyeing the umbrella and whispers "I got it at the Bumbershoot Music Festival last weekend. Isn't it so rad?"

"Well, listen," Slade starts, "I got your little tirade you sent me while I was enjoying a nice golf vacation with a new potential client. I didn't have cell reception. It wasn't until I hit the pass that I even saw that you'd called."

Liar. I say nothing.

"How dare you accuse me of putting you on the—what do you call it? "mommy track?" I don't even know what that *means*. This is just ridiculous. *mommy track*? What is that—your idea for a new brand of treadmill?

I form a fist in my free hand and get up and stand away from the table. "No, I—"

"So really this is about you and Clare," Slade interrupts, "Am I right? I thought you liked him!"

"This has nothing to do with whether I like Clare," I say, pacing around the outdoor tables, forcing myself to take deep breaths. " . . . but you can't just give Clare my job!" I say it just a bit louder then I intended. Ok, maybe a lot louder. Several people turn to stare, so I stare back and flare my nostrils a little.

"Whoa, whoa, whoa, missy. I can't give him *your* job? We haven't seen you in six months. Who was going to do all the work? Certainly not me— "

Why hasn't Starbucks added a punching wall to their outdoor landscaping? I wonder.

"Slade. I've been on *maternity leave*." I speak slowly and annunciate my words, as if I'm my mother while traveling overseas speaking loudly so "they'll understand English." "I'm coming back. On Monday. I mean, I did just have a baby if you recall?!"

"Oh, you say! I believe that was actually six months ago, and didn't we just have this conversation *three months ago,* and then you extended your leave again, and then again? It seems to me that you are far more interested in the mommy demographic than the working world."

Is he serious? I really can't tell.

"Okay, okay," I say wanting to lighten the mood. "Ha ha. Let's move on."

"I have moved on which is why you called I believe," Slade laughs. I can hear people chatting in the background and wind brushing by his phone, and I can just picture him in my mind, sitting on a patio overlooking the golf course with a gin and tonic in one hand, cigar in another, yucking it up with this potential client. Sealing the deal the old fashioned way. And then he goes on. "The truth hurts, Moore. How easily you've been replaced."

How easily I've been *replaced?* Fuck, fuck. Fuckfuckfuckfuckfuck. A feeling of dread overtakes my body and I feel angry tears start to well up around my eyes – but I won't. I won't let him do this. If he fires me I'll have to find another job. But where? This wasn't Madison Avenue with an agency on every other block. I'd probably have to go work the register at Nordstrom and be humiliated every day when neighbors and friends come in to shop and say, "Oh, Anna, I didn't know you had *changed* jobs." They'd awkwardly ask me if I had always been interested in retail and I'd pretend that I was but wanted to really understand the business by starting from the ground up. Or I could joke that I needed a complete wardrobe overhaul so decided to get the discount while I'm at it. Or I just become a stay at home mother, eat pot brownies with my mother and get fat, fatter than I already am. And then because we won't have any money, I'll have to resort to couponing and then *worse*, blogging. I'll become one of those annoying women that chronicles every fucking internal thought she has about parenthood! I'll write nonstop posts on Facebook about the joys of being really present with my kids now that I'm not distracted. I'll write tips about how to disconnect from electronics after school and then I'll ask all my friends to share my posts because I'll be surrounded by my own thoughts so much that I'll start to think they're really awesome. And then, slowly people will un-friend me, or look the other way when I approach them, and then I'll start drinking too much because my writing about being a stay at home mom will even bore me to tears. Ugh. . . my life is fucked.

"You can't do this," I sort of scream, but its actually more of a whimper. A plea, as if I'm saying, *you can't really do this, can you? And you can't let my nanny in waiting hear you do this.* Maybe I should have Maria start filming me and launch my own YouTube channel. Look, it's the Anna Moore Show! Live at Starbucks! Act two of her fabulous series. You all loved her in "My Daycare is a Shitbox." Now she's really shining in "My Boss is a Slime Ball."

I'm wondering if I should hang up on him and just show up Monday and squat in my office, like a sit in, or a work in. Or perhaps I should just explain the Family Medical Leave Act to Slade. I'm about to start in when I begin to hear a snicker on the other end of the phone.

"Oh Moore. You haven't been around to attend to my needs. Did you really think I'd let you off the hook that easy when you've been cheating on me with another man in your life?"

And then, Slade starts laughing. It's a slow maniacal, evil, cartoon character laugh, and he doesn't stop. I look around and hold the phone a few inches away from my head. Has he completely lost it? I picture myself on the witness stand or inside a lawyer's office taking a long deposition. *How exactly did Mr. McAllister fire you? Please explain. And then what happened? He began to laugh. Is that correct, Ms. Moore? Approximately how long was he laughing?* The stenographer takes it all down without emotion.

"Ahh, ahh, ohh, oh my God, Oh!" Slade is wheezing and can barely catch his breath. He's really huffing and puffing now. I picture him clutching his chest dramatically, or maybe he's rolling around on the floor, knees pulled up around his mid section. Perhaps his laughter is now levitating him up towards the ceiling.

I'm not laughing. It's not funny.

"Why are you still laughing?" I growl. "What's so funny?"

"Oh, oh god (more laughter and high pitched yelping sounds) yes, oh yes it is . . . oh, you were so good . . . (coughing and gagging sounds). Ah, ah, oh, ah . . . (cough, burp, gasp)."

"Slade?"

And then you think he might have had a heart attack, Ms. Moore? Because he was laughing so hard, is that correct?

Oh, I could kill him right now.

"IS THIS SOME SORT OF JOKE?" I hold the phone directly in front of me and shout into the mouthpiece. My one-woman performance really has a following now. I half consider taking off Max's baby baseball cap and turning it inside out so that people can drop their coffee cards inside.

"Oh, oh, I wish I could see the look on your face!" Hiccup. "mommy track! Oh, I really had you there, didn't I?" he squeals.

I'm about to hang up, about to tell him where he can stick it, that I'll see him in court, that he's acting like a three year-old and needs a serious time out, when all of a sudden he switches back to Mr. Hyde—or, Mr. Slade McAllister, as it were.

"Okay (hiccup, cough, clearing of throat). So let me tell you what's going on with the Bayview account." And just like that his tone is all business and professional. I picture him straightening the corners of his freshly ironed tangerine polo shirt. The one he wears on every golfing trip.

"What?"

"You're totally right, Moore. We need you back. You should see the comps Clare put together. They're a disaster. You have to fix them. You're the only one who can fix them. Clare doesn't get the new mother demo at all. He thinks it's all about expensive strollers and anti-aging facials. I'm putting him on that butt-hole whitening cream account instead. That should make him happy."

"I'm hanging up, Slade," I say, as I try to surreptitiously fix the wedgie from my left butt cheek that's been inching its way further up my butt with each pace of this call with Slade.

"No, no, no, no, no, no," Slade hiccups, still recovering from his laughing fit, apparently. I wait and lean against the concrete wall while he sighs and coughs and composes himself, though the urge to hang up is still strong. It's almost like there are magnets on my fingertips, pulling them over to the 'end call' button on my phone. "Seriously, I actually really need to talk with you about my meeting last week with Asenzer. It went *very* well," he says with an understated accent on the very as someone might say they're the *right* kind of family. "You know what this means don't you?" I want to say, "that we get into their country club?" But I don't.

I exhale loudly. I *do* know what it means. Even I can't resist the lure of a new potential client. And a big one at that—household name status kind of big. I look over at Maria making googley eyes towards

Max and inch closer to our table. "That you'll get discounted sleeping pills?" I say.

"Well . . . that certainly would be a bonus, now wouldn't it? I think there might be some laws against that kind of thing, but don't think I'm not going to try," Slade pauses. I mention sleeping pills and now he's having a little drug fantasy. "Anyway, as I was saying . . . I think we may have a real shot at landing this account. And well, we need to land it for the sake of -- I mean, we really need to land it. Just come back and wave your magic angel dust so we can do it . . .."

"You mean *pixie* dust?" I roll my eyes again, and Maria looks up at me with a curious expression, almost like a twinkle in her eye.

"No, I mean angel dust. Isn't that what it's called? PCP? Hasn't that been approved by the FDA yet? I'll find out if it's one of the drugs Asenzer is making. I'd like to get my hands on that as well. You know . . . we could put together a campaign that is truly far out, Moore."

I allow myself to exhale finally, and Max lets out a whimper.

"Here's the deal, Moore. You have to come back, and you have to come back now. We need you to win this account. See you Monday."

I look over at Maria. Can I really hire the first person I interview? I feel like I need more time to figure this out, but my mother would just call it God working his magic so I decide to go with that too. "Slade, I—"

And then he hangs up.

Ok, I guess this is a done deal!

"Sorry about that," I say to Maria, shaking out my arms out.

She smiles at me with a look that says *I don't want to know what that call was all about.* All ten fingers are splayed out on the bistro table as she lets her turquoise nail polish air-dry. I sit down. The wind is blowing steadily now and I fan out my upper arms to let the breeze air out my armpits.

"Okay, where were we?" I say.

"I think we were talking when I would start," says Maria, waving her fingers in the air, jazz hands style. *Were we?* "And you know that cutie pie has been making baby faces at me, so may I?" She holds out her arms for Max.

I un-strap him and hand him over. Instantly I feel as if a major weight has been lifted from my shoulders, which at 17.5 pounds of fleshy baby goodness, it definitely has. The tops of my shoulders cry out in relief. Max's eyes light up, and he lets out a loud squeal, kicking his head toward Maria.

"Oh, I miss this age soooo much," Maria croons as she cuddles Max as if she were about to breastfeed him. He does look pretty cozy over there on the other side of the bistro table, which gives me an equal sense of horror and delight. *And* she's figured out a way to hold him that doesn't mess up her freshly polished nails. "You are just so tasty I could eat you up," she gushes. And then she does. She actually starts nibbling on Max's toes, which makes Max giggle and smile. She squeals, dislodging her mouth from his foot. "Oh, and look at these little earlobes," she says, holding one of them daintily between her fingers. "They are so soft of fuzzy. I could just wrap myself inside a little baby earlobe blanket."

Instead of suffering from the stranger anxiety that is supposed to be at its peak at this age (according to Dr. Sears) Max starts head butting Maria as his way of asking for more. She nuzzles his nose and gives him butterfly kisses on his doughy cheeks.

"Oh, there are so many fun things we can do around here Maxi Moo," she croons. "We can go to story hour at the library, music class at the community center and we can make picnics to take to the park. We can do baby massage and we can speak *en Espanol* and help your mommy get her work done. And I'll show you all about what *I'm* learning in school, my little *muchacho.*"

Well, then. They seem to be hitting it off already! "Do you have experience with toddlers too?" I ask, realizing that I should probably consider Lucy and Franny too. I still have whiplash from the call with Slade. My mind is replaying the conversation over and over again like a wind up doll. The more I think about it, the angrier I get.

I get the sense that Maria is picking up on my sour mood but she's doing everything in her power to either ignore it or change it. "Oh, I just looovve babies. You don't understand. I could just hold them and kiss on them all day." She pauses to kiss Max on the forehead, which results in more smiling and giggling for both of them. I manage a half smile. Maria caresses Max's toes and pulls him in closer against her enormous breasts. "Oh, but I love older kids too," she says, looking me in the eye and suddenly taking on a convincing tone, letting me know that she fully understands that the job involves three children and not just one six month-old baby.

"I think family is the most wonderful thing in the world. I just love having older and younger siblings, and I'm going to show your children all my family traditions – how we have dance parties and how we make birthday gifts instead of buying them and how we like to tell stories with contributions from everyone in the family. Oh we're going to have fun. Yes we are."

Max looks at Maria's chest, and I can tell he's thinking of lunch. He arches his back and turns towards me.

I look over at Maria, a potential nanny who shows up to her job interview in a clubbing outfit, but who seems to have succeeded in bonding with Max already and appears to have a real feel for my needs. I find myself not only okay with the idea of bringing Maria into my house on Monday, but also suddenly overcome with the sensation that the universe has just brought her into my life for some higher purpose. She's not what I expected, but that's not a reason not to hire her. In fact, I honestly can't think of one good reason *not* to hire her.

"Well, Maria, I'll be honest," I say, "I have a great feeling about you. Let's try this out. I stand up and reach my arms out to take Max back, signaling that we're about wrapped up.

"Oh my gosh, that sounds perfect, so this is great, this sounds like exactly what I wanted. I'm going to take such good care of your children. I was thinking $24 an hour would be about right for three kids, is that okay?"

What is this, I wonder, a one-woman effort to close the wage gap for women in the U.S.? I don't know what the going nanny rate is, but that sounds high to me, and if it sounds high to me, it will sound astronomical to Patrick. But I haven't done my research, and three children is a lot. So I say nothing and smile, a big stiff smile trying to hide the mental math I'm doing to calculate how much per week that would be. 50 hours times 10 would be $500 times two would be $1000 plus four times 50. $1200 a week. $4800 a month. That can't be right. Or can it? I'll figure it out later. "Okay then," I say.

"Oh, Maximo, you and I are going to have *so* much fun together!" Maria squeals as she jumps up, wobbling on her heels as she leans in to give him a big kiss on the forehead. "Oh, thank you so much! You are the best! I'm really looking forward to working for you and meeting the rest of your *familia*," she beams. "I have a really good feeling about us, you know?"

And then she leans in to give each of us a big wet kiss.

Three

I shuffle home in a semi-stupor. The inside of my mouth is filmy and bitter, and my mind feels hazy again. In the past forty-eight hours, I've fired my daycare, become a YouTube sensation, been fired and hired again, and now have to somehow come up with almost $60,000 a year to pay the nanny I've just hired who is basically a total stranger. I try to remember the saying about embracing change and going with the flow, and opening doors when God closes a window. Or if you're willing to travel the world for a teacher one will appear? The platitudes running through my head are starting to make less sense than ever.

Maria seems nice. Or has she just cast a spell over me? There was something about earlobe blankets, a lot of slurping and giggling, and frequent nibbling of Max's toes. I remember that clearly. The rest is kind of fuzzy. What exactly did she say that was so impressive that essentially resulted in me hiring her on the spot? Did I hire her or did she assume that I hired her? And does it really matter anyway, because I have to go back to work in a day?

My foot hits a crack in the sidewalk, and I trip awkwardly, nearly landing headfirst on the pavement with Max strapped to my chest. Maria has me drugged and Slade has me fired up.

So now the weight of the bad economy falls on *my* shoulders. *Oh hi Anna, sorry we've been ignoring you. Didn't really think you were coming back to work so we made a few changes in terms of staffing and creative direction. But unfortunately, as you saw, these were not the greatest decisions. And now? Now the agency will go under. Everyone will lose their jobs. Unless . . . unless you come back right now and save us!*

I picture myself showing up to work on Monday in a Wonder Woman costume, with a cape and spiky boots to kick everyone's ass in gear . . . especially Slade's.

My phone buzzes with an incoming text. I pull it out of my pocket and look down; it's from a number I don't recognize. The first thing I notice is the string of exclamation points.

"Thank you for hiring me!!!!!!!!!!!! I am sooo excited!!!!!!!!!! I am going to take such good care of your kids! We are going to have so much fun! Jajajajaja!!!!!!!!!!"

Just then Max starts howling. I look at my watch: it's a quarter past boob time and my breasts immediately start tingling and then leaking. "Sorry, Max!" I say, cradling his head trying to console him, "we've got to find a place to pull over." I look around. We're about mid-way between our house and Starbucks; there's nowhere I can go to sit down except a nearby park bench. Unfortunately, this particular park is always a scene. Drop by any time of day, save for lulls at lunch and afternoon naptime, and you'll find scores of nannies and stay at home moms lining the park benches surrounding the swimming pool-sized sandbox. Of course, the nannies and moms sit on different sides of the sandbox.

I plop myself on an unoccupied bench under a large maple tree by the playfields hoping to go undetected. This is the park where I used to come when Lucy was a newborn and I first weighed the decision of whether to stay at home or go back to work. No sooner do I have Max latched on, wondering what to do about my exposed mid section, when I see Colette. Colette is a SAHMWN, a.k.a. stay at home mom with nanny. We met early on in our careers, working at one of those destined-for-greatness dotcoms of the mid 1990s run by a pair of 25 year-old 'visionaries' who had the foresight to run the company into the ground eight months later. We worked long hours and were paid very little, sucked in by the promise of stock options and the possibility of going public someday. Colette was a hostess at heart, always volunteering her apartment whenever we needed a meeting place, and throwing great parties on a budget with pony kegs and chips and salsa. She always knew where to go to see great, undiscovered bands on the cheap, and had an uncanny knack for finding friends with boats on the most beautiful summer weekends. Even though she was gorgeous and seemingly could have her pick of men, she was a girl's girl and always made time for me. But then out of the blue, or so it seemed, she met her very own Microsoft millionaire. It was as if she had been waiting for him.

They married shortly after meeting, and as if she had read the "Girls Guide to Transforming Your Life After Marrying Well," Colette immediately started hosting parties where, instead of serving chips and beer, she hired a catering team to serve champagne and pâté. When, two years later, I married a lowly computer programmer who didn't even own a sport coat to wear to Colette's fancy parties, our worlds started slowly drifting apart.

"Hey you, looking good, is this Max?" she coos, strolling over to me with the enthusiasm of a peacock. The main benefit of having a nanny if you don't work—the ability to leave the house perfectly coifed—is well displayed on Colette. Dressed in a chic-but-not-over-the-top ensemble of white jeans, a thin linen sweater, designer sunglasses and flats, she has the appearance of looking both fully at ease and on top of this world. Even her blond locks don't display the slightest hint of dark roots. I decide that it's the white jeans, though, that give the SAHMWN her signature status.

While I'm fully aware that the most important thing in life is resting in my arms right now, I'm simultaneously struck by my immediate pang of jealousy. Was it the marrying the millionaire that made everything fabulous in her life or is it the full time nanny or am I reading too much into the white jeans?

But then she steps closer and I see the lips. It's the newly plumped profile that gives her the air of a mom with just a little too much time on her hands. No stain-free skinny white jeans in the world can make up for those lips, and I am instantly joyful that I fought for my job instead of giving up and walking away. She may have all the money in the world, but I still have my own lips.

I look at Max. He can still make everything else drift away. "It is indeed . . . I just want to kiss him all day long. Did you do that with Cole, and if so, when do you have to stop before child protective services starts asking questions?" I tease. I look over to Cole, sweetly digging in the sand. He's a year older than Max, but not anywhere as cute. In fact, he looks just like his dad – rich, donning his toddler quilted jacket and leather driving shoes, but definitely not cute. Will I go to hell for saying that about an 18-month old, I wonder? Plus, what kind of narcissist names her baby after herself? Ugh, this park is bringing out the bitchy in me. Reason number 132 why Anna Moore will never make it as a SAHM, let alone a SAHMWN.

"Um, sure I guess I did," she responds, slightly thrown by my question. I wonder if I subconsciously asked about kissing to make Colette self conscious about her lips. But then she sits down on the bench, pulls out a pocket mirror and starts reapplying lip liner. I stifle the urge to giggle.

"So . . . are you going to stay home now that you and are Patrick and outnumbered?" she asks, eyeing her mirror and pretending not to notice my fleshy midsection. With Colette, working was out of the question with just one, and I'm sure she figures for everyone else it's a matter of not if but when. I briefly wonder if I should lie, and say I don't know, to see if I'll be invited to some secret club meetings where Colette and her other SAHMWN's get together and laugh about how harried we working moms look.

"Nope. In fact, I'm going back on Monday," I say, instinctively pulling down the back of my top, and trying to sound upbeat. "Everything's all set. I pulled my kids out of daycare and just hired a nanny."

"You were doing daycare with *three*?" Colette looks dumbfounded by the realization. "Oh my goodness. I didn't know you'd been trying to manage all these years without a nanny. You should have let me know," she says with concern as if I had just told her I'd been living on the streets and cooking eggs for the kids on my overheating car hood. Colette looks up toward the sun, shakes her hair out like a model on a photo shoot, and then brushes away some imaginary poverty dust that must have somehow made its way over to her from me. I kind of want to give her a slight nudge so that she falls off of the bench and gets her jeans dirty. *That would make a good YouTube video*, I think.

But then I realize that Colette *is* actually sort of a nanny authority having hired a team of them over the years, so I might learn something from her.

"So, you've had the same nanny ever since Taylor was born, right? Tell me—what is the secret to a successful relationship?"

"Oh, yes we have," she begins, patting the tops of her thighs, obviously thrilled that I'm tapping into her expertise. She puts her lip liner back inside her purse. "Well, she's . . . how do I say this . . . " she searches for the words, looking up towards the monkey bars to our right. "It's worked out so well because she's . . . sort of, well . . . "

"What?" I lean in closer and lower my voice.

"She's . . . she's really . . . submissive."

My eyes widen.

"Does that sound bad?" Colette asks.

"Well, it's not what I thought you were going to say," I say avoiding the question.

"It's just that she's so pleasant and quiet. It's like I barely know she's there when I am home but everything's clean and I don't hear the kids except when I want to. She's really easy to have around, and she makes things run smoothly."

Wow. Ok. I know I'm not in the market for a subservient nanny. "I'm thinking I might need something a bit more," I say, readjusting Max in my lap. "I mean, maybe less housekeeper and more teacher, someone who can stimulate the kids. She's taking the place of their school after all."

Colette winces, but then quickly unfurrows her brow and loosens her lips. "I'm confused," she began. "You mean, you're taking them out of a preschool to be with a nanny? Why wouldn't you just do both?"

I'm out of my league, and I realized it too late. Colette probably has Myrna supervising two other nannies and a team of tutors on hand as back up. I like to read about families like this in my Chick Lit books about posh Upper East Side families, but I avoid them in Seattle. I wonder ever so briefly if I should run back to the CDC, and beg for re-admittance once they get their license back. I can bond with the other harried CDC moms over conversations about durable lunch containers and the best shampoos for repelling lice. They're my people after all.

"I just found this woman on Craigslist who seems to be a real find—she's a UW student getting a degree, or a graduate degree, actually, I'm not quite sure which one, but her focus area of study is early childhood education. She's fluent in Spanish, and she and Max practically bonded on the spot. She'll be great for now," I say confidently, dismissing the school subject.

Colette looks horrified. "Did you say Craigslist?" she gasps, eyebrows raised every so slightly until they hit a brick wall of Botox barrier.

I swipe Max up over my shoulder for a burp. "Yep," I nod.

"So this Craigslist nanny," she makes it sound like *Craigslist killer*, " . . . you're thinking that you'll skip preschool and just have a nanny . . . ?" It was not so much an actual question as a judgment. She looks up at the sky and contemplates the idea ever so briefly but then just as quickly dismisses it. "Well, if for some reason it doesn't work out, you know, we got Myrna through an agency, and they were just wonderful. Before she started, they installed nanny cams through the whole house and took care of all the screening, training and referrals. It was such an easy transition. I barely had to lift a finger. I could make a call to the gal who helped us if you want. I mean, maybe if you just wanted them to do a background check or something. I don't know if they'd do that for someone not in their roster, but for me, maybe she'd do you a favor."

I think of the ad copy for that agency. *So easy, you'll never have to lift another finger. Let our subservient nannies do all the work for you, and then disappear into the wallpaper when you walk into the room.*

"I don't know," I squint into the sunlight, feeling my crow's feet collecting more poverty dust. "I'd kind of hate to get off on a bad footing with her by being so secretive. And my mom's around too. She was going to watch Max fulltime anyway, so I'm sure she'll be over a lot."

"Oh that's sweet," a few drops of spit sputter out of Colette's plumped lips with the word *sweet* that betray their authenticity. What she really means is not that it's sweet, but quaint perhaps. As in, oh, isn't that quaint that the Amish use horse and buggies.

"When I had Cole, the night nurse we used with Taylor was on another job so my mother had to fill in and do the night feedings for the first couple months. It was nice to have her around."

OMG. It was nice to have your *subservient* mother around? I want to say this, but I don't, but I'm not sure that my jaw isn't on the floor. And then she saves me from having to cover the shock in my face.

"You know . . . " she's speculates, "with a Spanish speaking nanny, if you're consistent, your kiddos might actually get a lot further in language than even the pre-schools that offer language four days a week. So, you know, you'll be missing out on the other stuff, but that could be a nice leg up later on." She's probably calculating the potential advantage to having in home language immersion instead of a preschool curriculum. With Colette, everything is about weighing the subtle advantages. But my decisions are more black and white. In my pro and con columns, the pro is keeping my job and making sure Maria shows up for work on Monday. So I look her straight in her Prada sunglasses and confess. "Well, I'm kind of at square one. I'll see how it goes before I convert our house to a Spanish speaking one. After all, I don't go much beyond *Hola* myself, and look at me!" I tease. I probably just gave Colette more determination to consider language classes for her kids if they don't want to turn out like me.

It's the most time I've spent with her in seven years. Clearly Colette has not seen *My Daycare is a Shitbox* or she would have been gone already. But I'm thankful, at least in this instance, for her lack of cultural awareness in YouTube sensations. This visit has reaffirmed me after a shaky start this morning.

Colette cocks a half smirk-half smile and briefly looks down before responding. "Keep in touch," she chirps, and then stands up. "I'll be anxious to hear how your nanny is working out. Good luck."

And with that, she brushes more nonexistent sand off her white jeans to conclude our chat. "I must go. I'm heading home to drop Cole off with Myrna now. I'm *way* overdue for a pedicure. You'll love it!" she smiles sweetly as she picks up her pint-sized purse and turns to leave. "Oh, and Anna?" Colette pauses, momentarily lifting up her sunglasses to peer down at me, "if you get in a bind, be sure to call me."

"Oh sure," I nod and then look over at Max who has all of a sudden gotten very hot and heavy on my chest. I watch Colette scoop up Cole from the sandbox and walk across the sun drenched park, until I can no longer see her miniscule hips swaying in the distance.

My gaze focuses on a patch of sawdust just in front of me. A black ant struggles with something as it traverses up and down over the wood chips. The ant does not pause or investigate an easier route; instead, it simply trudges on up and over the peaks and valleys of its terrain. At first I can't tell what the ant is carrying; it's obviously a heavy load. Is it a dark leaf, a raisin, a piece of chocolate cupcake? And then I see that it's carrying two other ants.

I let out a loud sigh and look up towards the evergreen canopy overhead. Max slowly opens his eyes and looks up at me, his gaze full of adoration and contentment. He leans back against my chest, turning his head with his mouth open. Wordlessly, I lift up my shirt again and tuck his head underneath my top. At least now I know what I'm supposed to be doing, in this very moment.

"Come on Maxi Moo," I say, lifting him off my breast and back into the backbreaking carrier. "Time to go." No looking back this time.

47

Four

"She's coming tomorrow morning, and we're paying her $24 an hour? What do we get besides the babysitting? A gift with purchase?"

Patrick has just arrived home from his business trip, and is not impressed or amused with my spur-of-the-moment hire.

"Oh, come on," I say, not quite knowing what to say, and wishing that I had staggered the news. Perhaps new nanny this week, then next week, "Oh guess what, we're paying her." Perhaps, "Oh come on, its just a drop in the bucket when you think about what I'll be making after I win the Asenzer account." But I say nothing. There's nothing to say. We have to suck it up.

I'm sitting cross-legged on the bedroom floor amidst a cascading volcano of laundry, folding a white men's undershirt, just the way he likes it. Originally I did it the way I learned at The Rack in high school – fold arms and sides in, and then fold the body in half. I was a pro at display folding. But Patrick likes to put them in his dresser two stacks deep, so his way of folding begins with a vertical fold followed by two horizontal folds. He always wound up refolding my shirts. I could have a Gap worthy stack of shirts already IN his drawer, and he would take them out and refold them. So, as an olive branch, I start with the vertical fold hoping he'll notice and potentially soften. I get that folding shirts doesn't make up for a potentially major financial flub, but it's something to lighten his mood, I hope. Also, I think he's overreacting. Childcare for three kids is an expensive bullet we just have to swallow. Sure I can approach household budgeting with a bit of magical thinking every now and then (Oh, it will all work out somehow!), but Patrick is a hard core pragmatist, and I can see him working the numbers in his head.

"I didn't really have a choice," I say, shirt in hand. "I either go back to work tomorrow and win this new account or I might not have a job. What's the alternative?" I look at Patrick for a response. His body language softens slightly, but the expression on his face does not. He turns to me with a "huh" look. I return the look and cast both hands up in the air.

"Choice? What about the daycare where we've sent the girls for the past four years? And what about your mother? What about a neighbor?"

I glare at him. "A neighbor?!? There you go. It's that kind of answer that makes me really happy I hired Maria. Do you really not understand how these things work at all? We need full time care, not a mother's helper for an afternoon. See, you don't have to plan this but I do, and I actually have a full time job like you."

Patrick shrugs. "So a kid smeared poop on the wall, that kind of stuff probably happens everyday at a daycare. It probably happens here for all we know," he says, peering into the mirror to get a closer look at his nose hairs. Even after nine years of marriage, sometimes I still can't tell when he's joking or not.

"Patrick!" I screech, "he was finger-painting with poop, all over the daycare, and he was eating it and smearing it across other kids faces, chasing them and taunting them. And it was the kid with the pinworms. It's disgusting even saying it out loud. Blech! What are the girls supposed to do? Hide in the tree house all day for fear of another poop attack?"

"This isn't the Cold War, Anna. Kids aren't hiding under their desks for fear of a bomb being dropped."

"Nope, just a giant turd! And besides. I'm done. Yes, of course, they'll clean it up, and they'll reopen, but that was it for me. I cannot do it anymore without help. My mom's supposed to watch Max while high, and I'm supposed to really believe that she'll make it here on time every morning . . . in time for me to get the girls to daycare and get to work because you might be here or you might be on a business trip. We need this. I need it for my sanity."

The more I talked the more, the more I was convinced myself. I would find a way to make it work. I always did. I solved this crisis on my own in less than 48 hours, and I think it's a pretty damn fine solution.

Patrick throws his hands up in the air as if to say, *Ok, this is all on you. We may be married, but you dug this hole.* His eyelids flutter slightly, and his gaze moves up the towering laundry pile heap by heap until his eyes lock with mine. The bottom corners of his lower lip turn down as if to emphasize it. I feel an urge to lob one of his perfectly folded shirts at his head, or perhaps pull him into the pile and seduce him into a state of financial confusion.

And then I think maybe he's on the same page. He removes his shirt, flexing his arm over his torso as he yanks the fabric over his head showing broad shoulders, still *some* definition around the abs, and nice contour across his biceps. Then he unzips his jeans and carelessly kicks all of his clothes over to a corner, presumably for me to pick up at a later point in time. And then he does the strangest thing: He just stands there. Naked. Studying me, staring down at me, saying nothing. This is like a game of chess, I think. Who will make the first move?

Not a moment later, he has one hand on his hip and the other is scratching a butt cheek, like a cat on a carpet post. He sighs loudly, clearly exasperated. The moment is lost. More importantly, why have I never noticed how low his testicles hang from behind his penis? Or the little hairs that stick out from his scrotum that give the whole package the look of a plucked chicken? Must be the viewpoint from which I am gazing. Maybe I'm not in the mood after all.

"Anna."

I snap out of my daze. "Oh, so anyway, I'm not sure about the gift with purchase situation, but I think she'll be a really great nanny. I really do," I say, casually. "She was so animated during the interview, and she bonded with Max on the spot. She'll also teach the kids Spanish, and get this— she used to work at a daycare and confirmed my suspicions—no oversight!"

"Did her references support that? That she's the best thing since Mary Poppins? I'm assuming that's why she's so overpriced?"

I haven't called references, of course, so I just lean forward to grab more clothes out of the pile. "Haven't called yet, but I will soon, just didn't have time . . . ," I mumble, running a hand through my hair wondering what else he can possibly ask that will send me into a tailspin of regret, but then he heads for the bathroom.

"She'll be here tomorrow— you can ask her then," I shout, returning to the shirts.

"When we pay her $24 an hour," he snaps, leaning past the doorframe so I can see he's raising an eyebrow at me, "just be sure to tell the kids we're sorry we couldn't save for college for them; it was more important to learn Spanish." He disappears again and I hear the faucet turn on followed by a loud *zuurrrip* as he pulls back the shower curtain.

I let my head fall to my chin and return to the task of sorting and folding the laundry, realizing that my argument is pretty thin. How do I convince my husband that I just *know* that this is going to work out, that Maria will be great and it will be the calm in our household we are long overdue? What could possibly go wrong?

Midnight. Panic attack.

Patrick has been asleep for an hour. I did manage to eventually seduce him, but now I'm wide awake. That's the way it goes with orgasms. They're like sleeping pills for Patrick and caffeine for me. I marvel daily at his ability to turn off his mind like a light switch and go to sleep the second he closes his eyes while I lie there and feel overwhelmed by everything I must get done. I try counting sheep – literally I try counting sheep, and then inevitably I get to a number that reminds me of something on my to-do list and I go down a mental rabbit hole stressing about that. Tonight the number was low – 24 or rather $24.

Fuck. I'm totally awake now. Maria is hired; it's a done deal. The bigger question is: Do the kids need something else besides Maria? The image of Colette's turned up nose flashes inside my head. I hate that she's planted this seed on the day I had it all figured out, but she's right. I could care less about keeping up with the Jones, but Lucy is four and she'll be in kindergarten in a year. This is not the year to just have her with a nanny, even if I have confidence in that nanny. Ugh. I slowly sit up in bed. I slide one foot out of the covers and onto the floor. No noise. Good. Second foot on the floor. I gently press down, testing the pressure. Somewhere right next to my side of the bed is the creakiest floorboard in the entire house. If I hit it, it could set up a chain reaction of Max crying, then Franny, then Lucy, and then Patrick cursing. I'm confident I'm practicing some form of Tai Chi based on my movements. Safely standing, I turn and tiptoe across the room till I reach the door and gently pull it closed. Made it! I sit down in my office chair and lift the lid to my laptop.

Sticky notes filled with the names of preschools line the wall of the office above my desk. I hurriedly wrote them down after a spate of Internet research following my YouTube premiere.

St. Luke's

Temple Shalom Preschool

St. Anthony's Nursery School

St. Ann's

Clearly, I have my choice of religious preschools . . .

National Children's Growth and Development School

Seattle Children's Discovery Day

The Peak School for Early Learners

Cascade Academy

Marine Montessori

And then there are the schools that sound like early learning institutions, but who really knows?

So I turn to my friend Google. Please give me the skinny on these schools. St. Ann's, let's see what you've got.

"We're a traditional play-based nursery school that encourages learning through play. We believe children don't need to be rushed. In their own times and through their own natural curiosity, they find a love of learning at St. Ann's.

And Marine Montessori:

"Based on the teachings of Maria Montessori, we've developed our program with a profound respect for understanding our children as individuals. Our program focuses on unleashing the hidden strengths, talents, emotions and academic skills in each of our children.

Seattle Discovery Day:

"If you are interested in learning more about Seattle Children's Discovery Day, we invite you to join one of our information sessions held monthly. Please call our admissions director."

Perhaps our advertising agency should bring on some preschool clients. They all sound the same. I want them to have blaring vacancy ads on their home pages like a hotel. *Five spaces left, only $775 a month, comes with Crayola crayons and markers. A fully equipped playground and hot lunch included!*

I pick up the phone to call Seattle Discovery Day, the first school that told me nothing but at least invited me to call. So I figure I can at least leave a bunch of messages so I'm deluged with helpful information in return tomorrow.

"Thank you for calling the Seattle Discovery Day School. If you are interested in learning more about the school, submitting an application or attending one of our open houses, please call back after September 15th. For the upcoming school year, we are fully enrolled. Applications for next year will be available beginning in October.

I cross Seattle Discovery Day off the list -- so far, not so good.

I skip to the Montessori. Since they value the individual so much, perhaps they might value one disorganized but committed and loving mom with two amazingly happy and creative little girls? Maybe they even have weekly workshops that Maria could attend so the girls could get a drop-in style taste of real school like Monday math manipulatives or Friday phonics. I cross my fingers after I dial their number.

I breathe in and hold it, with a fear of exhaling until I hear the recording. I may be in luck after all.

"Welcome to Marine Montessori. We look forward to seeing you next week! If you are a prospective family, we look forward to meeting you at our first informational session in November. If you'd like to attend, please leave your name and contact phone number after the beep. Thank you."

Damn, damn, damn. This is a really bad idea to even be up at this hour but to be calling schools is the midlife equivalent of drunk dialing boys in college I decide.

I decide to turn to a safer audience -- the other insomniac moms of Seattle who are up trolling the NE Seattle Moms listserv.

The listserv is a necessary evil -- necessary when you find yourself in a hopeless situation and need a stranger's advice because you are too humiliated to turn to a friend or neighbor to ask, and evil because you never know whether you'll reach a friendly ear or a bitter mom using the board as her own personal whipping board.

Unlike lots of first time moms who mistakenly pick their real name as their username, my moniker of *spoonfulofsugar* puts me at no risk of being found out as long as I'm careful about not providing too much personal information.

I click on the "preschools" forum and scroll down the list of the most recent queries:

"What are the top feeder preschools for good elementary placement?"

"Should I send the admissions director a thank you note or something more?"

"Best schools for an aggressive boy?"

"Vegan schools — French immersion schools — outdoor only schools — which ones are you attending?"

Nothing relevant for me so I click on "new topic." My headline relays my tentativeness and hopefully will incite sympathy: "Late to the game, but hoping to find a preschool opening . . .

I thought I'd turn to the wisdom of this board to help me identify any school I may have overlooked that might still have openings. Thanks so much for your help.

I hear Patrick groan and the mattress squeak as he shifts his body in bed, hopefully not because he hears typing. Nah, who I am kidding. He sleeps like a rock.

I hit the refresh button to see if anyone has replied to the message yet. Views: 7. Replies: 3.

Not bad for midnight. It's a captive audience of breastfeeding moms—or vampires. I click the first reply.

"Not only are you late to the game, but you're about a year behind. Better start next year's application process now!"

Reply number two.

"Not sure where you are from, but this is a competitive market. People often think of Seattle as laid back when it comes to schools, but unfortunately, it's really no different from New York. If I were you, I'd homeschool them yourself."

And then—

"I just heard that there are some open spots at the Children's Creative Development Center downtown. There was some crazy mom who was obviously off her meds and blasted them on YouTube. But don't believe the rumors. The place is a-mazing! You should try there first."

I haven't noticed until now that on the scroll that shows which friends are also online, my friend Sarah is listed, so I send her a chat.

"Hey, it's me, Anna."

"SpoonfulofSugar?"

"I know . . . trying to be anonymous."

"Honey, WHAT are you thinking? Why are you asking COMPLETE strangers for advice . . . and mean ones at that!? I am your resource. Did you forget that???"

"Ugh, sorry, I'm actually not thinking clearly. Ran into Colette who gave me complete anxiety about robbing my children of the chance to have a solid pre-k education instead of "just a nanny."

"Don't be anxious. But … it's not a bad idea, and fortunately, I have an amazing idea for you. You are so late to the game that everyone has already gone home, showered and gone to bed. But I can help. I know of a new place and you'll fall in love with it. It's so YOU."

"What does that mean??"

"You'll see. Goodnight. XO."

Five

Ding dong. Governess calling! I hurry to put the last of the breakfast dishes into the dishwasher, press start on the coffee maker (pot number two!) and scurry towards the front door, picking up scattered kid shoes on my way. I stop at the hallway mirror and check myself before I open the door and then I notice the smell. I have body odor. *Motherclucker!* It snuck up on me out of nowhere. Or did it? I can't remember when I last showered, but I certainly need to this morning, and then get ready for work. Thank goodness she's on time, I think. I told Slade I'd be in a little late, and I wonder if any part of him might think that I'm going on a job interview. Who am I kidding? We both know that I'm still on the "mommy track," such as it is. I look in the mirror again. Yep, perfect picture of a woman who is in desperate need of help. That should start Maria off with a diligent work ethic. A small, very small, part of me is holding out hope she shows up in some sort of Governess get up. That would be the icing on the cake of this new arrangement.

I reach for the front door handle and a gust of wind slams the door back against the wall. Tiny leaves swirl at my feet. And the air, it smells fresh and brisk, a sense that wasn't there just a few days ago.

Fall. I look down. Greeting me on the other side of the doorway in teal-blue mini-shorts and a white tank top is Maria. She's much shorter than I remember. No heels this time—she's wearing flip-flops embellished with plastic rhinestones with her long hair pulled back in a ponytail. An enormous backpack like the kind I carried to high school takes the place of my longed-for carpetbag and her psychedelic umbrella is attached to the base with a carabiner. Maria bounds through the entryway and walks straight back to the kitchen. I hear the sound of sleigh bells and look down to Maria's ankle: tiny bells shimmer and clink around her feet.

"Oh, this is nice, really put together," she nods her head up and down confirming her pleasant surprise, and her glossy pink lips turn up with approval. "I can work with this."

"Great," I say, not really sure what she means, since I thought she was working with the kids and not the house. Maybe it means she's planning on some housekeeping and not just the *nanny-ing* of the kids. In any event, I'm confident that I am no housekeeper, so Patrick will be happy to hear that Maria's on top of the keeping of the house, whatever that means.

She looks up at me expectantly with an expression that tells me she's waiting to be told what to do. Of course she is. I'm an employer of household help now I remind myself and I mentally kick myself in the shin. I can criticize the CDC all day long but they were in charge. I just dropped the kids and ran. I anticipated only a feeling a relief not a surge of discomfort with an employee in the house that I have to instruct. People all over the world grow up with "help" in the house right? But the only people that come to mind are Prince William and Harry. And they probably have layers of layers of help to train the help that's training the help.

I suddenly feel in my gut that I'm doing this wrong. You're not supposed to meet someone and then leave her with your children five minutes later. I bet Colette had someone from "the agency" training the submissive one for at least a week before leaving her children alone in the house with her. I make an executive decision to stick around for just a bit longer. If things go poorly, my backup plan is to call Slade, give notice, compile a stack of coupons by the afternoon and make the first of my lentil surprise recipes by evening. But that's not going to happen. I'll be at the office by 11, maybe noon at the latest, ready to kick some slacker ad agency butt!

"Max and Franny are asleep, and Lucy is at her Grandmother's house," I blurt out, "so let's give you the grand tour shall we?" Then I start to ramble as I introduce her to our home. I guide her through our house showing her where to find everything she could ever possibly need throughout the day. I open up every kitchen cabinet, cubby hole, drawer where one might find critical baby gear—wipes and extra diapers, trash bags, bubbles, Play Doh, crayons, snacks, juice boxes, band aids and bongos. After this speed lesson in baby goods geography, I pause. Is she getting it all? I hope Maria is taking mental notes. I pause to stop and to my surprise, I see that Maria *is* taking notes, notepad in hand.

"I got it," Maria says, tsking me out of the kitchen with her hand, and then diving her head into our refrigerator. "Go get ready for work. If I need anything I know where to find you. I'll just get some food ready for when they wake up."

"Oh that's perfect," I say, standing in the kitchen doorway before I go upstairs. "You can do eggs and fruit or fruit and cereal for Franny, and for Max, he'll probably just want a bottle. He's really only on mushy bananas for food now. You know I need to write some guidelines down for you like about his nap schedule and how to make his bottles. Do you know all about how to do that?"

"Oh my gosh, completely. I mean, you can write everything down if that makes you feel good, but I think I can handle breakfast."

See! I want to say to Patrick, *Can she handle it? Yes she can!*

"Mommmmmeeeeeeeeeeee!" "Mommmeeeee!" The silence upstairs is now broken, concluding our orientation session.

"Hold on," I say. "*They have risen!*" I turn towards the stairs and am about to tell Maria to hang back for just a minute before I introduce her, but she's already lock step and bells behind me.

"I'm coming, Baby Doll," I shout as Franny continues her frantic mommy pleas.

I pause at the top of the stairs just outside Franny's door. A quick sniff of the air tells me it's most likely not a wet bed, so I turn around and say to Maria, "Why don't you stay out here for just a minute so I can make sure she's not a two-year old terror before I introduce you, all right?"

"Oh sure. Just tell me what you need." Maria steps back with jingling bells and leans against the hallway wall, silent. The last thing I notice before going into Franny's room is that Maria has a strange look on her face. She's motionless except for her eyes that are darting back and forth, like one of the Charlie's Angels right before they pounce with bouncing hair and loaded guns.

I open the door and see that Franny is wrestling with her purple garden canopy hanging over her bed. She'd spotted it in a catalog and had it have it. It was featured in a scene with little girls dressed in fairy outfits waving sparkly wands and flapping iridescent wings while delicately holding Easter egg baskets and dancing around the canopy. She begged for it for her birthday, and I caved. Then she insisted that we hang it over her bed like mosquito netting. It has become my nemesis ever since. Every time she got tangled in it which was often, she pulled plaster off the ceiling trying to free herself and inevitably got limbs and stuffed animals stuck in the netting. A year later it looked like one of those abandoned fishing nets you see on Discovery Channel documentaries that are full of ocean garbage and sad dolphins.

"Franny, what are you doing in that thing?"

"I wuz pwaying faiwy pwincess."

"It looks like you're playing Houdini." I say.

"Who's Deeni?"

"It means you are trying your hardest to smother yourself in this thing or pull the ceiling down to escape the house. *This* is why we shouldn't sleep with it around your bed."

"No, I need it. I need my gahden campy!" Franny wails.

"Do you want to have a fairy princess breakfast with your fairy dolls?" I turn around. Maria is in the bedroom wearing a pair of Lucy's fairy wings, flapping her arms and waving a doll above her arms in a sort of interpretive dance, including bell music, of course. She looks like a street performer at the Pike Place Market.

"Yes!" Franny exclaims, her eyes lighting up. "Who is dis Mama? Did you bwing me a weal faywee?"

"Hello Miss Francesca," murmurs Maria. "Mi yamo es Maria and I love to play with fairies." Maria kneels down so she's at eye level with Franny, reaching the doll over to her face and giving her an air kiss.

Franny hops out of bed and yanks her doll out of Maria's hand. "Mine," she snaps, "I want fairy bweakfast."

"Oh of course, my dear princess" says Maria as she turns to wink at me. "Let's go, let's go!" she whispers, taking Franny's hand. "But we must be very, very quiet and speak only in our special fairy voices."

"Howl long can she stay, Mama?" Franny turns back to me, holding Maria's hand.

"Oh, *si mia nina hermosa,* I will stay until the wind changes," she says.

In the shower I run through today's agenda. No Spanx this time, it's just going to be me with nothing to hide. YOWZ got off track, and I need to let my rolls hang out to get them back on track.

Dressed in a cute blouse and a pair of pre-pregnancy dress pants, lipstick applied, funky jewelry adorned and hair fluffed—I slip my watch over my wrist and see that I'm actually ahead of schedule.

The din coming from downstairs has gotten a little quiet, so I decide to take a few minutes to investigate. I quietly creep down the hallway and perch myself a few steps down where I can see glimpses of what is going on in the kitchen but hopefully remain undetected.

The stairs creak loudly as I squat down. I careen my neck out to get a better view, but almost topple over on my face. "Shit" I hiss quietly to myself. I need to get more creative here, so I get down on my knees and rearrange myself so I'm leaning down chest first with my legs behind me so that it appears as if I'm about to luge down the stairs headfirst. *There. Better view.* I hold onto a rail in the banister to keep myself in place.

"What's sat noises?" asks Franny from the kitchen.

"What noise?" asks Maria.

"Upstaywrs! On da staywrs."

Oh, crap. Don't look upstairs. Don't. Look. Upstairs! My heart thumps against the runner and I tighten my grip against the banister.

"Oh Franny, your mommy is upstairs, she's going to work today. Here—you want another piece of this apple?"

Phew.

I see Max sitting quietly in his high chair, smearing runny rice cereal all over his tray. "Oh, *Maximo*, look at you!" Maria puts her finger in her mouth and wipes off a bit of cereal off Max's cheek before scooping more cereal off the tray and letting Max suck on her finger. Oh gross, are her hands *clean*? Then she walks over to her backpack and slides a laptop out and perches it open on the table. Awesome, more germs. I wonder what she's doing but Franny asks the question for me.

"Can we watch Ewlmo?" Franny asks.

"No, no. No TV time . . . we're going to finish breakfast and then play. Isn't that more fun than TV, princess?" All the while Maria talks she's typing furiously and I wonder if I'm going to get a daily report of all their activities the way I did at daycare. This is brilliant, I think. I didn't even have to ask for it.

She shuts the computer lid and walks over to the microwave and places a plastic bottle and a sippy cup inside. I watch with horror as Maria closes the door. Everything seems to happen in slow motion as she lifts her finger to press the start button.

NOOOOOO! I silently scream.

"Okay, muchachos. I fix some yummy drinks for you and then we go to the park, si?"

I pull myself up and stumble downstairs as quickly and normally as I can, trying not to give myself away. "Hey," I say, entering the kitchen, scrambling to come up with some sort of plausible reason for why I have just appeared. "I just heard the microwave running and that reminded me that I needed to reheat my coffee before I get on the road!"

I reach up to hit the stop button and pretend to be surprised when I see the bottle and sippy cup inside.

"Oh, hey, Maria?" I say, hoping she doesn't pick up on the alarm in my expression. "I don't like to put any plastic cups or bottles in the microwave because of the BPA chemicals."

"Excuse me? What do you mean?" Maria shifts back and forth on her feet and leans in, looking at me, then the microwave, then back at me. "What is this BPA thing?"

"The plastic. It sort of melts a little bit and leaches out these really bad chemicals and can get into the kids blood streams . . ." I attempt to explain.

Maria gives me a look like I've just turned into Mrs. X. I silently vow not to micromanage her every move but safety is non negotiable.

"Oh, yeah, yeah sure, no problem," she says, flipping her hair to one side and clicking her teeth. "You like your kids to drink cold milk, that's okay, we can do that."

"No, no, that's not w-what I meant," I stammer. "The milk can be warm. You just need to put Franny's milk in a glass container first, microwave it, stir it, check to make sure it's not too hot, and then put it in a cup for her." Maria gazes at me wide-eyed as I go through the demonstration. I feel like some sort of control freak, but this is also sort of basic right I think. Even the kids stare at me with confused eyes.

"And Max's milk should never be microwaved—especially the breast milk." I open the refrigerator. "See these bottles in here, these are the breast milk bottles. You can tell because there's a layer of cream on top." It occurs to me that perhaps I could have gone over the milk situation in more detail.

"Sorry, excuse me?" Maria asks, peering over my shoulder.

"Never mind—see how these are different?" I hold up a breast milk bottle and a formula bottle. They look about the same except for a slight difference in color. Because the breast milk bottle has only been in the fridge an hour or so, the cream has not yet separated.

"I didn't know any of this before I was I mom either, so let's make it simple. Actually, the warm-up process is the same," I continue. I pull out a pan, fill it with a few inches of water and place it on the stove. "As soon as the water warms up, right before it starts boiling, turn off the stove and put the bottle in on top, like this." The bottle bobs up and down and then falls over into the pan.

"Umm, okay, that's basically how it goes. For now. I mean, for later. Max just ate so he doesn't need a bottle right now, and Franny, are you thirsty honey?"

"No Mama" says Franny.

"Well, okay, so did I hear that you guys were going to the park?"

"Yes, is that okay?" asks Maria. She looks over at the bottle toppled over in the pan.

I shift the weight on my feet and start to ramble. "Oh, hey, I forgot to ask the other day, but just you know, for a formality, do you have anyone I could call at the daycare center . . . you know, for a reference?" All of Maria's "you knows" are already rubbing off on me. I rummage around in our junk drawer and pull out a scrap piece of paper and a broken crayon.

Maria takes the paper and crayon and puts it back inside the drawer. "References? No, no, no. I don't do references. So old-fashioned. You'll get a feel for me right? And I'll get a feel for you. But if I just give you a number to call and they say I'm great, does it really mean I'm great? So silly. She smiles and clicks her teeth and then starts rinsing the kid's dishes and loads them into the dishwasher.

Is Maria serious, or is she joking? And she sort of actually makes sense, but then again, she completely doesn't. Colette's agency would have been all over this. But me? I'm handing my kids over to someone I met on Craigslist and asking her to please not microwave the breast milk.

I stand there for a moment longer, not sure if I should press the issue. "Don't you need to go to work?" Maria eyeballs the digital clock above the microwave. "This is a big day for you, no?"

"Yes, yes, of course," I blurt. I decide to lean on Mom, pot cookies and all, to see if she can come and hang out a bit today and check on Maria. So I add, "Oh, by the way, my Mom lives nearby so she might pop in to see the other kids when she drops Lucy off. Just didn't want you to be alarmed."

"That sounds fabulous. Family number one right?" Then she turns to the girls. "Okay, *muchachos*, let's go fly a kite!" I hear her say behind me.

Six

"Anna! You're Back!"

"Gloria, YOU'RE back!" We both squeal like sorority sisters and dance in place like we're about to pee all over the floor.

Gloria leans down and gives me a big, tight hug. "Where were you?" I ask, relaxing under the familiar scent of her gardenia perfume.

"What do you mean?" she responds, pulling away. She's dressed in an ethereal, gauzy dress and a military style jacket. On anyone else, it might look like a nightgown with a coat thrown over for a midnight dog walk. Not rail thin, 6-foot tall Gloria. Slade always talks about how he yearns for something really eye-catching and alluring for the front office, and yet I always thought he had that in Gloria, not that she's just another pretty face. She's been with the agency for just under two years, though it feels longer. I tried to bring her onto my team as a copywriter about a year after she had started, but she declined, saying she'd rather write words for herself during quiet times at the front desk than be paid to write words for someone else. "Um, yes, we'd all rather do that," I wanted to say to her, but she was actually doing it.

"You were the one who's been gone for half a year. I should be asking you that question, Gorgeous," she says in her thick Italian accent, which is kind of hypnotizing.

"There was someone here last week—some Goth looking—" I pantomime the application of thick eye and lip makeup.

"Oh, you must mean *Miranda*!" she smiles, reaching over to her desk to sort through some papers. "I got called in for a quick photo shoot, and that poor girl made a terrible mess." Gloria was occasionally asked by clients to be in their photo shoots, even after being presented with binders and binders of Seattle's top models. She reaches down for the log notes from last week, pointing to the scribbled entry:

Anna Moore to see Creative Director

I chuckle to myself as I walk down the hall to my office. I turn the corner and then come to a stop in the entryway. Everything is gone. The bobble heads are gone, and the smell of patchouli is no longer in the air. The photos and the clutter. They are all gone and they've been replaced with flowers from the Martha Stewart wanna-be florist I love and a glittery shoebox wrapped up with a floppy silver bow sitting atop my desk. Puget Sound glistens in the distance and the ferryboats seem to be blissfully skimming the waves. Yes, my little YOWZers, it's good to be back I think to myself. As sad as I was to leave my children, these minutes of freedom to do something for myself I remember, this space is part of why I am here.

A few team members huddle outside my doorway, snickering and whispering in hushed voices.

"Hey you guys!" come in! I urge.

"Open the box" they smile.

"Oh, my gosh, you shouldn't have . . ." I start, feeling guilty and giddy all at the same time. I sit down on my chair, smoothing out my skirt and take a closer look at the box. I pick it up. It has silver lettering on the outside—the script is flowery and takes me a minute to figure out what it says:

Daycare

"Uh oh," I say as I raise an eyebrow at the team in the doorway but they just keep smiling. "Open!!!!" one of them pleads, "just open it!" I feel like Alice in Wonderland. What sort of delights or horrors await? Slowly I lift the lid and peer inside. The box is full of multicolored tissue and glitter. I sift through the layers and finally lay my hands on something soft, rubbery and slimy.

Ewww!

And then I hear a click.

Suddenly there's a throng of people inside my office. The music starts. The team has lined up for what appears to be a choreographed dance routine, my own personal flash mob is welcoming me back to work.

M-m-m-m-my daycare . . . m-m-m-m-m-my daycare

"Stop!" I yell, waving the fake piece of poop at them, but I can't contain my laughter. I'm doubled over in hysterics, thankful that my lack of body armor is allowing my belly to move so I can properly breathe.

M-m-m-m-my daycare is a s-s-s-s-s-s-s-s-s-sh-i-i-i-i-t b-b-b-b-b-b-ox

There must be a train of ten people in and out of my office, stepping to the beat and breaking away for various routines. A few account reps actually get down on the carpet and attempt to break dance. Tears stream down my cheeks I'm laughing so hard. They get up, arms linked to shoulders and circle in and out of the office one more time before the song finishes up. At the end of the line is Clare, unsmiling and not dancing.

The music stops, Clare and I are standing eye to eye in my office. Everyone clears out.

Normally clad in garishly bright colors, today Clare is in all black — skinny jeans, a black button-down, black sneakers and black eyeliner. His beard is flecked with purple glitter. "Welcome back. And thanks for the demotion," he says.

"You didn't get demoted," I say, offering him a chair. I can see by his expression that this isn't going to go well. I sit down and look him straight in his smoky eyes and start again. "You knew I'd be coming back, so what's really going on, Clare?" I say, with more of a motherly tone than I intended. Early on in my career, a seasoned executive once confided in me, "if you can mother, you can manage" and I think of those words more often than I'd like to admit. Mainly because I think it's terrible advice. Mothering in the workplace early on led me to an office full of people crying about breakups, calling in sick when they were hung over from concerts and wanting to go bar hopping with me on business trips. When I started treating them like employees who needed to earn my respect, suddenly things started going much more smoothly – the work product was better and I wasn't picking up as much of the slack. And really, Clare was probably the last person in this office that I wanted to mother.

Clare's lower lip sticks out and quivers a bit. "Slade took me off the Bayview account," he says.

I nod without emotion.

"And he put me on the butt hole bleach account instead. This is so unfair!" He gestures with his hands and I am almost blinded by the bling. He has so many rings on his fingers he could put Liberace to shame.

"Why unfair," I ask. "Did he tell you why he took you off Bayview?" I wonder if Slade is going to leave it to me yet again to do his dirty work. I try to deflect. "And he gave you another account to run!"

"Butt hole bleach?" he spits, "you did hear me, right?"

"Well," I say, trying to figure out how to move on. Slade will certainly take on any account that pays, but I also don't want to wind up in another video on YouTube. And Clare is an actor so I decide to play it straight. "I know nothing about them yet but I'm sure if Slade brought them on board there must be something interesting about them."

"Anal whitening?! You find that interesting, do you, Anna? Well, the company's name is Nether Lights so perhaps we could team up on it if its so intriguing," he says this with a straight face.

I blink a few times and feel my face redden. "I'm sure I have a lot on my plate already, but I'm happy to strategize with you," I say, readjusting myself in my seat. "Certainly in my absence Slade was right to take it upon himself to assign accounts that he thought people were best suited —"

But Clare interrupts me before I can finish.

"I'm going to sue this agency for discrimination," Clare interrupts. He places his elbows on my desk and presses his knuckles together causing the rings to clang against each other.

"Ok Clare," I start smoothing my hair, a habit held over from childhood when things get tense. I used to chew on the ends but now I just finger it. I place my hands in my lap to keep them away from my head for fear that I may start gnawing away at any moment with my post baby long hair.

"Well, I can't speak to that. You'll have to take that up with Slade and HR, but you know, Clare, if you think about this from a creative standpoint, there's actually a lot of fun stuff you could do with this account -- get the Butt Hole Surfers to write some cool jingle. Geez they'd probably love the work about now. Even Bon Jovi who's way more relevant is doing that commercial for some cable company. And think about it - you could have them surfing while singing in white swim trunks! I'm thinking of like the GoGo's, what was that album cover where they are doing the pyramid while water skiing?"

"Really? *Vacation.* D'uh. I mean, seriously, how you could not know that? My mother played it constantly when I was a child. She can't be that much older than you. I bet you do that with your kids too." Yes, this account will be a perfect fit for him I decide.

"Anyway, I don't know what you're complaining about. You're being given a chance to take something that people are embarrassed to talk about and take it mainstream! Get the Kardashians to endorse it or something. They'll post anything on Instagram if you pay them." Did I really just say this? Sometimes my enthusiasm for the creative ideas makes me go a little haywire, but the clients love it… mostly.

"You always get the good accounts," he whines, first looking down at my hands and then turning to stare out my office windows. I notice that he's wearing blue mascara.

"I'm the creative director," I say, putting my chin in my hand, I'm getting bored with this. "I don't "get" the good accounts, I help make them good accounts," I continue, "We all do. That's why we work here, Clare. Because we share this talent and this passion." Twenty years ago I never could have imagined that I would sit across a desk from a direct report talking to them about passion and butt hole bleaching in the same 60 seconds. In fact, twenty years ago, when my mother suggested that the rhyming songs I used to make up for family birthday celebrations (*Happy Birthday dear Dad, you'll never go out of style like shoulder pads!* And *Happy Birthday dear Mommy, I hope we never lose you in a tsunami!*) positioned me for a great career in advertising, I responded by asking her if she hated me by suggesting that for a career for me. "*I want to own the company that needs the jingle, or at least star in the commercial!*" I screamed at her.

Now I can't tell anymore whether I'm passionate about it or whether I've just gotten really good at reciting the script.

I stare at him intensely for a few beats until he turns to look me in the eye. I want him to see that I'm not bullshitting him, that we're in this together. We're still on the same team. And he needs to get over his temper tantrum.

I half expect to see a softening in his expression but instead, he turns to look me in the eye and all I see is pure disgust. He stands up and starts pacing around the room. The white walls have holes and dark scuffmarks that I didn't remember being there before. It's like I've reentered a war zone.

"Here's what I know -- that I finally got a good account in a hot new demographic and that you waltzed in this week and are going to pull it from me," he says with a snotty voice oozing with sarcasm. "*You're* the mom. *You* get to show up with your cute little baby who drools all over the conference table and suddenly you're this hotshot mommy expert. *I* did the research! *I* lined up the focus groups!"

I remain seated and take a few slow breaths, choosing my words carefully. "Listen, Clare, I get that its no fun to be yanked around like between accounts or that you feel Slade has pigeon-holed you as a gay man and now have to lead an anal—"

In an instant, Clare's face turns purple. "I am NOT gay!" he shouts, stomping a foot on my floor so hard that my desk shakes underneath my elbows, causing my arms to slip off the table.

Is he kidding me? Do hipster straight men today have boyfriends and wear mascara? Is it like the new man bun? Clearly I'm making the situation worse, and he looks like he might punch me in the face with all those sharp rings. I get up slowly, take a few steps and sit on the desk facing Clare. I hear murmurs from outside my doorway and quickly walk over to close the door. Footsteps scatter.

"Time out, time out," I command. "Let's get something straight before we move on."

After another thirty seconds that feels like an eternity, and after I decide NOT to say that he shouldn't bring Stu to company parties and introduce him as his boyfriend if he doesn't want people to think he's gay, I finally figure out what I want to say.

Clare turns his head and gives me a sulking half nod, my cue to continue. "So, I don't care what you are and the fact of the matter is, the only thing that matters is your ability to produce on accounts," I say somberly.

Clare shakes his head.

"Now I KNOW that you're the one behind putting me on this account," he blurts out. His anger is ratcheting up, not down. "Well my sexual preference is none of your business!"

Clare wipes his eyes and smears blue mascara across his cheekbones. With the smudged eyeliner, it actually looks like Clare has a black eye, as if I've just spent the last 10 minutes punching him in the face.

There's a knock on my door, and Lauren walks in without allowing me time to answer. "Oh, I am SO sorry!" she says, taking one look at Clare facing the wall, and backs away.

Clare stands up, sending the chair clamoring to the floor and sprints past Lauren so fast that her hair kicks up a bit in the gust. "She's ALL yours!" he snarls, not clear if he's referring to me or to Lauren. And then looking at me, "For now . . ." he snarls.

"That didn't look like it went very well," Lauren gulps, looking over her shoulder.

Not wanting to make a disaster of an HR situation even worse, I quickly change the subject. "Did you have a good weekend?" I ask.

She smiles sweetly, walks over and places something in my hand. "This is for you," she says, quietly. I look down at the small bundle of dried green leaves tied in dainty string and look back up at her. I jump up to close the door.

"Lauren, oh my God," I whisper, "Are you trying to get us both fired?" So far I'm looking at both a potential lawsuit *and* criminal charges in the first hour back at work. Pot's legal in Washington State, but not at work. I peer through the half windows on either side of my door and scan the hallway to make sure nobody is watching us.

She laughs. "No, silly," she says, more confident than I remember. She pulls a pack of matches from her pocket and holds them up like she's showing off a product on QVC.

"Lauren! No not here!"

Lauren erupts into giggles and touches my shoulder. "Anna! Calm down. It's dried sage. What did you think this was? It's a Feng Shui thing. We need to cleanse this office, stat! I was going to do it on Friday after Slade made Clare move out, but the energy was so bad that I couldn't even walk in here without getting sucked into a vortex of negativity. I spritzed a little with Glade and then went out and got this for you over the weekend. Smell it. I got it at the farmer's market. It's been blessed."

"Blessed?" I hold it to my nose, inhale deeply, and then sneeze.

"Bless you!" says Lauren with a smile.

I reach over and hug her tightly.

"Come on," she says, "let's do this quickly, because the meeting will start soon, and I want to make sure that the energy in this place has shifted before you walk in there. Normally I don't believe in all that ritual mumbo jumbo stuff, but it can't hurt, you know?"

I close the blinds on my windows, hit the mellow mix on iTunes and Lauren and I slowly move around the room. The swirl of smoke surrounds us and I inhale, trying to calm my nerves after Clare.

"Ok let's go," she says, glancing at her watch. She looks radiant, reenergized and young, and I'm hoping the sage has allowed some of it to rub off on me too.

My energy has shifted, but I'm not sure in the right direction. Suddenly I have the sense of being old, like an aging Baby Boomer trying to reclaim her youth through New Age-y crystals and incense. "Okay . . ." I murmur, looking down at my own attempt at office fashion: gray pants and an ill-fitting blouse that I thought would hide my stomach but as I stand up I realize the silky fabric is just enhancing the effect, like cling wrap over a bowl full of Jell-O. I toss on a blazer as Lauren hands me a stack of files, which I protectively hug to my chest. We walk to the conference room.

I gather my materials in front of me, industry articles I pulled together over the weekend, and the last client status report I can find from before my leave. I'm sitting tall in the head honcho chair with my back to a wall of tinted blue glass, ready. I smell Slade before I see him – a mix of his beard oil and hair pomade and skin lotion. The man is a literal and metaphorical oil slick. I turn around slowly and greet him. He's looking especially dapper this morning in a dark suit, a slightly gaudy but all-the-rage bright tie and overly priced polished black oxford shoes. I make a conscious effort to put on my happy face. "Good morning Slade, so nice to see you!" I chime. But I feel the sides of my eyes struggling to lift up and meet the pitch of my voice.

I decide to stand up and go for the half hug after such a long leave. But he keeps walking by me towards the end of the table to assume his seat at the opposite end. And then Clare walks in and decides to scoot his chair right next to mine, crowding my position. He clears his throat, tucks an imaginary hair behind his ear and scans the room until he has everyone's full attention. I decide to take advantage of it.

"Ok, Clare," I say, "Let's get started. Why don't you lead us *one* more week and give everyone a update, while getting me up to speed, on where the accounts stand…And let me also publicly thank you, for your willingness to step up to the plate during my time away." I'm certain I can feel blood seething up from his core, but Clare won't dare scream at me in front of Slade.

He's come prepared and has all the materials ready as if he's prepared to publicly stage a coup.

"Well, as you know, Bayview Hospital has been wanting to improve their image . . . they've been losing business to the, ahem, *hipper* hospitals on the East side and no longer want to be known solely as a trauma center. We're going to broaden their reach. So, this is what we're proposing: less trauma, less drama . . . more *mama*!" Clare flashes the white cue cards for everyone to see.

I open my mouth to laugh, but I see only straight faces.

"C'mon, Clare," I gently prod. "Very funny… you're kidding, right?"

"No." He turns to glare at me with the authority of the permanent and not temporary creative director. "It's our repositioning statement." And now I realize that while Slade has seen these before, he's said nothing to Clare about them, leaving the dirty work to me.

Clare stands up and puts his hands on his hips, and I know what comes next. We've all been trained on body language techniques and how to appear powerful during a pitch meeting. Winning a client or selling them on a campaign is often not about how compelling the idea is, but whether you have the balls to sell it.

The first image shows a woman with a foot brace and crutches trying to balance a baby under one arm.

The copy reads:

A sudden injury can send your world spinning
Find solid ground at Bayview Hospital

I sit up straight, press my lips together and choke back the impending guffaw. "Okay, so on this one, Clare," I start to say, slowly, in my nicest tone, pointing to what looks like a hasty comic book image of a modern mom, "no mother would attempt to carry a baby and walk on crutches at the same time." I lean forward and rest my elbows on the table. No major attack here; just merely conveying a rational voice of reason.

Clare flashes me a florescent white smile. "I'm glad you brought that up," he sneers with an amazingly ill advised level of confidence. "I was originally thinking the same thing, but you know, when *I* met with them last week, they indicated that with the launch of their new birthing center, the hospital wants to target the woman who can balance it all – her children, her career, her health care. So . . ." he forcefully jabs a finger at the image, "I think everyone agrees we've captured it here."

I inch my seat forward and glance around the room. "Well, I am not quite sure this is what they meant," I say, with perhaps too much diplomacy. Slade is staying silent.

Clare stands back up and starts waving his arms around. "Sure they did. Have you not *been there* recently?" There is some crazy shit that goes on at that hospital . . . people smoking outside with oxygen tanks strapped to their wheelchairs . . . dudes being pulled off ambulances with knives still in them. I hardly think a mom with a baby and crutches is going to upset them."

I look around the room. Silence of the freaking lambs. Until I get to Slade.

"Moore, why don't you tell everyone the problem with this? Go ahead."

"So yes, Bayview is a level 1 trauma center, which is why, as you say, there's some "crazy shit" going on there," I say, raising my voice. I'm not exactly shouting, but my tone now ensures that I have the full attention of everyone in the room. "But this," I say pointing to his comps, barely able to contain my disgust. "This would send any thinking mother running for the hills at the thought of going to a hospital that would let a mother with a leg injury leave on crutches while holding a baby under one arm!"

Clare sits back down and spreads his arms out across the comps like Vanna White. The bangles around his wrists clatter loudly. "I'm sorry," he interrupts, "but how can you not know that women – especially mothers – are the hottest growing market, and what they care about are people who can help them with all the juggling they need to do in their life! I've been going to these 'marketing to moms' conferences," Clare rolls his eyes at me, exasperated. "Don't you *see*? We are appealing to Bayview's most important audience with this. It's no longer about Swiffers and Hot Pockets and Minivans. It's about juggling and balance. That's why we have the crutches in there. To remind women that there's no way in hell they can do it all. They *need the crutch*! Get it? Crutches = hospital. It's genius!"

And I was worried about MY job?! Now I'm pissed. Is this the best my team can come up with while I've been gone? Even if Slade had done the most minimal checking in on the team while I was gone, we could have avoided this and the threat losing a major hospital campaign. I don't buy it that Slade could be that out to lunch.

But then I don't have to.

"It's so good to have you back, my dear!" Slade walks down the length of conference room chairs with his eyes locked on mine and when he reaches me, he leans over and kisses my cheek. I fight the urge to wipe off the residue.

"So everyone," he says as he rolls back and forth on the balls of his feet and claps his hands. "Sorry to interrupt this absolutely, what's the word I'm looking for, intriguing, staff meeting, but I have a surprise. . . Kendall . . .?" As if he's Bob Barker asking one of those game show women to unveil what's behind door number one, Slade's assistant Kendall floats in toting bags that seem overflowing with goods from the drug store across the street. Young account execs and artists rush in and grab seats around the already crowded table. Clare has disappeared.

Kendall dumps out the hefty drug store bag onto the conference room table as if it were filled with Halloween candy. Packages of over-the counter pain medications, vitamins, St. John's Wort, fish oil and a few prescription vials clatter across the table. One of them skids across the tabletop and I grab it just before it hits the floor. Vicodin. It's empty but it has Slade's name on it. Hmm.

"Bad day already?" I joke, looking up at Slade.

"No. It's an *excellent* day, Anna. I called this meeting—well, this *group hug*, really, because we wanted to welcome you back. We've *missed* you so much. Kendall?" Slade scans the room looking for his assistant. "Where did she go? She was right here." He waves his hands in the air as if he's just misplaced his car keys.

I point to the doorway.

"Oh there you are, dear."

Kendall returns with two extra large cardboard boxes from Top Pot Doughnuts.

"Yes!" One of the more junior male execs sitting at the middle of the table raises his fist with a victory punch.

"Okay. Everyone grab a doughnut. Pick one that speaks to your soul." There are a few chuckles around the table as people stand and hover over the boxes, making their decisions. "Now . . ." continues Slade, once the boxes are nearly empty. "We're going to do a little exercise. Let's go around the room and each one of you is going to tell me three things. One: why you chose that particular doughnut. Two: what being creative means to you. And three: how we can showcase more of a 360 approach for our potential clients – an approach to show off our *best* thinking, and our most creative approaches to the challenges our clients are facing. The doughnuts are a *met-a-phor, you see.*" Slade caresses his candy-striped tie and grins, obviously feeling very pleased with himself.

"And what about the drugs? Is that for the after party?" I quip.

"Oh yes, the drugs. That's the most important part, and the point of this whole exercise. The drugs are for our latest client opportunity, everybody, and Anna will be in charge of putting together the pitch—

along with the rest of the fine people in this room of course. It is quite the opportunity and we need it to be top notch, top shelf, top dog, top of the world."

I look around the room. Half of the team members have already started devouring their doughnuts, wiping powered sugar and chocolate frosting off the corners of their mouths, while the other half seems to be entranced with the drug paraphernalia. I catch one junior account exec opening one of the prescription vials and tapping it into his hand to see if he can catch any residual dust.

"Does the team already know about this pitch?" I lean over to ask Slade.

"Well, not exactly," he winks at me, "they know that I've been working on luring in something big, but now they will!" Slade throws his arms up in the air as if he's already won the account. He pulls up a chair and shoves it next to mine so that I'm forced out of the head spot, causing a ripple effect around the table as everyone else readjusts their seats to make way for Slade.

He claps his hands together and rubs them rapidly back and forth before he begins, Slade's signature warm-up gesture. "As you know, the prescription drug market is changing the advertising landscape as these companies navigate new ways to approach the direct to consumer terrain. That's where *we* come in. Asenzer is in the finally stages of bringing to market a new anti-anxiety drug and their first target market is directed at women, because who's more stressed than them, right Moore!?" Slade slaps me hard on the back and then rubs his palms together, interchanging his slender fingers in a scheming little dance. "So good to have you back, Moore. Women's college graduate, our agency's top performer, busy mom with a new baby . . . you must have some anxiety issues you can tap into for this pitch, am I right?"

I meet eyes with Stephanie, who heads up PR for the agency, who mouths to me: "Oh my fucking God" from the other side of the room.

Slade continues as I muster a pained grin.

"We've been asked to submit a proposal to do a full treatment— product branding, campaign theme, print, TV, digital campaigns. You name it. It's a *huge* opportunity for us, and a *huge* opportunity that we need right now. So, I want us to think outside the pill bottle on this one—big ideas, what can we do that's never been done? How can we address this issue in a new way? What's the YOWZ prescription for them?"

Slade turns to wink at me. I lean in and open my mouth, preparing to facilitate a discussion, but he keeps going, waving his arms like he's gaining wind and about to take off. "We really want to show them our ingenuity that comes from being small and flexible – that's why they're coming to us. We're the only small firm in the group of bidders. No idea is too wacky. Let's throw it all out on the table. Maybe we pull together some sort of a sweepstakes for consumers. Whatever it takes to get them to sign with us." Slade leans back in his chair and sighs loudly, putting his hands behind his head. He's clearly very satisfied with himself thinking that the Publishers Clearing House model is how you promote a new drug.

"Uh, Slade?" Stephanie raises her hand halfway.

"Yes, my PR queen?" Slade jerks forward and the chair nearly slides out from under him.

"I'm pretty sure a sweepstakes is a no-no with the FDA."

"Nonsense!" He slaps his palms on the conference room table and I notice his nails are buffed and neatly trimmed. "Where's your *can do* spirit?" he seethes. "Let's forge a new path! You just worry about how to publicize this when we win it and create a tidal wave of other RFPs flowing in."

Slade leans back in his chair and grips the edge of the conference table and goes on. "We're here to break the rules! Our ad agency has no boundaries. Isn't that right . . . " Slade looks around the room, searching for a partner in crime, "Kyle?"

I feel the ground vibrating and look down to see that Slade's knee is bouncing at the speed of a hummingbird. I wonder if he helped empty out any of the prescription bottles before coming here.

Kyle, one of the newest members of the account team, springs to attention so fast that his doughnut slides across the table. "Yes!" He cocks his head and does a mini hair flip, brushing his long bangs off his forehead. "If we're not breaking some of the rules—or offending someone—then it's not worth doing."

"That's my boy," nods Slade with an approving grin, fingers pressed together.

"So." Slade gets up from his chair and stands behind me, rubbing my shoulder blades. Suddenly I'm thankful that at least I know his hands are clean. "The question for you, Anna, is how to take anxiety drugs for women, inject them with some psychedelics and make this campaign far out? You and I are going to San Francisco to make the capabilities presentation in two weeks."

I wiggle my shoulders and casually shake Slade off my back. "Okay Slade, let's focus on the capabilities and not pulling the Merry Pranksters back together."

"Ooh, Tom Wolfe, I like it Moore – that take no prisoners straight talking intellectual Smithie stuff will wow them." Slade adjusts one of his cufflinks back into position and moves over towards the whiteboard. "Let's move on. So, who wants to go first and tell me about their doughnut to get the creative juices flowing?"

Just then my phone beeps and I look down. It's Maria. A lump forms in my throat and I gasp. Something awful has happened to Max, I just know it. I click open the text.

Look up. Max and I are here.

Seven

Maria is standing just on the other side of the conference room where everyone can see her. Max is strapped to her chest in the Ergo baby carrier. Maria is waving maniacally and Max is flailing his arms and kicking his legs against Maria's toned bare thighs.

"You'll have to excuse me," I say, abruptly standing up and taking my phone into the hallway, feeling two dozen eyes scrutinizing the back of my head.

In the course of the ten seconds it takes to get from my chair to the other side of the wall, my mind goes straight to the nightmare scenarios again. Only this time my brain has conveniently converted the daycare death trap scenarios into nanny wreckage. The kids were playing in front of the house, Maria took Max in for a nap, and the girls chased a ball into the street where they were flattened by a truck. It feels like an eternity to get to Maria.

"What's wrong," I ask, out of breath, as I lead her by the arm down the hall trying to get her as far away from the fish tank as possible.

"Nothing! Are *you* okay? You are breathing so fast!"

My instinct is to reach out and strangle her, but I hold back, not wanting to set a bad example in front of Max.

"I just wanted to see how things were going with your first day back and all . . . and this little smoochie needed some fresh air!" she smiles, kissing his cheek.

I clear my throat, pretending to act calm.

"Where are the girls?" I say barely containing my mounting anxiety.

Maria's air is all breezy nonchalance. "Oh, they had a play date with your mom. I think they're at the library story time, and then they were going to have lunch. And it's such a nice day, so I thought it would be good to get out!" She tickles Max's feet and prances on her toes at the same time, causing the bells around her ankles to chime loudly. I see a few heads pop up from behind fabric partitions.

"My *mom* took the girls? Why didn't you call me?" I fume.

"Oh, I didn't want to bother you with *that*!" she purrs, tickling the bottoms of Max's feet again. He arches his back and looks up at her with adoring eyes. "You said she might stop by, and she did so we exchanged numbers so we can arrange that more often." I dare not say that it was just a lie to keep her on her toes. Now my mom and Maria will be chatting all day. Ugh!

"But how did you get here?" I yelp, picturing Maria and Max careening in the backseat of some grimy cab or pimpmobile—or God forbid, in the back of my mom's Subaru. Max's only car seat is in the back of my car.

"We took the bus."

Awesome. Taking the six month-old who you've known for less than a day on the bus? Good call.

But . . . I am *not going to be* a control freak, so I take a deep breath.

"Maria," I say, "this is my first day back at work and—"

"Yes, that's why I thought it would be so helpful for you to see Max. I just knew I had to bring him to you!" Maria interjects, swaying her hips back and forth to keep Max from fussing and the sleigh bells tinkling around her feet. For my sake, and nobody else's, I wish she'd put on a few more clothes before coming downtown. Still in her teal short shorts and barely-there tank top, her cleavage is partially covered up by Max in the front carrier, but there's still a lot of side boob action going on. I notice two male account execs conspicuously ogling her behind from their cubicles down the hall. I narrow my eyes and glare at them.

"Come into my office," I practically shove Maria and Max through the door.

"Listen," I say, lowering my voice, "I'm sorry I didn't spell this out earlier, but you can't just pop in on me at work. I need a little separation. Maybe not down the road, but on my first day, this is just not appropriate."

"But you worked at home this morning and told me that this is the new way mothers are working nowadays, integrating it all. You said that," she retorts.

"Never mind what I said," I say. "That was home. This is work. It's too distracting to have both of you here. I mean, I've barely been here two hours. Also—and I guess I should have explained this earlier—but the kids cannot just run off with their Nana. She's can be a bit, um, unstable at times. I mean, I know she's my mother and she's great, but . . . you know what, this is just too much for today."

"Oh. Okay." Maria takes a step back, startled by my tirade. Max bursts into tears, but as I reach out to stroke his head, Maria takes yet another step back and puts her hand on the handle of my door. "I just thought you might want to see Max, and Lucy and Franny were so excited to see their Nana . . . and she seemed so excited to see them, she's so funny, you know? But we can go now . . . ."

"Do you drive?" I blurt. It's the first thing that pops into my head. I need to know.

Maria raises an eyebrow and gives me a look that says: *what's with the non sequitur?*

"Do you drive?" I ask, again. "I know I should have gone over this during the interview, but I just need to know whether you drive or not."

A wave of realization washes over Maria's face. Now she gets it. "Oh, *driving?*" she responds, holding her hands at 10 and 3 o'clock to mimic a steering wheel. "Oh, no, no, no, no, no. I mean, I *used* to drive back in Colombia, but now that I am here in Seattle, I don't drive at all."

"So you have a driver's license." It's a statement, not a question.

"Oh, yeah, sure." Maria bends her knees up and down, stroking the bottoms of Max's feet until he stops fussing and begins to coo and squeal.

"Perfect. Do you have it with you? I'll just make a copy, and then I can figure out which days you can have the car and . . . ."

"Oh, Anna, you misunderstand me!" Maria tsks me with her index finger. "Now that I am in Seattle, I don't drive. This is the emerald city, no? The city of green living? Citizens for no carbon footprint? No driving for me!" She holds her nose and waves her hand back and forth to gesture that she will have none of that stinky business. "Your kids and I will walk and take public transportation!"

Lauren has just entered my doorway.

"Hi," she says, a little sheepishly, giving a sideways glance to Maria who is still dancing in place and holding her nose. "The meeting is about wrapped up, but I have some—I mean, I can come back later." Lauren gives Maria the once over and I can practically see the question marks swirling over her head in a cartoon thought bubble.

I think back to when I was 13 and new neighbors fresh from Arizona came knocking on our door asking if we had anyone old enough to babysit. My mother immediately volunteered me, said I was great and signed me up for a regular babysitting job with three children aged six months to seven. When I asked my mom if it was okay that I really didn't have any experience, she said, "Oh sure, it all comes naturally. You'll know what to do. Just don't drop the baby." Sure, there were times when, frankly, I had to turn to the seven year-old for help. In fact, I probably should have split my pay with her. Standing here looking at Maria, I feel like I could be looking at my 13 year-old self. I silently make a vow to give her more notes, more direction, more scenarios for everything that could possibly go wrong and what to do. I'll arm her with information and expectations and safeguard my workplace.

Lauren smiles sweetly at Max, and he immediately stops crying. "This is the research that Slade wanted you to have," she says, handing me a stack of files.

"Thanks," I say. Maria and Max are now hovering over my shoulder.

"What kind of research?" asks Maria. I can feel her breath on my cheek and inhale the scent of something fruity and sweet.

I can tell that Lauren is momentarily taken back by the question but answers her anyway. Lauren is good that way; she used to work in retail and is great when it comes to customer service. "Demographics and psychographics on modern moms, plus some women's mental health data," she explains, not dumbing down the marketing terminology for Maria's sake, which surprises me a bit. Maria, either totally in-the-know already or putting on a good straight face, nods accordingly and starts thumbing through the files I've just put down on my conference table. Lauren then lowers her voice, addressing me specifically. "This is some of the stuff I was helping Clare work on last week for Bayview, but . . . I'm not sure why Slade had him do that song and dance this morning, but we lost Bayview. They called this morning to say that they didn't need to see any more from us . . . ."

"What?" I practically shriek. "They were one of our biggest clients. Why didn't anyone tell me??"

"I thought Slade—" Lauren stammers, trying to piece everything together.

"Oh . . . my . . . God" is all I can muster, my hands reaching up to smooth my hair, "why didn't anyone call me in for this?"

"Well, I don't know the whole story, " Lauren takes her voice down another notch and looks out in the hallway to make sure no one is near, "but Clare and a few designers went ahead and pitched on Friday without Slade's okay, and the head of Bayview marketing point blank told him that there was a big misunderstanding with their goals, and that they were going to have their in-house communications team handle all marketing efforts for now, " she blurts before looking down at the floor.

"Ugh," I groan. There's a tightening in my chest. So Slade wasn't kidding about my job after all. I can tell there's more to the story, but I don't want to get into it with Maria and Max standing in my office. Maria's full attention is on one of the articles in the file, and she and Max appear to be reading it together.

Fuck. Fuckfuckfuckfuckfuck. Bayview was a REALLY big account. I can't believe we fucked this one up. Without them, the agency has only two or three other major accounts, which can't sustain us for very long. "We still have the Dental Association, right?"

Lauren turns and glances out towards the hallway again. "No, they decided to cut back."

"The League of Apple Growers? Tell me we still have that one." I'm doing that hair-smoothing thing again. If I don't stop now I'm going to have the greasies by noon.

"No."

"Lauren, good God, do we have ANY clients left at this place? Please tell me we have some big accounts." I know I shouldn't be verbalizing any of this, that I need to drop my voice about 10 octaves, that the professional thing to do would be to talk to Slade, but I'm still mad at him and can hardly handle eye contact, let alone a real conversation.

"We have some really big leads," she says, trying to sound upbeat, but we both know that this is a big fat lie. "And yes, we still have Georgetown Brewing and Tully's Coffee," she adds.

I sit down at my already cluttered conference table and rub my forehead.

Lauren lets me be and Maria continues perusing the contents of my files, as if she's standing at the supermarket flipping through women's magazines. I glance over to see that the particular document she's reading *does* contain headlines from women's magazines, in addition to news clips, research briefs and book titles.

When Worrying Becomes an Illness: How to Spot Your Anxiety Disorder
New Report Underscores Women's Mental Health Concerns
Prescription for Happiness: Are Drugs Right For You?
Anti Depressant Use Among Women Up 400 Percent
and the list goes on . . .

"Listen, Maria," I say, lightly touching her shoulder as she skims the articles with intense interest, "as much as I'd love for you and Max to hang out here, I really need to focus—"

"Oh, yeah, sure, sure!" Maria puts the files down and arches her back. She appears to be reaching for something between her massive cleavage and Max. I'm about to avert my eyes but then she's digging deep down in between her breasts and the next thing I know, she has an envelope in her hand, and she places it on the corner of my desk. "Here, I brought you this!" she exclaims.

"Oh goodie, another present," I think. Actually, it's probably best to let it sit there for a bit until the sweat dries. Do I need to open it now while she's still here? As soon as I look over to gauge her expression I see that she's holding her wrist up, glancing at her tangerine sports watch. "Oh my gosh! You are so right. We need to go. It's almost tea time!" Max lets out a burp and a giggle and then they're gone. I open the note.

Dear Anna,

I wanted to thank you so much for hiring me! This job is exactly what I wanted and I am learning so much already. I love your kids. They are so sweet and smoochie! Jajajajajaja! You are such a good mom, you do so much for everyone all of the time.

    I have a list of things you need to do for me:

- *I must have a key to your house*
- *I need a list of your friends with kids so I can organize play dates*
- *Premium cable so we can watch Spanish TV and your kids can learn new words*

Muchas gracias!
Your friend,

It's late in the day, and I'm exhausted from scolding Slade, tracking down my mother and daughters' whereabouts, reviewing accounts, attempting to salvage Clare's ego, reassigning team members to what little is left of our project work, and pleading with the PR director of Bayview Hospital to please take us back so we can continue to *YOWZ* them. I stuff the note inside my purse, adjacent to a wad of receipts and various flotsam and jetsam—a worn packet of gum, a grimy pocket sized vial of hand sanitizer, a diaper and something sticky that I can't immediately place. It's like I've just stuck my fingers inside one of those slots inside a haunted house and you have to guess the contents, usually something slimy and gross like cold noodles mixed with grapes or pumpkin guts. I remove my hand and stare down at a lollipop draped with strands of hair and lint and a clump of raisins stuck to a penny. What's that saying about the contents of your purse symbolizing the state of your brain? Maybe Maria can clean out my handbag instead of so enthusiastically riding public transportation to entertain the kids.

Without the daycare pickup, my commute home is laughably short, and I'm at home 17 minutes after I leave the office.

I enter our house through the back door opening to our kitchen. The kids' tea set is out and Maria's laptop is open on the kitchen table. I really need to talk to her about that, I think. I cannot have her Facebooking or trolling online dating sites or whatever it is she's doing at work. I close the lid and see that it's covered in purple and gold UW stickers and friendly looking Husky dogs. Her enormous backpack is plopped on one of the kitchen chairs, its sides hanging over the seat like Jabba the Hutt. I resist the urge to peer inside.

The house is too quiet. I poke my head into the basement. Nothing. I call upstairs, nothing. I open the front door, retrieve the day's mail. Nothing. Then I hear giggling coming through the kitchen window. I peer out and see Maria running along the border of the yard, Max in arms, being chased by Franny and Lucy, blowing bubbles behind them. There are two new Bratz dolls on the outdoor chairs, plus wrapping. So *that's* what Nana was up to, loading up the girls with more sexually suggestive plastic crap. The sun is still shimmering through the tops of the trees, and I realize that I'm just now noticing what a gorgeous day it is … it was. I put my arms behind my back and grab my hands and slowly bend down at my waist as my arms drop over my head. I hear too many creaks, and I feel like a candy that needs to be cracked out of a mold after sitting in my office chair all day.

"Maria?" I call out the open window. She stops in her tracks and looks up at the window, panting and giggling a bit. Lucy and Franny, barefooted in dirty t-shirts and pink tutus, reach her and topple her, but she manages to keep Max upright.

"Oh hi Anna, come out on and play with us. Right girls, Mommy can play now too right?"

Lucy and Franny shake their heads and continue tickling Maria. I slip my shoes off and walk out onto the back porch.

Maria and the kids march up to greet me, sweaty with blades of grass stuck to their cheeks and arms. It's almost six, yet the sun is still high in the sky; I am thankful for the northern light.

"Anna!" Maria walks right up to me and plants a kiss on my cheek, "how was your amazing day?"

I stand there, dumbfounded. The Moores were raised to show as little affection as possible. Yet another thing I failed to go over during the interview: kissing policy.

"Is it okay if I stay a little later?" She asks, batting her eyelashes at me. "I'm guessing you haven't thought about dinner for tonight so the girls and I are decided to put something together. It won't take long, I promise."

"Um . . . sure that would be great," I mumble, still recovering from the kiss.

"Okay, girls, it's cooking lesson time!"

I grab Max and tell Maria that I'm going to head upstairs to feed him and also check a few emails while she and the girls get dinner ready.

"Working at home still, eh?" Maria smiles, nudging me. "Breastfeeding and working and multitasking and so busy . . . there's a word for this, no? Super Mom, right?" She winks at me. Is she mocking me? But there's no time to analyze. I *do* have a ton of work to do so I blurt out an awkward "I guess so" and run upstairs, latch Max on the boob and open up the lid to the laptop.

Asenzer . . . Asenzer . . . show me what you've got. I didn't have much time to research the company earlier in the day, so I go first to the image of Thomas Paine, the Pharma CEO who Slade is wooing. The man I need to sufficiently dazzle in two weeks. So I can save the company. We *need* this account. Even more so now that I have a full understanding of how dire the situation is at YOWZ.

Facebook and Google are such gifts for account research. I remember one of the earliest and best lessons from my first ad agency internship: Target both the rational and emotional side of every client. What does this guy care about? It's certainly not the individuals that make up our agency, nor their specific need to hang onto their respective jobs. Those are my pain points. *I* need to win this thing so that they don't have to worry. Pictures of him at corporate events will tell a lot. Is he seen only in formal hand shaking poses with other senior alpha males? Or is he singing karaoke with the interns at the Christmas party? Is his Facebook photo a formal headshot? Does he have "followers?" That's a big clue. I had noticed that most down-to-earth CEOs I had worked with had Facebook pages that sometimes let you accidentally see a few photos, but otherwise, their accounts were locked and their lives were private. But cocky narcissistic CEOs, male and female, had activated the "follow" option on their page. I get it when Mark Zuckerberg and Kim Kardashian have follow options. I don't get it when a drug company CEO has one. He has a massive PR team doing communications for him, so he certainly doesn't need "fans" to hear him sprinkle his wisdom on Facebook.

Fortunately, there's no follow option, but there are bad privacy controls and I can see lots of photos. Regardless of the setting, the pictures all show one thing. There's never a hair out of place, a shirt un-tucked or a pillow out of place in what is presumably his living room in some photos. With dark brown helmet hair, a broad forehead with deep-set eyes, he looks like he's never had a disorganized day in his life. No George Costanza wallet in the back pocket of this guy! This is a disaster. What on earth does this guy know about frazzled women with anxiety disorders? Thomas Paine is the picture of calm. As the CEO of one of the biggest Pharma companies in the U.S., he probably has four assistants and at least two wives waiting on him at all times. Tom Paine, I will refer to you from here on out as T. Rx. What will you do T. Rx when I come in and introduce you to the frazzled American working mom you are trying to reach? I can tell you this T. Rx. You need me.

"Anna, you home?"

"Yeah, upstairs," I shout down to Patrick. I can hear his car keys land on the entry table near the foot of the stairs.

"You've gotta come down here."

Patrick stands over a pot on the stove, head down, with a look of dismay of his face. In one hand he holds a sporty all-weather laptop bag. It's blue and orange with a big software company logo across the front. In this town of hipsters with funky man bags, Patrick pulls off a cheesy conference give away bag with style. At least I think he does. In his other hand he holds a pot lid in the air. He stays in this position over the stove, his dark curly hair immobile, like a pensive Rodin sculpture.

"Hey Babe," I sneak up and grab him around the waist with one arm as Max tries to reach for a fistful of his hair.

He turns to give me a brief kiss on the lips. "What's up with this?" he gestures to the pot.

Inside is macaroni and cheese with what appears to be slices of hot dog mixed in and topped off with shredded carrot.

"Did you make this?" he asks with a raised eyebrow.

I shake my head. "Oh, my," I giggle, covering my mouth.

Patrick sighs, puts his bag down, opens the refrigerator door and gazes lovingly at his prized beer collection. "Hmmm… what shall it be… " he says in a singsong voice, scratching his head for optimal effect. "A smoked Porter to go with the 'lil smokies… or something hoppy to go with the 'lil bunny who plopped some chewed up carrot in the pot?" He selects a bottle, opens up the freezer door, removes one of his pre-frosted pint glasses and pours himself a beer, tilting the glass at a slight angle so the beer doesn't foam. He lifts up the glass, takes a sniff as if he is about to sample a fine wine and takes a sip. "Ahhhh," he sighs. "Much better."

I lean back against the kitchen counter with Max on my hip. Patrick seems relaxed tonight. Now may be a good time to warn him that our new nanny likes to visit our workplaces and that he should prepare accordingly.

But just as I open my mouth to speak, the kids bound up the basement stairs. "Daddy, Daddy, Daddy!" Franny and Lucy shout in unison, running forward to grab a leg. "Did you see what we did? We made dinner for you!" "Careful, careful girls," says Patrick as a few drops of beer spill onto their heads. He wipes their hair with his hand and puts his beer glass down on the counter.

"I *did* see what you did. What a *surprise*" he says.

"Just the way you lwike it Dada," says Franny. "I put da hot dawgs in da pot."

"Well, it looks so delicious, I want to make sure there's enough for you girls," he says.

"Oh, you like?" I turn around, Maria's cheeks are flushed and she's smiling from chandelier earring to chandelier earring. Patrick's eyes flash to Maria and then to me in our silent communication. I can't wait to hear what's behind the expression.

"I'm so glad you are happy with the dinner," she says with a coy smile, looking up at Patrick and me expectantly and stroking her ponytail. "Cuz, you know I wasn't sure. I know already that you two are so busy, so I figured anything is better than coming home and cooking right? Do you want to try it, it's yummy?"

"Um, sure, but . . . I think I'll just enjoy my beer first," says Patrick with a deadpan expression, looking back at me before taking a long sip out of his glass.

"You know, you two haven't officially even met yet," I say, reaching towards Maria and putting a hand on her shoulder. "Patrick, meet Maria, and Maria, this is Patrick. Gosh, it actually feels like you've been here more than just one day, don't you think?" I look at Maria and then at Patrick, giving him my closed mouth, wide eyed unwavering look. I'm hoping that he's able to telepathically pick up my message to say something nice.

Maria offers a hand to Patrick. "Well, it's very nice to meet you," she fawns, leaning her chest forward. Gone is the overly excited enthusiasm of her introduction to me, and it's replaced with a flattering seriousness I hadn't seen from her yet. "And I understand you work in game development," she says, followed by some batting of eyelashes. "I think that is so fascinating—and especially raising kids in this era. It must influence the types of games you want to promote. You'll have to tell me more about it sometime."

I can't remember when I mentioned this to Maria, but before I can think two seconds about it, Patrick has started his company pitch. I want to remind him that he's not explaining his business to an investor, but to our nanny. But Maria is utterly absorbed as Patrick goes on and on, and before I know it, Patrick is sitting down at the table, explaining to Maria the intricacies of the market and their new game release, which he hopes will smash the competition. I'm beginning to grow irritated and I'm not sure at whom. The girls are eating dinner and Max is playing with Cheerios and I wonder if since everyone is occupied, I should go back upstairs and continue to research T. Rx. But with Patrick having the time to hang out and drink beers with our nanny, my irritation begins to brew. This is lost on Patrick, although Maria repeatedly gives me sideways glances, as if to gauge my temperature before she puts her eyes right back on my husband. I lean against the doorframe and even surprise myself when I start tapping my foot. It's almost 7 o'clock now and I can't hold it any longer.

"I'm sure you two will have lots of time to get to know each other, but I'm afraid it's time for Maria to go." I glance at the clock above the microwave. Patrick's conversation with Maria just cost us $16.

Maria stands up and swings one voluptuous hip to the side. Bells tinkle around her feet. Franny and Lucy are chomping away on their dinners. "It's yummy, Mommy!" says Franny through a mouthful of food. I can see some bits of carrot on top of her tongue and a few limp green beans on her plate. My daughter is actually eating vegetables, so I count that in and of itself as a successful first day for Maria. End on a high note I say telepathically to her.

Maria slips her enormous backpack on her shoulders and tightens her ponytail, smoothing out her shiny black hair one last time before heading for the door. With his audience gone, Patrick has gone back to focusing on his beer, and I breathe a sigh of relief as I feel like I have my house and family back to me for the night.

We could lay gazing at each other for an eternity while the rest of the world drifts out of focus, I think. There's no self-consciousness about it when it's just the two of us. I can drift in and out of sleep—or be an active participant. Either way, I'm enjoying every minute. He shimmies over and nuzzles his face in between my breasts. Then, resting his head on one of them like his own personal pillow, he gazes up at me with his gorgeous baby-blue eyes and dives in.

Did it feel this good before? I can't remember. Slow sucking motions. His warm mouth sends tingles throughout my body. Is it just me or is there something strangely arousing (in a non-sexual sort of way of course) about breastfeeding?

That is, unless teeth are involved. "Ouch!" I yank Max off before he can do any damage. With two new sharp-as-razor pearly whites, my sweet loving baby boy test rides his new set of knives on my tender nipples—again. Sometimes he doesn't even nurse but rather just takes my nipple between his two front teeth and pulls, stretching it out flat like salt-water taffy, so far that I think it won't give any more and my skin will crack and bleed. And then, suddenly, thankfully, he lets go. *Not bad elasticity for 40*, I think.

But now my nipple is squirting milk like a mini geyser. I cup my hand over my breast but leave my index finger out as an added gesture to make my point. "No bite, Max! That *hurts* Mommy!" Max giggles and starts slapping my breast just in time for Patrick to emerge from the bathroom. I instinctively hold my breath for a few seconds hoping the plume of whatever is emerging with him will float by my nose and land elsewhere.

"Shut the door!" I gasp.

"It's fine. I didn't drop any bombs."

I groan.

Patrick spies Max's flailing hand.

"Oooh, can I have some of that? That's right Maxi, slap it!"

"Don't be gross! Max, come on, there's more in there. Just calm down baby." I turn to Patrick. "Come sit down for a minute."

"So, this is something new and different, lying here with *Max* on the boob!" Patrick sighs as he flops himself down on the bed and throws his arms over his head.

"So, what'd you think of her?" I ask.

"Nice tits just like you said, AND she knows a lot about gaming, and is actually interested in it," he smirks, looking up at the cracks in our ceiling.

I narrow my eyes and glare at him.

"I'm kidding. I'm kidding. She really doesn't know that much about gaming. But what a culinary genius she is, right, Ms. No Nitrates?" Patrick hops off of his side of the bed and crawls in behind me, wrapping his arm all the way around me so he can pat Max on his tush. With Patrick's body tight against mine, his chin resting on my head, I am happily stuck in the middle.

Later, as I'm flitting around the house, turning off lights in preparation for turning myself in for the night, I see the flashing light on the home phone so I check voice mail. It's my mom.

"Anna. You need to call me RIGHT away. It's about your babysitter!"

Eight

"Noooo Mommeeee! Noooo!" Franny arches her back as I attempt to put her shirt on. Down on my hands and knees, I flip her over and pin her shoulders to the ground. I yank the shirt on over her head but then she gets up and takes off toward the bedroom door. I tackle her around the middle and flip her onto my lap, holding her tight as she kicks my shins. I break out in a sweat as I attempt to hold her in place, forcing one arm through a sleeve and then the next. New reality TV show! Mother-Daughter Wrestling! Friday mornings at 8 a.m. PST.

"Come on Franny," I sigh, finally giving up. She yanks off the shirt I've just spent the last 10 minutes trying to put on and dramatically throws it on the floor. "No!" she shouts. "No! Mow! Showt!"

"Listen, Maria will be here any minute and we've got a preschool tour this morning. I need you dressed," I plead.

The cell phone and the doorbell ring at the same time. "Lucy, get the door, I'll get the phone!"

Lucy answers the phone.

"Hi Nana . . . " she says, twirling a clump of matted hair around one finger.

I scramble downstairs and reach for the door. It takes my eyes a minute to adjust to today's ensemble: a lime green terry cloth hoodie and matching short shorts with a fuchsia tank underneath. The weather has cooled a bit, and I am thankful she has covered up … somewhat. Still, she looks more like a character in an animated movie than Mary Poppins. Her backpack rests on her shoulders and there's something new around her waist I haven't seen before: a teal sequined fanny pack that shimmers around her waist. She looks up at me glumly, in solidarity with Franny's mood but then starts tickling Franny all over.

"Come on my little princess, it will be fun!"

"But I don't WANT to. No! New! Skoo!" She picks up a board book lying on the floor and throws it against the wall, leaving a small dent in the sheet rock. In the early days of our ad agency, Slade was prone to tantrums and would occasionally throw things as well. I was used to it.

Franny stands up and starts running up the stairs, still in nothing but her underwear. Lucy follows behind, coaxing her along.

"Hey Franny," says Lucy in a silky sweet voice, marching up the stairs. "I'll help you pick out a pretty outfit. We'll have fun. You'll see."

"Oh, Lucy, you are a wonderful child," I say, pushing myself up off the floor and wiping the sweat off my brow. At least *someone* is excited about the possibility of a brand new school. I turn to Maria who is picking up the remnants of the tantrum, a sweaty toddler sock and some synthetic filling from one of Franny's stuffed animals.

"So we're going to look at preschools today?" she asks, tightening her ponytail.

"Actually, you'll stay here with Max," I say. "I'm taking the girls."

Maria sticks out her lower lip and frowns, like I've planned a trip to Disneyland without her.

"You know, since I do know a lot about preschools, you could use my advice—" she says admonishing me for potentially relying solely on my own judgment.

Oh right, preschool whisperer. I pause, wondering if the nanny trailing along will help our chances at landing a coveted spot, or hurt us. Maria doesn't move. She's waiting expectantly for my approval. Maybe this is the kind of submissive behavior Colette was talking about.

"Deal," I concede, cocking my head towards the kitchen, "I guess we can tackle the dishes later. Can you finish getting the kids ready?" Maria salutes me like I'm her lieutenant and charges up the stairs two at a time.

I try calling my Mom back from the kitchen phone while Maria is upstairs with the kids, out of earshot. It rings and rings and rings.

No answer.

Lucy squeezes my hands tightly as we walk up the steps behind the bicycle shop. The cold stairwell smells of damp concrete. A woman carrying a yoga mat passes us on the way down. "Excuse me," I say with hesitation as I wonder if we're heading towards a school or a palm reader, "we're looking for—"

"The preschool? Oh yes, you're in the right place," she says. "It's at the top of the steps on the other side of the yoga studio. Just go down the hall."

"Thanks," I say.

Sarah was right. The location (at least in terms of distance from our house) was ideal: just four blocks away. The location above the bike shop on a busy arterial? Not ideal but not enough to back out just yet. I look over at Maria to see if I can gauge her reaction but she's entranced in her text messages. I think she might be giving me the cold shoulder after I said no to the premium cable subscription.

As we near the top of the steps we can hear the signing. Yogi chants? No, it sounds more like a sing-along DVD. I feel a surge of annoyance that I could be wasting my time here: are the preschoolers watching TV?

Good morning Carson, good morning Carson, good mooorrning Carson, it's good to see you now! Good morning Annabelle, good morning Annabelle, good mooorrning Annabellllle . . .

I knock gently on the door. "What's going on, Mama?" asks Lucy.

"What?" I say. I can barely hear her question through what sounds like the loud banging of a tambourine. We might be here awhile before they hear us knocking. Lucy gives me a nervous smile. Maria nuzzles Max and squeezes Franny shoulders. I stand tall in my work clothes, hoping nobody wipes snot on me. And then it occurs to me that Maria and I might look like a postmodern lesbian couple: The successful overweight career mom with a much younger exotic-looking trophy wife.

We wait through two more good morning songs before a lull in the music gives me an opportunity to knock on the door again. This time I do it loudly, with authority. An towering woman with short, spiky blond hair, red-rimmed eyeglasses and Chinese script tattoos running up and down each forearm opens the door. She's wearing a hibiscus print Hawaiian style mumu.

"Good morning!" she says to us in a thick European accent. "Zao an, ba ba," she says, squatting down so that she's eye level with Franny and Lucy. "Guten morgen, bon matin, sabaah al-khayr."

"Do you know what I just said?" she asks. Franny and Lucy shake their heads. "I was saying good morning to you in four different languages of our *vorld*: Chinese, German, French and Arabic. Have you ever heard any of those languages before?"

"Hola" means hello," interrupts Maria, stepping forward with a loud clinking of bells from her ankle bracelet.

"You must be *Ahhna*." She stands up and reaches out to shake Maria's hand.

"Actually, *I'm* Anna," I say, crossing my hand over Maria's. "This is Maria, our *nanny*."

Her handshake is warm and I immediately relax as her flesh touches mine. She must be sending me some sort of a voodoo relaxation energy waves because it's as if my sins from five seconds ago—and all of the missteps from five days ago, have suddenly dissipated. Wow. I could use a dose of that every day. I wonder if its included in preschool tuition or if could invite her to chant with my team at work each morning. Out of the box thinking, that's what Slade wants from us. He's got it.

She then kneels back down and puts a hand on Lucy's shoulder and then Franny's. "You must be *Frahncesca*, yes?"

Franny nods.

"And *Loocille*?"

Lucy looks up at me, confused. "Who's Lucille?"

"YOU are, silly," I say, caressing the top of her head. "Lucille is your full name."

"It is?" she asks.

My eyes dart around wildly. How is it that my eldest daughter doesn't even know her full name? Jesus. Thankfully, Ms. Mumu ignores our exchange. "My name is Miss *Ahnnnika*. Like your *mudder*'s name. I am from the *Nederlands*. Welcome to the Global Citizens *Ahcaademy*. This is our school. Please, come in and let your beautiful auras lead the way." Annika motions for us to step inside.

Franny looks up at me. "Tiaras?" she asks. I shake my head and shoo her inside the door. The entry way feels cramped—or maybe it just seems that way because we all try to shove our bodies through at the same time.

"Francesca, would you like to know what an aura is?" asks Miss Annika once we're inside. The carpet is filthy, and there are children's shoes and coats strewn all over the floor. Every square inch of wall space is covered in vibrant art.

Franny nods.

"An aura is like a magical halo that surrounds your *baaudy*." Annika raises her hands over her head and makes a swishing motion like she's caressing herself; only her hands don't touch her *bauudy*. "It is made up of many different colors. The colors change depending upon your mood. And we want to always have happy auras that make our *baaudies* feel good, yes?"

I want to ask "Is Auras 101 part of the school curriculum? May I see the syllabus, please?" but instincts tell me to go with the flow instead.

Maria, obviously not feeling the peace, picks up her pace and whips out her phone and begins texting with one hand while holding Max with another. They stroll ahead of us down the hallway and begin investigating the children's art that lines the walls. Maria peers inside a few of the rooms before turning back and joining our group.

Annika leads us to a big open room where half a dozen children and two female teachers of varying and indeterminate ethnicities sit in a large circle. The children (also made up of varying but indeterminate ethnicities) look up at Franny and Lucy excitedly. I'm aware of how I feel *very white* but also *very welcome* in this environment. What a contrast to the CCDC where the kids were predominately white but the staff was not.

"Global Citizens, may I have your attention please?" The children fidget and giggle but she clearly has their attention. "I *vould* like to introduce you to our friends Lucille and Francesca and their nannah Maria. And *der liddle broder* Max. Please *velcome* them to our *ahcaahdemy*."

One teacher pats the floor, motioning for Lucy and Franny to join the circle. A girl and a boy scoot out of the way and make room for them to sit down. Lucy sits down first. "Do it like this," says a round-faced Asian boy next to her, demonstrating how to sit, folding one leg over the other. "Crisscross applesauce."

Maria and Max join the circle and as Maria sits down and extends her legs, I hold my breath, hoping she doesn't expose any furry lady parts to the kids with her who-wears-short-shorts shorts. Then I needn't worry when she plops Max to sit in between her legs.

Just then my phone rings. I pull it out of my pocket and see that it's my mom. Annika gives me a look that says, *true Global Citizens don't answer their cell phones while in the ahcahhdemy,* so I silence my phone and put it back in my pocket.

We tour the preschool rooms. There is an art room, a yoga room, a library and a nature room. "Interesting" I say. "Is there a playground as well or is that the nature room?"

Annika looks at me sympathetically, a look she must reserve for the underprivileged, or the just plain clueless. She has just finished going over the basics of auras after all, something I've failed thus far to introduce to my children. I *do* have a lot to learn, I realize, and preschool is a great place to start. "*Vee* prefer the children to be at one with themselves and the earth whether they are indoors or out, and not have 'learning' time and 'play' time," she explains. "At the *Ahhcaademy* we blend our experiences to enhance the inner peace and well being of each child." I take that as shorthand for "no playground."

Before I have a chance to ask about the particulars, there is a ringing of bells and Maria is at my side, nudging my shoulder. "But the children go outside, right? Everything I've read shows a direct connection between lots of playtime outside and neurological development, you know." She smiles and looks up at Annika expectantly.

Annika gives me a subtle *who's in charge here—you or your nanny* glance while simultaneously flashing Maria a polite smile that could almost go the way of a full on snarl. I'm picking up on a trend here that Annika doesn't like to answer questions.

I realize that Maria has just left Max unattended in circle time. "Excuse me," I say, turning towards the front room, leaving one eye lingering on Maria, "let me just go check on Max."

"Oh, he's totally fine!" Maria interjects, pulling me back. "He really likes the tambourines, you know? One of the teachers is holding him. Stay and listen and I'm going to take notes for you!" She holds up a spiral notebook and a pen and begins writing before I have a chance to say anything.

Annika, all but ignoring her, continues giving me the spiel. "Here, let me show you our *veekly* schedule. I think you'll get a better feeling for our program that *vay*. Every morning *vee* start out with circle time and songs. Then *vee* break out into our groups – math, science, art, languages and reading. Then *vee* go for a *valk* — *vee* prefer not to climb on manmade playground equipment that leaches toxic chemicals into our young Global Citizens' blood streams that you probably are thinking of," she looks at Maria up and down as she's writing in her notebook. "*Vee* climb hills and pick flowers and look at soil and bugs and clouds. Whatever our beautiful universe is presenting us with that day. Then *vee* come back and have snack. On Tuesdays *vee* play soccer at the indoor arena. On Fridays *vee* do culinary and top Seattle chefs from around the *vorld* come in to prepare organic food for the chicken — excuse me, I mean, *children*. *Vee* only eat vegetarian at the *acaahdemy*. *Vee* focus on academics. Every child who graduates from the *acaahdemy vill* be reading at a first grade level."

"Oh my," I say, looking over at Maria this time, happy to have an assistant to write everything down. "That sounds like a nice program, and the chefs, they are included in the monthly tuition as well?" My heart goes pitter-patter.

Annika nods and leads me over to a table and hands me a packet. I look over at Maria and can see that she's written CHICKEN in all caps in her notebook and is now starting to doodle a chicken with long spindly legs and spiky hair kind of like Annika's. She catches me and flips the notebook closed.

"Here is an overview." I take a look at the flimsy one-color brochure and the marketer in me immediately thinks *why didn't they spend more money on this?* Maria snags a brochure for herself.

"Are you certified by the NAECE or licensed by the Department of Early Learning?" Maria interjects, looking at the flier and turning it back and forth in her hands as if she's missed something. "I don't see the logo here."

"We're in the process." Annika curls her upper lip and looks at me again as if to scold me for letting the nanny hijack the school tour. Her eyes are cool, yet trusting. I have such a good feeling about her. Why is Maria acting so weird?

"This year, tuition is $400 per month," Annika boasts.

What?? How much did I shell out every month to the CCDC for not even a quarter of what this school is offering? A rush of validation flushes over me and I feel giddy with the idea of everything falling into place. Sarah was right. This school is so *me*. I couldn't have dreamed up a better set up: close to our house, offbeat yet rigorous curriculum, focus on play, the environment, some organic sound bites thrown in there for good measure, and world peace. I almost feel a tear forming on the inner corner of my eye.

"I see," I say, measured and calm, hoping the happy dance in my head doesn't give me away. Maybe I should silently count to ten before asking where I sign on the dotted line.

"Here is the payment schedule." Maria reaches her hands out but Annika hands the paper to me. This year families pay tuition quarterly at the time of their enrollment."

"Okay . . ." I say, wondering what this means. She wants (vants) her money up front I guess. I'm sold, but Annika goes on to deliver an unsolicited soliloquy about the history of the school, her extensive credentials, the credentials of the staff, the building, and Maria continues to pepper her at each turn. The preschoolers have moved out of circle time and now they are playing various musical instruments. Franny is happily pounding on a traditional leather drum, while other kids bang away on tambourines, triangles and xylophones. Lucy is sitting on the floor with Max between her legs, and then dragging him like a stuffed animal over to look at the instruments. He jabbers with delight.

Annika walks us down the hall into her office. Towers of books and multicolored papers and folders are stacked on the desk and around the floor. Clichéd inspirational sayings line the walls, hand-written with calligraphy pen on dot matrix computer paper: "All you need is love," "don't worry, be happy" and "peace begins with a smile."

"*Vee* only have two spots left so if you'd like them, I *vill* need tuition by end of day, yes?"

"Oh," I pause, holding the piece of paper in my hand. Maria tries to give me a look that I can't decipher but just then her phone rings to the tune of "Moves Like Jagger." She pulls her phone out of the fanny back.

"Excuse me," she says, all of a sudden sounding professional, "I need to take this so I'll step outside."

Annika sifts through a stack of papers on her desk and hands me a contract. "I *vould* be delighted to offer these spots to Lucille and Francesca. Yes, then?"

I shift my purse to my other shoulder. "I'll discuss with my husband tonight," I say, picturing round two of my fabulous vertical shirt folding abilities, potentially followed by loading the dishwasher the way he likes, before diving in pre-school tuition. "In the meantime, are there any current families I could call?"

Annika puts on her reading glasses and peers up at me from her desk, looking impatient and slightly smug. "Didn't your friend Sarah refer you to our school? I *vould* be happy to provide you *vid* additional names but I may not have spots this afternoon. I only have availability for two additional children."

I pull out my checkbook.

"Hey girls, what did you think?" I ask, tossing packages of fruit leather to my backseat passengers. I'm giddy with the probably fleeting feeling like I've figured it all out – fabulous, although sartorially challenged, Nanny and under the radar progressive, and bargain-priced pre-school-signed, sealed and delivered. Yes! I allow myself a celebratory fist pump. Maria is outside on the sidewalk, pacing up and down the side of car, on an animated phone call. She pauses occasionally to write more notes in her notebook, so I take advantage of the delay and dial my mom's number, holding the phone to my ear as it rings.

No answer. Her voicemail to me during the preschool tour doesn't indicate anything urgent—just "calling you back dear!" in a singsong voice, followed by a click. I wonder how something so urgent could now become non urgent. Maybe marijuana induced hallucinations – another reasons the kids need proper, reliable, full time care.

"Umm, good," says Franny, fidgeting with the wrapper.

"Really good," says Lucy. "I like it a lot. But—"

"But what?" I ask.

"But I think Miss Ann—what's her name again, Mommy?"

"Miss Annika."

"I think Miss Ann-ekah needs a new hairstyle and new glasses, she kind of looks like a clown."

"That's not a very nice thing to say, Lucy!" I cough, trying not to choke.

"Sorry, Mommy."

Maria steps inside the car and hoists her backpack in between her knees with a cheerful sigh. She's beaming.

"What was that about?" I ask. "Date tonight?" And then I silently curse myself for asking. This is probably the first step in becoming friends with your nanny, which I definitely do not want.

Maria looks at me like it's not only a perfectly acceptable question, but she's flattered I asked. "Well . . . " she says, rearranging a spaghetti strap and stuffing her notebook deep inside her backpack. Her cheeks are flushed and she's speaking fast. "It was my advisor at school calling. Her grant just got approved!" Maria continues on about her educational research project, but in few seconds I realized I've sort of tuned it out as I turn on the ignition and pull out of the parking lot and start to think about what I need to focus on now that childcare is finally wrapped up. "Just some paperwork you need to sign," I hear her say after a few minutes, followed by "and I'll actually get you that reference you wanted, you know?"

"Um, yeah, right, sure," I say, distracted by a large truck in front of me that has just made a sudden right turn, sending its wide backside directly in my path. I hit the accelerator and go around, narrowly missing a head-on collision. "Sounds great," I say to Maria.

Just as we're rounding the corner up to our house, my phone rings. I look down at the vibrating numbers in my lap. It's a number I don't immediately recognize. Could be work. I answer it without thinking.

"Hello, Anna? I'm sorry to bother you in the middle of the day. It's Colette."

Colette. Colette? Oh, right, *Colettte*. What the heck is she doing calling me?

"Listen—I wanted to let you know about a preschool that has openings. My nanny mentioned it to me today."

I pull the car over to the curb. "Oh, wow, that's so nice of you, but I actually just committed to a preschool . . . " I say, feeling as smug and sassy as the leagues of Colette. I glance towards Maria and she raises an eyebrow at me, as if to say, "really, *we* just found a place, or did *you* just decide to settle for the first preschool you set your eyes on?"

"Actually," I continue, with an eye still on Maria, "If you want to give me the address I'll check it out for fun." If another opportunity drops in my lap, who I am to reject it before signing on to the *acaahdemy*. And I can always put a stop payment on the check if for some reason this one proves to be a winner.

"It's a little out of the way, over near Greenlake . . ." Colette continues, "but Myrna said they had openings and I mean, who has openings in Seattle?! You practically have to get on a waitlist before you're pregnant. Anyway, she says there's a cool indoor play space across the street. Anyway, thought I'd pass it on."

Maria fishes out her notebook again and writes down the address and directions and off we go. I get the sense she's happy I'm doing a bit more due diligence.

I call Lauren to let her know that I've got a meeting with a potential client—a huge stretch of a white lie. Less than a week back and I'm blowing off work for a decoy preschool preview, or in other words, having it all!

"It's gotta be around here somewhere . . ." I wonder aloud after we've been in the car for 15 minutes. We're already on the north side of the lake. I look down at Google maps. "Hmmm ... not exactly

Greenlake, more like Greenwood. I circle around and head north on Aurora Avenue. The scenery is getting seedier by the second: flop motels with hourly rates, floor sample liquidators, used car dealerships and prostitutes. In fact, I think I spot one now. If I didn't know better, she could easily be mistaken for a woman jogging around Greenlake in her blue fleece vest and black baseball cap. Except that her footwear is completely inappropriate. Ditto for the skirt. In Seattle, even the prostitutes wear fleece.

"There it is!" shouts Lucy from the backseat.

"What?" I'm too focused on the prostitute's curious fashion. Two hundred feet in front of her is a mold-streaked plastic white sign with purple and green letters that reads "ChildCare Now Enrroling." I'm not sure if it's the egregious spelling errors or the fact that there's a rusty playground surrounded by a derelict dog run style chain link fence swallowed by weeds facing a busy intersection—but I find myself pressing my foot down on the gas pedal. Maria looks up long enough from her phone in order to give me an approving nod.

"You didn't stop, Mommy! You missed it." I hear echoes from the back seat.

"That wasn't the one we're looking for," I lie. I turn on my blinker at the next light and turn right.

"McDonald's!!" shout Lucy and Franny with glee. I look up at the enormous structure including the indoor play space. Ah yes, *play space*. That must have been what Myrna was referring to. I'm fuming and I can't wait to bump into her again to gloat about the academy. Sending my kids to a McDonalds playground for childcare. God, did I really look that bad when I saw her or does she live in that much of a bubble.

With the steam almost literally coming out of my ears, Maria clearly senses trouble.

"Anna, you picked a good school. You cannot worry what other people think. You know what Dr. Seuss says, *Be who you are and say what you feel, because those who mind don't matter and those who matter don't mind...* You know this saying? Girls, you must know this right? Repeat after me girls, Be who YOU are and say what YOU feel, because those who mind don't matter and those who matter don't mind."

In the backseat there's a chorus of little voices saying that they can give two fucks what anyone thinks and I realize that Maria has deftly turned a fuming, shallow mommy moment into a female empowerment lesson. Go Maria.

Back at work, I try Mom one more time. The world of pharmaceuticals is calling, but so is the nagging thought in the back of my head that my Mother needs to alert me to something important. This is not based on a track record of frequently telling me things that actually are important. She's left me plenty of "urgent" messages in the past about the fact that I absolutely cannot miss an upcoming episode of *Hardball*, that she was about to leave for church in case I needed to reach her and that a singer named J Lo was engaged to Ben Affleck. All of these, among many other urgent voicemails over the years, necessitated multiple home and cell phone messages but I still had a nagging feeling.

"Why on earth have you been calling my phone all morning? What is wrong? Are my little darlings okay?"

"Mom. You were the one who called *me* with an urgent message last night about Maria."

"Who?"

"Maria, our new nanny."

"You have a new nanny now? When did that happen?"

I groan loudly into the phone. "Ugh, Mom, weren't you over here yesterday? I believe the two of you met before you took the girls out for lunch and Bratz dolls."

"Oh, oh, I remember now. Yes, I did meet her. I thought she was just one of your babysitters. She looks too much like a floozy to be called a nanny. Did I say nanny in my message? I hope not! Anyway, dear heart, I'm remembering now. It's VERY important."

"Yessss?" I cradle the phone in my neck and go to Google. I decide to start my mental health research with the keywords "frustrating" and "mother."

"When I was at your house yesterday I brought you some tomatoes and mint leaves from my garden, did you get them?"

"Yes, Mom, thank you" I say.

"Well. I also noticed that you do not have any emergency numbers listed by the phone or on the refrigerator for the babysitter! What if something were to happen? You cannot have a new babysitter in your house and expect her to reach me in an emergency if my number is not listed PROMINENTLY!"

For a split second I consider retorting, "Yeah, but you never answer your phone!" But instead I say, "You know what, Mom, that's a great idea. We should definitely let Maria know how to get a hold of you."

"Good."

"So, you don't have any concerns about Maria then?"

"Oh I suppose not. Well, I think she should put on more clothes when she's around Max. He seemed to enjoy her quite a bit. Hopefully you are okay with that."

Nine

Dear Anna:

I need you to do some shopping for me tomorrow. I am going to make for you my Sancocho! You never have time to cook for your familia. This is what I need:

- *Lots of garlic!*
- *Carrot*
- *Spanish onion*
- *Habanero chili*
- *Cilantro*
- *Chicken bouillon*
- *Chicken (the whole chicken!)*
- *Yucca*
- *Green plantain*
- *Regular potatoes*
- *Ripe plantains*
- *5 ears of corn*
- *Oreo cookies double stuff*

You can get the chicken at Safeway. The chilies you can get at QFC. The plantains and Spanish onion you can only get now at Pike Place Market. Mexi Mart in South Seattle is good for cookies and fresh tortillas. You will really like this dish. It is sooo yummy!

Your friend, Maria
P.S. The Oreo cookies are for me and not for the Sonchoco, jajajajajaja!

At the top of the paper the word CHICKEN is in all caps and there is a small drawing of a cartoon-like chicken with a dialogue box that says, "I cook you dinner, si?"

Christ. Now I need an assistant to help me run errands for the nanny. It's Maria's fourth day on the job.

Not a minute later, Clare walks into my office, all smiles, and drops off his resignation letter.

Dear YOWZ,

You suck.
I quit.
See attachments.

Sincerely (not),
Clare

The first attachment is the market research he's done for Nether Lights. It's a beautifully bound presentation deck entitled "You are all Assholes" in a contemporary, chic font. I wonder which designer helped him with this, because the production value is really excellent. I flip through page after page of creatively cropped butt hole photographs - some before and after shots (dark butt hole/lighter butt hole), some clearly pornographic, with people literally licking the butt holes, and others that are just silly, butt holes covered in snow, or decorated like chocolate sundaes with cherries on top.

"This is really well done!" I say, holding up the packet, "Thank you, Clare! Great work!" I'm actually being sincere. Aside from the objectionable photographs, this is one of the better presentation decks I've seen in a long time.

Clare huffs and starts to leave. I know what he's thinking: *I do my best work on my last day and finally get the appreciation I deserve!* And suddenly I feel bad for him. He really did think he had my job there for a while; I guess I'd be pissed too if I came back, and might even be prone to lash out. I reach out my arm and rotate it toward me for a few rounds, as if I'm reeling him back in. He doesn't come back inside the office but stops in the doorframe, arms crossed, eyes squinted, and lips puckered, as if he's about to spit.

I look down at the second attachment, a lawsuit notification. It looks a little fake to me, maybe because it's printed on YOWZ letterhead.

Dear YOWZ,

This notice is to inform you that plaintiff, Mr. Clarence Brendan Hall, is suing you for wrongful termination, sexual harassment, discrimination, assault and bullying. In order to avoid a long and painful, drawn out, highly embarrassing court case, you must deposit a sum of $1,342,568.98 into Mr. Hall's account by September 30th. If you fail to make this deposit, a bigoted, racist member of the Seattle Police force will grind your face into the pavement, leaving bloody streaks all over the city and a smear on your reputation.

"So, Clare?" I say, looking up at him. He's wearing purple jeans today paired with an extremely tight-fitting navy polo shirt with a popped collar.

Clare turns on his heels and waltzes toward me with long, overly exaggerated steps.

He pushes himself up against my desk and shouts in my ear, "WHAT?"

The corners of my lips turn up just slightly. "I was just wondering . . ." I pause, bringing a knuckle to my lips, "if you were really quitting, or if you are just trying out some . . . new material."

Clare's eyes narrow. "What do you think, Biat—"

"Ah, ah—" I tsk, lifting a single index finger in the air, "don't call me any more bad words or I'll have to file a fake counter law suit. I just asked you a simple question."

He leans his body over my desk again like an arc. He takes a deep breath and I instinctively cover my ears. "YES!" he yells.

"Oh my God!" I hear someone exclaim from outside my office. "That was so loud my partition is shaking!"

I remove my hands from my ears, swallow and exhale. "How did you and your attorneys come up with this amount?" I point to the number. My voice is calm, soothing. I'm dealing with a wild animal here.

"It's a complicated algorithm," he sneers, "for pain and suffering. Something you will NEVER understand." He's shrieking now and I resist the urge to cover my ears.

"Okay, fine," I say, rereading his letters. "I accept the resignation. But the lawsuit needs more work. There are a number of typos and a few dangling modifiers." I hand the paper back to him.

On his way out, Clare picks up the piece of rubbery fake poop I've been using as a doorstop and lobs it toward my head.

I duck, and it misses me. Instead, it skids across my desk, taking the Nether Lights presentation with it, sending butthole images all over the floor.

As soon as he's gone, I buzz Gloria and tell her to call security and have someone escort him out of the building.

"One down, 45 more to go."

Slade's words, not mine. After I deliver the news of Clare's departure, Slade stares out the window for a long time before telling me that if we don't land the Asenzer account next week, we'll have to go down to a skeleton crew of five or so employees before Christmas. I assume that I'll be one of those five, but I'm not entirely sure. He didn't even crack a smile when I showed him the Nether Lights deck.

I pull into the driveway and pause at the garage door. Stress has officially invaded my body, setting up a central command center in the knot just above my left shoulder blade.

As I climb the stairs, carrying two heavy loads of groceries, topped with a package of double stuff Oreos, I feel my chest heave and my thighs sway. For a moment I fantasize about being one of those tiny workout junkies who lifts enormous dumbbells at CrossFit and then burns every last calorie off on the StairMaster. If only we were rich! I'd hire a personal trainer, and I would be skinny, and I wouldn't have to put up with anyone's shit. And I would grow the chilies in the backyard that Maria needed to make us her exotic chicken dish. I wouldn't have to sell my soul to some helmet-headed Pharma CEO down in California just to win the chance to be his marketing campaign drug pusher. I would *be* the Pharma CEO. Hell, I'd make the drugs myself. But I'd be better than that—because drugs just get everyone addicted. I'd be brilliant and a total game changer and develop something entirely new. Like a real live magic happy pill that wouldn't be a pill exactly, but more like a prescription for life. Something beyond the psychobabble and happiness self help "projects." Something real. Something tangible. Something you could buy right off the shelves! It would be at the right price point, too. $29.99 or even $19.99, affordable for the masses and not some elite group of Botoxed yoga-toting freaks. And it would come in an attractive box made from recycled materials with no off-gassing byproducts. Now . . . if I could just package this concept and slap a patent on it . . . Where's Maria when I need a Dr. Seuss quote about not feeling sorry for myself?

I enter the kitchen and gasp. The grocery bags fall to the floor with a loud clamor, and my jaw drops to my belly button. My eyes are struggling to take in the scene. The first word that registers in my brain is "ransack." Canned food, pasta, cereal, oatmeal, sauces, seasonings, baking mixes, the fondue kit, the sushi canopy maker, the Easy Bake Oven, place mats, pickles . . . it's all splayed out on the countertops. There isn't an inch of space that isn't covered in debris.

I open up the cabinets. Except for a few staples, the shelves are clear. Everything has been wiped down, labeled and rearranged. Appliances that once lined the counters are now up on high shelves.

My eyes go to four empty paper bags on the floor that say "Food Bank" scrawled in flowery writing. Are things that bad for us that the food bank has already arrived? I haven't lost my job yet!

I walk towards the living room. Before I even get there I can tell that something is off. The light is different, and the padding of my footsteps gives off an echo I haven't heard before.

The furniture has been completely rearranged. The couches are pushed up against the windows, creating a sort of V-shaped window seat, the coffee table is wrapped with butcher paper, and each of the end tables, where fragile lamps once stood, are replaced by plastic cups filled with crayons and craft materials.

W . . . T . . . F . . .

As I make my way to the stair landing, I hear the deep beat of salsa music emanating from upstairs, along with loud banging and giggling. Steps away from Lucy's bedroom, I hear hammering and I stop.

If I were still at work, I wouldn't know what was going on. But I'm home and the mother in me needs to know. I need to make sure that Maria is not some kind of crazed psycho killer nailing my daughters to the floor or installing risqué artwork in their room.

I push the door open just a crack and see Maria on her knees, butt in the air and head in the closet hammering away. A black lace thong is sticking out of her jeans, and with every hammer it wiggles a bit.

And then I hear a man's voice.

I slam the door open and see a guy with a shaved head and tattoos covering each arm sitting on the floor with a My Little Pony in each hand, playing with my three children who are looking up at him with full attention and adoration.

"Ahh!" I shriek, stepping back. As if on cue, he drops the ponies and stands up. He walks over to me and reaches out a hand.

I remain standing in the doorway, hands firmly on my hips.

"Ash. Ash Black." He leaves his hand out for another moment, but when he sees that I'm not reaching my hand out in return, he adds, "I'm a friend of Maria's," and he reaches into his back pocket and pulls out a worn business card.

I take the card and look down.

Ash Black

Chim Chim-eree

Chimneys, gutters, landscaping, electrical, fine art, odd jobs

"No Job Too Odd!"

Lic: 243-58321

ash@chimchimeree.com

"At your service," Ash tips an invisible hat. "I do gutters, chimneys, yard cleanup and odd jobs like—"

"Ponies!" Franny chimes in.

"And furniture rearranging and kitchen ransacking?" I say.

Maria rushes in front of Ash, as if to take the first blow should I decide to hit him. "I am *so* sorry. Very, very sorry, you know?" as If I don't understand sorry and that is all that needs to be said. "I should have told you he was coming over, but I just realized this morning that I needed help with this one tiny thing—" she motions towards a series of multicolored milk crates along the wall under the window with the girls' books, socks, underwear, and hair accessories. The top of the dresser and mounted bookshelves that Patrick had installed just a couple months ago are empty. Franny's crib mattress is on the floor, flanked by decorative pillows and stuffed animals.

"Ash is my *friend*," she says, squeezing his arm, which I take as a signal that he is *more* than a friend, "and—"

"And he's my friend too!" Lucy interrupts, rushing to pull on one of his arms just as Franny gallops over to grab the other arm. "Mwy Fwiend!"

Sitting up on the carpet, Max picks up the two My Little Ponies lying on the floor and begins jabbering and banging their two heads together. "Yeahyaaah!"

I place my hands on my hips and huff loudly, contemplating my next move.

"I was already in the neighborhood and happened to have the tools for the job," says Ash, motioning to the tools strewn all over the floor of the closet. Max has only recently learned how to scoot along the ground like a soldier on the beaches of Normandy, but is doing his best to make his way over to them now.

"Mommy, look, now I can get myself dressed without waking you up," says Lucy, leading me over to the crates on the floor.

I look at Lucy, pink-cheeked and smiling. How can she be so proud when I am so horrified?

Maria sees the look on my face and sighs loudly, followed by a clicking of her tongue. "Tsk tsk on me. Oh, Anna, it was supposed to be a surprise. I'm so bummed. Aren't we girls?" Maria pushes out her lower lip like a pouting baby and reaches around to her backside to tuck her thong back in.

"Well, here I am . . . you surprised me. What is this? And can someone explain what happened downstairs as well?" I growl.

"Well, you know, children want to work, it's in their nature, at their core! And we stop them with all these shelves and heights and barriers. Our grownup houses and furniture keep them down, but this way," as she sweeps her hand across the room, "this way, we open up their natural ability to work and help run the household. We need to help them be independent! And you could really use the help, right?" she adds as if to say, this is all for your benefit, Anna.

I want to say I hired Maria to help me, not to help destroy my house and put my kids to work. I'm still smoldering so she continues.

"So I've been reading about how to set up Montessori-friendly rooms in your house. Isn't that just great? And this is just a start," Maria pulls her hands together like she can't wait to tell me more, or pray for forgiveness. "Basically everything the children need should be within their reach. So they can get dressed by themselves, and get in or out of bed by themselves, you know? Franny is in here now, so Max can have his own room, and maybe you and Patrick can have some alone time?"

I squeeze me eyes and squint at her. Since when did my sex life become her business?

Maria grabs hold of Ash's hand, and now they are both looking at me with solidarity. "I put some utensils for the kids in a place where they can reach them in the kitchen! And we cleared out your cabinets so that it is more child-focused too. The kids showed me the food you never eat so we're giving all of that to the food bank to help people in need! Isn't that wonderful? No need to store all those cans and let them get all dusty in the back of the cabinet!"

The girls erupt in cheers and giggles, jumping up and down on the crib mattress on the floor. While I have spent the better part of five years trying to keep things out of their reach, Maria has spent an afternoon undoing it.

"See Mommy, we can sweep togeder in herwe now!" Franny squeals.

I'm still a little confused . . . is this their idea of a game for the afternoon? Will she and Ash put everything back where it belongs before she leaves today? Or does she think it's really staying like this?

"I'm guess I'm just closer to the research than you are," Maria explains. "Studies show that parents read a lot about parenting and early childhood development the first year with their newborns, and then they really stop."

I've got to put a stop to this, I think, just before Maria leans over to give me a hug and kiss.

Ten

Week two. To include the husband or not include the husband, that is the question. The email instructions specifically indicate that all parents and caregivers are required to attend the Global Citizens Academy orientation meeting tonight, along with a treatise on how you cannot divide childcare responsibilities along gender lines. Annika's explanation is that even though the children will not be at the meeting, they will know (because they are such intuitive little creatures) when one parent is shirking their responsibilities. Patrick read the note and immediately volunteered to be the one to shirk his responsibilities. And, he added, "I'd rather shirk my responsibilities here at home by hanging out with my children than by going to a meeting run by a woman who doesn't actually have any." He did have a point.

I also wondered how Annika was able to get away with making this a mandatory meeting for both parents, without offering any child care options. Since Maria is the only one even excited about tonight's meeting, I halfheartedly wonder if both Patrick and I can shirk responsibilities and just send her. She seems to be acting like the early childhood education expert, after all.

I call my friend Sarah to get her sound and sane advice. "Fuck that, leave your husband at home." Sarah is her usual emphatic self. "Trust me on this one. The only guys who will be at tonight's meeting are the gay dads."

Sarah and I met in a neighborhood baby/parenting support group when our firstborns were still in the floppy infant stage and most of us new moms were delirious from lack of sleep and clueless from lack of experience. Not Sarah. She was bossing everyone around with instructions on the "right way" to hold a baby, the "right way" to change a diaper, the "right way" to have your baby latch onto your nipple (which she had no problem demonstrating with her own baby and her own nipple). Not surprisingly, she clashed right away with the group leader as well as a number of other new moms. She and I, however, hit it off almost immediately.

"Take Maria and leave Patrick," Sarah tells me. "He's going to be worthless anyway." I laugh as I look over at him, legs outstretched on the ottoman, beer in one hand and TV remote in the other. I know she's right. The only thing I'll get from Patrick attending is questions about why our children need to be able to chant in four languages.

Even though the sun is still high in the sky and I instinctively know that walking the four blocks with Maria would be good bonding time for us, we decide to drive to save time. Maria tells me this is good because she has some prep work to do in the car. I wonder what kind of prep work she can possibly get done in three minutes, but as I drive down our tree-lined street, I see that it mainly consists of fluffing her hair out around her shoulders and dabbing essential oils on her wrists and neck. "It's for calming nerves and focusing our minds," she says. "Want some?"

As I park the car and get out, I look over to see Maria rummaging around in her enormous backpack for something. I wait for her on the sidewalk, checking email on my phone. Suddenly the passenger door flies open, and Maria emerges in sky-high wedge heels, blazing red lipstick and turquoise chandelier earrings. The "I'm closer to the research" comment is still burning in my ears so I can't resist.

"Do you have plans afterwards?" I inquire.

She gazes down at her heels, and uses her right hand to fluff her hair off her shoulders.

"Oh this? No. I always say, if you look the part, you'll feel the part, you know?"

"Oh sure, I say," but I wonder what part of parenthood I've missed that requires chandelier earrings and high heels. Does the latest research indicate a fancier approach to parenthood or is it millennials watching too much Mad Men?

Mama Maria.

The Global Citizens Academy is decked out and buzzing with activity by the time we arrive. There must be at least two-dozen parents crammed in this tiny school, and I wonder if we're violating some sort of fire code regulation. I scan the room for a place to sit and see that there are indeed hardly any men here. Thank goodness I didn't drag Patrick. The crowd is an eclectic and ethnically diverse group of parents, which for this particular socio-economic overly educated slice of Seattle, means that everyone looks the same. My strappy sandals and tunic over leggings combo actually appears a little too flashy in this a sea of clog moms. Several eyes follow Maria as she struts in, wobbling slightly in her heels, nearly collapsing on the floor in front of the first row.

"Anna!" I see a bony hand dominated by an enormous diamond waving at me from the back of the room. Before I even register her face, I stiffen.

Colette pushes away her expensive-looking purse and sweater, making room for a seat and signals for me to join her. Her husband, Blake, sits on the other side, fully engrossed in his iPad, and on the other side of him is an older, expressionless woman, wearing black pants, a white short-sleeved top and a black fleece vest, sitting silently with her arms folded in her lap. This must be Myrna, the submissive nanny.

"Well, you're probably wondering what *I'm* doing here." Colette leans forward and props an elbow on her lap as she turns to give me her full attention. "After I talked to you, Anna, last week, then I bumped into Sarah, and I heard so many great things about the school, I just thought that Cole should enroll. What a wonderful opportunity this is- world peace right here in our little slice of Seattle! Who knew?" Her voice is so sweet the fillings in my molars hurt.

Annika walks to the front of the room with a guitar strapped to her chest, flanked by two staff members. One of them blows a *didgeridoo* to call everyone's attention.

"I got the last spot, isn't that great?" Colette whispers in my ear before clasping her perfectly manicured hands in her perfectly arranged lap. *Oh did you?* I think and glare and Annika.

As a concession, Patrick sent me off with a bottle of Balance Water®—bottled water infused with an Australian wildflower essence, promising to "assist with calming and centering of the mind." He picked it up at the specialty beer store, of all places, telling me it was "on brand" with tonight's orientation. I hate it when he does that: using my own terminology against me! I sip from the bottle anyway and lean back, listening to the opening ceremonies, trying to stifle laughter and stress in equal measure. Between the water and the essential oil, I think I just may be relaxed enough to fall asleep. But just as I'm zoning out, the music stops and Annika makes us all stand up. "*Velcome* Global Citizens!" she commands with all of the gusto of a Sunday morning minister, and I snap out of it with a jolt.

After her introduction, Annika makes us put away all the chairs. "Good. Good cooperation students!" she exclaims, pacing back and forth, pausing to correct one parent's stacking technique.

We must now sit in circle time.

Annika's posse passes out tambourines and triangles. We sing a few songs and hold hands with our neighbors.

Maria is sitting cross-legged with her notebook open, looking around the room furtively and scrawling notes like Harriet the Spy. I can see another parent leaning over her shoulder to see what she's writing, but Maria tsks her playfully and opens and closes the notebook peek-a-boo style, flipping pages and revealing nothing. Myrna, Colette's nanny, sits motionless, waiting for instructions.

I turn to Colette, attempting to solve the story problem in my head. "If both you and Blake are here, and Myrna is here, who is watching your kids?"

Colette smiles in a way that only a SAHMWN married to a Microsoft millionaire can. "Oh Myrna's just our head day nanny, so its critical for her to come to school orientation," she murmurs. "Jessica takes over in the evenings. She's amazing—she does a great job exfoliating the kids."

Next on the evening's agenda, Annika has us move into the yoga room and stretch out. She dims the lights and talks to us about the positive energy flowing through our *bauudies* and how important it is that we are part of this magical global community, all brought here together by destiny. Our children are part of a new generation that will love, not hate; be compassionate, not selfish; live in harmony with the environment, not destroy it. The music is soothing, and I close my eyes. I'm aware of nothing else except the faint sound of a ringing bell and the smell of incense. All of a sudden I feel someone's hands wrap behind my neck.

Ahhhhhh. Nothing quite like a good neck stretch on preschool orientation night.

After several minutes, Annika asks us to open our eyes. "Sit up very, very slowly my Global Citizens," she says, with all the care of bedside nurse. The lights are still dimmed. Images begin to flash on the wall and the music shifts to a symphonic melody.

"I hope what you've seen tonight has made an impact," says Annika, closing her laptop. "Without your support we won't be able to feed hungry children in China or save girls in Africa from violence and American celebrities. This is what it means to be a part of this community. Helping others. *Vee* are making a difference," she says. "Tonight, I'm asking everyone to make a donation to our foundation. Ten thousand dollars, five thousand, even one thousand if that is all you can afford." I panic. Did I miss mention of a required additional donation when I wrote my tuition check?

The lights go up a tad, and the envelopes are passed around the room.

Just then "She Works Hard for the Money" starts blaring from my back pocket, and I scramble out of the room to take Slade's call in the hall. Saved by the Slade.

"Yesss?" I yell-whisper, annoyed, holding my hand over the receiver as soon I'm out in the hallway.

"Sorry to bother you at home Dear, but I wanted to see if you were following this hashtag business on Twitter. There are a lot of really excellent looking women online right now, and they are all speaking in some sort of strange code. A lot of them are making humorous yet crass remarks, complaining about their lives and writing things like #Ineedadrink and #momchat. There's even a #mentalhealth tag that I found. We need to get on top and figure out how to corral these women before we go to San Fran next week. I think I've just found a sweet spot here with the target audience." I give Slade a virtual pat on the back for doing a bit of research.

When I walk back into the yoga room, one of the staffers shoves a rudimentary piggy bank in my face. It looks like an oversized toilet paper tube or a former oatmeal tin wrapped in kid art. "Can you make a donation?" she asks.

"I, um, well—" I stammer.

"This isn't for the foundation," she says, "but for carpet cleaning."

Colette gives me a playful nudge on the shoulder as she puts her checkbook in her purse and heads for the door. Myrna stands two steps behind her, as if she's awaiting instructions, like a bodyguard or a servant. Blake is nowhere to be found and I wonder if he was part of the group of dads who left upon hearing the words "circle time" and "yoga" and high tailed it to the pub two blocks away. "Anna, I am *so* glad we're here at this school together. Blake and I are going to be benefactors of the Global Citizens Foundation. Isn't that fabulous?" The corners of her plumped lips turn up just so.

I smile back at her. "Fabulous," I parrot back, patting her on the shoulder. "Just fabulous!" Isn't that what she wants me to say?

She grabs my arm and pulls me in closely. "Listen," she says, "we really need to grab coffee and catch up! You are so busy all the time— do you ever even have five minutes to even breathe? Let me do something—can I take you to lunch?" She pauses and looks around the room to make sure no one is overhearing our conversation, and then leans in even closer. "I'm working on something that I think would really interest you."

I want to tell her that she already pressured me to sign the kids up for school after already having a nanny so could she please just leave me be, but instead I rifle through my purse and hand Colette a business card. She looks at it and squeals. "Creative Director! Oh my gosh! This is so perfect. Can't wait!" She plants a kiss on my cheek. It feels rubbery, like the fake lips you can buy at the party and costume store.

"My assistant should be able to find a time for us to talk," I mentally make a note to warn Lauren about Colette.

Eleven

"Ouch!" A painful twinge shoots down my spine and into my right hip as I lean over to yank my suitcase off the turnstile. The corridor is bustling with travelers thumbing through email messages, pacing figure eights while jabbering away on cell phones, checking wristwatches, scratching noses, tapping out text messages. Such busy and anxious people! Ah, at least I'm not one of them. Oh no, not me. Not now. I'm calm, collected, and clear-headed. Cool as an ice cube floating on a lily pad in a Zen garden with a rudder and a GPS.

I spent the entire plane ride reviewing my slides, mumbling to myself, jotting down notes, mentally reviewing my positioning, my tone of voice, my jokes—and when I will subtly bug my eyes a bit at Slade, indicating to him when he needs to drive a point home. With every dry run my confidence grew and grew, to the point where I sensed that the passengers sitting on either side of me were eyeballing my presentation and facial expressions to see what the excitement was all about.

I've got this thing figured out. I mentally picture myself tomorrow, casually clicking the remote through the presentation deck while dazzling the Asenzer execs with my unwavering intellect, charm and wit.

I'm ready. Nothing—not Maria with her jaja notes, not Patrick and his brooding about the lack of bro-ha-ha over his latest game release, not Annika with her pithy peace emails, not housework, nor calling friends, nor coffee breaks nor anything that could possibly fall in the category of "relaxation"—got in the way of my preparations for this pitch. It was my laser-like focus, my attention to detail, my ability to ignore practically everything and everyone in my life that got me to this point. Between me, the brilliant junior designer behind the Nether Lights PowerPoint, two copywriters and Lauren acting as researcher extraordinaire, it was all hands on deck this week. The content, the colors, the font, the sound effects; it's pure genius.

As I trudge up the stairs in shoes that are pinching my feet, carrying far more belongings than necessary, a smile overtakes my face. The weight of the suitcase, the pinch of the shoes, the kink in my neck . . . it doesn't matter. The fact that I have a night alone to relax before the pitch is making me giddy. A night alone—in a hotel—with a mini bar!

I look at my watch. It's almost 4 o'clock. Let's see, so if there's no line at the car rental, I'll have time for a quick stroll down Fillmore to do a little window-shopping, maybe pick up some cuter shoes and some new lipstick, head to the hotel, meet my college friend Seema for a quick drink before dinner with Slade, and then maybe, just maybe, squeeze in a movie in the hotel room. Literal chills go up my spine at the mere thought of it.

Whoosh.

The tram whizzes up to the platform and comes to a halt. As I board the train, I'm greeted by a wall of men: men in suits carrying briefcases, men in fleece jackets on cell phones, men in dark denim tapping away on their latest iDevices. All men. Suddenly I feel like a pioneer woman blazing the trail for working women everywhere: Yes, Virginia, you *can* travel and have kids. Just don't expect anyone to give up their seat for you, even though you're slightly limping in your pointy-toed business shoes. I try my best to mentally channel smooth Claire Underwood strolling everywhere in her pointy heels. I bet a man would give her a seat, but not a single man even acknowledges me. Maybe this is what equality is all about, I think, somewhat despondently. Sheesh, couldn't someone at least have the courtesy to scoot over just a bit so I have a place to plop my derriere. I lug my gear over to the stripper pole in the center of the tram. The air is stale, a mix of B.O., leather and damp fog. The weather outside is overcast, with just a sliver of pink-tinged sun peaking through the clouds just above the tree line, reminding me that the dark days of fall and winter are just ahead. I brace myself against the pole, lodge my suitcase between my knees, secure my purse firmly to my shoulder and fish out my phone, joining the ranks of anti-social business travelers. I think about calling Slade to tell him I've landed, but then decide instead to keep him waiting for a bit. If he knows I'm here, I'll be stuck in a hotel room practicing with him for the rest of the afternoon and evening.

As the tram starts its journey to the rental car building, I wrap my elbow around the pole, careful not to actually touch the germy thing with my fingers, and start texting Seema.

Just landed. Can you come by my hotel for a quiiiiiiiiiiii

A sudden jolt sends my phone flying out of my hand. The train lurches violently from side to side. I lose my grip. I twist, turn, and contort in what feels like slow motion across the length of the train. I instinctively reach out to grab something—anything—to hold onto and brace myself but I can't stop! Colors and faces whizz past me in a series of milliseconds. I don't even have time to scream. Just as my body registers the sense of weightlessness, I fall. Hard.

I land with a sickening thud against the passengers sitting on the window seat at the end of the train. All I can think at the moment is that the driver has just made a really bad stop. But then the train starts shaking again from side to side, just like one of those trams at Universal Studios. Everyone in the car begins to yell the same word, and it echoes and reverberates inside our tiny death capsule. "Earthquake!"

My body hurts. The pain is excruciating and I feel smothered, like my head is in a vice and I'm gasping for air. And I have no idea what hurts or where I am. I blink, but everything has gone dark. It takes me a couple seconds to realize my face is resting in the lap of a rather large man and he's stroking the top of my head. I struggle to push myself off him, but my arm won't move.

"You got thrown pretty badly there. Take your time, and don't make any sudden movements. I'm a doctor."

Oh, nice. I think. I've made a soft landing into the lap of a trained medical professional and planted my face firmly in his crotch.

I attempt to lift my head again so I can get out of his crotch, but when I try, the pain in my shoulder is excruciating and all I can do is wince.

"Ahhhhhggggg…aaaooooouuuchh," I groan as I slide off his lap and rest my head flat on the floor, staring up at the ceiling of the train, panting and moaning with my mouth gaped open like a corpse. I pat my right arm around the floor trying to locate my phone. Someone hands it to me and I am immediately comforted by the reassurance it spontaneously delivers. I may be lying on the floor of an airport shuttle, but help, the hotel, and my family, are all just on the other end of that phone if I need them. Of course then I think that if I hadn't been holding the phone I may not have broken the fall with my shoulder. Damn.

"Folks, looks like we've had a little bit of a quake," says an all too upbeat voice coming from the speakers, "we're going to sit here for a minute to make sure there's no damage to the track ahead and then we'll pull into the station and have you on your way in no time."

Just go! I want to scream at the conductor, *I have a hotel room and glass of wine waiting for me!!*

As I lay on the floor I wonder if this is Karma? Like working moms shouldn't preemptively plan to enjoy work trips away from their family. I was excited about a night away, and so the punishment is to not only make sure I don't have any fun but to make me work one handed for the rest of the week? I decide instead to focus on positive thoughts. It's just a bruise probably, and the San Andreas fault did not in fact will itself to rumble for the exclusive purpose of ruining my night.

The emergency room waiting area is actually full of people with nicks and cuts from what I have learned on the news was a 4.7 quake -- barely a rumble by San Francisco standards, but enough to derail our collective evening plans. The gentleman who was so kind as to loan me his cushy lap on which to rest my head turned out to be a family practitioner in town for a conference. He insisted on taking me via taxi to the emergency room for what he suspected was not a bruise but a dislocated shoulder. My moans at every bump in the road did nothing to assuage his concerns that I was seriously injured.

Seema has pinged me. It's now 5:45.

Survive the "quake"? Call me when you get 2 hotel and I'll meet u for a drink!

I ponder the message. Of course she didn't mean to rub alcohol in my wounds, but as I look around the waiting room, tears spring to my eyes. My one night away, wasted in an emergency room. I inhale deeply through my nose and out through my mouth following the instructions on some meditation app Lauren suggested for me at the office. But it does nothing to calm me. I cover my face in my hands to keep my emotions and whatever else is springing to the surface, back inside.

Gulp.

It's not working. My chin quivers just like Franny's when she's on the cusp of totally losing it, and I swallow hard. In college, where emotions occasionally ran high, I was the one who never got caught crying over a boy who didn't call, a spiteful friend, a missed episode of *ThirtySomething*, or a grade that didn't turn out quite right. I was strong, keeping everything inside and not wanting to share my hurt or sadness or disappointment. It wasn't the healthiest approach but it got me through and kept me on track. So I can certainly choke back tears springing from a teensy earthquake accident in my forties, I tell myself. Self control. Self control. Self control.

I picture Annika and the kids at the Global Citizens Academy. All those peaceful *bauudies*. They could certainly teach me something about equilibrium and maintaining a sense of calm in the midst of chaos. My mind wanders to that fleeting moment I had on the floor of the yoga room last week, listening to the soothing sounds of waves crashing via a boom box on top of a toddler sensory table. Before Maria bent over and flashed her thong to a few unsuspecting gay dads, before Slade called, inciting a Twitter panic, before Colette invaded my personal space and planted her nasty plumped out lips on my face. How do I get back to that peaceful place? Even if just for a moment? I need this. My ass—and Asenzer—depends on it.

I inhale, close my eyes and pretend I'm sitting in the hotel room, glass of wine in one hand and remote control in the other. Out the window I spy just the tip of the Golden Gate Bridge. This is the hotel where Patrick and I spent the first night of our Hawaii-bound honeymoon. The discreet four-story townhouse tucked in a far corner of Pacific Heights overlooking the Presidio gave us the feel of city living and total remoteness all at once. My mind fills with the imaginary fog that's floating through the burnt sienna hued spans of the bridge and carries me off to a place of contentment… for about two seconds.

There. A little better. Then my phone starts vibrating in my hand.

"Anna, are you okay? I heard there was an earthquake?" Lauren's tone is full of concern and I feel the tears welling up again but I wipe them away with the back of my jacket sleeve.

"Well, if you can believe it, I'm in the emergency room, but I'll be fine!" I say, taking a deep breath, hoping she didn't catch the crack in my voice. "It's not a big deal, I just tweaked my shoulder a bit."

She gasps. Lauren knows me well enough not to press the issue. "Oh gosh, okay, well, I just wanted to let you know that Maria was trying to reach you when you were on the plane. She's called here three times."

"Thanks!" I say, hoping my overly cheery tone doesn't give me away. I change the subject. "Everything good with you?"

"Well . . . um . . ." I can tell Lauren is struggling to find the words. Something's up with her, I can almost hear the blood pulsing in her veins. Not that I would know anything about that . . . .

I lean over and cup my hand over the phone, knowing full well this doesn't give me an ounce of privacy, but oh well. "What, Lauren? Are you okay?"

"I really shouldn't bother you with this now."

"Bother me with what? Tell me!" I look around the emergency room. There's a woman clutching her side in the corner, a child with a gash across his forehead crying uncontrollably, an old man slumped over in his chair, holding up a bloody and bandaged hand. By comparison, my problems seem fairly insignificant. I cock my head to the side and wince. Ouch! Okay, maybe I do have a bit of a problem here, but Lauren doesn't need to know that.

"Uh . . . well . . . the office is abuzz with this rumor and some folks are starting to freak out a little bit . . . ."

I clench my jaw. The clenching seems to alleviate some of the pain, and gives me an opportunity to work up to speaking normally. "What rumor?" I keep my voice upbeat. Thankfully Lauren cannot see me now, grimacing, jaw open, staring at the ceiling, panting softly. I actually want to say that I don't have the time right now for office gossip and she's right that she shouldn't have bothered me with it. But I don't.

"Uh, well, people are saying that if we don't land this account, a lot of us will be out of a job by Christmas . . ."

"I see," I say, grimacing again, digging my nails into my thigh.

"Is it true?"

I have a choice. I can be completely straightforward with her and tell her the truth . . . or I can refrain from spreading bad juju on pitch day. I *need* everyone to be behind me tomorrow, regardless of whether they are physically present or not.

"Oh Lauren, of course it isn't true." I say. It's my voiceover voice. Not quite polished enough for commercial TV or radio spots, but just the thing for placeholder narration. And then, a bit to my own surprise, I add, "We practically have the account already!" I'm not exactly sure why those words just left my mouth, but instinctively I wanted to quash the rumor, and they just slipped out.

I am reminded of a book I bought for Lucy last year that I *thought* was age appropriate because of the juvenile font and the words "girls growing up" on the cover, but when my three and a half year-old started asking me what the fallopian tube illustrations were, I realized it was a puberty book and confiscated it. Thinking I could use a refresher, I read the entire book with great interest, especially the chapter entitled "How to Spot a Liar."

"We do?" Lauren sounds ecstatic.

"Yes! Of course!" I say, "Why would I lie to you?"

According to the *Girls Growing Up Guide*, the phrase "Why would I lie to you?" is in fact a dead ringer for someone who is in fact lying to you.

"Anna Moore?" a husky voice booms into the lobby. I look up and see a stocky woman with broad shoulders standing in magenta scrubs with folders stacked in front of her chest. Her boobs and stomach all kind of meld together in one semi circle lump. Her wide stance, her buzz cut, her head slightly cocked in the air, the curl in her upper lip . . . she means business, and I kind of like it. She'll get me out of here quickly I think to myself.

I stand and salute with my good arm to acknowledge my presence. She responds by pointing a scolding finger at my cell phone.

"Listen," I lower my voice now, eyes on the nurse who is glaring at me. "Gotta go, Lauren. If Maria calls again, just have her call Patrick. And tell Slade I'll be in touch soon."

Click.

I toss the phone in my purse with my bad arm and wheel the suitcase in with my good arm up to Miss Cross Face.

"No cell phones in the emergency room, no exceptions." She barks. *Even in the case of emergency?* I want to retort. But I decide the more compliant I am, the faster I'll get out of here. She escorts me to a gurney—not in its own room but in a room with two others separated only by a thin layer of see-through sheeting. It reminds me of that scene in *Gone with the Wind* where you see the shadow of someone amputating a soldier's leg. I decide to keep my head pointed straight ahead at the wall. I lay down as directed so she can take my temperature and blood pressure before filling out a chart. I wince as the clipboard grazes my shoulder.

Miss Cross Face is silent and sullen as she briskly wraps a blood pressure cuff around my good arm for a second time. She hasn't introduced herself so I look up at her nametag: Mel.

Mel pulls the cuff off my arm with a loud *rriiiip*. "Yep, you're pressure's a little elevated. We'll need to get that down before you leave."

"I'm not here for my blood pressure . . .," I start to say, but then on cue my phone starts humming in my purse which now sits on top of my suitcase. I want to dive for it but she's giving me that scolding look again.

"You need to rest, and you're not allowed to take any calls. We have to wait for the orthopedist to get here anyway. He's in surgery. It should be about an hour, so just lie back and relax." Her eyes narrow at me. It's the same look I give Lucy when she's about to be in Big Trouble.

Relax!?

"Are you sure I can't just follow up with my doctor in Seattle? See, I'm just here on business and my blood pressure is probably elevated because right now I'm supposed to be prepping for a meeting tomorrow. And I need my phone because my babysitter is trying to reach me to share some news, I have no idea what, but it's got to me about my *kids*." A larger lump forms in my throat, sitting on top of the earlier lump that I thought had gone away, but now I realize that I'm at risk for a whole stack of lumps piling up inside my throat that might gag and choke me any second. That's what it will read on the autopsy report. Cause of death: strangulation and suffocation due to throat lumps constricting airway.

Mel is unsympathetic. "You can't fool with blood pressure. How old are you again?" she says as she's eyeing the chart looking for my birth date.

"I'm sure my shoulder will feel better with a little more Advil," I croak. "Or something stronger? Something to help with the pain, allow me to sleep but then totally kick ass with this presentation tomorrow? Do you have anything like that? Of course, but not strong enough to cause those horrible opioid addiction stories I keep seeing on 60 Minutes. You don't give those out here do you?" Mel writes a note in the file. Now I worry she'll think that I'm actually aiming for a prescription. That's what addicts do right? They fake injuries in order to get pain pills. No, no pain pills for me. I sit up straight and smile so that she doesn't call social services on me. "How long did you say until the orthopedist arrives?" I ask pleasantly. I won't share any more thoughts with Mel, but I make a mental note to walk around the hospital before I leave and see if any cardio patients will loan me a beta-blocker for tomorrow. Even Gwyneth Paltrow swears by them to calm public speaking jitters, and I've never seen a 60 Minutes special on beta blocker addiction, so I decide it's a fine hospital fantasy to have.

Mel is still examining me suspiciously. She bunches her lips together, narrows her eyes and scribbles something on my chart. The chart is wedged in a space she's created between her stomach and boobs, like a natural shelf.

Instinctively I know that I should shut up at this point, that Mel is not my fairy drug mother, yet my mouth betrays me, and I blather on. "This is really unnecessary. Totally appreciated of course—but shouldn't you be focusing your efforts on the more serious cases here?" I nod in the direction of the moaning man on the other side of the curtain. "I actually just came here to appease this doctor who was on the tram with me when I fell. There are worse looking people in the waiting room. Maybe we don't need to wait for the doctor after all? I'm pretty sure everything is going to be okay and I can just get up and—"

Mel holds my chest with the wide expanse of her palm, keeping me from getting off the bed. "You sit tight," she orders, "I'll be right back."

I lay back and exhale loudly. *Uggggh*. The pain in my arm is excruciating, but I still curse the fat doctor who brought me here.

As soon as I no longer hear Mel's voice, I hop out of bed and retrieve my phone. Three missed calls. Maria, Patrick and Maria again. *Good Lord.* Without listening to the messages I tuck the device under the bed sheet to muffle the sound of the dialing. Meanwhile, I keep an eye out for a shadow resembling humpty dumpty on the other side of the curtain.

Maria answers on the first ring. "Oh, hello Anna," she says. Her words seem to have a hard edge to them.

"What's going on?" I ask, lowering my voice and feeling the inner ridges of my brow knit together in a unibrow across my forehead.

"You know, I've called three times, didn't Lauren tell you?"

I flinch, propping my bad arm up with pillows as I cradle the phone in my ear. "Well," I pause, "I've been on a plane, and as you may have heard, we had an earthquake here. I'm sitting in an emergency room now getting treatment. So…what's so urgent?"

"I can't watch the kids tomorrow."

What!?!?!

Just like that. As if she's the neighborhood kid that I asked to stop by for ten minutes while I ran to the store instead of MY FULL TIME NANNY that I hired less three weeks ago. I press the phone to my temple like revolver.

"I'm sorry," I clear my throat to push aside the words I want to say ("ARE YOU FUCKING KIDDING ME?"), but fear that will resort in a psychiatric consult or, worse—someone confiscating my phone. "What did you say?"

"I said, I can't come tomorrow."

I can't come tomorrow. I can't come tomorrow. The words bounce back and forth inside my head like a losing game of pinball.

"I wanted to be sure to tell you today instead of in the morning so you could make other arrangements," Maria says defiantly. She seems to be thinking she's doing me a favor. I'm envisioning her twirling her hair around her finger or cradling the phone on top of her perfectly working shoulder so she can finish painting her toenails.

"What do you mean exactly?" I ask, as if there is any need for an explanation, "I mean, the kids aren't sick or anything are they? And you sound fine . . .," I laugh nervously and then pause. What if she's in some kind of trouble and really does need the day off? But then I think, no, this is where I need to lay on the pressure . . . I wouldn't let anyone at work skip out on a big presentation regardless of what was happening. I would power through it and expect my colleagues to do the same. This is where she needs to be reminded of her role and the fact that I am really relying on her. This is a one-woman shop. I can't call in the substitute teacher here.

"You know, I *am* in San Francisco, Maria. You do know that, right? I can't just run home tonight."

"I'm sorry, Anna. I can't help you," her voice is all sweetness now, "I really have a lot of work today and a big meeting to prep for. Thanks for understanding. I know how busy you are too."

What????

A lot of work to do?

A big meeting?

Thanks for understanding?

"Maria. *I* have a lot of work today, and *I* have a big meeting tomorrow. Is this some kind of joke?" I'm practically shouting now. The lumps in my throat are gone, replaced by bubbles of boiling steam.

The man on the other side of the curtain groans loudly as if to verbalize what I cannot express in words.

"Anna," Her voice is all patronizing now, "I know you're upset but we should probably discuss this when you calm down. Ash is available if you want."

My heart thunders in my chest and I fight the urge to punch a hole in the wall with my good arm. *Calm down? Did she just say calm . . . DOWN?*

"Maria. Whatever it is, I'll help you with it when I get back. I can't handle this right now. I really can't. I'll pay you double for tomorrow. Triple, whatever you need. Please. I just need you—"

The line goes dead. Did she just hang up? My breathing is so shallow that I begin to feel dizzy and lightheaded and I break out in a full body sweat. My chest feels constricted. The room begins to spin. And then everything goes dark.

When my eyes slowly open, minutes, hours or an eternity later, I see faces. So many faces. I'm aware of voices and sounds but it's all so disorienting. Where am I? I can barely detect a dim white light though my tunnel vision. Next I experience a strange sense of being lifted, feeling weightless. Soft hands carry my body gently towards the bright light above me. Time and space stand still. I'm floating.

Bam! Back to earth as my body lands on the gurney and a surge of pain sears through every nerve and connected tissue. Mel's face comes into focus.

"Wha—" I gasp, trying to lift my head. My stomach does a back flip and I fear that if I try to speak, vomit will spew all over the room like a sprinkler system. *Well, at least I know I'm alive,* I think, though somewhat regretfully.

"Stay down!" barks Mel, pressing my head back down on the table as someone else wraps a blood pressure cuff around my arm. My bad arm. "Yeow!" I yelp.

The nurses switch sides and the blood pressure cuff goes on my good arm while an IV needle is placed in my bad arm. My body breaks out in a cold sweat. I feel horrible, inside and out.

I open my mouth to try to speak but the words come out garbled, but things are starting to come back into view. Mel's face hovers above me. "You just fainted. Your blood pressure is even higher. We're going to order an EKG. In the meantime, I need you to stay lying down so you don't fall off the bed again."

Mel seems more annoyed with me than sympathetic, as if she has more important things to do with her time than dealing with a fainting patient in the ER. "And NO TALKING ON YOUR CELL PHONE" she says, waving my phone in her hand before placing it deep inside my purse which is now sitting on a chair on the far side of the curtain—way out of my reach.

"Bu—" I try to protest.

"Don't. Move." she commands.

A few minutes later a different nurse pops his head in, someone I don't recognize. "Oh, sorry. Wrong curtain," he says.

"Oh, wait" I say, raising a finger so that my shoulder stays immobilized. "Would you mind handing me my purse? I just need to get some, um . . . chapstick."

He obliges, handing me the whole bag before closing the curtain.

As I wait for Patrick to pick up, I wonder: Did I ever discuss sick or personal days with Maria? Is this yet another area that I brushed over entirely in the interview?

"Hehrow!"

"Oh, hi dear sweet Franny, it's Mommy," I whisper, my hand with the IV attached cupped over the receiver.

"Hieeee! Mamamamamamama!"

"Can you pass the phone to Daddy please?" I plead, hoping she picks up on the desperation in my voice.

"Mama I wuv you," She blathers in response.

"Now, Franny, I love you too, but I need Daddy now!" I bark too loudly. The man on the other side of the curtain groans, followed by a "for Crissakes!"

Franny starts to cry and the sound of her wail mixed with the background noise of sitcom laughter fills my earpiece. Why is the TV on? I wait a few more moments, my heart beating as fast as the wings of a hummingbird.

Franny, I'm sorry sweetheart. I really am. Just go tell Daddy to pick up the phone. Please Patrick, pleeease pick up. I wait for what feels like eternity as I telepathically try to communicate with my family.

"Hey, who left the phone off the hook? Luuuucy?" I can hear Patrick's footsteps.

"Hello? Hello? Who is this?"

"Oh, Patrick, thank *God*!" I gush into the phone, so happy to hear his voice.

"Anna, is that you? Oh hey Babe, how was the flight?" It's his nonchalant voice.

Wait. How is this possible that my husband knows NOTHING?

My pulse quickens and the words spill out fast. "Forget the flight. I can't talk long because I'm being watched. And I'm being held against my will. And I need your help. You need to call Maria."

"What the hell are you talking about? Did you watch a CSI marathon on the plane?"

"No time for explaining. There was an earthquake. I'm in the ER."

"Earthquake? ER? Anna, what the—"

"Stop with the questions. There's no time to explain, or they're seriously going to put me on lock down if I'm caught. I'm barely hurt. I just need some Advil, but that's not why I'm calling!" Just then I readjust myself and a shot of pain sears through my shoulder and I recoil, holding my breath so that Patrick doesn't detect what's really going on. "Listen," deep inhale, "I think I just sprained my shoulder when the airport tram almost derailed during the quake." Exhale. Quick inhale. "And then there was this guy, this doctor, anyway, he forced me in his car and dumped me at the hospital. It's horrible here. No doctors but they won't let me talk on the phone and then I fainted and fell on the floor and Maria—"

"You fainted?"

"Ugh, you're not listening to me, none of that is important. I just need them to take out the IV and forget the EKG so I can—oh . . . owwwwwww." The pain is excruciating and I can't hold it back. "Ow. Ow. Ow. Ow. Ow!"

"Anna!"

"She's not coming in tomorrow! Maria's not coming in tomorrow!" I shout/whisper to convey the urgency without getting caught.

"What?"

I don't believe this. Why is he not understanding me?

"She. Maria. Our Nanny. Not. Coming. Tomorrow." I groan.

"Okay . . ?" Patrick's tone has now shifted; I can tell he's beginning to absorb the seriousness of the situation. "So . . . what's your plan?"

My plan.

This is where the cartoon version of Anna begins piping steam out of both ears. Suddenly he's not so worried about me anymore but about my plan.

"Well. I don't know what *our* plan is yet," I say, gritting my teeth, trying not to scream at him at the top of my lungs.

"Um, well, what's the latest flight you can get back to Seattle?" he says.

Oh my God! "I'm getting off the phone now!" I say in my bitchiest voice, and hang up.

Tears well up in my eyes for the fourth time today and I look down at the IV firmly taped to my forearm. Time for triage. Between tomorrow's client pitch and tonight's childcare emergency, the winds need to shift in my direction. I lay back and give in. I will be a good patient and maybe in waiting a plan will sort itself out.

Thirty minutes later I'm in the hospital gift shop dialing my mom's number with one hand while I'm pressing my IV wound with a bloodied piece of tissue with the other. You'd think Band-Aids would be easier to come by for those who make a jail break out of the hospital. Actually, it wasn't quite a jail break. The orthopedist, fresh out of surgery, spent two minutes moving my shoulder around before telling me I had a dislocated shoulder but no fracture. The pain of relocating it nearly caused me to black out again, but once it was done, with an ice pack and a sling to reduce movement, I was on my way.

No answer at Mom's house.

I briefly fantasize about telling Patrick to drop the kids off at the CCDC in the morning. He can adopt the role of "Clueless Dad" and pretend that he doesn't know that the family has a nanny now and just assumed this is the same morning routine as always. I think about calling Colette, then Sarah, then Lauren—begging her to skip work—and then finally, the elderly woman who lives across the street from us. She might be lonely!

Incoming text from Maria:

So sorry about not being able 2 come 2morrow! Should have given u more notice, but I have big deadline & I knew you'd understand b/c ur so busy too! U should come hm early, take care of ur arm & you & Patrick can spend time w/ your kids. They miss u and love u so much! When u come back, I'll stay late and you and P can go out on nice date. You need to spend time together and relax!! Enjoy your vacation in sunny California! Miss u! Your friend, Maria

Oh, the humanity.

Five minutes go by and my mom hasn't called back.

I gather my purchases and head for the door, trying to think of alternatives. I'm like a market research company scanning the landscape in search of people within a highly defined target audience.

Hello, this survey will take just a few minutes of your time. Press 1 for yes; 2 for no. Do you live in the Seattle metropolitan area? Are you between the ages of 18 and 74? Do you have previous childcare experience? Do you have any important meetings tomorrow—and if so, would you mind scratching them so you can be available for employment between the hours of 6:30 a.m. and 6 p.m.?

I hail a cab with my good arm and sink into the backseat.

Incoming text from Slade:

Are u here? I need to c u @ my hotel tonight

Incoming text from Patrick:

Do we have a nanny plan for tomorrow yet?

My phone rings and I fumble with my apparatus for a few moments before I'm able to answer. The cab driver, obviously annoyed with my sci-fi ring tone (which is a signal to me that my mother is calling) turns around to look at me with my sling, icepack and cell phone all stacked nicely on top of my shoulder. His eyes widen and he shakes his head at me.

"Ah, Mom" I sigh, relieved to finally have a sympathetic ear to lean on. The ibuprofen is kicking in, the city skyline beckons into view and I get the feeling like the day might possibly be saved after all.

"Anna? Is that you Dear?"

"Yes, Mom. Hey, are you free tomorrow?" Trying for the casual approach first.

"Yes, absolutely free. Well, except for art class and dog walking. Oh, and I was supposed to have lunch with Peg. Why?"

"Can you take care of the kids?"

"Oh my little darlings? Of course!"

"Oh, thank God." I let out a sigh of relief and nudge the ice pack to a new position.

"Why, what's going on Sweetie?"

"Oh, nothing, really," I respond, deciding that I will leave out the part about the earthquake and trip to the ER for now. "Our nanny can't make it and I'm really in a bind."

"Oh that girl? What's her name again?"

"Maria" I say, simultaneously attempting to readjust the straps on my sling and fish out the address to the hotel from the bottom of my purse.

"You know, I've had concerns about her. Did I tell you that?" Mom's tone is less than kind. It's the same way she used to talk to me when I tried to leave the house in fingerless lace gloves, an off-shoulder tank and sky-high bangs in 1985.

"No but I'd love to hear them sometime later—" My mind is elsewhere as the city comes closer into view. With the ice pleasantly numbing my shoulder, I suddenly realize that I'm exhausted and in desperate need of a drink.

"Well, I don't like the way she dresses like a reality TV star. Why don't you just stay home tomorrow, you could probably use the break, you're always working too hard."

"Mom, I'm in San Francisco."

"Oh, you're in San Francisco! How lovely! Are you going to see cousin Carol?"

"Ugh, Mom, can you watch the kids or not?"

"Yes, yes, yes I can. Calm down Anna Louisa."

"Okay. Thanks so much, Mom. Love you! You're the best. I'm in the taxi now but I'll call you from the hotel to work out plans."

Chardonnay, here I come.

The hotel meets all of my expectations, and then some. Decorated, yet accessible, eclectic, yet traditional, impressive and still low-key, the lobby/ library is also sporting a cozy bar accented with the kinds of accessories that could fill up several Pinterest boards.

Heaven.

As soon as I get up to my room I throw myself back onto the bed, just like in the commercials, with a loud sigh, followed by a whimper as I land awkwardly on the pillows behind me. The numbness is starting to wear off.

I fish the phone out of my purse and dial my mom back to shore up plans.

"Hey, Mom, so about tomorrow…can you to be at the house at 6:30 a.m. or even 7 would be fine, but if you want to just go over and spend the night so you don't have to get up early, that might be easier on everyone."

Silence.

"Spend the night? Oh, no, no, no. I think I'd rather just show up early. Muffin Top won't do well overnight." My sister and I begged her to choose a different name for her dog, explaining the modern meaning of a "muffin top," but she refused, telling us that muffin tops existed long before the "misogynistic" term of describing women's overhanging bellies came into the vernacular. "It's not my dog's fault that those low-rise pants look so *stupid*," she explained. Poor Muffin Top. A Chow mix with an extremely fluffy forward half, she does resemble a bit of a muffin top. I'll give her that.

"Just tell me where I take the girls to school honey."

"Patrick will give you directions. It's The Global Citizens Academy on 34th, above the yoga studio."

"Oh, for crying out loud. That's the name?"

"Yes, Mom, the girls go there. And you pick them up at one o'clock. It's very important that you get there on time otherwise I'm charged a late fee."

"What? What did you say? There's a *late fee*? Oh, for goodness sakes. Your children are not library books! That sounds fishy. Hold on, what is the name of the school again?" I can hear the click of computer keys in the background as I prop myself on the bed and search for the remote.

"The Global Citizens Academy," I yawn, bunching up the pillow behind my head and clicking on the TV.

"And who runs it?"

"Annika. Annika Verbeck. She's Dutch, I think. Why are you asking?" I scroll through the TV menu impatiently until I find what I'm looking for: Pay Per View. "You don't need to talk to her, Mom. In fact, it's better if you don't." Why is my mother asking so many unnecessary questions?

"Well, my goodness. It says right here that she is a horrible, awful person!"

"Mom!" I clench my teeth and click the TV off, tossing the remote onto the bed, "what are you *talking* about?"

"Well. I just did a search on your Dutch master and saw this, um, what do you call it, an online review?"

"Fine, read it to me," I sigh, rolling onto my back, staring out the window. This isn't the room where Patrick and I stayed with the view of the Golden Gate. Instead, I gaze across at an apartment building above a bustling taqueria.

"Okay, here it is. Director Annika Verbeck—*if* you can even call her a Director—

See, right there, the reviewer doesn't even think she's deserving of the title!"

Just then I see something flutter outside my window—a bird, probably, but suddenly I'm overcome with a fantasy where Mary Poppins pops in through my hotel window, grabs a few notes, and flies her umbrella on up to Seattle. Maybe she can jab some sense into my mother while she's at it.

"Okay, okay. Here's what it says: 'Director Annika Verbeck is a complete fraud. She is operating without a license and the state, the *State*—Anna, did you hear that?— has issued a number of fines against the school. My child cried every day at drop off the first week, and Ms. Verbeck had the audacity to tell me that this was 'normal!' Then two teachers quit, claiming that they'd never been paid. Who runs an illegal preschool, lets kids cry and doesn't pay the staff? DO NOT send your children to this school. It was one of the worst experiences for me and my family."

"Is that it?" I ask.

"No. There are a number of exclamation points as well. This woman is really upset."

"Any other reviews?" I sigh, "Because this woman sounds like a nut. It's completely normal to have your child cry at drop off, especially the first week. That happens all the time. And moms like to vent and exaggerate on those message boards. It's only the angry ones that use them."

More computer key clicking. "Hmm, let me see. Two more."

I rub my forehead with the hand that's at the end of my good arm. "I don't want to hear them."

"Didn't you check this preschool out before you signed up Lucy and Franny?"

"I did. What's with the third degree, Mom? My offer from before stands. I will gladly listen to your concerns as soon as I get back from San Francisco. But right now, I'd much rather go down to the lobby so I can drink a big glass of wine. I've been through a lot today. Can I go now?"

"Oh, that does sounds like a nice idea. I wish I could come there and do that with you. I should come there next time you have to go. Wouldn't that be a nice idea?" she says seemingly forgetting the task at hand. "Anyway, don't worry about the school too much tonight. We'll figure it out. Just go have your wine."

Click.

I assume that means my mother is showing up, but I can't be entirely sure. Maybe I'll keep working the phones from the lobby bar once I'm adequately hydrated.

Coffee in one hand, laptop tucked under my sling and purse slung over my wrist, I walk precariously into an enormous conference room. The image of Clare's hospital comps, the one with the mom balancing her baby and crutches, briefly flashes through my mind, mostly because that's exactly who I feel like right now. Maybe he was onto something.

An assistant places small tchotkes at each seat around a very large conference room table: pens, jar openers, letter openers. She looks up briefly and accidentally drops one of the jar openers, which makes a loud clamor. "Oh my goodness, do you need help?" she asks, rushing over to lift the laptop from under my armpit.

"Oh, I'm *fine*," I smile. "Everything," I say, lifting up my chin, "is under control."

Slade enters the room, rapidly reading through emails on his smart phone (or at least he's pretending to be) as he walks.

"Good morning," he says to me, sidling up to my right shoulder with a brief nod and a wink before returning to his phone. "So, was it good for you last night?" I inhale a whiff of his cologne. Not bad. I gotta hand it to Slade, he's all about the personal details, from his slightly artsy yet highly distinguished eyewear, to the colorful cufflinks on his wrists, all the way down to the unmistakably confident way that he walks in those expensive oxfords. Slade even *smells* on brand. Meanwhile, I'm wearing my go-to black suit. It's from the Point of View department at Nordstrom, definitely not the most fashion-forward section of the store, but more importantly, the suit fits me nicely (extra thanks to the five pounds I've lost over the last couple of weeks due to stress and not having time for regular sit down meals) and even under the circumstances, I still feel confident, smart, and pretty. Normally I'd wear my hair up for a big meeting like this, but today it's down around my shoulders, perked up by my favorite styling products. Did I remember to put on deodorant this morning under my sling? I cast my nose ever so slightly downward. I did. Phew.

"I tried you several times," he says under his breath. "Did you not get any of my messages?"

"They didn't allow cell phones in the emergency room," I smile, nodding towards my sling. "Sorry about that."

Slade raises a perfectly groomed gray eyebrow as he examines the contraption around my arm. "Oh, I thought it was just a prop, but no, an actual conversation piece. How nice." Slade opens up his pinstripe suit jacket and places his phone inside an inner pocket.

"So, are we ready for this?" he asks, stretching his arms out to check his cufflinks. It isn't a rhetorical question. "I'm worried we didn't get in a practice session last night—"

Just then the Asenzer entourage enters the conference room.

I recognize T. Rx immediately, and my heart flutters a bit with anticipation. He's shorter than I imagined he would be from the photos, but otherwise looks exactly the same, perhaps even more commanding. His suit is a standard shade of dark gray, and he's wearing a white shirt and a red tie with a pattern on it that feels slightly dated. Not exactly a turn on, but it'll have to do. If this were a fashion contest, Slade and I would definitely be threads ahead.

"Tom Paine," he says, extending a hand. He looks at my sling, switches hands at the last minute and gives me a firm handshake first followed by extending a hand to Slade. So much for the conversation piece. I want to blurt something out about how I received my injury via stripper pole within the first 30 minutes of arriving in San Francisco but decide against it.

T. Rx takes a seat at the opposite end of the conference table and leans back into his chair. As everyone else gets situated, Slade makes the rounds with the female staff and I fire up the presentation. After weeks of researching this company and staring at his photo, I thought that seeing T. Rx in person would give me some sort of new insight into his personality. Deep down, what does he really *want* from this campaign? Press? Trailblazing a new category? The satisfaction that comes with helping people who suffer from a debilitating condition like anxiety?

And then it hits me. Money. All he wants is the money. Of course! All drug pushers are the same: they don't care about side effects or social consequences or the wars that may break out as a result of their actions; it's just business. I look over at T. Rx one more time and think to myself, *numbers guy*. That's what Slade would have said, had I spent the evening in his hotel room instead of dousing my shoulder in Chardonnay. *Keep it about the numbers.*

"The number of women who report anxiety is on the rise," I lead off with the click of a button as I launch the visual presentation, voice steady and strong. "Four times as many women are affected as men." The bullet points slide in according to my cue and I pause, making each point.

- One in four women will experience severe anxiety at some point in their life.
- Anxiety affects four times as many women as men, regardless of racial and ethnic background or income.
- It's the number one cause of disability in women.
- Married women experience it more than single women, and it is most common among mothers with small children.
- And yet … only about one-fifth of all women who suffer seek treatment.

I look around the room. T. Rx is typing something into his phone and the other execs look mildly bored.

So I pick up the pace and move quickly to the meat of the pitch, the YOWZ capabilities. TV, radio, print, web, market research, trend-scaping, social media, PR, viral marketing, mobile marketing; sweepstakes. Slade's contribution started and ended with the sweepstakes, but it actually morphed into a fine idea – a contest of nominating people who have overcome struggles, kind of like a Make a Wish Foundation for overworked parents. Sure it's a cover for the fact that we'll just be trying to sell them a happy pill, but why not share some great stories while we're at it.

Some of the slides include capabilities we've never done before, but Slade and I decided to throw some bells and whistles into the presentation. Perversely, it makes us look like we know what we're doing.

T. Rx's eyes light up and his gaze is only on me. It emboldens me this feeling that I'm connecting, that my words are having an impact on him. It's part of the thrill of this job. How to reach the client? What can you say to make them sign? Oh, there it is. I said something that hit him in just the right sweet spot. No more looking at his phone, no more looking at the door to the conference room. I connected. I glance at Slade and the twinkle in his eye says that he knows it too.

The first to speak after our laptops fold down and I click off the projector, T. Rx folds his knobby hands onto the table and leans forward. He's wearing a big gaudy gold ring with a big blue stone in the center. It's a ring I would expect to see on one of The Sopranos, not at a conference table in San Francisco. He probably made big money back East and moved West with his California trophy wife who wanted to come home. The skin is bulging around it. He can't get it off I bet. It makes me feel constricted and I start to lose the swoon from the presentation so I look away.

"So, what I really want to know is . . ." he says in a low, slightly raspy voice, "do you understand today's mothers?"

"Oh, do we ever," interjects Slade, jumping in ahead of me. "Anna is not only a creative genius, but she's living the life. Tell him, Anna."

I love how Slade interchangeably wants me to either admit to or deny that I have children depending on which client we are speaking to, but this one was no surprise. So I dive in, "I am a mother," I start. I'm about to say I'm your target audience, but I quickly realize he doesn't want his target audience running his campaign. "And I'm an educated, working mother doing it all. Or at least trying to, right? That's what we were told we could do – have it all. But do it all well or easily? While coifed and cultured and conquering?" The alliteration just rolls out of me and I'm not sure where I'm going with it but I still have his attention. Slade on the other hand is starting to raise an eyebrow ever so slowly, so I wrap it up. "I guess what I'm saying is. I see it. I see it everyday. Near and far I'm surrounded by the women you're trying to reach, and I understand them, how they work and how to speak their language."

"I guess what I'm getting at is . . ." he goes on, leaning his enormous body back in his enormous chair, "is to avoid a Motrin Moms clusterfuck with this ad campaign."

"Oh, of course," says Slade, looking at me and acting like he knows what he's talking about. Does he? I'm the one who followed the Motrin Moms campaign with great interest: how the "wearing babies as fashion accessories" and the "If I look tired and crazy people will understand" cause I'm a mom. The "we feel your pain" strategy fell apart when a handful of irate bloggers brought it down via a well-crafted, and well deserved Twitter crusade.

"We'd put together a social media strategy that includes the major mom influencers so we'd avoid something like that. Anna is our in-house social media expert."

Now he's treating me like I'm his daughter.

"Well, that's certainly a start," says T. Rx, still looking unconvinced. "You can never underestimate the power of an irate mommy blogger. In fact, they may be just the type of patients we're looking for." He laughs, leaning back in his chair again, coughing into his fist. Flashing the ring. Not a moment later he sits up and adjusts his large frame within the confines of his high back executive chair. "But what I'm really getting after here is something a little deeper. Have you seen this?" He opens up a leather folder and pulls out a folded over New York Times article and pushes it across the conference table like a toy boat. I reach for it but Slade grabs the paper first, opening it. "*Blue is the New Black. Maureen Dowd. Women are Getting Unhappier.*"

"Oh yes, I read that," I say.

"And . . . how about this one?" He slides another article our way. This one is from *New York* magazine: *All Joy and No Fun. Why Parents Hate Parenting.* Or this? *Why Women Still Can't Have it All. The Atlantic.* Anne-Marie Slaughter.

All of a sudden I feel a little exposed, like T. Rx has unveiled the personal journal entries of my closest friends, coupled them with the angst of our current generation, and now has a convenient solution in the form of one neat little pill.

"Women are talking about this already," he smartly says. I've underestimated him. "Are we going to speak their language? A real campaign of real moms talking about real struggles and pulling together these leading voices that are already out there doing it?"

It's a brilliant strategy, actually.

He shoves the articles down the table and I glance at the quotes that are marked with yellow highlighter.

Mothers are less happy than fathers.

A wide variety of academic research shows that parents are not happier than their childless peers, and in many cases are less so.

Studies have found that parents' dissatisfaction only grew the more money they had, even though they could buy more childcare.

"Well . . ." I say, looking around the room, searching for the right words. Slade is definitely not going to help me out on this one. I can tell from my peripheral vision that he is leaning back in his chair waiting for my response. I'm on my own.

T. Rx sniffs and looks down, pulling his tie straight.

"As it relates to your advertising campaign for this new anti-anxiety drug," I continue, "Listen, this is a very real issue. On the surface, of course, much of this debate is rooted in the pressures that are put on today's women in terms of juggling career and family and having it all . . ." and then I pause. "But anxiety is not a debate. It's very real and it can be debilitating. It can make you question everything, and it can make you lose everything. And the women who suffer from it need a very real way to feel better and in control of their lives—" I look around the room hoping to meet at least one eyeball that flashes me an ounce of integrity. " Maybe they've tried therapy and medication or other medication, but our job is to show these women, and their doctors of course, that's there's a new avenue they can take while seeking help. Help in the form of an anti-anxiety drug that will change the pharmaceutical landscape for generations to come. Your drug. Axiphan."

My eyes flash to the trinkets around the table emblazoned with a tacky Axiphan logo. If we win this account, the name will have to change. Axiphan could be anything: a software company, an allergy medication; dog food. I don't tell them this now though. Now my only job is to make everyone in this room feel super smart and important, while at the same time, giving them more than a few reasons to trust me. I sit down, fold my hands in my lap and lean forward with my chin slightly cocked, pulling my shoulders back as best as I can without yelping out in pain. My body language says: *We're in this together. Let's get to work!*

"I like the way you think," smacks T. Rx, using his arms to lift his body up and farther back into his seat. "Helping women. That's what we're all about. Am I right?" He looks around the room and his gaze is met with unanimous nods. It's a successful pitch, but I sort of want to throw up in my mouth that this guy is saying he's the man to help women. I focus on the fact that he's hiring me to help women instead. And just then, T. Rx puts his fist on the table. "Okay, let's do this thing," he says.

Twelve

"But we haven't said our prayers yet," pleads Lucy.

"Yeah! our pwarers," echoes Franny, tiny fingers pressed together in the steeple position, kneeled up against the side of her mattress on the floor, wiggling her tush back and forth.

The girls' bedtime stalling techniques are getting more advanced. Thanks to the Global Citizens Academy, they are now praying for things like reduced carbon footprints and organic, sustainable food for children in south Seattle. Lucy's prayers in particular could go on forever. "And I pray for bunnies . . . and the bees . . . and the Canadian geese that are getting rounded up by our government and sent to gas chambers. Peace for Geese! And also for momma's shoulder . . . so she can feel less stressed and more re*laxed* . . . ." And here's my opening to cut her off.

"Okay, that's plenty for tonight sweetie, I love that idea. I think I'll go relax my shoulder and my mind in my own bed now," I say, patting her on the back as I pull back the sheets to both twin mattresses on the floor so the girls can climb in. The girls are in the same room now "thanks" to Maria's foresight and attempts to bring our family "closer together" whereas Max's crib has been moved out of our bedroom into

Franny's old room so that Patrick and I can "better communicate." The garden *campy* has been sold on Craigslist. It's fine. These things needed to happen and Maria was just the catalyst, though admittedly, all of it is making me a bit tired. I slump on the edge of Franny's mattress and rub my eyes. Even though I should be feeling better by now, I'm still in recovery mode from the San Francisco trip. The pain in my shoulder has subsided, but the combined trauma of the injury plus winning the pitch has taken it out of me. I feel a slight pang of guilt that my own daughter has recognized my short temper for what it is. No regrets though—landing the Asenzer account was critical. I just wish I had a clone to jump in and do the work now. There is a ton of it ahead of me, but I'm still employed—and so are the rest of the team members at YOWZ – *and* I didn't have to do anything untoward to win him over, except maybe put up with some mansplaining about women and anxiety to get the job done. But hey, I'll be writing the ads so … I've successfully done my job. So the little bit of craziness and chaos to get here was worth it. If I weren't still feeling the twinge of soreness in my shoulder blades, I would totally be reaching over to pat *myself* on the back right now . . .

"But Mommy, Mawea's not here yet!" Franny chimes in, pudgy arms crossed in front of her chest, refusing to get into bed.

My heart skips a beat. What on earth is she talking about? Maria? Good riddance. Maria who left me in a lurch last week and made things weirder with my already weird mom. Maria who now has "meetings" that are apparently more important than mine? If I had a few ounces more of energy, I'd be scheduling some important meetings of my own this week—in the form of nanny replacement interviews. But I'm too exhausted. And oh yes, I'm trying to be "chill" now.

Another problem: the girls obviously adore her. And Max is now beginning to squeal words like "Maah" and "Maahiiii" whenever she's around. Even though I'd like to think that this is a precursor to him being to clearly articulate "Mama" or even "Let's take a trip to Maui," I suspect that more than likely, this is a sign that he is indeed bonding with Maria. And therein lies the problem.

Huh.

What do you do with a problem like Maria?

"For the song, we can't go to bed 'til we do the song," pipes Lucy from her perch under the fairy print covers.

"What song?" I retort. Even though I have just made a vow to be less bitchy and more present, twenty seconds later I now find myself clenching my fists and looking up at the ceiling, silently saying a bedtime prayer of my own: *Please, please, please, just go the fuck to sleep!*

I take a deep breath and turn towards Lucy, who has buried her head and started fake snoring.

Clonk! I hear the front door unlock with a thud. Keys slam against the front table. I cringe knowing that the vase is probably wobbling, but I don't hear a crash. Lucy sits up in bed and smiles with wild enthusiasm. Static from the sheets is making her hair stand on end; she looks like she has just stuck her finger in the happy socket. She yanks Franny by the hand and they scurry out of the room.

What the—?

"Oh, *muchachas*," I hear Maria squeal and she pounds up the stairs. "My little princesses, are you ready? Spit spot, my little ballerinas. This is Mommy and Daddy's special night!"

Special night? *Spit spot?* Is that some kind of cleaning party?

Oh, fuck.

I pull the door shut to Max's room as I march down the hallway. No sense in him waking while I push Maria down the stairs. Special night? My special night was last week in San Francisco I want to remind her.

Oh, she's no dummy though. Maria sees the look on my face, holds her finger to her lips and gently takes me by the arm, leading me towards the master bedroom. She's carrying a garment bag over her shoulder. Franny and Lucy follow closely behind, hovering and giggling. I decide not to say anything because I suddenly wonder if Patrick is in on this too.

We open the door to find Patrick completely naked except for his boxer shorts, hunched over on the bed trimming his toenails. He's so engrossed that he doesn't look up when we come in. Maria clears her throat and I suddenly break out in laughter. I'm not sure what is funnier: the fact that my husband was just caught in an awkward position or that Maria is so bold as to seem completely comfortable in front of him when he doesn't have any clothes on? Or is it because I've given up? I was so close, *so* close to an evening of peace, but here she is.

"Anna, sit down. Patrick, sit up!" Maria commands with militaristic hand gestures, as if this is the first day of boot camp. Tonight's ensemble includes low-slung bell-bottoms that are frayed around the heel and a zip-up hoody that says *chillax* on the back. As much as I'm dying to hear what on earth she's doing in our bedroom at 7:30 on a Thursday night, I find myself more intrigued by this sudden authoritarian role she's taken with us. Is this how she keeps the kids in line when we're not around? Patrick mindlessly slips a hand inside his boxer shorts and scratches an antsy testicle.

I sit down on the edge of the bed just as Maria launches into her soliloquy in front of my cluttered dresser. "So, you know, I feel really, really bad that I left you in a bind last week . . . ."

My teeth clamp down on my tongue at the same time as Franny and Lucy climb up and sit on my lap.

"But more than that . . . I can't help but notice that you two haven't gone out on a date since I've started working with your *familia!*" Lucy and Franny both giggle at this statement; I'm not sure why.

I look over at Patrick to gauge his reaction. He's still half focused on picking at his toenails and flicking dead skin on the carpet. I know he's thinking in his head, this is *your* deal, the CDC never barged into our house at bedtime.

"So I thought, I'm going to make it up to you! Give you some alone time . . . together!" Maria smacks her lips and then giggles, looking quite pleased, patting her thighs. Lucy and Franny clap wildly and then stand up to join her. Patrick fiddles with a dangling toenail and begins to lean over to bite it off, but I thwack him on the head before he can.

"So THIS is your night! I'm babysitting the kids and you two can get mooshy mooshy at a downtown *restaurante*! I made reservations for you! Oh, and Anna—I brought you something special." The grin on her face makes her look almost deranged. Patrick and I remain seated, mouths hanging open. "Don't say anything, you don't even need to say thank you," she squeals, tickling Lucy and Franny behind their ears, "just go and get dressed and get pretty for your *muy guapo* husband!" Maria looks down at Patrick's shorts and hands me the garment bag. "Patrick will love it I know," she flashes me a smile and then winks at Patrick. I look over at him, still sitting there in his boxers, but his expression is moving from calm but clueless to mildly irritated like he's watching *Kim and Kourtney Take New York* instead of *Maria Takes Over the Moore Family*.

"It's just a little bit sexy, so I think you'll be ok with it, and I just know it will look awesome on you," she says, before finally handing over the goods.

The garment bag is so light in my hands that it feels empty. I open my mouth to protest, but she shushes me and swallows a giggle. What would I even protest at this point? The date? The staring at my husband in his boxers? The dress? The bedroom changes? "I won't take no for an answer!" she sings before twirling high on her toes and departing the room. "Come downstairs when you're dressed. We have one more surprise," she sings down the stairs.

Why is she bringing me clothes to wear on a date with my husband? My mind flashes to the clothing she's seen me wear in the weeks we've known each other. When your uniform consists of barely-there tank tops, terry cloth short shorts and platform wedges, the working mother wardrobe is probably a pretty grim sight. Still, I'm not sure I'm up for this. Surely the evening can be salvaged. We can just send Maria home, get the girls to bed and forget the last five minutes even happened . . .

But then, as if he's reading my mind, Patrick, who is now stepping back into his clothes, a pair of pressed khakis and a blue button-down, looks at me and says, "I bet you will look hot in it. Let's go!" He winks at me before heading into the bathroom.

At Maria's instructions, we sit on the living room couch wedged up against the wall, and I shift uncomfortably, crossing and uncrossing my legs until I find the right position, to provide sufficient coverage. One of us has already flashed Maria tonight; she doesn't need to see up my skimpy dress even if she is the one who gave it to me. Patrick's opened a new beer and is entering his field notes into his iPhone.

The lights go down, and Maria appears at the curve of the banister. Lucy is shining a flashlight onto Maria's face, and I can hear Franny sniggering at the top of the steps. Wielding a toy microphone, Maria starts the show.

"Ladies and Gentleman, we're pleased to present tonight's main attraction. Singing for you this evening, the dynamic disco sisters!"

As Maria whoops and hollers and tries to make up for the admittedly stale audience that Patrick and I are being, I see Lucy and Franny slide down the banister with feather boas sailing behind them. Maria, with her microphone still in hand, walks up to me, strokes my cheek with the tip of her feather boa, and then Patrick's. With the showmanship of a Vegas performer, Maria pulls her hand back to the microphone and gushes, "the girls and I prepared a song for you, something so special to get you in the mood!" And then she winks at us, turns on her toes and walks over to hit play on the boom box. Franny and Lucy, who have been standing like statues with their heads dramatically looking down, now begin swaying from side to side, holding hands and singing like little angels over the beat of the music.

> *Listen to the ground, there is movement all around*
> *There is something going down and I can feel it . . .*

I look over at Patrick to gauge his reaction, but he's entranced by the performance and won't stop caressing my knee.

On the waves of the air
There is dancing out there
If it's something we can share
We can steal it

And that sweet city woman
She moves through the light
Controlling my mind and my soul

When you reach out for me, yeah, and the feelin' is right,
Gimme the night fever, night fever: we know how to show it!

The night fever, night fever: we know how to do it!
Gimme the night fever, night fever: we know how to show it!

Maria and the girls shimmy and float around the room once they reach the chorus. Our living room floor, which now doubles as a dance stage because the furniture has been rearranged, is dusted with wayward purple and pink feathers that have fallen off the boas. Images from the pervy Grandpa in *Little Miss Sunshine* flash in my head.

The girls give a final flourish and fall onto each other into a heap on the floor in a giggling fit. Without missing a beat, Patrick takes my hand and leads me out the front door, pausing for a moment to blow air kisses to the girls and Maria.

The hostess walks us through the restaurant to the back where a tall, inviting and thankfully dimly lit booth waits for us. I say a prayer of thanksgiving that no one I know is in the restaurant, but the hostess made up for that by turning back to face me and give me once overs several times on the way to the booth. I wanted to bark, *Haven't you ever*

seen a belly button before? But I resist and try my best to own it. There's no hiding it now.

Our server approaches the table eager to welcome us and rattle off specials, but I cut him off. I'm not in the mood to smile patiently through a list of things I don't want. It's late, I have to work tomorrow and if I have to sit here in this dress, I'd like to numb my self-consciousness as quickly as possible.

"A Lychee Martini, one Singing Fish Satay and a large order of Lettuce Cups. Please!" I follow up with a stern look that says: *Don't even THINK about commenting on my outfit if you hope to get a tip.*

Patrick gives me an approving nod before asking umpteen questions about the microbrews on tap. Finally he decides on Black India Pale Ale. Whatever that is. A few silent moments go by after our server leaves our table. I look down and see the folds of my stomach through the see-through dress and sit up straighter. This outfit would be a great diet. All you have to do is walk around in a sheer black dress which highlights every bodily flaw you can imagine, and then accent it with a hot pink slip underneath to ensure that everyone notices you. I suppose I should be flattered to think that Maria thinks I can pull off the same dress that Princess Kate pulled off in a college runway show. Hell, I may have actually chosen to wear this in college too, if I was drunk. But that was twenty years and twenty pounds ago.

"I cannot believe you made me wear this," I spit. "I mean, I bet even Maria wouldn't wear this out!"

Patrick shrugs. "I didn't want to hurt her feelings. She seemed so excited. And you do look hot," he adds, eyeballs scanning the bar, making me wonder if he's checking to see if any of his colleagues are lurking. "Maybe you should have Maria take you shopping," he teases.

I raise my eyebrows at him. "It's a good thing this table is between us right now or I'd smack you! How about she takes YOU shopping? I mean, clearly, she's comfortable seeing you in your boxers; you could invite her back to the dressing room for help with zippers and such."

"Alright, alright, alright" he says turning on his Matthew McConaughey *let's just settle down now* voice. "But she's right. We haven't been out in a while. Look around. There are actual working couples, probably actual parents too, out on dates, having a good time. You know, this could be us more often," he wiggles his eyebrows a few times at me.

He's got that look on his face—the one I distinctively remember from when we first met. Patrick and I were both a few years post college, drinking beers at one of Colette's parties (this is well before she met Blake and moved her summer parties to their yacht), and Patrick kept looking over and smiling shyly at me from the safety of his gaggle of software buddies. I was feeling insecure in the dating department, and honestly could not tell if he was checking me out . . . or if he confused me for some long lost cousin or something. I'd had enough go-nowhere hook ups at Smith to wonder if I would ever have an actual relationship. But once he walked over and started to talk to me, his whole demeanor took me off the defensive. Here was a nice guy, a really nice guy who was probably checking me out, but who also just wanted to get to know me. I had to slowly hang up my hang-ups one by one to make it work with this genuinely normal nice guy.

Patrick looks like he might be salivating.

"Are you hungry?" I ask, sucking in my gut.

"Yes, very," he says, with lowered eyelids and a sultry tone to his voice.

Ew.

It was just weeks ago that I had to work really hard to seduce him in order to seal the deal with Maria, and yet here I am kind of dreading the idea of having to put out tonight. I make a note to tell Maria that being able to stare down at my stomach roll does not to put me in the mood. And plus there is so much work to do! And I am so tired! Oh well, I'll cross that bridge when I come to it.

I study Patrick's face for another few moments. There's something about his expression that triggers a nerve. At first I can't quite place it but then it hits me. He looks just like Max, right before he's about to devour one of my boobs. That's it! Like father, like son. Men are so exceedingly simple, I think. Eat, sleep, play with boobs. Max has taught me so much about men. They really are such simple creatures. If only I'd had a baby boy before I started dating, I could have relaxed more and put the analysis to rest.

"So, where do you think Maria wears this when she's not loaning it out?" Patrick asks, leering over the table to try to cop a feel.

I think about the sweet Maria from the interview who described herself as not paying too much attention to dating right now because she wanted to focus on work. Did she wear this to college parties or does she wear this to clubs? Or does she wear it while making mac 'n cheese with 'lil smokies dinners at her apartment followed by spoon-feeding Ash? Does she bleach her butthole? And what kind of person represents the sweet spot of the target audience for this butthole whitening cream anyway—and if Maria and her friends are part of the demo, can she help me line up some focus groups with some of her friends? And what is up with her and this Ash guy anyway? I assumed he was her boyfriend, but she was so quick to say *nononononono, he's jusmyfriend* and I now wonder, what does *justmyfriend* mean to someone like Maria? Is that code for "friends with benefits?" Or what do you even call relationships between twenty-somethings these days? As I ponder these questions, it dawns on me for the first time that I don't know how old Maria is. She looks so young, but since she's in grad school, she must be at least 24 or so.

"How old do you think she is?"

"Who?" Patrick dips his head under his menu. Just then our server brings us our drinks, we move the menus out of the way so she can put them down. Patrick lifts up his beer and clinks my glass with a sly smile.

"Maria."

Patrick grins knowingly, "Oh, *Maria*," he says, wistfully, "You mean, you didn't notice when you checked her driver's license . . . you did check her driver's license, didn't you?" He looks me in the eye for a few excruciating moments before slapping the palm of his hand on his forehead *I Could Have Had a V8* style and exclaims "Oh, right! She doesn't drive! I almost forgot!"

He's being mean, and now I wish we could go back to the lust phase of tonight's evening. I take a long sip of my martini, and rub his calf with my foot under the table.

"Do you think she'll call someone over for a little night fever while we're out?" It's the first diversion that pops into my head, and I instantly regret the question. Why do I keep bringing the conversation back to Maria?

"Um . . . no. I don't think she's that type . . .," Patrick's voice trails off as he reaches for my foot under the table with one hand, while studying the menu with the other. How does he know whether or not Maria's that type? My eyes go back to the listings on the page. Black Pepper Scallops or Princess Prawns? I rest my elbow on the table, prop my head on my palm and look at Patrick, thinking. He's rubbing my foot now, and it feels pretty good. Although, I can't sit up straight, suck in my gut and have my foot rubbed all at the same time, so I slump down in the booth.

Maria is right. We haven't been out on a date in months. I don't even know how to carry on a conversation with my husband. So far, it's just been a series of awkward comments and conversations with myself in my head. Someone could eavesdrop on our conversation and just as well think we are on a first and last date, or our 300th. Is this why my parents got divorced? Did they fail to recognize how important it was to spend quality time as a couple? But then I remember all the bad babysitters I had as a child. My parents went out all the time and left my sister and me alone with some doozies.

"We had a sitter who was having sex with her boyfriend on the job once, when I was little," I blurt.

"Of course you did," Patrick drops my foot, lifts his Dark Pale Whatever Ale and takes a long sniff before putting the glass to his mouth.

"What do you mean 'of course'?" I say indignantly. "If Maria is home right now, having night fever with someone, then we have to go home," I say. I think about her offer to have Ash stand in as her replacement when I was in San Francisco.

Patrick raises an eyebrow and then looks a bit surprised, like he just came up with a brilliant idea. "Oh, I know! Maybe this wasn't a thank you/I'm sorry for last week. Maybe it was just an elaborate scheme to get us to turn over our luxurious master bedroom with the dirty sheets and all of the kid crap in it, so that she could have an evening of passionate night fever with some dude. I'm sure that's it!" I know he's joking, but I can't help feel my stomach somersault underneath the transparent fabric. The visual of Maria and Ash going at it in our bed is too disturbing. Would she . . .?

I take another sip. "You obviously never had any bad sitters as a kid," I mutter.

"That's not true. I had this sitter who showed me her turd in the toilet once, does that count?" Patrick smiles.

"Gross!" I almost snort lychee-infused vodka out my nose. "Why would she do that?"

"She was trying to set an example, I guess," he says, still examining the menu. Damn, I really can't decide what I want to eat."

"Set an example in what way exactly?" I glance at the menu, "Order the Tuna Manada so we can share it."

"I vaguely remember that it had something to do with potty training. Although that's not the part I remember as vividly as the big nasty poop."

"Wow. So how old were you, two or three? And you remember this?"

"I don't know . . . I might have been three or four."

"And you weren't potty trained yet?"

"Ok, can we talk about something else?"

"Well, I had a sitter who made us watch that awful movie Bad Ronald when I was like five. It gave me nightmares for the next decade," I say. Patrick looks unimpressed. "Bad Ronald. How could you not know that movie? 1970's made-for-tv movie about the creepy boy who lives under the stairs of his house after his mother dies and the new family moves in and he spies on the girls." Oh God. I realize our stairs look just like that nook where Bad Ronald lived. I bet Ash could outfit a makeshift bed under there in no time with his handy man skills. Maybe I should glue that door shut or fill it with cement.

Just them my phone beeps. A text! I look down:

Are you enjoying your date night? Jajajjajaja! Kids are sleeping -- everything is fine. Have a nice dinner!

"Phew," I say.

"What?" Patrick asks, wiping a bit of heavy beer foam from his upper lip.

"The kids. They are asleep."

Patrick sighs loudly, and then burps into the back of his hand.

Our server brings our appetizers. The lettuce cups look like a gourmet version of a toddler meal, one of those you'd see in a high-end magazine like *Sunset* or *Real Simple*. I pick up a lettuce cup, hold it in front of my mouth like a dainty taco and pretend that someone is about to take my photo.

"So…. how's work going?" I ask casually, now that the conversation has steered away from sex and feces.

Patrick starts to answer my question but my mind trails off again. My eyes follow his mouth moving up and down and I can hear his voice, but it's not registering. It's like I'm watching a silent movie over on the other side of the table while I sink my teeth into a high-end TV dinner. First I go back to Maria and Ash. I don't know her well enough to think that she wouldn't have him over. After all she introduced him to the kids and had him over to the house without our permission once already. What's to stop her from doing it again? Then the word "Ash" makes me think of smoking and how I used to smoke in college. I rarely if ever get the urge now, but when I'm falling behind in work and I feel like I don't know where to start, all I want to do is light one up and take a nice long procrastinating drag. I could go for one now in fact. And that makes me think of my French college roommate who smoked so effortlessly and went through life effortlessly. Was it the fact that she was French and it was genetic or was it the cigarettes? Nicotine's supposed to actually cause your heart rate to speed up but I swear there's a calming element to it. I look up from the lettuce cups. Patrick is staring at me.

"So?" he asks. "What do you think?"

"Oh," I smile and nod, as if I've been listening. "I think it sounds good."

Patrick puts down his beer. "Did you hear a word of what I've been saying for the last ten minutes?"

"I'm sorry. I got distracted. My mind's been racing all week. Tell me again."

"So, not a word?"

I look at him and try to piece together bits of what I heard on the fly. It's like when you're driving and suddenly you've reached your destination but don't remember all the familiar landmarks along the way like your mind was on autopilot.

"I know you're talking about your new game release and the guys at work," I manage to pull together. "Tell me more, seriously," I say sincerely.

"Anna," he says, eyebrows knitting together, giving me that condescending look again.

"Yes, Dear?"

"It's clear you didn't hear a word," he scolds. Now I feel like I just failed a third grade reading comprehension test. "This is why we're here tonight. Do you get this? We're alone. You're not at work, you're not teaching the kids to read. You're not cooking. Can we pay attention to each other for an hour?!"

When did I become the problem? Am I the only one not paying attention? I thought it was both of us. I want to quiz him on my trip to San Francisco and whether he know the slogans I'm coming up with or the alternative names to Axiphan.

"I get it. I'm serious. Tell me more. And by the way, when did my distraction become the only problem here Mr. *What's our plan for the nanny'* while I'm in San Francisco?"

"Jesus." Patrick slams his napkin down on the table. The diners adjacent to our booth look our way and I impulsively sit up straight and suck in my gut. "Are we going to play tit for tat now?" He's angry. I am no longer his luscious piece of meat wrapped in saran wrap.

"Let's start over. I'm sorry. I want to listen," I say, raising my eyebrows. "What did you want to tell me?"

"You know what?" he sniffs. "It doesn't matter. Let's just go back to the grind, and eat our food and we can work on our phones in bed when we get home. Sweet life."

I think Maria's plan has backfired. Was Patrick always this upset or did the dress and the date stir some fleeting memory from long ago that we used to have more time for each other when my brain wasn't one long to-do list?

"Of course it matters," I say. I want to reach my toes over to his crotch, hoping this helps sooth his nerves. But I decide it's too soon.

"Do you even care?" he asks.

What? Don't I care too much already? How much caring can a woman of my generation even handle?

"Yes of course I care," I respond, impassively.

"I don't know, Anna," he swallows hard and fidgets with the napkin. "You were so intent on hiring Maria -- she was going to wave some sort of magic wand and make everything better for you -- but now you seem so wrapped up in whatever she is doing or *not doing*, and then when you're not focused on that, you're freaking out about your own job. I'm just getting kind of sick of it."

There was a time that I could write a list of everything I wanted in my life on a short little list. In high school: to get a date to the prom, a new pair of cool jeans, the "it" sneakers, to win the swimming championship. In college: to be able to afford a winter weekend dress and enough gas money to contribute to road trips to Yale and Williams for the weekend and, of course, to pass my classes. And in young adulthood: to land a job, work hard, get promoted, get married and have kids. And now . . . now that I "have it all," I'm a little foggy on what comes next. What do I want? I feel like I've been too busy to give it much thought. Can I hire someone to write that list for me?

Maria is asleep on the couch wearing my cashmere wrap sweater that I considered wearing out over the slut dress but then left haphazardly on the bed when Patrick urged me to forgo the cover-up and show off my "sexy self." She has it on backwards, Snuggie-style. Without makeup, I'm struck by how childlike she looks. Her skin glows under the lamp, and her facial expression is one of complete contentment and peace.

Her computer is open in front of her, groaning away. I shut it down and tap her shoulder. She stirs slightly and raises her arms over her head to stretch.

I rouse her and ask if she needs a ride home. It's begun to rain outside, and I don't even know if the buses are running at this hour. I look over at Patrick. He'll take her home, won't he? I'm tired and need some sleep.

"Oh, nononono, I'm okay, I've got a ride," she replies, groggily, reaching for her phone and unclipping her weird bird umbrella from her enormous backpack. "Ash is taking me home -- he's waiting outside. But it was good right? Just what the doctor ordered, no?"

I look up at Patrick who is trudging upstairs to bed. I want to go hug him and have it just be the two of us for a minute together to make things right before we go to sleep. I look at Maria. She's grinning wildly now.

"See, my little bit of magic, works wonders, you'll see."

And with that she pranced outside.

I won't bring it up to Patrick again, but I wonder why Ash just happens to be outside while Maria is happily sleeping inside. I'll find out on my own.

Thirteen

As soon as I close the door behind Maria I head upstairs to check on the kids. I check on Max first. Sound asleep. Then I enter the girls' room. Rosy-cheeked and smiling in their sleep, they look so peaceful. The comforter is jumbled, the pillows are out of place and there are overturned laundry baskets on the floor. But they are drifting away happily to Neverland. Franny is hugging the feather boa that, thankfully, is not wrapped around her neck.

I stand outside their door and think about how to salvage the night with Patrick. I'm consumed with regret about the dinner. Maria wanted us to have a fun night. Patrick wanted us to have a fun night. And me, what's wrong with me? I can't go out at 7:30 on a weeknight anymore? I can't spend the evening laughing with Patrick about what a ridiculous dress I had on. We could have recreated the girl's hilarious and completely age inappropriate dance routine and sung Night Fever ourselves while stumbling into the bathroom to make out. We could have gone out dancing after dinner or done shots at the bar or actually talked about whether or not Maria was working out with her crazy house rearranging and disappearing acts while I'm away. But no, I take the blame for this one.

Suddenly I just want to be held by Patrick. I decide to just say I'm sorry I fucked up the evening and give him a big bear hug and snuggle in bed. That's the benefit of marriage. You can turn it around quickly with a few words when someone loves and understands you warts and all. But when I walk into the bedroom I see he's assumed *the position*. Not the carnal knowledge position. The position he's settled into comfortably is the lazy married person's evening entertainment position. He's lying stretched out across the bed, on his stomach with his face at the end of the bed, and his feet on the pillow. This is key so that his face can be closer to the screen. He's got the remote in his hand and the credits are already rolling for the beginning of *The Killing*. We came late to the series, especially considering that it's set in Seattle, but it's our latest and greatest on-demand series addiction now that *Breaking Bad* is over, which became our addition once *The Wire* was over, which became our addiction once the most recent seasons of *House of Cards* and *Orange is the New Black* were over.

"Ready for another one?" he asks? Sadly, I know he means another episode and not another orgasm. I nod and say sure. The sight of him eager for a night of TV watching has taken the wind out of my sails. And I am in fact, ready for another episode. I don't get my hug, but I also don't get a cold back to me with the lights out. I like to think we watch good TV but really, deep down, I know it's like the upper middle class version of heroin. When you're deep into a series, you've got to get your fix, or your Netflix as the case may be, no matter what. Even if you've already watched two episodes and it's coming up on midnight…just one more hit. That'll do it. You'll be satisfied and able to hang on until tomorrow. And then you can't control it – you find yourself wanting to watch a couple minutes of the next episode the next morning on your commute. Even though you're groggy from staying up late. But you can't stop. Because at the end of a long day when work was crazy busy, and the kids had speech and girl scouts and swim lessons, and dinner is not coming together the way you'd like, sometimes you just need a little escape. Tonight that "relaxing" escape comes in the form of a murder mystery. I wonder what the treatment for this condition – Netflixoria, the mild euphoria you experience from binge watching addicting series – could be. Maybe we should go after that market.

1:00 a.m. Patrick is sound asleep and I'm wide awake. Two hours worth of talking about murders in Seattle has not had the same lulling me to sleep effect that it had on Patrick.

If fact, some of the creepy characters in the show remind me of Ash which remind me of Bad Ronald. So I decide to research nanny cams, taking breaks every 10 minutes to check on the kids to make sure they are still breathing.

The technology has definitely improved since Nan discovered the teddy bear in Grayer's room and made her own video for Mrs. X, and this pleases me. Gone are the clunky VHS tapes and wall-mounted cameras. Surveillance has moved into the digital age, and I am delighted to see that I have a wide array of cams to choose from: wall clocks, objects d'art, faux kitchen appliances, faux books, faux toys and more. With this assortment, I suspect I must be the only one without a camera. There's nothing wrong with keeping an eye on your kids during the day I tell myself. I order a system that will connect cameras in the kitchen, living room and upstairs bedrooms. And for bonus measure, I throw in a doorbell camera so I can see if Maria's taking any visitors throughout the day.

Patrick and I were a few years into marriage, sans kids, when the *Nanny Diaries* hit the scene in 2003. Of course Patrick never read it, but collectively, among members of my book club and the college alumnae crowd, the consensus was that Mrs. X was a bona fide biatch. The fact that she had allegedly attended Barnard (fictitiously) and then in the movie had gone to—gasp—Smith, was horrifying. No Seven Sisters graduate would treat another woman (women's college alum or otherwise) so horribly, let alone sit so idly.

But back to the book. Like I said, at the time, I sided with Nan. We all did. Who wouldn't? Aside from drinking on the job and saying nasty things about her boss behind her back, she was a pretty good nanny and she loved that awful little turd of a kid. The only person who disagreed with me on this prevailing sentiment was my own mother. I loaned her my copy of the book and we subsequently engaged in a heated argument over who the more sympathetic character was: Nan or Mrs. X.

My mom sided with Mrs. X, citing all the horrendous babysitters she'd hired when we were kids. "Don't you remember Jill and her boyfriend Dan, who told you girls she was going upstairs to do some "laundry" in the master bedroom, and then Elise went outside and asked you why they were "doing pushups" and not laundry?" I did, and in fact, I recalled this memory more often that I'd like to admit. It sadly even came to mind in the middle of losing my virginity when I wondered if I was "doing it right" or if I was supposed to look more like I was doing pushups. "Or Roger, who told you when you were just seven years old that Rod Stewart was a "fag," and then when you asked the logical question "What's a fag?" she said that he had sucked on another man's penis for so long that his stomach was full of pints of semen, which caused him to pass out on stage, and then he had to be rushed to the hospital and have his stomach pumped?"

I vaguely remembered this one too. Thanks for the refresher, Mom! Apparently there were a number of bad sitters, and my mother issued this caution: as soon as you have kids of your own, you will experience your own share of bad sitters too. They're not all like Mary Poppins. You'll most likely wind up wishing you didn't have to deal with them at all. I thought about this now. Could my mother be *right?* I held so much sympathy and compassion for poor Nan. But alas, now I'm channeling Mrs. X.

In a mere matter of days, I have the entire house bugged. It costs me a small fortune, mostly based on that fact that I had to arrange for a surreptitious off-hour installation. The whole system is set up with motion detectors and infrared sensors and I can watch the footage almost in real time from work.

I don't say anything to Patrick about what I'm doing. Why make him worry?

"She's on the phone, again . . . ," chirps Lauren, popping her head in my office.

Things have been busy—really, *really* busy—since we landed the Asenzer account and every day at YOWZ feels like whirlwind. The dampness of fall has set in and our office windows are steaming up from the level of activity.

Bayview must have received my telepathic memo that we have an entire team devoted to researching women's health now, so they're back. Microsoft, wanting to get a head start on some consumer print ads for their new Excel product targeted at busy families is back on board the client roster as well. Tully's and Georgetown Brewing? Buzzing as usual. And as for Nether Lights . . . well, let's just say we're going with a kitschy snow globe theme for their holiday launch in mainstream and health media. We couldn't afford the Kardashians, so we had to go with Lisa Rinna, the housewife willing to do anything for a buck. It's going to be the biggest trend in Beverly Hills since vaginal rejuvenation. We have a healthy enough budget for some well placed holiday TV ads on Bravo and a few print ads in pornography magazines, a first for my career. It's going to kick some snow white ass.

"Ugh, again?" I ask Lauren, glancing to the ever-growing pile of sticky notes on the left side of my desk.

Lauren gives me a half smirk. "Well, she says she knows you are here. She says that unless I'm the worst assistant in the world, she knows that I have been giving you the messages." Lauren looks over to the stack on my desk. "Do you think I might be able to put the call through this time? Please?" Lauren presses her palms together prayer style and gives me a curtsey. "She's starting to ask me really personal questions about my income and my exfoliation habits."

I hold my chin in hand, thinking.

"She says she knows it's almost lunchtime and that you need a break."

"Fine," I say, "put her through."

"Oh, Anna! My gosh, it's really you!" gushes Colette. She's talking fast and sounds annoyingly upbeat, I wonder if she's confused bath salts for "bath salts." "I've been trying for *weeks* to get a hold of you! Is everything okay? I keep thinking that I might run into you at preschool drop off, but I never see you there! You are working so much and you need to take care of yourself, so that's why I'm calling."

I pause. "I do have a full-time job," I say, steadily, "But I assure you, I am fine – it's just a job, not Ebola, so no need to worry.

"I know, but it's just been so… long, and I feel like now that we're in the same school, and I still never see you. We really have to do something about this!" I look outside. It's overcast and dreary and the streets are soaked with rain. The last time I saw Colette was the second week of September, when the air was still dry, a distant memory by Seattle standards, but still, preschool orientation wasn't *that* long ago. And besides, there were years that went by where we never so much as called each other or sent a Christmas card, so why now?

"I haven't been at the school . . . that's why I have Maria . . . ," my voice trails off as I scan through 250 emails on my computer screen.

"Oh I *know*! I was just hoping to see more of you -- see if I can help … that's really why I called." Colette's tone changes, "I actually have a project to talk to you about, and it's somewhat urgent. Can I take you to lunch?" she pleads. "I think you'll agree it's an amazing opportunity." The desperation in her voice is a little painful. "What are you doing right now?"

I look at my computer and think for a bit. I've got a ton of research to do, comps to review, a meeting later this afternoon . . . and I want to take the nanny cam surveillance for a test spin. It's the first day it's in operation, and I need to check in and see what Maria is up to. I was planning on grabbing a sandwich and sitting down to enjoy the action.

Plus, whatever "opportunity" Colette may present is most likely not something I will be interested in. I'm reminded of a guy I had a crush on many years ago at one of my old jobs. I nearly peed my pants when he asked me to lunch, enticing me with the words "business" and "opportunity." In my mind, the pairing translated as an invitation to a romantic partnership where we would first make-out for hours before opening a joint bank account, and I'd be momentarily struck by how many millions were in there already. Or . . . we would skip lunch, make out in the executive suite at a fancy hotel downtown, and then he would ask me to lead the creative team of his new high tech startup.

Alas, lunch with him did mean that there was a brief comingling of finances – that instant we both fished out cash from our cheap wallets when it came time to pay. For the hour leading up to that tender moment, I had to endure the Amway pitch. And then it hit me. Colette's probably going to pitch me to "join her team" for Rodan & Fields. Or maybe Stella & Dot? Nah, her jewelry is way more upscale than that. Oh no, I've got it. India Hicks, the former Princess Di flower girl who now led a lifestyle empire from her home in the Bahamas with her gorgeous husband and four kids. Those were the premiere modern day multilevel marketing businesses for women who didn't work and didn't need to because they were married to hedge fund managers or Silicon Valley entrepreneurs, but wanted to do a little something on the side. That consisted of nonstop Facebook posts about how they were kicking back and earning money while they slept thanks to these amazing businesses. I bet anything she's trying to expand her empire and will pitch me on the ability to make extra money while on her team. Those schemes pissed me off. Not only because most people barely make any money and embarrass themselves on social media as they constantly hawk their teams, but more because women raising kids and working should be able to have flexibility in their jobs without becoming Avon ladies. I think I'll ask her, if it's such a great opportunity, why don't I ever heard about men selling any of these products? And I'm tired of being pitched to. There's nothing more annoying when I spend most of my days scheming my own pitch techniques.

I click open the nanny cam software on my computer. "I can't . . . I'm sorry. Not today," I say to Colette, emphatically. "Maybe some other time."

Back to the nanny cam. It's too bad my girls aren't old enough to submit to reliable lie detector tests. The day after our dinner out when I drilled them about Ash's whereabouts during the evening, they made up a fantastical story about going outside to watch Patrick and I drive off into the sunset, and then Maria's friend Ash just *happened* to drive by, and he *happened* to have a bunch of colored chalk in his car from the dollar store and then they spent some time (neither child could verify how long) drawing intricate scenes on the sidewalk and on our driveway. With each new scene, Ash had a new story to tell, and then they all "went places" in the story. And this is where the narrative diverged a bit, depending on whether Lucy or Franny was retelling the story (I interviewed them separately, part of my detective work). Lucy said they all rode on a merry-go-round and Franny told me she petted some pigs and goats that made her sneeze a lot. Got my goat, eh? I don't think so! I understand that the ability to tell tall tales is actually a developmental milestone, and that kids often have trouble separating fantasy from reality. . . but with my house now bugged I'm ready for the truth.

"Oh Anna, I *really* need to talk to you!"

"Some other time, I've got to go now," I need to turn Lauren into one of those LA-style assistants who screens the pitches ahead of time and only gives me the digest version if she thinks it's worthy of my attention.

Click.

SitterSpy, the software program that runs my nanny cams, is displaying three new events and one real time live stream. The thumbnails are arranged like little YouTube videos. I can save them, name them and organize them by categories. I click on the first one. It's from this morning, in the kitchen. The din is so loud that the audio is distorted on my computer, and I can't make out any of the voices. Seeing my house like this, on video, gives me a new voyeuristic perspective and it's not a good one. It's one thing to see those messy hoarder type families on TV but quite another to see your own cluttered spaces reflecting back at you on the small screen. Also, to my horror, *I'm in the video*! Maria is calmly feeding the kids and wiping down counters while I bounce around the room, looking frantic and crazed, muttering nonsensical phrases under my breath as I rush in and out of the room to grab my keys, shoes, purse. Jesus, I look like hell! Would it be bad to ask Lauren if she could automatically schedule my hair appointments every two months I wonder? Not really resume building stuff, but if I look good, she looks good, right?

Click. The second one is in the upstairs hallway. The kids' clothes are all lined up in a sort of assembly line, including socks, shoes, and even a toothbrush at the end. She calls out Franny first, then Lucy, and they both sit down and dutifully get themselves dressed. Max scoots around on the floor and Maria tickles him all over before unzipping his jammies and pulling a shirt over his head. Nobody whines, nobody cries . . . they're just doing it. Huh. It looks so easy from afar.

Click. Third time has got to be the charm. Give me some action here! There's no way things can be going *that* smoothly. This one's live so I check my watch: 1:14pm. Preschool is over. Everyone is in the den, and at first I'm so shocked by how quiet it is that I check the volume on my computer. Franny and Lucy are snuggled up on the loveseat, with a blanket draped over their legs and picture books stacked next to them. Lucy is mock reading to Franny, flipping through the thick board book pages of *Brown Bear, Brown Bear* and Franny keeps putting her head on Franny's shoulder. Max is in his bouncy seat on the floor, kicking back and forth but looking drowsy. Maria is talking to him softly and stroking his head, but I can't hear what she's saying above the din of Lucy's story telling. Then Maria gets on her knees. She's doing something but the camera angle is such that whatever it is, I can't see. What I *can* see is her butt facing the camera and a teal lace thong peeking out. It goes up, and then down. Up, and down. What is she doing? Jane Fonda's exercise tape? Is Ash over at our house again?? The kids are paying no attention to her whatsoever, in fact, all three of them look like they're about to nod off. Did she drug them?? I wish I could run home and adjust the camera angle to a wider lens so I can see what's going on.

And then, as if my prayers have just been answered, I can see. She moves the laundry basket over within camera range and finishes placing all of the folded clothes inside. Then she hands Max a pair of socks. No ordinary pair of socks, but one of Patrick's made to order sock burritos.

"Oh Maximoo, see how Maria likes to make a burrrrrito! *Juslike* this! This is the way your daddy likes them!" she croons. "Do you love your daddy? I know you do! He's such a sweet man!" How the hell does she already know how Patrick likes his socks folded?

I watch for a long time. I watch as Max drifts off to sleep, then Franny, then Lucy. Maria quietly picks them up one by one, carries them to their beds (SitterSpy flashes 'new event' three times—displaying a brief new video every time a kid gets placed in bed) and then she returns to the den. She walks over to the wall of books on the north corner of the room and scratches her arms and back a bit as she browses the selection. Suddenly I feel self-conscious about our book collection. Too much chick lit and self help? I do have a number of titles up there from my book club years that I'm proud of, but I'm afraid the rest is . . . well, representative of the way things are right now.

Maria bends over and scans all of the titles on the second shelf up from the bottom. *What To Expect When You are Expecting, Misconceptions, Backlash, Raising Your Spirited Child, I Don't Know How She Does It, How to Shit in the Woods* and *Lean In*. Maria pulls out a few parenting titles and puts them down on the end table. Next she sits down, opens up her laptop and begins typing.

Slade walks into my office and I gasp, quickly clicking out of the SitterSpy program. "What are you doing, Moore? Did I startle you? What were you doing just now, looking at porn?"

"N-no!" I stammer.

Slade wants to know how it's coming with the mental health research and if I've lined up enough 'crazy bitches' for the focus groups.

Which gives me an idea. I think I can arrange for that.

Fourteen

"Moore! Why did you make me go to that . . . that awful conference? It was actually not really even a conference . . . what would you call it . . . it was as if the narcissist's mother ship landed in town and all the wackos came out."

I swivel around to face Slade and hold my hand over my mouth to keep from snorting out loud. He looks like he could use a stiff one, and it's only 10 a.m. Too bad I don't keep a mini bar in my office.

"Welcome to my world, Boss!" I grin.

In an effort to get Slade a bit up to date on real life anxiety in women – rather than the Jacqueline Susann *Valley of the Dolls* version playing in his head – I sent him to a monthly gathering of self-described anxious mothers at a Seattle Meetup group called "Mommy Angst." It was led by a local woman who said she was recovering from her former life as a stressed out mom, and now she wanted to share her wisdom with all the moms who haven't seen the light yet. Apparently he didn't find it as useful as I had hoped.

"I don't understand . . . were they happy this month? Normally it's a really nice mix of pissed off divorcees, crazed workaholics and narcissistic parenting bloggers."

The sessions were sort of a strange combination of bragging and complaining about your life all at once, but there were some juicy nuggets in all that whining – like the woman who hated her husband, but had finally reached her sexual peak at 46 so was looking for anonymous sex on listservs or the women who thought it was so detrimental to work outside of the home and not be there for your children that they came up with crazy work at home schemes like creating an online coop of women who pump their breast milk for years after they were done breast feeding their own kids and selling it on eBay to support themselves and the women who can't produce. Their words not mine.

"Oh come on. Honest to goodness, that was nothing but a fucking bitchfest. And these women! What is their problem? The ones who don't work outside the home are criticizing the ones who do even though they all have these little side so called businesses making candles or inspirational CDs; the ones that work too much moan to each other about how hard it is but then they carry around these articles about how kids of working parents turn out better, and flash it like its their drivers license or something. And oh good God, I need something stronger to drink. Either they have too many kids or not enough, their husband travels too much or not at all. There was not one word uttered there that was not about these imaginary problems that are making them anxious and they need to figure out how not to be anxious. I wanted to scream at them – wake the fuck up. Talking about all your anxious parenting problems is *making you anxious*. Get a real hobby! God save them."

"Welcome to the mommy wars," I smirk. "And that would be, Asenzer save *them*! Slade, *this* is our target audience. Don't you get it?"

"Okay," he shrugs, rubbing his brow, "but let me tell you something. Once we're done with this anxiety campaign, we're going back to Asenzer to pitch them on a new drug" he points a slender index finger towards my face, "the drug that everyone else needs just so they can sit in the same room with these women."

"Isn't that called beer?" I smile.

Slade crinkles up his nose and huffs out of my office.

I swivel back to face the computer. I myself was fairly caught up in one of Anne-Marie Slaughter's *Atlantic* pieces on the myth of the work life balance, or more precisely that balance is something only a very privileged few will ever be able achieve (a.k.a. afford), and that "the majority of American women who have caregiving obligations are persevering in the face of seemingly impossible conflicting pressures." Yes! It makes so much sense. We're all talking about it. And Mr. T. Rx thinks he has the solution, and it's my job to make people think he does. But does he? I decide to put my moral compass aside for a minute and dig into the comments. Anonymous online comments are the greatest contribution to social research since the invention of polling.

Just then Lauren solemnly walks in and drops off the preliminary focus group findings on my desk. "I know this is totally unprofessional," she gulps, backing away from her own spreadsheets, "but I didn't know how else to organize this in order for it to make sense . . . so I just used the terms the women used to describe themselves." She's about to leave, but I stop her as soon as I glance down at the categories:

Losing My Shit
Slightly Crazed
On the Verge
Mildly Insane
Fucking Nuts
Beyond Help

"Very interesting . . . ," I say, glancing up at her above my glasses. I have to wear my glasses all the time at work now; my eyes have nearly given out with so much screen time. I scratch my forehead. "So, what do you think?" I ask her.

"What do you mean?" She stammers, backing away from my desk.

"Of the data? Of these women? What do you think?"

Lauren gulps. "Uhhhh . . . honestly?"

"No, lie to me. Yes, *honestly*. I just want to hear your opinion. There's a lot of information here." I flip through several pages of research and hope Lauren can at least top line it for me before I dig in.

"Well . . . uhh . . . ," Lauren looks all around the room, anywhere except directly at me. She shifts on her feet and grimaces like I've just asked her to spell out a dirty word.

"Out with it!" I say.

"Well . . . okay, I'll say it: reading all this stuff actually makes me not want to be a mother."

I look at Lauren and smile. She continues. "I mean, I know we're actively searching out people with issues but . . ."

"But . . . what?"

She dances from side to side a bit more. "It's just that . . . all of it sounds so *awful* but also kind of *normal*. I mean, we screened out everyone who would potentially have something really bad going on in their lives, like a serious mental illness, a death of a spouse or family member, or a cancer diagnosis, or a terminally ill child . . . uh . . . so I guess that's why I just don't get it. Sorry." Lauren drops the rest of the files on my desk like a hot potato and practically runs out of the room.

A few moments later, Slade is back in my office, elbow propped inside the doorframe.

"Moore, are you sure you're on the right track here? I'm counting on you. I hope we're not betting this campaign on these whiny moms down the street. I was hoping for something that could offer a panacea for the yearnings of American culture. Like Viagra."

Ugh, now I'm the one who needs a stiff one.

"Listen." I reach down and grip the corners of my desk. "Would you rather I send you over to the law firms downtown? Maybe you could rent an empty office across from one of them and use your binoculars to spy on the women working 'til 3 in the morning and then sleeping under their desks and crying when they look at the pictures of their kids that they never see."

Slade's mouth hangs open. "Oh, I see . . . did I touch a nerve?" He starts backing out of the office. He makes it all the way out of the office before adding, "And maybe it's best to keep photos of your kids out of the office for now . . . ."

"I'm ON TOP OF IT." I shout down the hallway. And then I whisper, "fuck off" after I'm sure he's gone.

That was probably Slade's ten minutes of work today. But as I kept reading through the emails from the working moms spewing venom at the "self righteous, Jesus loving, mini-van driving she-slaves," I had to wonder, are we anxious because we don't have the right man or the right job or enough money or the best skin? Or is it really that we've made "award winning parenting" or "having it all" so much of a goal that we all feel like we're letting ourselves or someone else down? In trying to have it all and be perfect, are we just sabotaging it all in the end? That, and I also wonder why the SAHMs always also get saddled with being Jesus-lovers and working moms get labeled as sex-starved. And uneducated moms turn complex social and political issues into a veritable freak show. But that's not what I was here to figure out.

All I need to do now is get all of them to want a little something to take the edge off and make nice!

I was jealous of Slade's nonchalance and ability to see the campaign for what it is: just another advertising blitz aimed at yet another target audience. Yet I can't ignore the fact that this one tweaks a nerve a little too close to home. Perhaps I can convince T. Rx that, as part of his campaign, he needs to donate some money to some sort of foundation for girls to save the next generation of women for this angst.

I flip through the clippings on my desk and pull out "The Happiness Doctor," a flyer I picked up at the Northwest Women's Show last week. *How to increase your happiness! How to stop the negative influences of others from taking over your life!* If happiness is a state of mind, should we pay this guy to start talking about the benefits of medicine or should we pay him to get out of town?

"OH FUCK, what am I doing?" I groan.

Lauren pops her head in my office. "Everything okay?"

"No." I press my fingers hard against my brow bone. "Can you get me some drugs? See what we've got in the first aid kit in the lunchroom. The stronger the better."

"How about a martini for lunch instead?" I don't have to look up. I know who it is, but how did she get in here? How did she get past Gloria?

I almost hated to admit it to Colette, but her whisking me off to lunch was just the thing I needed to get through the rest of the day. The heavy drapery, the ornate carpeting, the gentle clinking of silverware and pouring of ice water goes a long way to calming my nerves. And after all my years in Seattle, I had never been invited to the Sunset Club – perhaps the oldest (if not the hoity-toitiest) ladies-only club on the west coast.

We get seated in our plush, high-back chairs and I look across the table at her. As always, her hair is a glossy, sleek mane of perfection. She smiles at me as I attempt to smooth down my own frizzy mess in between sips of water that taste like they were melted off a glacier. "I'm so glad you were able to join me today, Anna," she says, with a slight lisp. She must have had a recent injection as her lips look freshly plumped I think, and I try to overlook the fact that she's beginning to look more and more like a female impersonator.

I put my napkin in my lap and lean against the table. "So, what's up?"

Colette takes a tiny bite of arugula mixed with sliced pear. She chews for a long time, swallows and wipes the corners of her mouth daintily with her napkin before responding. "I'm starting a foundation," she says.

"Wow, that's great!" I respond clumsily, as now with a mouth full of food, a stray piece of lettuce flies out of my mouth and lands on the tablecloth. I slide my plate over ever so slightly to cover it up. "What's it about?"

"Well . . . that's what I wanted to talk to you about," she says, stroking her soup spoon as if it were a personal pet. "It's a bit of a sensitive issue, so I hope this doesn't come across the wrong way."

"Sensitive?" I ask. "As in classified? I'm great at keeping secrets. I still haven't told my mom who shot JR, and she can't find the episode on Netflix."

Colette looks around the room and lowers her voice before responding, not picking up on my joke.

"It's a foundation which will support working mothers who are struggling," she says, not quite making eye contact.

"That's terrific!" I blurt, shocked that something like this would even be on her radar. "Like Dress for Success, or Welfare to Work?"

"No, not exactly. . ., " Colette goes back to stabbing her salad, but not eating it. "Those programs are wonderful, and they serve a real need for a certain audience . . . but I'm focused on a group that no one is paying attention to yet. I'm still in the early stages, but I know I've hit on something. And no one is watching out for this at risk population. They are lacking a collective voice." She looks up at me tentatively.

The feminist in me actually likes what she's saying and wants to hear more. I knew there was a reason I've stayed in touch with her all these years I tell myself. She isn't completely out of touch after all. I've misjudged her. But I say yes to too much. I'll just tell her that I support the idea but really have no more time for anything. But then I can't resist.

"How can I help?" It just comes out and I find myself genuinely meaning what I've just said. Call it feminist brainwashing: all someone has to do is say 'women's issue' and 'cause' in the same breath, and I'm on board.

Colette's face still doesn't move, but there's something about her expression that makes her appear as if she's done a good sell.

"Wonderful!" she exclaims. She picks up her purse from the side of the table and pulls out a packet of information and a brochure. This isn't a low-budget media kit; instead, it's four-color, glossy, and extremely tasteful. Very appealing. I tell her this.

"Oh, thank you," she replies, demurely. "I really appreciate your feedback. It's intended to be perceived as aspirational for this underserved audience, so it's really good to know that you like it."

"And who exactly is the audience?" I ask, tearing off a large piece of bread.

Colette looks around the room and reaches an impeccably manicured hand out towards me on the table before responding. "You are," she says, lowering her eyelids. "It's a foundation to support management-tier working mothers who earn less than $300,000 a year," she looks at me and bites her lip, which for her really takes effort. Then with a touch of faux embarrassment says, "I hope I'm not being too bold to assume you're in that category."

I gulp, unable to fully swallow the last bit of sourdough roll I've just stuffed in my mouth. It sits there in my throat and I look around the room for a waitperson to refill my water glass so I can flush it down.

"I want you to be our spokesperson," she says, hands on the leather-wrapped steering wheel of her $70,000 SUV as she drives me back to the office. "Be the voice of our cause. I know it's a lot to ask, and you have a lot on your plate already . . . ," she sighs, checking her hair in the rearview mirror, "but will you at least think about it?"

I roll my head down and then over to look at her. "As much as I would like to be the poster child for your charity," I start to say, but she interrupts me.

"Listen," she says, reaching over to place a bony hand on my thigh, "I know you think you don't need any help, and you're probably thinking it's silly for me to be putting this foundation together. You look around and see so many other women less fortunate than you. But think about this. *Really*, think about it. I mean, think about the *real* needs in our society. Upper middle class women *are* at risk. You are the backbone of our society, and yet, are you getting all the support you need? Are your needs and desires being fulfilled? Are you keeping it all together? If you ask me, the answer is no. You need our intervention and you need it now."

I sigh. I wonder if it was the Craigslist nanny ad that suggested to her that I was "at risk" or the lack of a yacht club membership, or hell, lack of a yacht for that matter. We're now out in front of my office, so I click my seatbelt open and grab the door handle to let myself out. "Just one question," I ask before leaving, "how exactly will your foundation support these 'poor' and yet 'upper class' working mothers?" I do air quotes to try to highlight the ridiculousness of the situation according to Colette, but she gladly dives in with her proposal.

Colette beams at the chance to share from her heated leather seats. "Spa treatments, pedicures, back-up childcare, mental health counseling, and infrastructure-related initiatives like nanny cams, weekend retreats, consultations with stylists and, of course, continuing education in the form of symphony and theatre tickets. It's the little things that can make such a big difference in a person's life. Think about it!"

Fifteen

More than 30 million Americans are currently taking some form of anti-anxiety medication, including one in four women in their forties. And of course that doesn't include all of the other "remedies" (natural or not) that people use to self-medicate their way through anxiety. My own research, combined with dozens of studies I've pulled up in the last hour, collectively points to a very sobering fact: we're all pretty much trying to drug ourselves.

Even the women in our focus groups who said they had never gone on anything cite four or five-cup coffee drinking habits during the day, and then "a glass or two" of wine or spirits at night, to take the edge off. "Because Mommy needs her medicine," more than a few of them said.

Some women swear by therapy. Some are addicted to exercise. Others devour self-help books by the dozens. All of that was to be expected. Botox, however, was a surprise. Apparently, it wasn't because you didn't look old anymore and therefore had less stress, but because if you can't look sad you can't feel sad. So apparently there is really something to that song from Bye Bye Birdie, *Put on a Happy Face.*

I decide to call my mother for some perspective. Are we really that different from other generations, or as some of those new age doctors would have us thinking, did we inherit this anxiety from our parents' wartime and depression era brand of anxiety?

"Oh hello sweetie, I'm so glad you called. I was just sitting down with a bag of chocolate chips for dinner," she giggles, "I can't stop eating them!"

"Mom, that's not good for you. You need your protein, especially if you're carrying Max around." And then I think, well duh, there's one answer to my question. My mother's been addicted to sugar her whole life to feed her anxiety. Sure, the marijuana may give her the munchies every once in a while, but for her the sugar is definitely feeding a deeper craving.

"Mom, when you were younger, did you or your friends take anything, like pills or anything like that, do take the edge off, you know what I mean?" My mother was already married at the height of the beat generation, and besides she was always sort of square, so I know she didn't do any mind enhancing psychedelics. But she had to have done *something*. Just because you're a nerd doesn't mean you don't get stressed.

"Oh sure, well, we mainly had cocktails. None of these fancy beers or wine that you kids drink. I only ever drank scotch or gin," she gloats, as if I'm a lightweight.

"Oh come on, Mom, there must have been some crazy and wild people who needed something beyond social drinking, right? You know, screaming kids, husband cheating – Mad Men stuff – what'd you do in those cases?"

"Oh, like drugs, sure. I mean everyone had Valium, I suppose. And then your Aunt Carol took a Phenobarb whenever Uncle Tim drove her nuts, which was pretty much all the time. That would help her deal with him. God he was such a crank!" I do remember him as being a crank, always red in the face, smoking and yelling at his kids when we went to visit them once a year.

"But when things got really bad, you were sent to the hospital to *rest*," she adds as if she's talking about a day spa.

"Wait! To *rest*, at a hospital? That doesn't sound very relaxing," I say, remembering my own recent visit to the hospital all too well.

"Maybe I'm getting confused. Maybe that wasn't something you did to yourself, but something that your husband would do to you. Now that I think about it, yes, I think a friend of mine from college got sent away to rest. I don't think I ever hear from her again," she seems to shudder at the memory. "Sweetie, you're not thinking of doing drugs, are you? Don't do drugs. If you need help with anything, I'll order you some vitamins from my doctor."

My mom also had a doctor who sold expensive sugar pills to treat all sorts of ailments. That and her medical marijuana were all she did now.

I need to know more about this remedy that T. Rx has up his sleeve. Is it really an elixir for the stresses of modern life? At this point, I'm not sure I really care, or have the time to care, or the ability to be concerned -- I still have to put together the ad campaign and make it sing. I'm just curious. What does it really *do*? We've done all the research on the target audience, gathered the demographics and analyzed the psychographics. I *know* what these women want, and I have a pretty good read on what they need. My question now is: Can it deliver? And if so, where can I get my hands on some?

As I'm waiting for T. Rx's assistant to put me through to the product knowledge team, I pull up three tabs on my browser — Facebook, SitterSpy and Gmail. I cradle the phone in between my ear and the crick in my neck and wait, staring at the screen.

My mom's having a field day on Facebook. She posts her schedule, and then likes her own post and comments on it. I'd make a point to tell her that she's doing it all wrong, but no one's following her anyway. Except for me of course. So I throw Mom a few 'likes," and ask her to be sure to pop in.

Then there's more local SAHM promoting their businesses -- workshops on gardening, connecting with your kids over the holidays, reconnecting with your husband in the evenings. Oh, wait. Here's something. More market research.

Damn! Advertising *Xanax* in ecards, that's cute. I've got to up my social media strategy for Asenzer's upcoming mommy's little helper. I'm thinking a Hamilton-like campaign. Viral rap songs on YouTube. That could be the ticket.

Lighten up, yo, ladies and look at the day!

The founding fathers built a country, what have you got to say?

Child-rearing, bosses-fearing, people jeering, is that all?

Keep your spirits up and don't take that fall!

Ok, maybe not.

"Asenzer product knowledge, this is Jennifer, how may I help you?"

My adrenaline is pumping, and I try to steady the hand that is holding the receiver. "Jen! Hi!" Despite the fact that I've never spoken to this woman before in my life, Jennifer is suddenly my new best bud. Can she hook me up with some product samples? Jen declines, explaining that the drug is not yet on the market, and if it were, it would still require a prescription. I was just kidding of course. Plus, they are still early in the game in testing and haven't completed clinical trials yet.

"Ok, so let's dig in. Tell me exactly how this will work and how it differs from others on the market."

Pen and pad of paper at the ready, Jen leads me through the scientific lingo: "neural pathways of anxiety," "Amygdala's sensory triggers" and "GABA activation." Always the multi-tasker, while I'm listening to Jen, I click over to another window and see that my husband, Patrick Farrell, and my nanny, Maria Garrido Perez, have just become Facebook friends. Mere seconds later I see that she's written something on his wall in Spanish:

tan grande para conectarse con usted jajajajajjajajajajjajajajajajaja.

Why did I waste my time in high school taking French? And more importantly, why am I paying a nanny to chat on Facebook with my husband? While Jen continues on about drug physiology, I launch the real-time video on SitterSpy. Sure enough, there's Maria, typing away on her laptop in the den. The girls are putting together a puzzle and Max is kicking back in his bouncer. My eyes narrow, and I glare at Maria.

Jen explains the finer scientific points of existing anti-anxiety treatments and how each one impacts the brain. I know I'm the one who asked the question, but now she's starting to lose me. "Uh huh . . . oh yes . . . I see . . . ," I mutter, taking notes and asking questions that hopefully sound at least semi-intelligent.

All of the sudden, Maria is waving. I don't know why, but instincitvely I look behind me, thinking she's waving to someone in my office. What's wrong with me? It's a *spy* program, not Skype.

Now Jen is really laying down the science. I'm not totally tracking, but I register words like neurons and synapses and pre- and and post-synaptic cells. I won't be writing any actual scientific copy, so I'm not too worried. I just need to make all the side effects scream *Don't be worried to try me*! I cross my fingers they don't find out that loose bowels are a side effect.

On SitterSpy, Maria seems to move closer to the camera and starts talking. I don't dare touch the volume button on my computer and risk blowing my cover with Jen, so I try to lip read. She's very animated about whatever she's saying. Maybe she and the kids are putting on a play.

I lean in to get a closer look. It's almost like Maria and I are nose to nose on opposite computer screens.

All of a sudden, Jen goes silent. "Are you still there?" she asks.

I snap back from the screen. "Yes, yes—uh, sorry, I was just looking at my notes here to see if I've got everything," I lie. "Let's see . . . where were we . . .? " I stumble, "Can you go into a bit more detail on the competitive landscape for me."

Now Maria has all three kids in the frame, and everyone is waving into the camera. In an instant a wave of heart racing panicked nauseousness engulfs my body. I try to swallow, but my throat is dry, and I gasp, coughing into the phone. I feel like I might faint. My neurotransmitters are going haywire.

"Jen, I'm sorry—something's come up and I've got to go." I blurt, and hang up.

I click the volume button on my computer with the speed of a hummingbird, but it's too late. They're gone.

What were they doing? What was she saying? Did she just figure out that I've bugged the house? I try to click back to the beginning but I can't. SitterSpy doesn't work that way. Had I not watched the feed in real time, it would have saved a video for me, but because I did, it's gone. Poof.

Shit.

I talk myself down. It's not as if she had some random dude over to the house and rearranged all the furniture and gave most of our food to the food bank. It's not as if she were flashing her thong at me and clicking her teeth or writing me rambling ransom notes. That's all been done already. We're past that phase now.

Still. I need to know what is going on. Why were they waving ... at the camera? Maybe there's someone *else* in the house. A tiny creature living in the bookshelves next to the hidden camera. That's it. They're playing a make believe game and they're talking to elves!

I click through to all the other cameras. Other than the house being a complete disaster, everything is in its place. The kids have finished up the puzzle and are now drawing on top of the former coffee/now sensory table.

Focus, Anna, focus. It's not that big of a deal. A little waving and smiling never hurt anyone.

Time to get back to work!

I open up my inbox and the ALL CAPS message blaring at me from the screen nearly causes me to fall over.

"WHAT?" I growl, throwing my hands up in the air, kicking the chair back from my desk with a quick shove.

Lauren pokes her head inside my office. "What happened? Everything ok?"

"No . . ." I sigh, embarrassed that she's just witnessed my tenth mini tirade of the week. I *wish* it was Slade. Then at least this would make sense. Bitching about one's boss is totally socially acceptable. Now I have to explain myself. "It's not him . . . it's actually not even work related."

"Oh . . . sorry," she says, "Can I help anyway?"

"No, I'll handle it," I say gruffly, inching my chair back to my desk. As I exhale, my nostrils flare like a big angry bull. I roll my shoulders three times, but I know it won't help. I'm still pissed.

"I'll be right there," I type and then hit send, and then I get up and grab my coat.

"I have a doctor's appointment," I announce to the team, a flat out lie. Well, perhaps it isn't that much of a lie. In this case I am the doctor and Annika at the Global Citizens Academy is my patient. The anxiety campaign will have to wait as Annika personally sees to it to increase my own anxiety levels.

The sky over Puget Sound is dark and gray when I leave the office. Sensing that the clouds will burst with rain any second, I resist my better judgment to stay on the straight and narrow by walking directly to my car, and round the corner instead. I need this, I tell myself. It's just one drink. I'll be okay. It'll help me relax. And if I'm relaxed, I'll be better able to focus, during the meeting . . . and hopefully less likely to flip out at her.

All of the bottles are perfectly lined up behind the bar. I inhale deeply. The aroma itself is enough to calm my nerves, even for a tiny bit. *This is why I love this place*, I think. *This is why I keep coming back*. I may have a teensy addiction problem but so what! So does everyone else I know.

"Tall Americano," I say, "with room for milk." I bark out my order from memory like an alcoholic at happy hour.

With one long sip, I feel whole again, ready to face the world. I push the glass door open with my elbow and realize that it's now pouring rain and I've left my umbrella in my car four blocks away. Screw it. If I show up looking like a drowned cat, so be it.

The doors to the Global Citizenry are locked when I arrive. Shaking out my head like a dog, I knock on the door. A few moments later Annika arrives. "Come in," she says, looking a little tired despite a valiant effort at hiding it in a vibrant red and black sleeveless floor-length dress. She doesn't comment on my hair or the mascara that I know is smeared on my cheeks. The air inside the school is dry and warm and words of thanks are expressed in construction paper along the walls. Thanksgiving is next week. Standing in the entryway, I take off my scarf, coat and boots. I'm about to crack a joke and ask where the grown-up cubbies are located but decide that Annika's aura might not in the mood for humor right now. I just hope we don't have to sing the greeting song to each other before getting started. I need this to be quick.

She nods with silent approval as I put my boots inside Lucy's cubby and hang my coat inside Franny's, as if this is what any logically thinking parent would do. Normally worn spiky and short, I notice that Annika's hair has grown out into more of a pageboy bob. From behind, with her head tilted down and cocked to the side just so, I swear she looks just like Julie Andrews in *Sound of Music*. Maria with tattoos running up and down each arm, that is.

My jaw instinctively tightens as I walk towards her office. It occurs to me that perhaps I'm feeling some contempt for this whole emergency situation. On the one hand I get it: Annika and I are both professional women, and it's no fun to deal with on-the-job stress. On the other, I just don't see why she can't she just deal with this on her own?

"Here, sit," Annika commands, pointing to an oversized chair adjacent to her cluttered desk. I wince slightly at the sight of her dark armpit hair curling over the fabric of her sleeveless dress. The chair swallows me and I sink down feeling as dwarfed by my surroundings as a miniature Alice in Wonderland. Piles of files, newspapers, books, pottery and other miscellaneous tchotchkes line the walls and fill the bookshelves. Her desk is stacked high with towers of unopened mail. I don't know whether to be happy she's focused on the children all day or scared that she's so disorganized. Although she can't be *that* disorganized if she successfully got me to drop everything and come over for this "emergency" meeting.

Thankfully, Annika gets down to *beeznus* right away. She's got files, handwritten notes and photographic evidence. "So many disruptions," she says, opening up the files and allowing me to peruse her documentation. "I just had talk to you about this unacceptable behavior so that we can be united in trying to fix it."

She stares at me intensely as I flip through her notes.

SCHOOL SKILLS
Ability to follow verbal directions:
Both of them have the ability to follow verbal directions, but often choose not to.
Ability to walk in a class line:
Yes, but the two of them often play around in line and disrupt the other students. They need to learn how to keep their bodies to themselves.
Demonstrates patience with self and others:
This is a skill we need to work on. It is fine to express feelings but not emotional outbursts or meltdowns. We do not tolerate meltdowns at the Academy as we feel it only encourages them to act out more.
Ability to communicate, share ideas:
Both of them are good at communicating their ideas and like to share, although a fair share of their ideas are inappropriate.
Imagination/creativity:
As the director, I do not appreciate being second-guessed on what is imaginative and what is not.

"This behavior is very much affecting the students in a negative way . . . and the other members of the *comooonity* . . ." she goes on, pointing to her notes.

I plunk my head back on the chair and let Annika continue for a while until she starts repeating herself. "Neither one of them is even trying to meet these objectives," she says, finally closing the files and folding her hands over the stack to signal that she's done and it's my turn to respond.

I crack my neck and roll my head around in a few circles before attempting to sit straighter. "Thanks for bringing this to my attention," I say in a professional tone. "We'll work on these things at home, and I'm really sorry about the disruptions to the school environment. Although I would like to know how widespread these complaints are, or are they just your observations?" And then I pause, considering my words carefully, deciding to go for the direct approach. "Also one thing I'm wondering though is . . . why do Maria and my mother have to adhere to the same standards as the preschool students?"

Annika scrunches her lips and her cheeks fill with air and I already know her answer before it leaves her mouth. "BECAUSE . . . we are ALL Global Citizens!" She throws her hands up in the air and points to peace quotes stenciled around the walls.

Oh, right. Almost forgot! Never mind that I would never be able to fulfill the volunteer hours required at the school if it weren't for Maria and my mother. But I think my work here is done; it's time to get home. I flash my best "I'm done here" smile and grab my purse.

Bent forward, in that awkward stooped over position necessary to put on boots, I'm beginning to stand up and loop my scarf around my neck when suddenly I feel a hand on my shoulder. "Ack!" I jump and stumble over my boots, nearly falling on my butt.

"Unclench your fists!" Annika bellows.

I look down at my hands. In one hand I've got my purse and the other is my umbrella. What is this, a hold up?

"Your tuition is overdue," she says, unblinking and calm.

I thought I had paid for a whole quarter back in September, and now it's only mid November. Nevertheless, I reach for my checkbook and quickly scribble out another check. "Here," I huff, shoving my feet into my boots.

"Thank you," she smiles, pressing the check to her heart. "You don't know how much it means to have your family be part of our *commoonity*. But what I meant earlier is true. You must unclench your fists, and you need to start putting in some weekly volunteer hours here in the classroom. You can't delegate all of them. It will help with your aura."

I raise my eyebrows.

"Your aura is almost black."

Your aura's nuts, I think.

"I heard that."

When I was a kid, I remember the sense of *almost* being in big trouble. Perhaps worse than the actual act of being busted, the anticipation was terrifying. With one look, or one intimidating raised eyebrow or sharp-angled hand on a hip, my sister and I were reduced to a pool of submissive pulp. Even the mere hint of pending discipline caused us to cower behind closet doors or quake under our beds.

But I don't think I have that power now. My kids giggle when I try to give them time outs. I'm not intimidating, and my kids don't fear my disappointment at all. How did my mom do it? I need to know, especially since I'm planning to turn those tactics back on her. I mean, what a report card! She needs a serious reprimand. C'mon Mom, follow the damn rules at preschool! I know you're doing the school a huge favor by volunteering your time and getting more involved with your granddaughters, but really?

But first, Maria.

I'm home early and enter through the back door extra quietly . . . hoping I'll stumble on some gem of misbehavior that I haven't been able to pick up via the nanny cam. I stand in the basement step for a few moments, listening, putting my hand on the wall to pick up some sense of vibrations. *Thump thump thump.* The pitter-patter of little footsteps. *Clatter, bang, thwop.* The sound of the dishwasher being loaded and closed. *Clunk, roll, bonk.* A sippy cup tossed on the floor.

And then I hear it: a man's voice. I *knew* it! Ash is here again! Damn it! I *told* Maria he couldn't come over anymore, so what is he doing here?

I take the last few stairs two at a time and pounce, surprising everyone in the kitchen.

My mom, Maria and Ash are all sitting at the kitchen table, drinking tea. They look up, not surprised to see me.

"Well, well!" I exclaim, feeling triumphant in my surprise attack.

"Hi Mommy," says Franny, nonchalantly.

"Mamamamamammama," says Franny, running over to hug me.

"I'm glad you're here," says my mom, lips pursed together, looking up at me over her glasses. All of a sudden my body fills with dread. She has that *you're in trouble* look on her face, the one I know all too well from childhood.

"Sit down. We need to talk to you."

Sixteen

"Why are you home early, you didn't get fired did you?" queries my mom from her perch at my kitchen table. She has a bright patterned scarf tied neatly around her neck and her white shirt looks crisp. She's definitely not high on her cookies.

I exhale through my nose and put down my purse and keys on the counter. I am so not in the mood for this now.

"No, I did NOT get *fired*," I growl. Ash and Maria look relieved, though I detect a hint of disappointment on my mother's face. My father was laid off so many times, it just may have become a habit for her to ask. Ash takes a long sip of his tea and looks out the window, with his fingers wrapped around the mug, not making eye contact. Maria gets up and moves over to the sink.

"Well. I suppose that's good then. Given the circumstances." My mom eyes Maria first and then Ash. Maria begins washing out Max's bottles with one hand, and tickles his chin with the other. Max is sitting tall in his high chair, wheeled up next to the sink. He squeals and giggles and pounds his fists on the tray as if to ask for more. I smile at him, but his eyes are fixed on Maria. Franny and Lucy are rolling out clay on the floor to make their own figurines and then play acting with them. "And then the nanny says. . . don't worry about it, if your mommy doesn't know about it how can she be mad about it." Lucy holds up a wobbly green clay figure and then pantomimes, "That's right, baby, we're going on an adventure. No school for you today even if Mommy said so, I'm in charge now!"

My mom catches me staring at my daughters with my mouth hanging open. "Anna!" she shouts, "Close your mouth or you'll look like a cod fish. What, are you worried that they are going to make a mess? Life is full of messes! Now get over here and please sit down; we need to talk to you."

I plop my butt down in the kitchen chair as instructed, and look my mother in the eye. She's older now, less intimidating than I remember from my childhood days. The laugh lines around her eyes indicate good times in years past. I *must* have had a good childhood, I think. I do recall more of the happy memories than mad which means she must have been a good mother . . . I turned out okay . . . *didn't I?*

Still, I'm having a bit of a visceral reaction. "Okay, what's up?" I ask. Trying to sound calm here. There's a strange man in my kitchen whom I don't trust along with a nanny my kids worship, and my own mother has obviously turned both of them against me. Neither Ash nor Maria will make eye contact with me, yet they keep giving each other knowing glances.

"It's about that preschool of yours . . ." my mother starts in, adjusting her glasses. "Did you meet with her today? She told us she was going to . . . that bitch."

"Mom!" I exclaim, looking over at the kids. Lucy and Franny are still engrossed in their clay and not listening to the conversation. Ash scratches the back of his neck with his long, bony fingers and looks out the window.

"Well, she IS! And that's not all. That woman is a pathological liar, and probably deranged. There's no peace-building going on over there, I can assure you! But there's a lot of slave labor going on while she does who knows what in her office . . . gives herself more tattoos? She has *us* all doing the work. She never paid her staff, did you know that?

For months! So they all left. Ash and I are leading ALL of the art activities, and Maria has taken over the preschool curriculum!"

Really? I look over at Maria over at the sink. Her lips are puckered and her eyes are wide. She gives me a quick nod as if to say, *yep, it's true. I tried to tell you earlier but you wouldn't listen. Your mom is right! Lah dee dah, lah dee dah.* She's up on her tippy toes, twirling around the cabinets, cheerfully putting things away. I almost wonder if she's enjoying watching me get the third degree.

I stare at Ash's face until he looks me in the eye. I never got a good look at him before. With his shaved head and arms full of tattoos he is both frightening and beautiful to look at. Almost like a piece of art. His eyes are soft and sparkly, and when he finally looks at me I finally see what Maria and my daughters see in him: he's stunning.

Ash puts his mug down on the table and rests his fist in his cheek. "It's true," he says, lowering his voice and leaning over the table towards me, "that lady is One Hot Mumu Mess." Then he leans back and adjusts himself in his chair. "But your mom and I are getting a chance to do some really wicked art in the sensory room," his face lights up and he looks towards my mother, who gives him a smile and a squeeze on the shoulder, "the mixed media collages the kids are doing are pretty awesome. I'm actually working with a gallery downtown on potentially putting together an exhibit. But that weirdo Dutchess wants it to be a fundraiser for her school and I just won't do it. Especially now that I've seen the books." Ash goes back to sipping his tea and looking out the rain soaked window.

"You've seen the books?" I ask.

"I've seen it all," Ash turns to me, briefly, with a shrug, and then goes back to looking at the trees swaying in the wind.

"The place is about to go up in smoke," interjects my mom, tightening the scarf around her neck, "four families have left already. Maria says she's not even legal. You need to pull the kids out of there as soon as possible, but we don't want to leave the other kids in a bind so we're trying to figure something out first."

"I just paid tuition for another three months," I grumble, looking outside. The rain is really coming down now.

"Oh ANNA!" Mom throws her arms up. Ash scratching his neck and Maria rolls her eyes ever so slightly, pretending that she's making googly eyes with Max.

"Oh please, Mom," I'm trying to downplay the situation. It's not that much money. That's not the issue. I want to explain that if Colette is still there -- the one who was so militant about using a nanny search agency -- then I feel slightly better, until I realize that at some point she'll probably blame me for the shoddy research. Or thank me for leading her to a deserving charity case; one of the two. Maybe it's part of the foundation work for her kids to co-mingle with some of these at-risk upper middle class children.

"I can't deal with this just now. I had to leave work early to talk with Annika, and now I need to make up that time," I get up and look at my watch, signaling that it's time for everyone to leave. Mom gets the hint and stands up as well, huffing and walking over to her purse on the counter. "Sorry, but I just need to digest this."

"OK dear, you take your time. By the way, how are you enjoying your surveillance?" My mom asks casually as she roots around for her keys.

"Excuse me?" My pulse starts furiously beating in my eyelid and I feel like its lurching across the room with each thump. What is she talking about? There's no way she can know. No way. Just act calm. Calm, calm, calm. I lean back against the kitchen counter and take a deep breath willing my eyelid to surrender.

Ash gets down on his hands and knees, helping Lucy and Franny put away the clay. Maria wipes down Max's high chair tray. Neither one of them makes eye contact with me, and suddenly I'm embarrassed for them as well as myself. Why is my mom causing a scene? Is there no family privacy anymore?

"Your new nanny cams . . . how are they working out for you? It must be so hard for you to be working all day and only be able to see your dear sweet children via web cam. But it must be strange too . . . kind of like watching animals in the zoo, no?"

"Mother!" I hiss. "WHAT are you talking about?" Lucy and Franny cover their ears, and Max lets out a quick wail.

"Dear, don't be upset," she sneers. "I mean, it was so expensive, so I was just wondering if you feel like it's all been worth it, that's all."

Oh, how I want to strangle her right now. "How—" I start to blurt, but she interrupts me.

"How do I know? My goodness, Anna. There are cameras all over your house, and Ash installed them! How can any of us *not* know?"

I brace myself on the ledge of the kitchen counter and glare down at Ash on the floor. He lifts his head and smiles at me, sheepishly. "Uh, yeah. . . " he says, rubbing a tiny ball of clay between his fingertips, "I was. . . uh. . . part of the electrical team that did the installation. I'm sorry. I mean, I wish I knew earlier that you wanted something like that, and I could have done the job myself and gotten you a better deal. The maintenance fees that security company charges are pretty outrageous."

Blood rushes inside my head with the force of a fire hose, and I feel I might faint.

"One thing I could still do though" he smiles, standing up, with just a hint of an evil grin, "is install cams in Miss Annika's office . . . to see what she's up to at that school when we're not there running it . . . if you want."

I usher the three of them towards the door and grab Max out of the highchair, holding him firm against my hip. Lucy and Franny first give my mom a group hug, and then Maria, who murmurs something to them in Spanish. Ash gives them each a fist bump and then whispers "watch this." The next thing I know, he sails down the front steps and clicks his heels together over the bottom two stairs. The kids squeal and clap with delight.

It pains me to make the phone call, but given that the stakes are mostly against me, I feel that I have no choice.

"Anna!!" she shrieks, practically the moment after I dial her number. "I knew you'd come around!"

I clear my throat. "Oh, no. Sorry," I say, and then pause.

"Oh."

I can hear the heavy disappointment in her voice.

"I'm actually calling about the preschool," I mumble.

"Mmm hmmm," she coos. I don't know what to make of the response. Colette could be doing anything on the other end of the phone. Laughing at me, twirling her hair, smiling, frowning – actually, I wouldn't know if she would be smiling or frowning, maybe she doesn't either.

"I've been hearing rumors," I say.

"It's all true," interjects Colette. "Every bit of it. Whatever you've heard, I'm sure of it."

I open my mouth to respond but she keeps talking. "Your mom and Maria have been amazing. They're down to a skeleton crew, of course, but I think we'll have this thing wrapped up by the end of the year. I can't say much more, but know that there is a plan in place. Did you pay tuition?"

"Yes" I sigh.

"Good."

"Good?"

"You'll see."

The kitchen fan is on high, and I'm standing by the stove stirring risotto with Max next to me in his high chair, finger painting the tray with mushy banana, when Patrick arrives home. He comes up behind me, giving my shoulders a firm squeeze and a light tap on the butt. "Que tal?" He asks, and then launches into more Spanish. Something about "bonita" and a string of other words I don't register. I turn to look at him. "Are you insulting my cooking?"

"No, no!" He says, putting his messenger bag down. "Glad to see you cooking! And you're home early!" He pauses to give me a quick kiss on the lips. "I actually wasn't even sure it was you standing there over the stove. I'm so used to seeing *Maria* during the dinner hour, enjoying a quiet candlelit dinner with *her* while we both wait for *you* to come home, and then as soon as you do, I get to spend more quality time with Maria while I drive her home. Honestly, I think we've really reached a new level of intimacy. That, and my Spanish rocks. It's just a surprise to see you, that's all!"

Now I feel guilty.

"Daddy, Daddy, Daddy, whatssat fing on your face?" asks Franny, galloping over to greet him.

"Oh, this?" grins Patrick. "This is for work. Wanna feel?

"Nooo!" squeals Franny. "Zats yucky!"

"I wa! I wa!" squawks Max.

"What's going on?" I ask, opening the lid to the broccoli on the stove. "Look at Daddy, Mommy," says Franny, pointing a small finger.

"What honey?"

"His face! Fat fing on his face!"

"I don't see anything," I say, making a half turn away from the stove to glance at Patrick.

"Really?" he asks, cocking his head. "Wow, Anna, at least I make an effort to notice your haircuts."

"Did you get a haircut?" I shrug, wooden spoon in hand, "I can't tell."

"Noooo," he says, stroking Max's head, "it's more like, what *didn't* get cut," he says, pointing to his upper lip.

"OH MY GOD!" I scream, dropping the spoon. "Patrick, no! That's horrible. It's like a pornstache. OMG I can't believe I didn't notice. No, no, it's awful. Take it off."

"Hey," he says, covering Max's ears, "there are children present."

I glare at him.

"Don't worry. I know it looks kinda bad now but that's because there's not much there. Once it grows in it's going to look *so awesome.*"

I turn back to the stove.

"Oh, come on. It's supposed to be fun." He comes back behind me, this time pressing his chest against my back. Max grabs a fistful of my hair. "Ouch!" I yelp. Patrick takes Max's fingers, uncoils them from my hair. "Oops," he says. I feel something wet and heavy on the back of my head. The banana. I give Patrick the *You're In Trouble* look.

"Sorry," he says, reaching for a paper towel to wipe off my head. "It's just for fun. Whoever can grow the best mustache by the end of the month, for No-shave November, as a fundraiser."

I keep stirring. "But what about the merger? I ask, "doesn't that kind of look bad to have a bunch of guys with half-grown mustaches running around the company with potential investors coming in and out of the office?" Patrick's company is up for sale. He isn't nervous about it, which ironically makes me more nervous, but I have to trust him. Slade would never let me grow a mustache, which is why I pluck and bleach on a regular basis.

"We look great!" Patrick flashes me a cheesy smile. "It's a morale booster," he says, raising his arms up to the ceiling. "And besides, there are some pretty . . . exciting developments going on," he says, stroking his mustache fuzz with an evil grin, "Which I'd be happy to tell you about after dinner. The icing on the cake, if you will."

"Yeah, sure," I answer, wiping off my hands on a dishtowel and stepping into the stairwell. "I've got a lot of work I have to do tonight, so maybe it can wait til after that. LUCY! TIME FOR DINNER!" I'm not going to tell Patrick about my afternoon today with Annika and then Maria, my mom and Ash. I'm not.

Lucy thumps down the stairs, half-clothed Barbie doll in hand.

"What's for dinner?" she asks, looking up at my hair and then at Patrick's face and then Max, kneading the rest of the mashed up banana in his hand. "Ewww," she says. "That's *basty*."

"Basty?" asks Patrick.

"Bad plus nasty equals basty. Basty."

Thank you, Lucy, for today's word of the day.

After dinner, I stand on a chair putting glasses away on the top shelf while Patrick leans back on the counter, eyes glued to the news, alternating sips from his microbrew with cursory wipes of the kitchen table. He obviously has no clue about the nanny cams or our double payment of tuition or that my formerly super solid foundation is beginning to crack and crumble around me, and there's no need to tell him. Until I can sort all of this out and develop a new plan of action, there's no sense in alarming him.

"So, uh, there could be some big news," he says with a loud burp, placing his beer down.

"Uh huh," I mumble, turning my head away from him so I don't catch a whiff of his *basty* burp. I pick up a glass from the dishwasher, following Patrick's eyes over to the television set in the corner. "What's going on? Turn it up."

Patrick looks at me. "No seriously this is important," he says.

"Okay," I say, talking to the back of the cabinet as I rearrange mugs, "then turn it up. I'm listening. And, if you see any of the drug company ads come on TV, poke me, okay? I need to take notes on all of them. Even the erectile dysfunction ones."

"There could be some roles changing in the company," Patrick says as I continue unloading the dishwasher and stacking plates with a loud clamor. "It's related to what's going on in D.C. Something big."

"Yeah, ugh, I'm not sure I have time to worry about politics right now," I hold a bottle of cleaning spray in my hand and pause to look at him.

"Well, not politics, about the company in DC," he says, taking another swig of beer, running his fingers over his mustache fuzz. "I think there might be a good opportunity for me."

"Yeah, but does anything ever change over there?" I spray down the sink and grab a sponge.

"Actually, it could change everything."

"Oh, no it doesn't. People always say that. But just look at those guys," I wave a fork towards the television set, "they're just a bunch of talking heads."

"I'm not talking about what's on TV right now, Anna. I'm talking about the bigger picture. About us. About our family, about job opportunities."

I lift up the Dust Buster from the charger. Patrick looks at me, walks over to the sink, puts his beer glass down. "You're not listening to me," he says.

"I was going to watch it with you. I just wanted to finish this up first," I say, feeling like it was nice for once to spend a minute in the kitchen not doing work. And besides, seeing the state of our kitchen on SitterSpy has been eye opening.

Patrick sighs, leaves the room. I turn on the vacuum and suck up the crumbs from the kitchen floor.

I stare at the computer screen, dazed, tired, exhausted. How hard can it be to come up with a new drug name? There's nothing brilliant about any of these names. They could be sci-fi fantasy characters or obscure car parts or tasty dishes listed on a foreign menu.

Prozac. Paxil. Zoloft. Cymbalta. Lexapro. Effexor. Xanax. I see no commonality except for the frequent use of x's, y's or z's and I wonder what that means. If you're at the end of the alphabet, then you're at your wit's end, and you need our help?

If it weren't for the *advertising* we'd have no idea what these names meant at all. Oh right, advertising, that would be me.

The office door creaks open. "Anna?"

"What?" I groan.

"Nothing," says Patrick, dressed in maroon and blue plaid pajamas. "Why are you so jumpy? I was just—"

"Just what?" I groan.

Do you sometimes feel angry at the world, like nothing is going right?

"Just checking on you to see how you were doing. Is everything—?"

"Not okay," I say, rapidly tapping my foot.

Do you experience symptoms of anxiety or changes in mood?

"I'm just trying to figure out this anti fucking anxiety campaign." I curse through cupped hands over my face.

"Okay, well, um, maybe you should take a break. I'm just letting you know that Max is asleep and the girls are in bed, and they would like you to tuck them in."

"Can *you* do it?" I whine.

Are you not feeling like your real self, do you sometimes blame others for your problems?

Patrick stares at me, dumbfounded. "Sure, I'll do it, my pleasure," I say, with an eye roll, pushing away from the desk.

Do you no longer enjoy the things you used to love and cherish?

"This isn't like you," he says as I pass him in the doorway. "This client is making you wiggy. Do you think they could give you some free samples?"

I give Patrick the finger.

Do you sometimes do or say things that you might regret later?

"Sorry, but, listen, hon, I have some good news if you ever want to hear it. I'll be in bed. . . *waiting.*"

Ugh. Not tonight . . .

Are you experiencing a loss of libido and sex drive?

Talk to your doctor. The NAME OF THE DRUG THAT YOU ARE TOO ANXIOUS AND UNFOCUSED TO GIVE A NAME TO . . . can help.

And then, two hours later, it comes to me, as all brilliant and half-baked ideas do, sitting on the toilet followed by a vigorous brushing of teeth. Balenxa. The name of the drug will be Balenxa. Sounds like balance – a cliché concept that I hate, but still, an aspiration that women across America will do almost anything to achieve. Balance plus some sort of drug sounding name because of that critical X. I run back to the office and do a quick Google search on the name. Nothing comes up. Yes!

Draft Script: Opening Montage

Busy mom juggling it all. The music is upbeat as the montage quickly cuts through a half dozen or more snapshots of her life – at work, at the store, fixing dinner, smiling at her kids and husband, working out, driving, sniffing a candle. We don't see her face, just all the actions she's doing. Upbeat music changes to ominous music, something bad is about to happen.

Narrator: "In today's busy world, women juggle it all. . . but really, how long can you keep up the balancing act?"

Scene 1

Cut to mom pulling up in her driveway and then cut to her walking into her kitchen. It looks like a grenade went off. Zoom into woman's face. She's alone, looks stressed.

Narrator: "Life is full of bumps in the road. Sometimes things can get messy."

Scene 2

Cut to children running all around, jumping and screaming. The mom says nothing, goes to a cabinet. Music is suspenseful. The camera flashes to the kitchen knives, an open window above the sink; the woman's furrowed brow. What's she going to do?

Narrator: "And maybe you're not sure what to do. Maybe you feel like you're the only one. Maybe you feel like you have to do something drastic."

Scene 3

The music changes again. The woman is drinking a glass of water. At this point in the ad BALENXA is taking up one quarter of the screen. She has mellowed out. She's patting her children on the head. Everyone is smiling, helping put the kitchen back together. Keep going with the smiling and the cooperative gestures as the narrator reads through the list of side effects.

Narrator: "BALENXA is here to help. Talk to your doctor to see if BALENXA is right for you. BALENXA is not for everyone. If you have heart disease, if you are pregnant, or thinking about becoming pregnant, if you drink more than three alcoholic drinks in one day, or think about drinking more than three alcoholic drinks in one day, if you have allergies to poultry or eggs or methamphetamines or cat dander, BALENXA may not be right for you. Common side effects include dry mouth, nausea, memory loss, sleeplessness, drowsiness, annoyance with your husband, heart attack and death. Call your doctor immediately if thoughts of harming your mother or your child care providers ever occur.

Seventeen

The shopping bags crunch into each other and ricochet against the side of the car as I round the corner. The back tire skids into the sidewalk curb and one bag briefly goes airborne before crashing back down to the bottom. I tighten my grip against the steering wheel as if to will some sort of protection to the bags and miraculously safeguard the bounty of holiday loot in the back of the wagon.

Six boxes of white lights, 40 votive candle holders, 12 feet of garland and one mistletoe, along with two cases of wine, mixers galore and enough frozen hors d'oeuvres to keep my guests from driving home too drunk. This is the sum total of what I hoped would transform the house to look festive enough for my Slade-sanctioned holiday party, otherwise known as the party I was being forced to throw to kick off the holiday season. The Asenzer folks are dragging their feet on setting a date for the final review of the campaign, and the team is getting antsy. There would be no holiday bonuses, and no real holiday party without Asenzer signing off on the marketing blitz we were about to present. The "Moore Holiday Cheer" open house, as it was branded on Evite, needed a bit Moore help and Moore creativity if I was going to pull it off in two days.

With the door keys dangling from my lips and shopping bags triple stacked down each arm, I attempt to spit the keys into my hand but they fall on the floor instead.

"Maria?"

". . . esta señora es una. . . ." I hear her voice in the other room. For a moment I wonder why she is answering me in Spanish since she has already heard my broken tenth grade version. The floorboards creak in the dining room. Back and forth, back and forth. She's pacing.

"Maria?" I really want to put these bags down on a clean surface, but where? Remnants of some sort of holiday craft project are strewn all over the counters. Construction paper, cotton balls, pipe cleaners, paint, glitter glue, sippy cups. What is she doing with the sippy cups? Not using them to wash out paintbrushes, I hope. Oh yes, she is.

"Maria!" All I hear is more Spanish. She sounds animated and irritated. What's going on with her? I can basically pick up "fiesta. . . . bebe. . . . el morso. . . ."

Between the animation in her voice, the cracking of her gum, and the clicking of her shoes on our old floors, it's beginning to sound a bit like performance art. Is this an act of defiance? I brought her more treats today as part of my peace offering. Every few days since the "discovery," was made public, I've been bringing Maria little gifts to try to make up for the nanny cam gaffe. Lip glosses, stuffed animals, and rhinestone-embedded pouches with coffee cards inside. She oohs and ahhs with sounds of extreme pleasure every time I bring her something new, followed by an affectionate arm wrapped around my shoulder and a kiss on the cheek, but I'm still not convinced that my tactics are working. My little bribery/guilt dance goes something like this: I get home late (as usual). She, Patrick and the kids are either sitting at the dinner table giggling and laughing like the picture-perfect modern family, or she is upstairs bathing the kids. I take her aside and offer the gift. She squeals and twirls on her tiptoes and tells me how nice I am and how I "shouldn't have," which for some reason just makes me want to buy her more stuff. I haven't actually brought myself to issue a formal apology yet for having the nanny cams installed, mostly because

I'm not sure if I am truly sorry, or if an apology is actually warranted. And Patrick still doesn't know. At least, I didn't tell him. And then I start to feel like shit. And guilty. Like I'm a horrible person who's harboring secrets and doesn't even know why. Which starts me down the familiar path -- I've failed at being a sliver of a decent boss, I suck as a mother, and I have no idea what I'm doing anymore. Down, down go these spiraling thoughts that cling to the insides of my brain like a clogged drain. My nanny hates me. The kids love her, not me. She cooks; I don't. She's organized; I'm a fucking mess. She has full-on conversations with my husband; I can barely eek out a text message to the guy without first having to fling myself over a wall of resentment over that hideous mustache he is continuing to grow despite the fact that it's now December. I'm sure it's just to spite me. Oddly, one thing that does make me feel better are my daily excursions shopping for her in the middle of the day. With each little piece of jewelry from Claire's or candy from Bartell's or Hello Kitty pencil set from the gift shop in our office lobby, I picture winning her over. How happy she'll be. How the gifts will mend our relationship to the point where our bond is so tight. I might actually begin to release my vice grip on my unwillingness to trust her.

Except there's this one strange thing she does every time I offer a new gift. As soon as she's done gushing, she waits until she thinks I'm not looking and then she rushes over to her laptop, opens up the lid and enters information into some sort of spreadsheet.

The Double Stuff Oreos rest on top of one of the shopping bags that's causing my forearm to throb and shake. I also took out a large amount of cash from our bank account for her holiday bonus; but she doesn't know that yet. Click, click, click. Shimmer, shimmer, shimmer, jabber, jabber, jabber. Who is she talking to? And then I distinctly hear three words I most certainly recognize: "*Crazy, baby* and *mom.*"

Is she talking about *me?* Suddenly Maria darts into the kitchen and slides the last few inches, finally grabbing onto the sink for support. Bells tinkle around her ankles. She looks like she's seen a ghost. She sputters, "Oh, um, hi Anna" before turning her attention back to the phone.

"I just need your help for a second when you're done . . ." I interrupt, motioning to the bags cutting off the circulation in my fingers. Maria presses the phone to her ear again. She suddenly decides to start speaking in English. "Oh, yes, yes, of course. Thank you so much. Muchas Gracias. Feliz Navidad." She's all business now.

When Maria ends the call, I smile a little too eagerly at her, hoping to lure her into my holiday planning den. No confrontations, just collaborations.

"So, I got some stuff for the party here. I was wondering if you could just come down and look over everything with me? I just really don't know how to pull all this together right now, and I need another set of eyes." All part of my new approach. We're a partnership. We trust each other. We work together to support the family and we're so in tune that she can see where I need support and I can see when she needs some validation.

I know things will get better once Asenzer signs off on the campaign and Balenxa is finally percolating in the blood streams of millions of anxiety-ridden women. *Then* I can relax.

I scatter the contents of the bags on the guest bed. As I look around I realize that I hadn't even considered the time needed to clean up/redecorate/overhaul the basement before the party. The idea of a coworker seeing the laundry room/playroom/guest room/overflow kitchen/cricket sanctuary makes me cringe. For a split second I contemplate asking Maria to help organize this room, but then quickly decide against it. Better to do everything myself. And keep shopping.

"Okay, so, here we go," I say as I gesture to the two Costco bags and head to the freezer. I start unloading bags of frozen shrimp, spanakopita triangles, mini pizzas and stuffed mushrooms, and separate out bricks of cheese and boxes of crackers to put upstairs. "Do you think that ought to do it? Do you think we can work some magic with this?" I look at Maria and babble on. "I mean, there's nothing really super holiday-ish here, but I figure as long as I have enough wine, it'll be okay, right? I mean, it's only about 30 people. Do you think this will be enough?" I look over at her expectantly.

Maria surveys the loot and then stares up at the ceiling. I look up to see if she's identified yet another flaw in the room. Perhaps a ceiling leak or a spider nest, but realize the kids are upstairs, unattended.

"Oh my gosh. The kids. You're right. I'll go get them and then we can talk about the party," I say, heading towards the stairs. Maria instead plops down on the bed, cracks her gum and gives her hair a good flip. "No, they're fine. Max is sleeping and Franny and Lucy are watching How the Grinch Stole Christmas. . . but I have to tell you something." She looks up at the ceiling again, choosing her words carefully. "I feel so badly with the holidays coming up, but I might actually need to. . .

Yes, yes, what is it dear?

"I might need to . . ." she struggles a bit to get the words out, snapping her gum and looking around the room, everywhere except directly at me. This is it! Our big bonding moment! She's going to confide in me and let me in on her innermost private thoughts and desires. I'll be like the mom whose shoulder she can lean on. Wait – no, that's creepy; I already have enough kids. Instead, I'll be like the older sister, or the wise friend, or . . . the cool boss. Yeah, that's it – the cool boss! Why didn't I think of this role sooner? It's perfect for us! I look over at her, lips firmly pressed together, working up a facial expression full of compassion and concern. I smile at her, urging her to get it out. *Whatever your sweet heart desires . . . I can do it.*

Maria finally blurts it out. "I might need to take the week off."

The words hang in the air and I wait for some clarification. The *week*? Meaning this week? Or next week? I'm hosting a large party in two days, Asenzer is flying up early next week for the unveiling of the advertising campaign and . . . oh, sweet Jesus.

"I just can't get everything I need to get done with. . . "

I can't help it. I was trying so hard to be nice, making a real effort towards trust and friendship and being a cool boss but those feelings are now gone. The tension between us is suddenly thicker than the family pack of lip-glosses I just bought her at Costco. "Everything you need to get done!?! This is your *job*, Maria! Can't you do what you need to do for yourself during your time AFTER work? That's what I have to do and I have three kids and a husband!" I stop and Maria looks over at me and examines my face for a few moments. Despite the conflicts we've had I've never actually yelled at her. So much for my new approach.

Back with her head tilted towards the ceiling, Maria rolls her eyes slightly as if she has an imaginary audience and slowly blows a bubble with her gum before it pops without a trace of residue left on her face. "You know, Anna, you don't need to make this so personal. I know you're stressed, okay? *Everyone* knows you are stressed." Second eye roll. "We all know about all of the problems you think you have." Third eye roll, a smirk and some snapping of gum. "You're not the only one in the world, you know."

The words hang in the air between us. How did I get to the point where my nanny is berating me for being busy and a stress case — and now it's *my* fault for getting angry when she suddenly needs time off during the busiest week of the whole year? I am ready to launch the biggest prescription drug launch since fucking Viagra and I'm not allowed to be stressed or selfish?? Miserable, overly narcissistic, stressed, anxiety-ridden women all over the globe will never see any relief unless *I* bring this campaign to fruition!

Maria must be reading my mind or adding up all of the new stuffed animals she now has in her collection thanks to me because she now rests a conciliatory hand on my leg. "You know . . . in my country, we are so happy all the time. We are the happiest place in the whole world, did you know that?

No, I didn't know that Colombia has stolen Disney's brand identity, I want to say, but instead I just look at her and let her continue. "And its not just because of our coffee or Shakira. In my country, we don't worry about being stressed at work or worry about eating frozen food from Costco or microwaving breast milk—" her voice trails off as she pauses to stretch her arms behind her back in a kind of yoga move.

She's performing now, almost as if she actually has an audience. And then I wonder – does she? Our house is bugged; I know that for sure. But I never told the security company to put cameras in the basement. But that was before I knew that Ash was part of the installation. Suddenly I feel self-conscious. If this room is wired, who might be watching me now? Oh, wouldn't that be a nice product placement. Anna Moore™! Limited edition. Download now on YouTube or Hulu while supply lasts. I look up towards the ceiling and try to find the cameras, smoothing down the stray hairs that I know are frizzing around my head. I don't see anything – just dust, the rusty heating vent and a bad paint job.

"We don't let these silly things bother us. We know that everything will work out somehow if we focus on what matters. But I know you have a lot going on. So, actually, you know, since you need help with the party, how about I do this for you?" Maria continues, her hand now stroking my hair the way I do Franny and Lucy's when I'm trying to calm them down. "I will work for you tomorrow and the next day. And then I will come to party and you won't have to pay me extra for that. I will do that in place of a day next week, and then you can just pay me for the week and won't have to pay me extra for the party." Her tone is condescending in that she is calm and not getting emotional whereas I am a mess.

I stare at her, not sure I got all of that. "I need to look at my calendar and—" I sigh, "we need to work out the days together. I just can't decide that right now," I say.

Maria roots around for something in her back pocket. "Here, I wrote this list out for you. I knew you might need help with the party, you know, because you don't really cook or entertain or anything. So just get the stuff on the list, and I'll take care of it."

Premium brand tequila
Premium brand rum
Pork Loin, 4 ancho chiles, 6 guajillo chiles, cumin, chocolate, cloves, garlic, thyme, vinegar and cinnamon
Strobe lights

Extension cords
Fireworks or sparklers
Lady Gaga Megamix

With the final marketing campaign plan due to Slade in two days and with Maria leaving soon, I have no choice but to pull an all-nighter. The irony of having to make this heroic effort to finish my work so that I can spend the following day prepping a party where I'll be entertaining my boss is not lost on me.

My eyes glaze over at the graphs of millions of anxious women the research firm has sent me. How did I get here again? My nanny has hijacked my career, my kids barely know I exist, my mother, my nanny and my nanny's *jusmyfriend* are conspiring against me, and my husband barely speaks to me anymore. Living the dream! Happy Holidays to me! It's party time.

The doorbell rings and I rush to grab it. Shit —who is here so early? I'm dressed, but still schlepping around the house in my slippers, and I haven't done my hair or makeup. I open the door and take a step back. I'm both relieved and taken aback. It's Maria – thank God – but she's dressed in a skin-tight white lace mini dress that barely covers her crotch. On her feet are white patent platform heels, and on her head is a white feather fanning out so high it nearly grazes the ceiling. "Sorry I'm dressed this way," she smirks, "but I just got back from church."

The party is buzzing by the time Slade and his wife Liz show up. I see them walking up the stairs to the house and shout out to a few friends: "Okay, everyone on their best behavior, Slade the Blade is here!" I'm actually feeling a bit jovial – and a bit buzzed – after just one drink. I take their coats and usher them over to the makeshift bar atop the sideboard in the dining room, steering clear of Maria, wherever she is.

"Martini? With an olive?"

"Make it two martinis, four olives," he says, looking over his shoulder towards the hallway. "Moore, this is great. You need to do this more often. What's this – an exotic dancer you hired for the party? Kind of unexpected for a stalwart Smithie like you, but I like it, it's fresh and unexpected; it's a little grist for the millstone if you know what I mean. We should put this kind of unexpected creativity into our work. Remind me about that tomorrow, will you Dear?"

"I'll be sure to make a note of that," I say, reaching for the gin.

"Oh, and by the way, *Slade the Blade* has a nice ring to it. I'll take that as a compliment, Moore. Just between you and me," he says with an air kiss.

I pour the gin directly from the bottle into the martini glass, but am suddenly stricken with the thought that this is uncouth somehow. Should I have asked shaken or stirred? Is that cheesy or hip? I have no idea what I'm doing. As I'm busy contemplating bar etiquette, the gin drizzles over the rim of the glass onto my hand but thankfully Slade doesn't notice. He's standing with his back to me, surveying the crowd. I quickly alleviate the overflowing martini into the second glass, add a splash of vermouth and the olives. I have no business being anywhere near the bar, but the drinks actually look pretty and the house does appear somewhat festive. Who knew strobe lights and a garish garland made by the kids would do the trick? See Anna, you *can* throw a party together at the last minute. Or did Maria do that?

I stand there for a few seconds holding the two martinis out in front of me, waiting for him to notice, but he doesn't. His eyes are locked on Maria who is standing in the hallway, inadvertently dusting off our photo frames with her feather headdress. The doorbell rings, but before I have a chance to move to grab it, the door opens and in walks Annika and Colette. They're smiling and laughing like old friends. Both of them take one look at Maria, openly laugh out loud, and head in the opposite direction, toward one of the food/sensory tables in the living room. I can't believe I invited them. No, wait. I didn't. Maria did that. She told me yesterday that since she'd integrated some of her party planning into the preschool curriculum, she had no choice but to invite both of them. But why would they come together? Anyway, I don't have time to think about it for more than 20 seconds, and since nobody has told me anything, I figure it's not any of my concern anyway.

"Where's Liz? Did we lose her already?" Slade says to himself, turning around to grab the drinks, just before he heads directly for Maria.

The din downstairs is definitely loud, yet somehow I am able to hear wailing in the kitchen. It's the baby monitor.

Hoping I can use Max's cries as an excuse to pull Maria away from Slade, I look for them in the dining room, but they aren't there.

On the other side of the room, my mother has glommed onto Patrick's boss. They appear to be deep in conversation. About what, exactly? Doesn't matter. I'm just tickled pink by the fact that I have a nanny and a grandmother at the work party I'm forced to hostess, but I'm the one going upstairs to soothe the crying baby.

I run upstairs and arrive on the landing to see that Lucy has "caught" Franny with a fishing net. Franny is lying on the floor writhing like a nearly dead fish. Lucy is standing above her saying, "Die now! I need to take you home and eat you!"

Max is whimpering in his crib, apparently jolted awake by the sounds of the fishing tournament. I gently but firmly remove the net from Lucy's hand and put it on the top shelf of the linen closet. "Where is Maweya?" asks Franny, her dripping nose headed towards the skirt of my dress for a quick wipe.

I gently grab her head just in time. So instead, she wipes her nose on my sleeve.

"Lucy," I plead, "Mommy will give you $10 if you make sure Franny stays in her room and if you read quietly. Deal?"

"Deal!"

Now, I'm paying a sitter and my daughter. Awesome!

Finally, I tend to Max. Last, but easiest to soothe, he is sitting up in his crib whimpering. I take him out of his bed and sit down in the rocker and cradle him as if he's still a newborn. I whip out my boob from the confines of my wrap dress; he's asleep in a minute. I briefly contemplate staying here. It's so quiet and soothing in his room with the white noise machine drowning out the downstairs commotion. But just then a vision of Patrick settling into the couch and inhaling Maria's pork fest while ignoring the guests startles me into action.

The party is crowded enough now that the room is humming. Patrick isn't on the couch, but neither is Maria. Did she forget that she agreed to watch the kids tonight?

My mother has moved onto Slade. She is sitting on the couch between Slade and Liz, and she has that "I mean business" look on her face, her head nodding vigorously at her own words and her finger tapping Slade's leg to drive her point home. I cringe at the thought of what she might be saying. Is she telling him that he works me too hard, he needs to give me a raise—or worse—he needs to give me a more flexible schedule so I can properly take care of my children?

I squeeze my way through some of Patrick's fleshy friends. They all came solo, wearing old jeans, sporting messy facial hair and smelling of beer. I should go and say hello, but rescuing Slade from my mother takes precedence. I wedge myself in between the couch and the coffee table and try to delicately sit down on the table without causing it to come crashing down. One of the unforeseen benefits of Maria moving around the furniture three months ago is that we now have plenty of room for the guests to mingle. I look down and notice that my breast has not been properly put away inside my dress. Although my nipple is not visible, it is fairly obvious that one breast is safely tucked inside my bra *and* my dress while the other is merely resting on top of my bra. My mother notices right away, making rapid head jerk motions in the direction of my wayward boob. Slade, however doesn't look anywhere near my upper half. He's scanning the room. For whom, I wonder?

As soon as he turns his head I quickly slip my breast back into alignment. One of Patrick's colleagues makes eye contact with me from across the room as soon as I do it. "Honey, did you know that your agency is going after one of these big pharmaceutical companies?" my mother asks.

"Yes, Mom, as a matter of fact, that's my account."

Slade isn't listening. He's still scanning the room and getting fidgety, like he's searching for the perfect opportunity to get up off the couch. Can I blame him?

"Well, I'm telling Slade that it's a crooked business. You know they just pay all the politicians these huge campaign contributions to get these drugs approved and then drug us seniors. You know that, Anna. I've shown you Dr. Ford's newsletter."

My mother's medical advice came exclusively from a large print newsletter she received each week that curses Western medicine while extolling the virtues of the exclusive line of Dr. Ford's vitamins to cure everything from cancer to Alzheimer's. The "doctor" is actually a doctor in philosophy, if you read the fine print, but that doesn't seem to bother her, especially since he wears a white lab coat in his marketing images.

Slade considers my mother's words with an earnest look for a moment, then curls his lips up and shakes his head. The next thing I know, Annika squeezes in between them. Her plate of food is overflowing, and she looks ready to devour someone.

I excuse myself to go find Patrick, and, of course, stop at the bar on the way.

As I pass through the front entry, three of Patrick's colleagues are walking out the door. I wonder if he even ever knew they were here. Determined to stop the party from bleeding guests so early in the evening, I head out to the back porch. Colette squeezes past me through the sliding glass door. She smiles sweetly and strokes my shoulder, but doesn't open her mouth to say hello. She smells faintly of smoke, and I soon know why.

Patrick is in his glory. Beer in one hand, cigar in another, holding court at our patio table. He doesn't notice me at first and I catch a glimpse of how he must conduct himself at the office. His mustache is at its full girth now, and it looks awful. The cigar smell is overpowering and instinctively, I hold my breath to keep from vomiting in my drink.

"No, Dude, I saw this show on Lock Up about all these gangs in D.C. So maybe we design a new shooter game where the gangs get extra points for drug dealing," I overhear one of his colleagues say, grabbing Patrick's cigar out of his hand so he can take a quick puff.

I look out towards the back gate and see smoke. My heart skips a beat but then, through the fading plume of smoke I see a tall, dark figure lingering near our rhododendrons. Another one of Patrick's work buddies, I think, but something about the figure is familiar. And then I see the eyes. Even in the darkness, I can see. They're sparkling.

Ash.

He motions me to come towards him, and I walk behind Patrick and his colleagues, unnoticed towards our back steps and down towards the grass below.

"Let's do it." He whispers, blowing smoke up towards the sky.

"What?" I giggle. I'm a little tipsy now, I'll admit, but *what?*

"It's time. I've got the keys. Your mom and Maria have the kids covered. Let's go. You and I. We can sneak away now and do it quickly." He's whispering in my ear and it tickles. I hold his arm and let out a snort.

"Shhhhh," he says, grabbing my hand. "Be quiet. Nobody can know."

I look up towards the deck. Patrick and his buddies have gone inside. It's just me, Ash, the cool damp air, his smoky breath and the stars.

"What are you talking about," I say, giggling some more.

"Sober up," Ash commands, putting out his cigarette. "This is going to be the quickest installation I've ever done, so I need you to pay attention." And with that he whisks me off to his car.

What does he mean by "installation" I wonder, as I stumble towards the passenger door.

Pulling up to the front of the Global Citizens Academy sobers me up enough to realize just what Ash meant by installation, and enough to realize that what we are about to do is highly illegal. Bugging a preschool. Who does this!? Apparently I do. I ask Ash why he didn't just do it on his own time, or take Maria along and not me, and he mutters something about how I'm the client, since I write the checks to Annika. I'm the one with the vested interest in her illegal activities. I'm the one who can turn her in. If grandma or the nanny initiated the surveillance, nobody will believe them. It isn't "legit." I'm the one who can file the lawsuit or the complaint. This doesn't really register with me, other than maybe providing a good motive and some profile information on me once the police are involved. I almost ask him to take a flattering mug shot of me while he's at it, because now he's acting like an undercover cop. But Ash assures me that Annika is too disorganized and too much of a pathological freak to ever figure out what we've done, and both the police and the Department of Early Learning are too laissez-faire to ever go after her without anything resembling hard evidence. In my semi-buzzed state, this makes total sense, enough to get me to follow him in.

Ash installs cams in her office and all of the playrooms. They are tiny devices, perched on top of dusty figurines from far-away lands and embedded strategically within her posters on the walls. He works fast, and his fingers are so nimble; I feel a slight rush as I watch him work. It seems all too easy to accomplish. After a few minutes, though, my adrenaline wears off, and I'm uncomfortably aware that I'm standing in my daughter's preschool after hours with . . . a . . .criminal. I walk over to Annika's CD player and hit the play button. The sounds of waves crashing onto a beach, backed by a few harps and seagulls fill the room. I exhale and roll my head around in circles around my neck until I get a bit relaxed and woozy.

"Shit!" Ash exclaims, suddenly, backing away slowly from his work with a panic-stricken look on his face.

In that one word, it hits me. I don't know why Ash is saying shit, but I know I need to get home.

"We need to go," I yell, remembering my house full of guests, my mother on the couch with my boss and my husband and nanny entertaining my employees with nobody watching over the sleeping children. "Pronto," I command.

"No shit – let's get the fuck out of here," Ash barks.

Ash quickly and wordlessly picks up the rest of his equipment and motions for me to head towards the door. He turns off the CD player, takes out the disk and inserts it into his pocket. "Good thing we know it's the right CD, right Anna?" he says, standing in the middle of the room, projecting his voice as if he were auditioning for a new role as a not-very-convincing errand boy. "This is just the one that Annika wanted us to bring to the party, right?" He nods vigorously at me, my signal to nod vigorously in return. Then we split.

The car careens down the street, and the tires squeal around the corner to my house. I grip the armrests for dear life and breathlessly ask him to explain what just happened. "Somebody got there first," he shouts over the house music blaring. His words are clipped, and the veins in his neck are pulsing, causing his tattoos to come alive.

"WHAT DO YOU MEAN?" I shout back over the music.

Ash turns the music off. "I *mean*—" he looks at me, beyond frustrated that he has to spell it out, "her office is already bugged. Another company – a higher end one – has already been there. Their cams are everywhere."

"Oh shit," I say, stating the obvious. "We're fucked!" I slump down into the seat and close my eyes. I was just trying to please my fucking boss with this stupid party, and somehow this led to a new low point. I can see my face, blurred out to protect my identity, playing on the evening news as the anchors announced that they had apprehended the suspects and were awaiting trial. "Honest to god," I say out loud, but then continue the conversation in my head. This sums up my life. Try to do a good deed even though I'm probably already maxed out and shouldn't have hosted a company party on such short notice with no time to prepare. Mixing people that have no business mixing. Throwing it together at the last minute when I really should have just taken a break for myself. And then I get tipsy, leave the party with some sketchy dude, and commit a felony. And why? I can't explain my actions to myself anymore. They make no sense. And now? Now, I'll go to jail for breaking and entering. People will joke that I'll be well-prepared for the women's prison scene having gone to Smith. *Orange is the New Black* and all. But really, I'll have to binge watch OITNB again before my departure date to figure it out. And of course, I'll have to pay Maria double what I'm already paying her so that she can cover for Patrick's business trips since I won't be there. He and Maria will probably fall in love over their family dinners, and they'll break the news to me together on visiting day. I'll have no choice but to scream bloody murder and break something or someone when I get back to my cell. Then my sentence will be extended, and I'll be really fucked…or not. Maybe it will be like "the rest" my Mother talked about, and I'll have time to read, and relax, and work on my biceps. I'll come back from prison relaxed and refocused.

"Not necessarily," says Ash, interrupting my daydream of doing time in the state penitentiary.

"No?" How so? I mean, at this point, don't we just turn ourselves in?" I ask, slumping down in the seat.

"No! Chill out and sit back and see what happens. We don't know yet who else is bugging her. Just act normal, if you can . . ." Ash pulls the car into park, and I start to cry, burying my face in my hands.

"Oh fuck, don't do that!" Ash whines, digging for something under the driver's seat. It's a flask. He unscrews the top and offers it to me. "Here. This will make you feel better. I guarantee it." Two or three swigs later, I do feel better. I'm thinking there could be a silver lining to time in the pokey. If I can write about my experiences like the OITNB woman, or even Theresa Guidice, I can parlay it into a respectable outcome. And Patrick will take me back!

"Anna, get out! We need to go back inside," Ash says, like a real (tattooed, shaved-head) gentleman. Ash has come around to the passenger side door and helps me out of the car. I lean on him as we enter through the back gate. I can hear the beat of "Party Rock Anthem" pumping from the house as we slowly make our way through the back yard. From the sliding glass doors, I can see that the party has turned into a line dance, with my mom, Slade, Liz, Colette, Annika, Lucy and Franny following Maria as she leads the dance moves. Maria is holding a very awake and alert Max in front of her, who appears to be punching his fist into the air. Patrick and his few remaining work buddies are hiding in the kitchen.

Ash opens the kitchen door for me, and as soon as he does, I stumble over the doorframe and my left boob falls out of my wrap dress for everyone to see.

What happens next is a bit of a blur. Patrick immediately starts shouting at me that "where the fuck was I," and that the party is a "colossal fucking disaster" and attempts to throw Ash out the back door. I start to shout back, but instead erupt into a maniacal fit of laughter. I've now exposed my breast at a work party—not once but twice -- and the sight of mild mannered Patrick shouting at me from underneath his handlebar mustache reminds me of Yosemite Sam. Maria intervenes, but instead of turning off the music, she smiles at Ash, flips her hair over her shoulders and turns up the speakers, taking hold of his slender hands as she leads him to the makeshift dance floor. The next thing I know, the party is hopping to "Moves Like Jagger," with a shirtless Ash playing the role of the Adam Levine, and

Maria lip-synching to the Christina Aguilera vocals. Patrick has disappeared.

Not a few minutes later it seems, everyone has left the party. Like someone rang an invisible bell, or flashed the lights and then poof, they all disappeared out the doorway, even Maria, Ash and her ever-present hulking backpack. But I know it wasn't the invisible bell. It was the drunk mother and boss coming home from a mid-party outing that sent everyone scampering.

Just as I survey the kitchen, wondering if I should clean now or save the mess for tomorrow, the phone rings.

"Hello, may I please speak with Anna Moore?" It's nearly 9:45, exceedingly late for a school night but not for the police, so at first I panic. But there's something about the voice sounds too formal, like maybe she's a telemarketer or a professional fundraiser. I wish I hadn't answered but now it's too late.

"Speaking, may I ask whose calling?" I say, leaning against the counter. I'm still a bit tipsy.

"Oh, hello Anna. My name is Barbara Hegarty, Maria's thesis advisor, and may I just say that I'm so, so sorry it's taken me this long to call. Maria told me at least two months ago that you needed a reference, and I just found your number again. It's so wonderful what you are doing for her, and we really appreciate the chance for our students to have first-hand real life experience in the areas they are studying."

"Um," the room spins around me and I clutch the counter, trying to keep myself from falling onto the floor.

"Hello, Anna, are you there?"

"Yes, yes, I'm here," I gulp. "I'm just a bit confused. What is Maria working on?"

"Her thesis. You and your family have provided an excellent case study, which will allow us to really pinpoint the most systemic issues facing today's modern mothers. Thank you again for agreeing to be a part of this important research. I'm happy to answer any questions about Maria, but since she's been working for you a couple months now, I'm guessing you have all the information you need already?"

"Yes, I got it. But thanks for calling."

When I finally head to bed sometime after midnight, I notice that Patrick has fallen asleep with the bedside lamp on. His large suitcase is open and clothes are neatly stacked inside, including the sock burritos that Maria has been folding for him. Things he never takes on short business trips – like hardback books, his running shoes, his suit (a suit!) and cologne (cologne!) sit inside the cavernous cavity. I turn off the light and pull the covers up to my chin, replaying the horror video of today in my head as I stare out our bedroom window into the dark and rainy night. Patrick murmurs slightly and turns his body towards me. Odd, since everything about tonight indicates that he is about to leave me.

"Who called?" he mumbles, gargling his words. He's not even going to remember asking me this question in the morning, after he's already left me.

"Oh . . . that was Barbara, Maria's thesis advisor," I sigh, speaking towards the wall. "Yeah, so apparently she's writing a paper on us. So, how was your night?"

Patrick grunts, and then his breathing slows and his arm begins to feel hot and heavy on my shoulder. I stare at the wall for several minutes, waiting for him to say something or acknowledge anything, but now I know for sure that he is asleep. Since I'll likely be awake for hours, I take the opportunity to keep talking.

"I'm sorry about the party tonight," I say, feeling tears begin to well up in my eyes. "It really was a fucking disaster. And you're right. I'm a mess. I probably need an intervention or something." The salty floodgates have opened and are really flowing now, and I'm slurping back the snot in my head as I speak.

It's easy to pour your guts out to someone who you know isn't listening, so I continue. I wonder if this is what therapy would be like, if I ever made it long enough to get there.

Patrick lifts his arm off me and flips his body over to the other side. I reach for a wad of tissues on the bedside table and blow my nose, loudly.

"Are you sick?" he mumbles in his sleep.

"Have you been listening to what I've been saying?" I ask, in between honks.

"Sleeping," he murmurs.

"Sorry. But what were you trying to tell me the other day . . . when I was working. What is it?"

"Igotajoboffer." The muffled sounds don't make any sense to me.

"What?"

"Joboffer."

"Did you just say job offer?"

"Mmmhmmm."

"Apromotion."

"A promotion?"

"Mmmhmmm."

"To what? In which department?"

"Deeshsee."

"Did you just say D.C.?"

"WashhingtonDeeshsee."

I jerk up, turn on the light and stare wide-eyed at my husband. Patrick yanks the covers over his head. "Turn that OFF!" he shouts, though his words are somewhat garbled in his half-asleep state. I lean over and fumble with the light switch. The lampshade spins and the base wobbles back and forth on top of my flimsy bedside table. I fear that the whole thing is going to come crashing down. Lamp, table, books, magazines, pens, tiny scraps of paper, me. But then the wobbling stops, and there's silence. I sit, immobilized, staring out into the darkness, my eyes stinging and puffy. "Are you . . . going . . . to D.C.?" I ask with a sniff.

"Yes, early," he grumbles from underneath the comforter. Then he punches his pillow a few times and flips his body away from me. "Tomorrow morning, now let me get some sleep."

End of conversation.

So that's it then, I think to myself, just before I cry myself to sleep.

Eighteen

My eyeballs ache as I exit the plane and walk into the terminal . . . hoping, pleading, yearning mentally for a coffee shop to greet me . . . anytime in the next five seconds, before I collapse, would be awesome. When I booked a last minute red eye flight I was somehow under the impression that I could get a solid five-hour stretch of sleep. But apparently, airlines consider Seattle to Washington via a two-hour layover in Detroit a red eye. Not that I've been able to sleep much lately, seeing as though my marriage has just completely fallen apart and my nanny is about to publish a paper about what a colossal mess our family has become.

Just as I'm passing a cardboard cutout President, thinking about how he may have the most stressful job in the world, yet still manages to look calm on TV, I spot the McDonalds. I'm desperate, and I've had exactly one hour and fifteen minutes sleep in the last two days so it will have to do. I order a sausage, egg and cheese biscuit, hash browns, a large orange juice and a black coffee. I know I'll feel nasty and greasy after I eat this, but I already feel nasty and greasy so at least there's no change there. It's a means to an end.

As I reach for my order I get a whiff of my breath and almost wretch. Coffee. Coffee. Must. Have. Coffee. I grab the piping hot cup and tip back my head. The searing heat gives me a jolt and makes my blood shot eyes water, sending tears down my face. My whole body jitters, shaking off the fatigue, and my tongue is burnt to a throbbing, aching crisp. I wonder if burning my tongue and throat has killed off the bad breath germs and if the grease slick down the back of my head makes me look like I've finally had the time to straight iron my mane. And if so, will Patrick find this sexy when I try to win him back?

Shower first -- then save marriage.

Balancing my coffee and juice on top of one another in one hand and pulling my suitcase, biscuit and soggy hash browns with another, I head down the open corridor, awake enough, at least, to walk. Outside the glass doors I can see that the taxi line is mercifully short. As I walk through the automated doors I feel the unseasonable sensation of a faint, yet distinct cloud of moisture enveloping my face.

"Where you going, Ma'am?" At the front of the taxi line, a middle-aged African American man with a red cap hands me a flyer with a map of the city on it.

"Dupont Circle. The Westin," I say, putting down my bag and beverage tower and hastily removing my trench coat. "I'm here to save my marriage," I add. He looks over towards a cab coming down the shoot and doesn't respond, so I try again. "Is it me or is it a little humid here?"

"Could be. Supposed to be in the sixties today," he says nonplussed, and certainly not looking humid himself in his black down jacket.

"Is that a bit odd for this time of year? I mean humidity in December is kind of strange, right? Even with global warming?" I ask.

But the political humor falls short. "Never know around here," he says, waving his arm to flag the next car. "We had snow last week, heat today, could have an ice storm tomorrow," he says as if he's not only the taxi line boss, but an old time local weather sage. A taxi pulls up and he remains stationary with his flyers. No tip required here I guess. I load my bags into the cab myself. I take this as an omen of pending single motherhood.

In the cab there's an evergreen air freshener hanging from the rear view mirror, and I decide that it's there to mock me. In Seattle we don't need evergreen air fresheners; we just roll down the windows! Then it hits me: What if saving my marriage means that we actually *move* here? There's something about the way Patrick's suitcase was packed that leads me to believe that the deal is already signed, sealed and cinched with a D.C. approved golden emblem of approval. And then I realize: Even if I'm not successful in patching things up, I'll *still* have to move here. There's no way around it. I clutch my purse to my chest like a bag lady, imagining myself moving to a tiny apartment where I'll only get to see the kids on weekends or on limited days of the week (Patrick will have full custody since I will be deemed too crazy and unstable. He'll only have to show the judge my mug shot once they figure out I broken into the Academy) and the visits will be supervised by a stern-looking social worker – just like the one Robin Williams had in *Mrs Doubtfire*. And the kids will look at me and think terrible but true thoughts like: *Why can't we have a mom who is normal?* And *Why did our mom have to become a YouTube sensation?*

But then, a moment later, my breathing returns to a non life-threatening rate. What is *wrong* with me? The divorce papers have not yet been delivered. The police have not yet put me in jail for illegally bugging the preschool director's clutter-filled office. I have not yet been assigned a social worker! I should *be* so lucky to follow my husband's career across the country! God knows he's suffered putting up with mine. I take another long swig of my McDonald's coffee and wolf down my breakfast in about 30 seconds. I finish the orange juice in two long gulps. There, I feel better now.

Buurrrp. Or not.

The kids. I hope they are okay. I silently pray that the hand over from Maria to my mom went well last night. Having to leave for the airport straight from work has caused me more anxiety than I'd anticipated. Did they bathe? Brush their teeth? Stay up too late? Is my mom reading Maria's graduate thesis, *Anna Moore's Mood Disorder Manifesto,* to them as a bedtime story? I'm in this weird limbo land where I've lost all trust for Maria and respect for my mom. How could they?? So blatantly plotting against me. Maria taking such good, detailed notes for her graduate studies and my mom providing her with all kinds of background info and data points. Unforgiveable! When I confronted Maria yesterday, the best defense she came up with was that I'd signed off on the whole thing earlier this fall when I put my signature on some forms she'd handed me one evening. Now she's taking most of the week off to finish up her paper and present it to the academic committee at UW. The thing is, I don't even remember approving this, tacitly or otherwise. I think I was under the impression that her early childhood education studies would be limited to the kids. How wrong I was! The title of Maria's paper is *It's All About Mom: Early Childhood Education and the Modern Distractions of Parenting.* I look down at the draft I forced her to print out for me peeking out of my purse and shove the crumpled papers down into the shallow depths of my laptop bag, out of eyesight.

Not now. I fish my phone out of my purse and call my mom's house. I just need to know that the kids are okay.

Ring Ring.

No answer. Hmmmm. Maybe I dialed wrong. I'll try again.

Ring. Ring. Ring. Ring.

Still no answer. My mom must be deaf. She's always telling me she can't sleep so I can't imagine why she wouldn't be up with Max by 6:03 am Pacific time.

Except that it isn't 6:03 Pacific time. I check my watch. It's 5:03. Whoops, bad math. Sorry, kids!

The cab zooms along the water, and soon all of historical Washington is whirling by the window – the Washington Monument, the Capitol, the Lincoln Memorial. I rest my dirty head against the window, and for a tiny moment I feel a surge of excitement at seeing the sights. Wouldn't the kids just love to see our nation's capital? I almost wish I'd brought them. But then I remember that I'm here on an altogether different sort of family trip: A *save the family* vacation.

If I'm successful, perhaps I can pitch the concept in a new line of resort programs for the Westin, including on site couples therapy. Stop, I tell myself. It's my crazed focus on work that got me here in the first place.

I dial Patrick's cell. Might as well get this over with before I lose my courage (or completely fall apart – whichever comes first) and tell the cabby to go all the way around the traffic circle and return me to the airport.

"Hello?" I can barely hear his voice on the other end and wonder if in my sleep deprived fog I've called the wrong number.

"Patrick?"

"Yeah. What is it?" He must have his hand cupped over the phone, because his voice sounds hollow, like the *wa-wa-wa* sounds that the adults make in the *Peanuts* animations.

"We need to talk," I say, my voice suddenly cracking. So much for keeping it together. I inhale and brace myself for the response.

"Not now," he says, and I can't tell if he's irritated with me or just being professional. "My meeting starts in 20 minutes."

"Okay, are you staying at the Westin?" I choke, tears now blurring my vision of all the patriotic sights outside my window. I reach for a greasy McDonald's napkin and dab my eyes.

"Yes, why?" He's all business. Probably preparing himself for the disengaged and unemotional tone he'll take with me from here on out. He'll get a better legal standing that way, I'm sure of it.

"Nothing," I sniffle, "I just need your room number . . ." sniff, "so we can talk later . . . ." My voice trails off and as I pause – before I can say "I love you" or "Good luck with the meeting," or "I've fucked up so badly and I don't know how I'll ever make it up to you but I'm on my way, Baby"— Patrick spits out his room number, sighs loudly and hangs up.

Good. I mean – not *good*, but now I have a room number and confirmation that he is indeed here for a meeting and not a sex trip. I sit up a little straighter and tuck the wadded up snot rag/greasy napkin inside my coat pocket. I'll have time to clean myself up and think about the exact words I'll use when I call Slade and explain that after working late last night on the final pitch materials, I ordered Chinese takeout and came down with a horrible stomach bug and that is why I won't be coming into work today. I'm way too old and way too senior for him to think I would be anywhere else but at home wretching. I haven't faked being sick since calling a college professor senior year to tell her I was too ill to come to class when in reality I'd road-tripped to Dartmouth, drank too much, and attempted to pick up guys who clearly weren't interested in me. But that was then. I'm a different person now . . . now I only manipulate men if it's absolutely necessary—as in the case of near marriage failure—or lying to my boss about my whereabouts two days before the biggest meeting of the year. Or, come to think of it, leading on a major pharmaceutical CEO and allowing him to believe I actually give a shit about the stupid drug he's about to launch.

Ugh.

The traffic circles are making me woozy. This one, the third or fourth we've circumnavigated since leaving the airport, has a magnificent statue of some sort of military figure on a horse waving a sword or a flag or something triumphantly as if to say, "Yes, we did it."

Yes. I can do this, I coach myself. I can win Patrick back—not through trickery and manipulation, but by way of truth, love and maybe even some good make-up sex. The lying and cheating at work can stop too. Just as soon as I save my marriage, hire a new nanny, find a new preschool and launch this drugged-up marketing campaign, I can get back on track. In the meantime, I'll just walk Slade through where I left all the finals on my desk, and promise to check in throughout the day. I left the video on a DVD, four printed out copies of the script, four printed copies of the final PowerPoint presentation and four copies of the client take away book. Slade will never think to ask why I got sick right when I got so organized. This may be the most unprofessional thing I've ever done in my entire career—but I can't let my marriage go down without a fight.

Suddenly, I feel dizzy and ill. The fifth traffic circle of my trip. *Whooaaaa.* What's left of my coffee spills onto my jeans, soaking them through.

My motor skills have gone to shit with no sleep. And my thoughts are getting pretty loopy too. That's what happens when you're sick, I think. Remember, I'm sick. Food poisoning. I need to channel this feeling for my call to Slade.

The hotel staff gives me a strange look as I stumble up to the counter. *What, haven't you seen a woman on the verge before?* I want to ask. "My husband is staying here," I say to a woman with her hair pulled so tightly into a ponytail that her eyes slant upwards and her smile appears to be permanently pasted on her face. "He arrived ahead of me . . . I took the red eye . . . that's why I look so bad . . . and *smell* so bad, whew!" I flap my elbows a bit for good measure as I sway on the balls of my feet, then I casually mention the room number so she knows I'm not a *total* freak. I hand over my ID – my Washington state driver's license that lists me as Anna Moore not Anna Moore Farrell, damn! She looks at me with quiet concern as she types away on her computer, and I pray that she doesn't make me call Patrick to verify that I am indeed still his wife, or worse, hail the police to come cart me away. "If I can just get a key . . . I can get showered and then I'll stop stinking up your lobby . . ." I blather on, hoping this does the trick.

It does! She hands over a folded card with a room key inside, careful not to let our fingers touch. "If there's anything we can do to make your stay more pleasant, don't hesitate to let us know," she calls after me as I walk clumsily towards the elevators.

I push the heavy hotel room door open and kick off my shoes. I'm so exhausted that my ears are ringing, and I nearly trip over the USA Today lying on the floor. I flop my body onto the bed. Ahhhh, better. The Heavenly Bed is definitely living up to its name. Note to self: Consider using a photo of a woman laying on the Heavenly Bed in the Balenxa ads. Maybe a partner opportunity?

I reach over in search of something to write with and pick up the binder on the bedside table. Let's see . . . fitness center, onsite dry cleaning, room service; list of local babysitters. Maybe as part of my peace offering I can tell Patrick to take a job here and we can all just move into the Westin. I'll just have to get the staff to sign non-disclosures so they don't write about us too. Clean up will have to wait until I hear from the kids so I try my mother again.

"Mommy!"

"Oh, Lucy sweetheart, you're alive!" I let my head sink back on the white pillow sham and don't even care if I leave a grease stain.

"Hahaha. You're silly, Mommy." I hear the television blaring in the background and what sounds like clanking and pounding of utensils on top of a table.

"Is Lucy there? Is she alive too?" I murmur, sinking further into pillow top sham heaven.

"Franny! Mommy wants to know if you are alive! ARE YOU ALIVE?"

"More Fooot Woops!" I hear Franny shriek in the background faintly, but the sound is muffled by the pillow around my head and by a voice that resembles my mom's, but I'm not totally sure. And then I hear dear sweet Max jabbering away in response to Franny, something that sounds like "sbjshduferghadat!"

Without warning, my breasts burst. Max. My baby. Hungry baby. Baby needs Mommy. I double over to my side and clutch my chest, but it's too late. The milk geyser has burst. I pumped before I got on the plane last night and should have done it again before I even *thought* about searching out McDonald's coffee. Oh my god, it's like a flood.

"Girls, I'm so happy to hear your voices but I have to go. Call you later!"

I hang up the phone and fall to the floor, frantically rooting around in my suitcase with one hand and holding my boobs against my chest with the other. Where is the damn handheld breast pump? My fingers locate the tip of a Ziplock, and I rip it open without eying the contents. I'm about to sigh with relief when something wet and slimy bursts in my hands, spraying the inside of the suitcase.

Shit!

White globs of my favorite hair product—Bumble & Bumble Grooming Crème—

mixed with an exploded trial size of Nether Light's *SupaFresh Anal Whitening Ointment* drip from the lining and a puddle of the stuff coats my clothes. In my haste to release the breast pump from the depths of my bag, I tip the whole suitcase over and my 500-count Costco ibuprofen empties into the mess, sending rust and white-colored streaks all over everything.

Okay. Could this trip *get* any better?

First things first. Most of my clothes are now ruined, and I can't do anything about that. I might be able to salvage a bit of the hair product if I'm careful. Good hair might be a higher priority than clean clothes at this stage; I'm not sure. And as for the white butthole situation, I'll take this as I sign that I'm not supposed to "go there." I only brought the sample as a joke anyway, thinking that if things went in the right direction with Patrick, I could offer it up as an extracurricular evening activity. *Hi Honey, dinner was so lovely. As a show of affection, can I whiten your butthole for you while you watch the football game?*

Since I'm 'pumping and dumping,' neither the relative cleanliness of my breasts nor the breast pump really matters, so I hastily screw the sticky breast pump nozzle to the pump attachment and attach the suction cup to my left boob. I start squeezing and watch my nipple get sucked into the plastic funnel, milk spraying the inside like a pressure washer.

Ahhh . . . relief.

With one hand pumping, I dial the front desk with the other. "Hello, Mrs. Farrell," she says. "How can we help you?"

"There's been a bit of an accident . . . in my suitcase," I grumble over the squeaking sounds of breast pump. "I'm going to need some more towels . . . and a new toothbrush . . . and some Advil if you have it."

Done.

Next.

"Slade McAllister's office. Kendall speaking." Damn. Damn. I was hoping to get voicemail.

"Hi . . . Kendall . . . this is An . . . na." My spur of the moment effort to imitate someone with food poisoning has me sounding more like a stroke victim instead.

"Anna, is that you? Doesn't sound like you?"

"No, I'm SO sick. Ate something. Bad. Last night." I look over at the mess I've made on the floor and quickly make myself visualize eating it in an effort to sound truly repulsed. I have quite the gag reflex and it kicks in handily.

Knock. Knock. Knock. Knock. Knock.

Crap. I'm topless with a strange contraption attached to my boob, and I'm on the phone.

"Kendall?" I say as feebly as possible. "Can you hold on one second?" I put the receiver down, wrap it with a sticky hair-volumizer-soaked towel and grab a new towel in the bathroom to cover my chest (and the breast pump.) It creates an odd tent-like effect but it'll have to do.

Knock. Knock. Knock. Knock. Knock.

I open the door and a thin man in a stark white uniform hands me a stack of still-warm towels and about 10 personal-size travel packets of Advil. He maintains eye contact, not once glancing at my chest. I'm so thankful for the shred of dignity he just afforded me. I grab the loot, whisper a thank you and close the door.

"Sorry, Kendall—" I cough into the phone, remembering too late that I have a stomach issue and not a head cold.

"Did someone just bring you something in a hotel room?" Kendall asks suspiciously.

I laugh nervously. "Ha! No . . . you heard that? No . . . just a friend dropping something off. I can't leave the house in the state I'm in . . .

so ill . . . so ill." I put my finger down my throat and make some gagging sounds into the phone.

"Oh, God, um, sorry. Feel better. I'll let Slade know!" she blurts.

With half of my day's work now out of the way, I lug my suitcase into the bathroom and rinse it out as best as I can in the bathtub. I scrub my clothes with a damp washcloth, hang them on top of the toilet, and take a luxurious 15-minute shower. Since I'm not at home, I reason, I can take longer showers because the people in DC aren't as big eco freaks as they are in Seattle. The wiggle room on my carbon footprint just got a little wider.

The heat of the shower zaps whatever minute amount of energy I have left in my reserves and I find myself swaying under the stream of water, unable to keep my eyes open for more than 20 seconds, and I almost pass out. I turn off the water. Moving about as slowly as a senior without a walker, I climb out of the tub, palms pressed on the walls. I gently dry myself off, comb out my wet hair, fill a glass of water, slip the 'Do No Disturb' sign outside the hotel room door and (since I have no clean clothes) climb into bed completely naked. I open up a packet of Advil and toss back the pills, willing my aching head to match the fatigue of my body and just surrender. The housekeeping guy was extremely generous with the drugs, and since I don't want them to go to waste, I open up the remaining packets and place them inside my empty pill bottle beside the bed. I look around for a recycling bin in the hotel room to toss the wrappers. Not seeing one, I just leave them on the table, promising myself to sort the trash later. If I have to pack it back in for the return trip to Seattle before I find a recycling receptacle, so be it. It's the least I can do, seeing as though I already usurped more than enough natural resources by taking such a long shower.

I'm asleep before I know it. At some point I'm aware that I'm dreaming, and it's one of those vivid dreams where you can almost hear what's going on, it feels so real. Patrick is calling my name. He sounds hollow and far away, yet his voice has an urgent tone. He needs me to answer him, to say something, to offer some sort of explanation of how and why we stopped communicating, but I cannot respond. I try to move or open my mouth to speak, but I'm incapable. I'm totally mute. Now it's presentation day, and I'm walking on a treadmill, performing for the Azenzer team. I'm carrying two weights on either arm—those obnoxious ones with the handles that look like grenades. One is labeled "work" and the other reads "kids." T. Rx calls me out. "Where's your marriage in this equation? Where's your husband?" he shouts, fists in the air. "Don't you give care about that?" He continues, proselytizing about the campaign and the target audience, how modern women have become narcissists and how he's not going to spend a dime on this campaign unless we can make "Stand By Your Man" part of the message. I open my mouth to speak, but the words don't come out. I look around the conference room and see that Patrick is there, but he's turned away from me. Has he given up on me? *Again?* I want to say something—I want to reach out and touch him and caress his face, but I can't. The weights are too heavy, and I have nowhere to drop them. I can't stop the treadmill and if I let go of the weights I'll get really hurt. This is a total nightmare.

And then, suddenly, everything gets loud in my dream. There are a lot of voices clamoring for attention, and I hear the words "drugs," and "overdose" and "pills. Perhaps hundreds of pills." And then: "Check the vitals. NOW!"

Golly, Jee, this dream is getting *in-tense*, I think to myself, right before the 230-thread count Egyptian Cotton sheets and down comforter are rudely ripped off my body.

My eyes open.

There are men in the room.

One of them has his hands on my chest.

The other one is holding my wrist.

I jump out of bed.

And I scream bloody murder.

"That was nice . . . I could put up with your freaky stressed-out self if you funneled more of it into sexual creativity more often . . ." Patrick smirks. "You could be the poster child for middle-aged women at the height of their sexuality!" He rolls off of me and flops himself face up on the bed, smiling contentedly and scratching the wispy hairs on his chest.

I pull the comforter up to my chin and stare up at the ceiling. Maybe this is where that saying, "be careful for what you wish for" is apropos. *Yes*, I'm ever so thankful that this was all a big misunderstanding and that I got exactly what I wanted (make up sex and a promise from my husband that our marriage is not on the brink of collapse) BUT . . . was it really necessary that I came *this close* to having my stomach pumped and had to explain over and over again to countless paramedics, the Westin's housekeeping director, PR director and General Manager that no, I did not come all this way just so I could surreptitiously break into my husband's hotel room and attempt suicide?

"No—and what a back-handed compliment *that* is. I am not middle aged... I'm ...oh, I don't know what I am." I sigh and roll over to my side, staring out the window, smiling.

The candlelight flickers between us, and I take another sip of wine, gazing at my husband. He's aged a bit, but his good looks have not disappeared. In fact, he may even be more attractive to me now than when I first met him. Certainly more so than last week. Now, at least, the mustache is off. "I don't know what else to say," he says, "I love it. I love everything about it. It's everything I've been looking for," he says looking directly in my eyes eagerly awaiting a reaction.

I haven't heard Patrick so enthused about a job in years. He goes on and on. The new green LEED certified building that houses his would-be new office. The new team in D.C.—a group of young, intellectual techies that are fun and nothing like the pasty, nerdy and egotistical programmers at home. The charge to focus on new product development and go head to head with their main East Coast rival. The budget, the perks; the senior management position. I barely recognize the man across the table from me. It feels like I haven't seen him in a very long time.

"Well, that's good because after this pitch I might not even have a job so it might be our only option," I say, picking at my food, all of a sudden feeling a pang of jealously over Patrick's enthusiasm for his new job.

Patrick puts down his glass of wine, and the smile eases off his face. He looks down at his plate and then up at me, and then reaches for my hand across the table. "Anna, I'm serious. I would really love to take this. I don't want to put your job in jeopardy, but Hon, would this really be upsetting to you? Forgive me if I'm wrong but you haven't seemed ecstatic about your job lately. You've gotten kind of . . . nasty and negative. About everything. And that's understandable . . . you have a lot on your plate. Your job is demanding. So are the kids. I know that sounds mean and I'm not saying you're mean. I'm just saying that maybe the combination of things is having this effect on you. Maybe its not the combination, maybe it's the job and a change would do you good too."

Patrick takes one look at my face and backpedals. "Okay, maybe that's not it." He's searching for the right words. It stings to hear that I've been a bitch this whole time, yet I know he's right. I'm about to respond and defend myself, but he continues. "Listen, clearly, you're, I mean, *we*'re going to have to find a new childcare situation anyway. You never have a minute to yourself, and that's all fine and good if you love what you're doing. But do you? Sometimes I look at you and it seems like the more you do, the unhappier you become."

I let his words linger in the air as I take another drink of wine and peer over at the distorted image of my husband through the curve of my glass. This is the first time he has actually verbally acknowledged how much I'm juggling. I didn't really know if he knew.

"Honestly? It hasn't occurred to me lately to think about whether I'm happy or not. I don't have time, " I say, hearing my voice crack. "I used to love what I do. And I still do in some ways. But I just don't know anymore . . ." I let go of Patrick's hand, pick up my glass and swirl the wine around inside the glass, staring until it finally stops spinning and sloshing.

I really didn't. I was surprised to hear myself say this. It was almost as if I was afraid to say it aloud because now that I have, it opens the door for change. Patrick looks at me, giving me his full attention, listening to my confessional. "I don't know anymore," I continue, "What is happy? Is happy just having a steady and good paying job because that's what I've been focused on for the past couple years. Keep the job, keep the kids clothed, try to get six hours of sleep a night and try to go for a run once in a blue moon. And even if I did have time to really enjoy my work, I don't because I've been so anxious about Maria and second-guessing her every move, or I'm worried about whether Franny's okay at school, or if Max is getting enough to eat. And then when I'm with the kids I'm worried that I'm not doing my job and I'll get fired and we'll lose the house. And you know what? I *hate* that. I hate it! I just need to hit the reset button. It's life I know, but when did it become so much to handle?" There, I said it. I surprised myself just then, throwing it all out there, and not even being afraid of his response.

Patrick says nothing, gazing at me intently. Not drinking, not eating, just really, really looking at me, like he's visually thumbing through the most fragile, paper-thin layers of my soul, pausing to examine and consider each one. My eyes are red now and I wipe my checks with the back of my hand, taking a deep breath, feeling my shoulders shudder. He lowers his chin, a barely detectible nod, letting me know to continue. It's almost like he *knows* I need to get this toxic shit out my system. So I go on. "And yet, on the other hand, I really don't want to lose that side of me. I don't want to move here just because I'm a little bit neurotic and momentarily overwhelmed at work. It's complicated," I sniffle.

Patrick reaches across the table and grabs both of my hands with both of his, and holds on with a firm grip. I look away as more tears stream down my face. I don't even know why I'm crying, really, but I do know that something has to be let out. I wipe my eyes and nose on my shoulder—the only clean top I have – er, *had.*

"Honey, we don't have to make any decisions tonight. But let's think about this. And I want you to realize something. This doesn't mean that you lose your job or lose your identity or lose *anything.* All this means is that, if you want, I can help shoulder a bigger share of the burden for a little while you figure out what you want to do. And if that means, keeping Maria on and doing some shopping with her so she can pick out more cool dresses for you, I'm cool with that too."

I'm laughing and crying at the same time now, and our server drops a box of tissues off at our table with an understanding smile. Patrick stands up and walks to the other side of the table and kisses me on the mouth. Snot, tears and all.

I have no idea where my glasses are, but in the blurry haze I can see the message light flashing red on the hotel phone. Why on earth would anyone be calling us here instead of our cell phones? I check my purse. Oh my God, where *is* my cell phone? I haven't seen it since . . . well, since I nodded off before my near drug overdose, and that was over eight hours ago.

A bottle of wine with dinner, two scotches for Patrick and a Drambuie for me means we stumbled back to the hotel room, and promptly fell asleep.

"Did you hear the phone ring?" I ask Patrick. But he's completely still and snoring like a bull.

You have five new messages.

Good Lord.

Message one:

"Oh, hi Anna, it's Maria. I'm wondering what you want me to tell Slade? He keeps calling here and says he cannot reach you on your cell phone, and then he wants to keep talking to me. My presentation is tomorrow, so I really don't have time to talk to him, you know? Also, your mom? She's not picking up her phone. What do you want me to do with the kids? Click.

Message two.

"Anna, this is Slade. *Maria* gave me your number . . . in D.C. Are you boning Obama? I'm going to need pictures. Whatever you're doing, it better be good. Oh and I hope you are "feeling better" with whatever "sickness" you have. Actually, never mind. I already know. Maria just told me all about her paper, and I've requested a copy through my connections at UW. Please call me ASAP."

Message three.

"This is Annika Verbeck. I am calling to let you know that your Maria did not show up today and therefore the *comooonity* did not get their Spanish language and cultural immersion curriculum. You *vill* either have to make up *zee* hours or pay additional tuition. School *zis* dismissed now and nobody has come to pick up Lucille and Francesca. *Vat* do you vant me to do vith them?"

Message four.

"Anna, hey, sorry to bother you. This is Ash. Listen, I don't want you to freak out or anything, but I figured out who installed that other set of cams at the Global Academy or whatever it's called. We need to talk."

Message five.

"Anna! Oh my God! Oh my God! It's Mom. I just got here with Max and we're standing outside the doors of the preschool. Everything is locked and boarded up! Nobody is here! I was just a few minutes late because I took Max with me to art class and there was some traffic on the bridge and oh my god! Where are the girls?"

<h1 style="text-align:center">Nineteen</h1>

Cell phone. Where the hell is my cell phone? Patrick is face down on top of the bed. The booze fumes radiating off his body are so intense that the layer of air above him is starting to ripple. Oh my God, what have I done? I try to shake my head in disbelief, but the alcohol sloshing around in my brain is quickly drowning out my disjointed thoughts.

But then I see it. Peeking underneath some Westin stationary on the desk by the window is my phone, right where I left it about nine hours ago after I stumbled out of the shower. Just before my accidentally on purpose "drug overdose." Ah yes, I remember now. I turned off the ringer.

23 new messages.

I thumb through the call history, looking for a sign, a clue—anything that might help me locate the girls. If only I'd hooked them up with GPS bracelets before I left . . .

Maria.

Slade.

Maria.

Mom.

Mom.

Mom.

Mom.

Mom.

Mom.

Mom.

Mom.

Colette.

Mom.

Mom.

Mom.

Mom.

Mom.

Mom.

Mom.

Mom.

Mom.

Something about the pattern indicates to me that my mother doesn't have all the answers. So I call Colette.

"Hi . . . " she says, ever so sweetly after picking up on the second ring, and not at all surprised to hear from me. I can just picture her waltzing around her gleaming kitchen with all her high-end appliances without a speck of dust or crumb of food on the floor. "Listen—hey, so everything is fine, totally fine. Lucy and Franny are such sweethearts! Aren't you girls?" I hear them talking softly in the background, and before I can let out a sigh of relief, she continues. "They are having a wonderful time, so not to worry. Take as long as you need." Patrick is now lying face up on the bed, mouth gaped open, and there is a noise coming out of the back of his throat that sounds like someone attempting to gargle with snot. I move to the bathroom so I can better hear all about how wonderful things are back in Seattle.

"I was just wondering though, while I have you, since it is getting late—do you know where Max is? The girls said you had gone to D.C. and hadn't taken him with you. So I've been trying Maria, but she isn't answering her phone. So then I got to thinking: Are you sure she's doing a good enough job for you? I mean, because if she isn't, our charity services are right here ready to step in and help. I'm assuming Max is with her, but I wasn't entirely sure, since she didn't bother to pick up the girls from preschool today."

"Uhhh, I start to say, wondering how I'm going to get myself out of this one without first stopping to show off my "bad mom" card, but Colette interrupts me.

"You know what? You don't even have to tell me. If you have another back-up arrangement that you prefer, that's totally fine. Fine! It's just that since the mission of our social services organization is to rescue ALL members of a family, so I just wanted to make sure he was accounted for."

And then I think: What does she mean by "rescue?" Like child protective services . . . or foster care?

"Max is with my mom," I blurt. "He's fine," I think. Better to say as little as possible with Colette. I still have to get on the phone and work through logistics with my mom.

"Oh, of course. That's wonderful. I know how much older women like to coo and goo all over those little babies! I'm sure she just *adores* having him all to herself. But if you change your mind and you'd like to *keep your family together*, or have Max in a secure, pet-free, toxin-free, BPA-free, TV-free, all-organic environment . . . perhaps I could have one of my CPR-certified, perfect driving record, early childhood education degreed drivers pick him up for you? We have a van especially for this purpose."

I take a step back and lean against the bathroom wall, pressing my shoulders against the cold tiles to steady myself and align my thoughts. Just what kind of operation does she have going on over there? But she keeps talking. "Listen. Your delightful dear girls can stay as long as you need. We've got a great set up here as part of our pilot program, and I am just THRILLED that you are able to participate! Oh, Anna, you wouldn't believe how great this is—we've gotten so much interest from the UW, national child welfare organizations and women's groups, and we've got some of the best early childhood education experts in the city working for us! AND, as soon as you get back in town and are ready for the full treatment, oh, do I have a surprise for you!!" she squeals.

Uh oh. I'm pretty sure I've about had all the surprises I can handle this year.

"Have you ever had Reiki?"

I sit down on the toilet lid, shaking my head in disbelief. "No," I mutter. Colette is completely off her rocker. She's like the Energizer bunny on Red Bull. "Have you ever had a Hydrating Salt treatment? Or a Seaweed Wrap? Yes? No? Oh, it's doesn't matter, you're doing them anyway! I've also got meditation classes, yoga, a nutritionist, a therapist, and a wellness coach lined up for you. I. AM. SO. EXCITED! It's all free for you and built into our program. I just need you to sign a few teensy forms as soon as you get back but that's it! Oh—do you want to talk to the girls?"

Five minutes later, I'm jabbing Patrick in the shoulder blades with my elbows to get him to wake up. He grunts and farts but STILL doesn't move. "Patrick!!" I shout, shaking him and slapping his butt.

No movement.

So I start pulling at the tiny hairs along the back of his neck.

"Unh," he grumbles, swatting at me like I'm an annoying fly buzzing over his head. Finally, he opens his eyes and sits up, leaning his wobbly head against the headboard.

"The kids." I say, "I need to talk to you about the kids!"

"Are they hurt?" he asks, stupidly, squinting up at me, using his hand as a visor to shield the light from the bedside lamp from his eyes.

"No . . ."

"Do you know where they are?"

"Yes."

"So what's the problem?" He slumps back down on the bed and buries his head in an oversized pillow.

"Colette took Lucy and Franny hostage as part of her foundation designed to undermine all working mothers."

"Oh, yeah, yeah . . ." Patrick lifts his head up, slowly, like a turtle. "I read about that in the paper. I didn't know she was so well connected. That's cool we get to participate."

"WHAT?" I ask.

Patrick mumbles something and nods toward the *Washington Post* on the floor.

NIH, Gates Foundation Fund Seattle-Based Non-Profit Focused on Nation's Working Mothers

Programs to include Emergency Back Up Childcare, Counseling Services, Wellness Treatments

Patrick has fallen back asleep, so I give him another thwack. "We NEED to get back to Seattle now so we can rescue the kids!"

He lifts his arm up, looks at his wristwatch and says to me, "No . . . *you* need to get back to Seattle and give your damn presentation. Doesn't your flight leave first thing in the morning?" And then he flops his head back down on the pillow.

In the cab on the way to the airport, I reach down and pull the hard copies out and look down. Four months of work, four months of brainstorms, four months of focus groups, late nights and lost hair now rests in the palms of my hands. All for the promise of our largest client ever.

Find Your Balance

These are the three words emblazoned across the front of the packet. Our slogan. All that effort summed up in three pretty little words. Either they'll love it or they'll hate it. Whatever their take, though, it's certainly new in the anxiety world. For all the women who don't identify with the wind-up-doll metaphor, or the woman curled up in a ball in a corner, Balenxa offers something new, unexpected and totally drug/drool worthy. I picture it now: *Find Your Balance* in the train station. *Find Your Balance* on the side of a bus. *Find Your Balance* in *Self* Magazine. *Find Your Balance* in a 15 second spot at 4:06 right after Ellen does her little shimmy dance and women across America think to themselves: *Why don't I give a shimmy?* Oh yeah, because I'm anxious! And then they'll see our ads, run to their doctor/drug provider and voilà! T. Rx and the Asenzer team will be more filthy stinkin' rich than they are already. And I will have done my job. And we'll all be on more drugs. The End.

But I shouldn't be so cynical. Maybe once we all start feeling a little better, a little more *balanced*, Balenxa could launch just the type of women's revolution we've been looking for. Yeah, that's it: Once all of the over-worked, over-stressed, juggling-way-too-many-balls-in-the-air women discover this new drug via our kick-ass advertising campaign, there's no stopping what women will be able to achieve next. Glass ceiling? Shattered. Equal rights? Women in charge! After all, there are no laws against performance-enhancing drugs in the workplace, cyberspace, playground or classroom.

I brought the master copies marked up with me so I could practice. I am the lead presenter in the pitch and will sell the idea. Slade will merely introduce me and conduct the schmoozing before and afterwards. I look ahead to make sure there aren't any more traffic circles approaching before I attempt to read the script.

"For years our society, and in fact, pharmaceutical companies like yours, have drilled into women's heads that they are sad, that they are lonely; that something's not right and that there's a little pill to help. But they're missing the point. Today's modern woman—the woman you are trying to reach—is a woman who doesn't feel sad or lonely. She feels stretched, she feels hurried; she feels chaotic and out of sorts and she wonders why. All the right pieces are there but she's spinning so fast she can't enjoy any of them. She wants to find her balance."

I've written myself a note to pause here. An old reminder so I don't rush—the Achilles heel of my presentation skills, along with occasional dry mouth. Note to self: Does Asenzer manufacture any dry mouth medication? Google that shit later.

"That's why we're proposing the "blissfully balanced" campaign.

Then I'll cue the music and start the show. Dramatic opening, campaign theme, music and video; our sure-fire trifecta of attention grabbers.

On the plane, with a gin and tonic wobbling ever so slightly cupped in my hand, I read through Maria's paper one more time. About midway through, I have a crazy thought: If I step outside the fact that the research is based on *me*, tilt my head three-quarters to the left and squint my eyes into deep-thinking little slits, I can see this thing in a whole new light. Maria has actually done me—and my Balenxa presentation—a huge favor. I decide to pull out some pertinent bullet points and include them.

Today's modern mother . . .

- Is more focused on what's organic than being organized.
- Does more due diligence on BPA plastics and breast pump reviews on Amazon than hiring a nanny.
- Equates multitasking with multivitamins. More = better.
- Would sooner throw money at a problem than reduce her emotional clutter.
- Wonders why her life is so "chaotic" but refuses to consider the source.
- Tosses back Advil in an attempt to solve indiscriminate thinking – not inflammation.
- Is convinced that drugs are the answer – just hasn't found the right one.

The turbulence is unsettling and the pilot pipes in, telling us we must turn off all electronics and stow our tray tables for the duration of the flight. With nothing to read and no ability to get any work done, I have no choice but to cinch my seat belt and sit tight with my own thoughts.

For two hours.

Which is so much more horrifying—and enlightening—than I ever could have imagined.

All of the self-loathing, all of the negative thoughts, all of the worry, the dread, the anxiety, the guilt, the sense of being overwhelmed, of never doing enough, or never doing it right, or wanting things to be better. I throw it all into the mix and let it slosh back and forth.

I think about all of the awful and ridiculous things I've put up with/faced/endured since going back to work and who is to blame . . . Slade . . . Maria . . . Clare . . . Maria . . . Annika . . . Maria . . . Ash . . . Maria . . . Colette . . . Maria . . . my Mom . . . Maria. The pattern is clear to me now. There is one person—and one person only—who is responsible for the current mess I'm in. And that would be . . .

Me.

A smile slowly emerges across my face.

Why didn't I see this before?

Why did I have to travel 3,000 miles to Washington D.C. and bounce 10,000 feet (give or take) up in the air for me to see the situation for what it is?

All of a sudden the bottom of my seat drops about 500 feet and I feel like I'm on an amusement park ride that I never intended to be on. As I reach for the barf bag in the seat pocket in front of me, I'm overcome with the premonition that this is not going to end well. The plane is going to go down. I grip the armrests, as if to prepare myself for impact. *Nooo*, I pray, *not now*! Just when I figure out the key to the universe and my own internal happiness! Please, God, don't let me be one of those people who dies too young with too much unfinished business. It's too much irony on top of too much irony! My tattered soul and wretched life has a purpose now! I know what I need to do! I know how to make things right! I have a much of a better idea of who I want to become. Please? Pretty please with a cherry top? Bargaining with God has never been my forte so I hope it'll do.

I sit eerily still through the rest of the plane trip, eyes closed, palms pressed together, thinking calm thoughts. I read somewhere that meditating can really help save the soul so I mentally begin chanting the first thing that pops in my head.

Balance.

Balance. Thinking about being balanced through the turbulence.

Balance. So balanced right now I really can't see it another way! I'm like a freak of highly balanced nature, walking on an unsteady tightrope at 10,000 feet in the air.

Balance, balance, balance. A thing of beauty. So fluffy and soft, carrying me up and over all the bumps and hurtles in the air around us.

Balance. The overhead compartment above my head groans and rattles with the latest jolt as the plane shudders in the storm. La la la la! I am so balanced! I hardly noticed that at all. All I can think of are calm and peaceful thoughts.

Like balance. An abundance of balance! And . . . butt holes.

Wait a minute – *what?* I don't know how or why that image just popped into my brain, but I let it stay there, not judging the words, not giving them a label, like "good," or "bad," or "totally inappropriate." Just a little alliteration passing through.

And then, just as I get back to focusing on being balanced, two amazing things happen.

1. I start to feel better. Clear-headed. Refreshed. A little bit happy. Even, dare I say, balanced. The ridiculousness of it all makes me giggle a bit and that, too, makes me feel more in control.
2. The plane lands without incident. The breaks screech and the fuselage shudders as the plane slows to a manageable clip, but otherwise everything— including my own internal universe—is intact.

I let out a sigh of relief and even though I'm not entirely sure why, I'm proud of myself for weathering this storm.

Muffin Top is the first to arrive. It's early evening by the time I get to my mom's house, and I've missed an entire second day of work. I did check in with Slade and the team during my layover in Detroit, but was not able to find a quiet place to talk so I know I missed out on maybe 70 percent of the twisted tongue-lashing Slade was lobbing my way. I apologized profusely but in the middle of my heartfelt confession, a nasal Midwestern voice blasted through the overhead speakers. All I caught Slade say in response was a perfunctory "You don't need to do anything else; it's all ready to go," so I thanked him graciously, assured that everything will go off without a hitch tomorrow.

"Mama! Mama!!! Lucy and Franny skid along the tile floors, landing on the inside of the front door with a delightful thud. From the side glass panels, I can see my mom step up behind them and slowly unlock the door. Franny bounces off the doorframe and lands into my arms as I stumble through the doorway, scattering leaves and pine needles in my wake. The wind is still blowing pretty hard.

Oh, how I've missed them. I look down at my daughters, taking note of how different they look to me. In some ways children are like puppies, I think. They grow and change in a mere matter of days.

But there's something else that I can't quite place my finger on. Lucy's hair is matted down on one side like clumped dog fur or the beginnings of dreadlocks. Franny's head looks like a bell, as if her hair has been stuck inside tightly knit cap or a Jell-O mold. Either that or she's slept in pigtails for three days. That's right, Monday morning, after the holiday party, I put her hair in pigtails. Which means . . . she/they likely has/have not bathed since then.

As I pull my daughters in close, I catch a whiff of what I can only describe as some pretty pungent Baby B.O. It's a sweet and sour mixture of scents, kind of like stale gummy bears and chocolate soaked in urine. I turn my head and cough into my shoulder.

"What did you girls do today?" I ask them, petting their dirty heads.

"We've been eating Gwamma's mookshakes and garwola bawrs!" says Franny with a huge smile. The corners of her mouth are a chalky brown.

"What?" my mother and I ask in unison.

"Yeah," says Franny. "Grandma keeps them in her fridgerwayter."

"I do?" asks my mom, suddenly looking a bit more wide-eyed than her eyelift normally allows.

All four of us step into the kitchen. On the counter are three Slim-Fast shake cans and four half-eaten Special K bars. Ah, well. At least they weren't eating Muffin Top's dog food, which has actually happened before or worse, Grandma's special cookies.

Max is in mismatched snug fitting two-piece cotton jammies, with one dirty sock dangling off his left foot. The way my mom is carrying him, the pajama bottoms are pulled down just enough to reveal that the diaper is on backwards.

If I had left the girls with Colette and allowed her swat team to swoop over to my mom's house and "rescue" Max, I would not be witnessing this scene, I tell myself. The girls would be fluffed up after their junior spa treatments and Max would be properly exfoliated and diapered, drifting off to sleep listening to Beethoven. But instead I did what I thought was best for my children, which was to have my mom rescue them from Colette. I guess I shouldn't be all that surprised that everyone looks and smells like hell. They're alive and happy and unscathed, and I've "kept the family together," such as it is.

"Have the kids already brushed their teeth?" I ask, gathering their things and holding out a fleece coat for Franny to slip her arms into. A seemingly innocuous question that I would ask of anyone—Maria, Patrick, the 13 year-old sitter down the street—during a hand over at 7 p.m.

But my mom snaps. "Not on my watch!" she snaps gleefully. "We were too busy having fun right girls, no time for teeth brushing at Grandma's."

I grab Lucy, Franny and Max, gush over how much I appreciate everything she's done for me and the kids, how she really saved me this week and how I'm so sorry that communication systems broke down, all the while thinking that what my mom needs is a spa day and some Balenxa and I'm mentally trying to figure out how I can set her up. Maybe I'll send her over to Colette.

On my way home, I call Maria. We haven't really spoken since before I left for D.C. Just exchanging of voicemails and cryptic text messages. I don't even *really* want to talk to her now, though I need to. With all that has happened over the last two days (let alone the last four months) someone needs to clear the air. And yup, that someone needs to be me.

As I stare at the wide expanse of the road ahead, it occurs to me, perhaps much too late to save my relationship with Maria, that I've been playing this whole thing wrong from the very start. I'm the boss. She is my *employee*. It's pretty simple. How and why did things get so complicated and out of control? Probably by me not being clear with her about my expectations and her filling in the blanks with her own ideas on what's best for my kids. Rearranging the furniture. Starting to teach at the preschool instead of telling me there was a problem. Having her boyfriend co-nanny with her. Assuming the role of the mother at family dinners with my husband. And of course, writing a Goddamn thesis on how neurotic I've become! And yet, I let this happen. And why? It's not like I'm new to the role of management. Being a parent, delegating tasks to Patrick, organizing activities—my *job*, heck, pretty much everything I do outside of this one thorny relationship is not as strife with conflict and passive-aggressive nuances.

It's going to stop.

I look over my shoulder and see that all three kids are sound asleep so I pull over the car. The last thing I need in my life is to get into an accident because I'm having an intense conversation with my nanny on my cell phone.

Maria picks up on the second ring. "Hi," I say. "We need to talk." My stomach lurches but it's the good kind of nauseous, like that icky feeling you get right before diving into a pool to win the race or open your mouth to ask for a raise. I know that no matter what happens now, I'll feel better after having this conversation.

And I do. It's a good talk. In fact, I realize that this is the perhaps the first time I've really paused to fully listen to her. Hearing myself speak, I sound like a grown-up. My voice is calm, I'm choosing my words carefully and my thoughts aren't scattered all over the dashboard. Maria sounds more mature to me too. Or, has she been the one acting like an adult all along and it's my first time taking a stab at this role?

Either way, I feel as if a huge weight has been lifted. I let my head fall back on the headrest and watch as the trees outside sway back and forth gracefully like ballerinas across the stage, noticing for a few moments how beautiful a windstorm can be. But now it's time to get moving. I sit up straight, readjust my seatbelt and turn on the ignition. It's time to go over the routine for tomorrow, I tell her, but she stops me.

"Nonono, I'm sorry Anna, I think you misunderstood me," she says. "You and I, we're all done now. My paper is finished, and I present my thesis tomorrow. And everything is good for you now, no?"

"Uhhhh . . ." is all I can say. I have just finished thanking her excessively for bringing clarity into my life and helping me move on to a new chapter. I guess I didn't anticipate that the end to this particular chapter would end so abruptly.

"I am just so happy that I was able to help," she continues. I feel like I'm reliving a breakup conversation from my 20s. The one where I was about to call it quits with the lame-ass boyfriend (and had actually taken the time to mentally write a script that wasn't overly hurtful or mean), but then was trumped by him being the first to tell me we were through. Intrinsically, I know that in these situations it's easier to be the breakup-ee rather than the breakup-er, but it still stings. "Oh, Anna, you had some tough things you needed to figure out! It is so hard to be Super Mom, you know? It's messy sometimes. But you are doing it. I always believed in you, you know. Hopefully we can stay in touch. But right now it's time for me to say adios."

A-d-i-o-s?

"But—but-but-but—I owe you money!" I stammer, thinking of the only thing at this point I can use as leverage to lure her back. The presentation is tomorrow morning.

"Nononono, Anna, you don't owe me anything. We're fine. I know you're so busy, so you may not have checked your bank statements in awhile, but I didn't cash many of those checks, you know."

My eyes grow wide. "You didn't?" She's right; I have no idea what's going on with our accounts.

"As part of my internship with you I could only accept a certain salary. It was in the paperwork I gave you."

Paperwork? Oh right, the paperwork that I signed but never read.

"The $24 per hour was just part of my research," she explains, as if she is merely recapping old information, "to see how much stressed out moms would be willing to pay."

I guffaw loudly into the phone. So loudly that I've woken up at least two of the kids, and now I can't stop laughing.

Maria is laughing too. "There was another mom who was part of our study who thought she was paying $35 an hour!" she snorts. "She was really desperate, you know?"

I laugh for a few more moments and then force myself to pull it together. "Okay, listen," I sigh. "Can you come over tomorrow and say goodbye to the kids? I feel like we should do that, you know, to have some closure." One last desperate attempt to lure her back, and could she maybe drag out those goodbyes long enough for me to present to T. Rx downtown?

Lucy pipes in from the backseat. "Are you talking to Maria, Mommy?"

I turn around to face her. Her cheeks are rosy, and I detect an air of wisdom and clarity in the expression on her face that is reflected back in the rain streaked window in the dark of night. "Yes, sweetheart, I'll be off in just a minute. You'll see Maria very soon."

"No . . ." says Lucy, her voice trailing off as if she already knows something I don't. "But can you tell her bye bye and thank you?"

"We've already said our bittersweet goodbyes, Anna," Maria interjects as the rain and wind slaps against the side of the car. "It's time for me to go now. I love you and your *familia* so much."

Click.

And then she's gone.

Tears stream down my face as I start up the car to drive home, and I'm not sure if this is a residual effect from my laughing fit, relief over this relationship that I knew needed to end finally being over, or if I'm crying in advance over not having any childcare tomorrow. I turn on the windshield wipers on high. It's really coming down now.

"Mama?" Franny taps a pudgy finger on my shoulder from her perch in the middle car seat as we pass a row of houses lit up with twinkling white lights. The trees sway and the strands of lights wrapped around the long branches bob up and down above us.

"Yes, Dear?"

"Mawyea said something weyud today. She said she was only staywing with us until the wind changed. What does that mean?"

Twenty

As I lug my suitcase up the basement stairs with one arm and carry a snuggly Max nuzzled in my shoulder in the other, I detect that something is off about the scene that awaits us. There's a smell. It engages with my nostrils in a way that reminds me of an earlier era, like that brief time span after college and roommates but before marriage and kids when I could always count on coming home to a clean home. I inhale deeply and turn on the lights in the kitchen, and nearly lose my hold on Max once my eyes fully absorb what my nose has already detected. Everything is gleaming and spotless. I reach for Lucy and Franny's sweet little hands as we survey what has been done: the appliances and furniture have all been rearranged—back to their original placements. The construction paper is off the coffee table and the living room no longer looks like a makeshift preschool space. The house is immaculate. It's as if a *feng shui* consultant and a HGTV decorating team descended with furniture dollies and color wheels in hand, plumped up the pillows and smudged the entire house with good energy. I can't believe my eyes. The house is a better version of itself, like a Pinterest board filled with comfortable and elegant shabby chic (with less emphasis on shabby) interior design images that I could stare at for hours.

Lucy leads me toward a note on the kitchen counter topped with a wrapped gift from GlassyBaby and a spray bottle of lavender water.

Dear Anna,

Thank you so much for letting me spend time with your familia. I love you all sooooo much! Here are some things I thought you might like. A GlassyBaby for when you need a few moments of serenity, hope and healing. And the lavender water smells nice, no? I found out about it in one of those funny novels I saw on your bookshelf. It was good info for my research! Jajajajajaja!

I close my eyes and let out a very long sigh.

In bed, I stare at the ceiling for a few minutes, thinking about yesterday, today and tomorrow. The pitch is tomorrow morning at 10 a.m. T. Rx and the Asenzer execs are probably snug in their Heavenly Beds, channel surfing and mentally stroking their dicks as they watch all the other national pharmaceutical advertising campaigns, wondering if ours is going to blow the competition out of the water.

And yet again . . . I have no childcare.

But then it hits me: I'll show up at the Global Citizens Academy first thing in the morning and sweet talk Annika into keeping Max. So many families have withdrawn in the past few weeks; my kids are practically the only ones left. And since Annika had no problem accepting my doubling up of tuition payments, I feel justified in asking her to handle one extra child. I'll have to take the rest of the day off after the pitch, but that's okay. I'll know the status of my future by noon either way. If T. Rx and his team feel blissfully balanced after my presentation, everyone at YOWZ will be slurping down a celebratory liquid lunch. If not, well . . . I'll just hang a proud SAHM placard around my neck, sign onto Medium as I'm cleaning out my desk and start railing against the pharmaceutical industry by afternoon.

When I arrive at the preschool the following morning, I notice that the signage has been removed from the door, but the lights are on inside, so I knock and wait, pressing my ear to the door to see if I can hear any singing.

Ash, surprisingly, comes to the door. He's wearing a cobalt blue work suit with a tool belt around his waist that makes him look like one of the Imagination Movers. "Hi!" I say, cheerfully, ushering the kids through the entryway, but he stops me, inching us back out into the corridor.

"You didn't hear?" he says, sticking his neck out to make sure the hallway is clear. Yoga class is in session; we can hear the faint chanting of "ohhmmmmm" a few doors down.

My eyes flash down the hall and stop on a quote, stenciled midway on the wall:

"Everything happens for a reason. People change so that you can learn to let go, things go wrong so that you appreciate them when they're right, you believe lies so you eventually learn to trust no one but yourself, and sometimes good things fall apart so better things can fall together."

—Marilyn Monroe

An amateur mural-style painting of Marilyn in yoga pants and a jog bra doing a downward dog frames the quote on the wall. I think to myself . . . is this oh so wrong . . . or . . . oh so right?

I shake my head, trying to absorb the truth and absurdity of it all.

Ash lowers his voice. "I left you a message. Anyway, Annika—" Ash looks down at Lucy and Franny and pauses, as if to re-sort his words to kid-appropriate format. "Basically, the Global Ciz is no longer. Colette's foundation is taking over the facility, and I'm getting it ready for her. We're closed here for a bit, but Colette does have a new temporary set up in her carriage house. That's where the rest of the kids are right now. It's pretty sweet if you ask me."

I weigh my options: Colette's *suite* child care, hiding out at the yoga studio, going home and taking ill under the covers, or hauling the kids with me on a field trip downtown so they can watch Mommy present the Balenxa campaign from outside the fish bowl. I hug Max to my chest and look down at my watch: I still have precisely 65 minutes to figure this out.

"What happened to Miss Annika?" Lucy asks just before we turn to leave.

"She's on a plane to NeverNeverLand—I mean—the Netherlands," Ash says with a wink and a slight tapping of his heels. And then he leans in and murmurs excitedly in my ear: "Colette and her genius spy cams. She had enough evidence to send the Dutchess to jail but got her to hand over the assets—I mean, debts—and plopped her on a plane instead." The girls are still looking up at Ash quizzically so he adds for their benefit: "There were some problems with her aura. It needed some fixing so she had to go home for a while. That's all."

Lucy and Franny seem more than satisfied with this explanation.

Sandi is sitting at the front desk when I open the doors to the CCDC. Holiday music and cut out paper snowflakes fill the lobby. Sandi is wearing a Christmas sweater with a wreath on it and multi colored drop earrings in the shape of outdoor lights sway from her earlobes. "Oh hi, Anna, what a surprise!" The forced enthusiasm of her greeting sets me back a bit, but I am undeterred. Neither one of us have forgotten the "incident" that landed the CCDC on the evening news and me into YouTube stardom.

"Jeannette told you I was coming, right?" I smile, ducking under a low hanging snowflake. I *did* call ahead and arrange this. Actually, "beg for" might be a more accurate description.

"Well . . . no, I mean oh, yes, there's a note here I see," she fumbles, leafing through the papers on her desk. "What can we do for you today?" She looks at me quizzically from under her over plucked eyebrows.

So I tell her the situation.

"Oh, we'd be delighted to help . . . if we can," she says, noncommittally, slowly flipping through a few papers before tapping away on her computer. I glance at my watch. Nine twenty-three. The clients will be here in just a few minutes. My heart thuds against the wall of my chest like an anxious knock at the door.

Finally she looks up. "Good news," she says with a pink frosted grin.

Phew.

"I have room for Lucy and Franny in the PreK room. It'll be $215 per child per day, plus a $50 registration and activity fee for each of them," she continues, getting up to retrieve some papers from the printer stationed behind her desk. Sandi's stark white underpants are showing through her thin black leggings.

"And . . . Max?" I ask.

"Sorry," she says. "I don't have any spots available in the infant rooms. Would you like me to put you on the waitlist?"

My pulse quickens and a stab of pain hits my chest as if I'd been wearing my bra backwards and some obnoxious kid has just snapped it like a slingshot. "I really just need a place I can leave them for a few hours. I have this huge meeting and—"

"Oh, I understand," Sandi replies with a slick grin. She shakes her head at me and her earrings sway back and forth like tiny porch swings. "That's why I always encourage parents to plan ahead. Good, safe, consistent childcare is hard to come by in this city, so if you find a solution that is a good one, I usually advise parents to hang onto that. Kids need consistency. A routine."

Had I not undergone my "transformative" and "enlightening" experience 16 hours ago, Sandi would likely be dialing the paramedics right about now, witness to me writhing on the floor in agony. Instead, I calmly ask her if she has any back up options. She puts a finger to her lips for a moment and then pulls out a card from the mess on her desk and hands it to me. "Here," she says, holding it towards me like a stick of bland sugarless gum, "I don't know who these people are, but maybe they can help."

In a Pinch?
Merry Poppins Emergency Childcare Services to the Rescue!
I call the 1-800 number. Colette answers the phone.

As I make my way to the elevator bank, I take a few moments to mentally brush off any lingering ill will that may have stuck to my consciousness in the last half hour. *Bad juju be gone!* (One more mental note: add that one to my ongoing list of clever slogans for product lines aimed at the formerly stressed out/newly focused and calm mom demographic). I survey my outfit. No suit this time—instead I'm wearing a chic wool pencil skirt with a funky herringbone pattern, an emerald green silk blouse, dark tights and killer patent heels. The Fashion Police could not have picked out a more flattering ensemble for me. It's bold. It says, "I'm confident, creative and I'm doing things my own way (and you're going to like it!)" Even better -- the high-waist cut of the skirt means there's no need for any vice-grip body shaper business. My hair is up, showing off the elegant-yet-artsy chandelier earrings that graze exact spot on my neck where my kids like to snuggle.

I step into the conference room at 9:49 a.m. The room is set up, ready to go. Slade's assistant, Kendall, is at the head of the table, testing the A/V equipment. When she sees me she rolls her eyes, passing on a message from Slade to me, no doubt.

The Asenzer executives are mingling in the back of the room, talking amongst themselves. I throw my shoulders back and prance to the other side of the room, vigorously shaking everyone's hands with a two handed shake like I'm Hillary Clinton on the campaign trail. Jen from product knowledge introduces herself to me. I clasp her hand and smile. She is a refreshing sight from the handful of middle-aged men in dark suits covering the rest of the room. Then I greet T. Rx, put a hand on his shoulder and lean down to plant a kiss on his cheek. I feel good about this, it's the holidays, I'm ready to go and I'm even having warm thoughts towards T. Rx.

Slade enters the room, smelling of the latest designer cologne. "Can I get anyone coffees? Waters? Meds?" There are a few chuckles as people call out their orders.

"I'll take a pill," I turn around and flash Slade a smile. He glares at me for a moment, and then the corners of his mouth turn up in an evil little smirk.

As Slade and Kendall pass out the coffees and waters, I take my position at the head of the table and fire up the presentation. Already I can tell something is off. The slides are all in the wrong order and someone has inserted a video clip that appears to be three to four minutes long. I've had NO time to review any of this.

Fuck.

But then I remember: I'm a different person now. Anna Moore version 2.0 doesn't freak out any more! I don't let outside events control my feelings. I control my feelings. I reviewed all of the new product specifications on the plane last night. Everything is going to be fine, fine, fine. All I have to do is walk these surfer boys from California through a couple of slides.

I take a deep breath.

Balance.

A slight tingle starts at my fingertips and makes its way to the crown of my head where it spreads down to my ears, as if someone has just cracked an egg on top of my head. I pretend that it's just a bit of imaginary pixie dust being sprinkled my way for good luck.

But now I have to pee. It comes on suddenly, like when you enter a steaming hot bath and there's a sudden change in blood pressure and you just end up relieving your bladder right then and there because who would ever know? Except *everyone* would know if I peed my tights right now, so I dig my patent heels into the carpet and look up at the overhead screen. Damn it. Why did I order that double tall macchiato while I was waiting for Colette's emergency childcare "Merry Minivan" to swoop up the kids?

As soon as I hit the play button on the opening video montage, I know I've been set up. I look around the room. T. Rx is stroking his chin, Slade is running his tongue underneath his lips, and Jen is giving me a wide smile. There's a flash of yellow behind me. I fight the urge to turn around and see who is lurking behind the fish bowl and puff my chest out for added authority instead. I squeeze a few Kegels too, hoping the pee can stay where it needs to be. I do the only thing that I think stands a chance at saving this presentation, which is to adopt a stoic yet cheerful expression that says: "All of the views and opinions expressed in the following presentation reflect not only my own personal compass, but the whole philosophy of our entire organization." I'm totally, *absofreakinfragilisticlootely* on board with whatever happens next.

And then the familiar beat of "My Daycare is a Shitbox" fills the room.

The first few seconds of the video montage are of me, of course, and I fight the urge to cover my face and hide under the table. Just keep smiling, I tell myself. Smile, smile, smile. Keep those tits up. Laugh with an air of mature nonchalance like you are really enjoying this. This is *your* show. A few of the execs glance my way for a few beats to gauge my reaction but then tilt their heads back up towards the screen once they see my sparkling white super wide smile. I look over at Slade, and he gives me a firm thumbs up. It's working. Everyone's smiling and chuckling now. This is good; they're getting relaxed. I start snapping my fingers and swaying back and forth to the beat, adopting a sort of makeshift line dance. If nothing else, it distracts me from my overwhelming need to piss.

Just when I think the humiliation is over, Clare's face takes over the screen. He looks maniacal, but also like he's playing with the audience. His hair is a different color too. This must have been shot recently. Now Slade and Clare are both on screen, faces nudged together like a happy May-December couple. They're singing a sort of catchy little rap song.

Who's crazy?

You, girl!

Who's crazy?

You know it, girl!

Who's crazy?

You go, girl!

The next three minutes contain videos that could have only come from one source: SitterSpy. Anna Moore, in her bathrobe, standing in her disaster of a kitchen, reminding Maria yet again not to microwave the breast milk. Then there's Anna, again, downing a handful of Advil. Anna, still in her work clothes, opening a bottle of wine with her car keys. Anna guzzling coffee straight from the pot. Anna rushing to the TV screen in the kitchen every time a drug ad airs and then scribbling down notes on the back of preschool art projects. Anna's voice edited with choice phrases like "I'm about to lose it!" and "This is nuts!" and "Are you insane?" The whole time, Gnarls Barkley's voice sings through the background of the presentation, then Willie Nelson, then Patsy Cline. *You must be craaazay . . . crayyyzhee . . . craaashzay . . .*

When Taylor Swift starts in, I can't take it any longer.

"You'll have to excuse me," I say, calmly, and then as soon as I'm out of eyeshot of the fishbowl, I sprint down towards the women's room.

"Ahhhhhhh," I groan, as soon as my butt lands on the toilet seat. It's one of those huge, lawn-hose style pees that keeps going, and going and going . . . .

Finally I flush, yank up my tights and open the restroom door. Jen is standing by the sink with an expression on her face that I cannot place.

I'm about to open my mouth and say something, but Jen shushes me. As I lean into the sink to wash my hands, she takes a step closer.

"Here. Do you want to try something?" I raise my eyebrows and watch as Jen roots around in her purse and checks under the bathroom stalls for feet at the same time. A moment later she's holding out a prescription bottle in her hand, only it isn't an ordinary looking prescription bottle. It's shorter and fatter and the childproof cap has a type of locking mechanism that doubles as a spoon-like dispenser— almost like one of those plastic scoops you'd use in the bulk food section or at the candy shop but cuter and way cooler. I stand there, not saying yes or no but staring curiously at this contraption, wondering what it is and wondering what it contains.

The next thing I know, Jen is spinning the top like a padlock. After a few spins it makes a satisfying click and the lid opens with a slight flick of her wrist. A tinkling of piano music begins playing from a small electronic chip inside the lid. And the smell, oh my God, it's the smell of heaven! "What is it?" is all I can think to say. I'm mesmerized, enchanted and curious all at once.

"Here," she offers, using the scoop to lift one pill, which she daintily places in the palm of my hand. It's beautiful. A translucent chestnut-brown sphere stamped with an eggshell blue B. I look inside the vial and see that they're all different colors. Some of them are even two-tone, with surprising and enticing pops of color. Now I'm giddy and salivating like a kid in a candy factory. "This is *it*," Jen beams. "You did this! You deserve this! Isn't it amazing?"

"But-but—" I stammer. I have a million questions for Jen. Mainly, is this the real deal? Is *this* Balenxa? I thought she couldn't share any details on the drug until . . . until the trials and testing were 100% complete. Which might be the case now. And if this is *it*, how could I be responsible for this beautiful product in front of me—meaning the package and the design, when "this" was never part of the scope of work? All we were ever supposed to focus on was just the marketing and advertising campaign.

"No time to talk, you gotta get back to the meeting," she explains. "Just take it. On the tip of your tongue. Like this. It's completely safe, and will make you feel better." Jen scoops out another pill for herself— this one's pink and white—and pops it in her mouth. "Mmmmmm" she says, "See? Better already. So clear-headed and balanced." And then she gives me another wink and a playful nudge from her hip as we breeze through bathroom door.

As I unveil Balenxa's national marketing campaign, Jen smiles at me from the back of the conference room like a coach or an old friend. My body begins to tingle and feel energized; I'm almost euphoric. I look around the room full of men literally gazing adoringly at me. Including Slade. Wow. Could this be the effect of whatever illicit drug Jen just slipped me in the women's room? I'm feeling the twinge of giddiness but the pangs of guilt as well. I'm sure this is highly illegal. And yet, I reason, now at the very least I'm having the opportunity to experience the product for myself. I feel amazing. I take a drink of water before moving to the next slide, noting to myself that whatever drug I have just ingested does not produce dry mouth. I'm just sipping water because it's an effective way to pause, and also because my bladder now has plenty of room.

I end with the final two slides, letting the brand messaging linger and fully sink in for my captive audience.

"And when it's time for a cure-all remedy, it's time for Balenxa," I conclude, feeling the carpet fibers beneath my heels ground me more securely than ever before.

Anxiety. Be Gone.

Blissfully Balanced™

I get a standing ovation. The thunder of hands clapping makes me feel like I've just given the best performance of my life. I stand there, slightly dumbfounded but also confidant and pleased with myself. Good vibes radiate from my *bauudy* like a rainbow of colors with a pot of gold at the end. It's a few more moments before T. Rx commands everyone to sit down, including me, while he takes the floor.

With his hands clasped together, he nods his head a few times and clears his throat before speaking. "I would just like to say . . ." he pronounces, pausing to give me and Slade a slight bow of his head, "that we are so impressed by how tapped into the target market you are. Not only have you and your team done an amazing job of putting a stupendous campaign together, but you, Anna, you were willing to go above and beyond by going undercover to do your research, which is extremely commendable." T. Rx pauses here, letting his colleagues fill the silence with quiet applause and a few "oh yeahs." I feel my face getting flush, but I just keep smiling. I just can't help it. "We have the utmost respect for you," he continues, rolling his heels on the floor. "Like the trailblazers Gloria Steinem and Barbara Ehrenreich before you, the on-the-ground, from-the-trenches research you did will forever change the lives of millions of overwhelmed and anxious women." T. Rx pauses again here, and I note that he's really good at the whole pausing thing. I should do more of that, I think to myself. More pauses. Good idea. "What I mean to say is," T. Rx continues, "you really nailed it in your role as the stressed out modern mom. Blissfully balanced. Ha! It's fucking brilliant."

I'm so caught up in the second round of applause and confusion and crazy-good feelings being bestowed on my aura that I almost miss it when Clare walks in, wearing neon yellow pants and black shirt. His hair is blond now—frosted tips with dark roots. He vigorously shakes everyone's hands, taking full credit for the video montage and the first phase of our market research. Clare glances my way in between handshakes. We don't exchange words exactly, but the communication that passes between us is – well -- what can I say. It's like we're both in on the same joke.

Just then something outside the window catches my eye. It's a glorious, crisp, post-storm winter day in Seattle. The sun is out, a rarity this time of year, and the view from the 56th floor is magnificent. The snow-capped Olympic mountains, the gleaming blue water of Puget Sound; Bayview Hospital sitting proudly on top of the hill. Seagulls float like gliders in the gentle wind. I turn around and scan the room. Slade is schmoozing it up with T. Rx and the Asenzer entourage. Clare and Kendall flank him, taking follow-up notes like cub reporters. Jen is on her phone. I walk closer to the window.

And that's when I see her.

Maria.

Psychedelic bird umbrella in one hand and her enormous backpack in the other, she's floating past our building, waving at me and clicking her teeth. She's mouthing something. I can't make it out, though if I were to make an educated guess, I'd wager what she's trying to communicate to me is *jajajajajajajajajajajajajajajajaja*.

I'm hallucinating. Oh my God, I'm completely out of my tree. What's wrong with me? I feel the pangs of a panic attack coming on, and I turn around to grab someone, something, anything before I scream and point out the window. And then it hits me. There's no reason to panic! I'm fine. The kids are fine. The marriage is fine. The career is fine. Even the childcare is fine. All of it, fine. If Maria wants to fly her umbrella outside . . . .

My heart rate slows, and I look outside again.

She's gone.

Jen follows me to the bathroom. I've just given her that look that says, "We need to talk."

As soon as the door closes behind us, I feel safe to talk. "Thank you," I say, giving her shoulder a squeeze. "That pill you gave me, was that Balenxa?" I whisper.

Jen smiles and opens up her purse once more, handing over the entire bottle. Oh my. *More* drugs for Ms. Moore? Aside from my brief hallucination, I think I might be smitten and possibly addicted already.

"You signed an NDA and a non-compete, right?" Jen looks up at me from under her glasses.

"Yes, of course," I respond. We do that with all of our clients, I want to remind her, plus, what am I going to do, go mix up some Balenxa in my kitchen and sell it, lemonade stand-style out on the street?

Jen kicks open the three stalls in the bathroom with the flick of her heels to ensure that we're the only ones in the room. "Just checking," she says.

"So . . ." I venture, staring at the bottle in my hand, wondering when she's going to get to the point about dosages and side effects and what else I need to know so that I can keep feeling this good for the rest of eternity.

Jen pulls me close and whispers in my ear. "It's just sugar," she murmurs.

"It's just WHAT?" I shriek.

Jen rushes to the door and presses her body against it, ensuring that nobody walks in.

"Shhhhhh," she hisses in a loud whisper, "YOU CAN'T TELL ANYONE."

My mouth drops open, but no words come out.

The rest of Jen's explanation doesn't make any sense to me – at least until she gets to the part about the extensive clinical trials and the millions they spent on testing one drug combination, and then another, and another, all the while comparing it to the placebo results, which basically means that women in the target audience—defined by mild (not major) symptoms like stress and occasional anxiety—the placebo always worked better than whatever drug combination they were working on. In other words, it was the sugar pill that did the trick.

"See, Anna, isn't it great, look what you've done!"

I still don't know if I should believe her. "What about the prescription?" I ask. If it's just candy . . .?"

"Don't say candy. It's not candy. It's a fine grade of pure cane sugar sourced directly from Hawaii. Local. 100 percent American. They're thrilled you know, because they've lost so much business to the corn syrup farmers and synthetic sweeteners!"

I'm still not fully comprehending. All that work . . . all that stress . . . all those late nights . . . for a spoonful of sugar?

"And as for the prescription," Jen adds, "you and I both know that people will do practically anything to land a good prescription drug. It's value add. It's vanity. It's the elusiveness. It's the brand identity! I learned all of that from *you*." Jen gives me a final nudge in the ribs before we exit the bathroom.

Just before the elevator doors close, Jen hits the stop button. "Oh, almost forgot," she grins, fishing in her purse. "Here. I know you'd asked for the side effects so that you could begin putting the print and TV ads together. There aren't many."

Balenxa.

Side effects may include sweetness of breath, a tingling of the tongue, increased energy, muscle relaxation, giddiness or euphoria. Some patients have been known to experience appetite suppression, or increased appetite. Children under the age of 18 should not take Balenxa because hyperactivity is known to occur. Do not take Balenxa if you are diabetic. As always, talk to your doctor about other medications you are taking and see if Balenxa is right for you.

Epilogue

"Breast kiss."

"Huh?" I open my eyes and grimace at a much-too-bright sliver of sun sneaking through the blind and directly into my eyes. I squeeze them shut again quickly, but I am awake enough to suddenly have that panicky feeling of not knowing what time it is.

"I unt Breastkiss." Max's porcelain skinned, cherubic round face is inches from my own.

"I don't understand," I say groggily, reaching over to stroke his wispy brown hair, my other arm draped across my chest.

"He wants *breakfast*, Mommy." Franny, my speech impediment-free, four year-old translator has just entered the bedroom. It's amazing what a few months of speech therapy can do for a child.

I lift my head and look over at the clock: 7:45. Perfect. Thanks to my new schedule, I no longer need an alarm clock; the kids do a good enough job. I dislodge myself, limb by limb from the dam of pillows I've built and I lift my arms up above my head, grasping my hands together, willing my body to waken. I pull myself to sitting and slide my feet out of bed. I land on something soft and fluffy.

Something loud.

Tiny squeals of laughter fill the room as Lucy and Franny get up and gallop around the room underneath my red bathrobe like a dragon in a Chinese New Year parade. I reach over and start tickling Lucy under her armpits. She yelps and falls to the floor, giggling with delight. She's so big now that it feels almost like I'm groping an adult person so I back off just a bit. Max catapults himself into the pile, followed by Franny. I start grabbing for body parts and tickling whatever I can. The breathless squeals are intoxicating and I savor the moment.

"Okay, my little *muchachos*, Mommy has to get ready for work now," I say, untangling my robe from the floor and slipping my arms through the sleeves.

"But Mommy, you don't go to work anymore," hiccups Franny, her hair standing on end from all the static in the room.

"I don't go to an office sweetie, but I still have *work*," I say, opening up the doors to my closet and peering inside.

"She works at Starbucks now, Franny," Lucy explains in a motherly tone to her sister. I catch her bossy expression in the mirror behind my closet door, and it reminds me of someone I used to know.

"I don't work at Starbucks honey, I go to Starbucks to work sometimes, but I don't actually *work* there . . . I just work *there*. Oh, forget it. It doesn't matter. Okay, girls, you need to get dressed for school. I'll meet you downstairs for breakfast.

I stare at the contents of my closet. Nothing in my career to date could have prepared me for such a dilemma on how I'm supposed to dress for today. Skirt and top? Too dressy. Dress and boots? Too funky. I got rid of the suits a long time ago; now I spend most of my days in mom jeans or workout wear. And what am I dressing for again exactly? Is this a business meeting or a coffee date or a play date?

"Hmmm tink tink tink!" Max verbalizes the conundrum running through my head. He looks equally as concerned as he furrows his brow and taps his head for an answer.

Wondering how I got here? Well, it didn't take long after the pitch for me to run home and draft my resignation letter.

My first attempt:

Dear YOWZ,

You suck. I quit.

Sincerely (not)
Anna Moore.

I was so disappointed with my complete lack of originality that I couldn't bring myself to deliver this sad rehash to Slade.

My second attempt at a resignation letter: A video monologue rant, listing all of the reasons why Balenxa will most certainly fail and YOWZ will take the fall. But after multiple retakes and editing the thing for more than an hour, I realized that this too, was sad, unoriginal and highly self-incriminating. I would need some genius sound mixing and effective wipes for this to even pass the realm of acceptability.

The third and final attempt is so boring and professional it's not even worth printing here. I skipped the tirade and the sarcasm. Rather, I simply wrote that I would be resigning my position as Creative Director because my husband had accepted a job in Washington D.C., and we would be moving across the country.

And here we are.

And . . . I'm not exactly sure what I'm doing. Well, I do, sort of. I'm my own boss, for one. Two, I get to do whatever the hell I want. And three, all I do at work is laugh. And I still get to put my skills to good use.

It started out as a joke, of course. I really did start railing against the pharmaceutical industry the afternoon after the presentation, but I thought it was way too subversive for anyone to notice. Patrick and I made an alcohol-fueled video to the tune of Ice, Ice, Baby. Dressed as a rap version of T. Rx., Patrick put his beatboxing skills to work as I sang, Pills, Pills Baby. We sent it to a few friends as a joke, giggling through lyrics that list side effects, but promised sweet, sweet reward, just for popping a few pills

Yo, I don't know,

Down your throat, you just may glow

See a moonbeam, you think you're losing your handle

Tossing them back like that champ Brandi Glanville

You would have thought I learned my lesson following the success of *My Daycare is a Shitbox*, but who knew I would strike gold twice. People started sharing the video like crazy. Only this time it wasn't embarrassing. I wasn't worried about what the Seattle moms or people at YOWZ would think of me, and it was cool at Patrick's job to be known as the star of *Pill, Pill Baby*. The next thing I knew, women started reaching out to me with requests to produce funny viral videos. Progressive DC lobbying firms reached out to me to write songs about climate change, family medical leave and same sex marriage rights. Seeing humor as key to getting people to connect on issues now that Jon Stewart was off the air, soon I was spending my time doing two of my favorite things – trolling 80's music sites for great songs and writing funny jingles. My mom was right in the end -- my talent for rhyming did prove to be essential to my career.

And Patrick and I are better now. We have a new daily routine that I call "pill talk." Kind of like pillow talk but with out the -ow. See, I still take a few vitamins (nothing crazy, just the basics), but I do it after dinner instead of first thing in the morning. I found it to be easier on the stomach, and it keeps me from pouring myself a second glass of wine if I'm thinking healthy thoughts. Patrick does the dishes while I make myself a cup of herbal tea, and then we both sit down at the kitchen table for ice cream (him) and supplements (me). It's hardly any time at all, maybe five minutes, or ten, but never longer than 20. How is it possible that a relationship can change that much for the better with such a simple ritual? And why have I stopped being so neurotic all the time? These are the questions I pose to the universe that I am still trying to figure out.

But now, my biggest dilemma is what to wear. Colette is in town for a meeting with her growing nonprofit and wants to meet for coffee. She has some money from partnering with some heavy hitting foundations and is thinking she could have a few videos to win people over to her cause. Colette's thinking is: if government programs can help upper and middle class (she's broadened her reach) moms and kids early, issues like childhood obesity and mothers being forced out of the workforce due to high childcare costs can basically be eliminated. She's on the speaking circuit and with her new bulletproof Callista Gingrich-style hairdo. She's been a huge hit in D.C.

Colette has her kids in tow and wanted to know if it was okay if she brought them to the meeting. Of all people! Of course I told her it was okay. Who am I, the mom who lets all her messy quirks hang out online, to be the one who claims it's not professional to tote your kids to a quasi business meeting with another mom at Starbucks. In fact, Colette was the one who specifically told me to bring a kid or two as part of her on-the-ground testing on real life scenarios for self-employed working parents. She's talking to Howard Schultz, too, about offering better play areas in select stores, staffed by baristas who also want to gain valuable early childhood education experience.

Speaking of early childhood education. It took some time before I was able to reestablish contact with Maria. It was she who insisted on a "cooling off" period and claimed that I "needed some space." Silly me to think that she would be the one who needed some space, seeing as though she *might* have been spotted sailing off into the distance above the skyscrapers in downtown Seattle! But whatever. She was right. Distance in our relationship was a great thing. She had some time to enjoy the perks of graduation, travel, and then look for employment in her field long enough to discover that the job market still sucks.

So now she's working for me. Kind of. She choreographs the more complicated video skits we're producing. She really has a knack for that, as well as a great Shakira-like thrust of her hips. She's not working too much though so she has time for planning her wedding to Ash. They both stopped through D.C. on their way back from a European vacation not that long ago. I'm not really sure why—perhaps out of the goodness of their hearts, they paid a visit to Annika in a town outside of Brussels, reporting back to me that she's up to her old tricks; telling everyone that she'll be back in Seattle in no time to open up a brand new school: The Global Peace Academy. I'll be sure to tell all my friends to be the lookout for that one. Or not.

We bought a row house in D.C. with a carriage house in back that was remodeled into an apartment. Previously rented by college kids, we weren't really sure what to do with the space, but as soon as my mom came to visit and laid her eyes on it, she decided she was moving. It had everything she needed: brightly colored walls, vintage fixtures, grandkids next door, and the best museums in the world within a four-mile radius. And medical marijuana is legal in DC now so she's got everything she needs. She's in heaven. She's more than happy to watch Max all morning while I work, we have lunch together and then, by the time I pick up the girls from school, Max is napping and I've gotten in a solid five hours of hilarity.

Clare was hired within a half hour of my resignation letter and took back his old post as Creative Director. I'm actually really happy for him. I hear that he and Slade are tight in a dysfunctional yet highly collaborative way, kind of like the Seattle version of Michael Scott and Dwight Shrute. Somehow it works. Even Lauren doesn't complain. She tells me that work is really interesting and that some clients have even signed on just to see the show tunes-style presentation antics that are now de rigueur for the agency. Rainn Wilson is even doing some ad spots via our agency for select accounts.

Balenxa, of course, is the hottest sensation to hit the over the counter drug market. I see moms all over town sporting the little pill bottles like the must-have accessory. No more prescription drug vials stuck behind medicine cabinets. No more murmurs about who's on drugs and who isn't. The stigma is completely gone! Of course I haven't said anything. Why bother? Especially when everyone looks so happy. It really has become the panacea for stressed-out moms. I have to give Jen a lot of credit. The packaging has now expanded to include customized pill colors, customized mp3 "moods" (kind of like ring tones) and other accessories like carabiners to clip Balenxa on the strap of a handbag, or cute carrying cases to hide personally-identifying information. With all of the accoutrements—and because Balenxa offers an "experience" beyond what any other ordinary pill that is simply popped down the back of the throat can offer—this is a drug that does what it's supposed to because it forces its users to slow down. It's not something you can just do on the fly. The pill won't even be released into your palm until you sit down and listen to five minutes of calming instrumental music, waves crashing on the beach, monks chanting, whatever your pleasure. Don't even get me started on what this has done for the music industry.

As I push open the glass doors to Starbucks with Max beside me, wearing my skinny jeans, a tunic, and wedge heels, I think to myself: It's no longer about the glass ceiling. That was shattered years ago. Now it's about the choices we face and sometimes about the risks that seem too frightening to take.

I'm no longer afraid. I always had the chance to redefine the rules and shape a new role for myself, I know that now. And it's a realization I can now appreciate. For some reason, I just couldn't see it before.

A new attitude kind of helps too. Instead of whining about what I don't have, or who's doing what, I'm more focused on the things I can actually control and the things I actually care about. Perhaps most importantly, I'm having fun again. Life is interesting that way, you know? Besides, everyone knows laughter is the best medicine.

End

Acknowledgments

I want to thank Allison for making this happen. Thank you also to MaryAnn for her amazing editing skills and Andrea for always being available for ideas and feedback. And I also want to thank Sheila and Peaks Island for helping me get to the finish line. And finally to my mom for sharing her love of books and great writing with me.

About the Author

Amanda Orr lives in Washington, DC with her husband and two children. She is a graduate of Smith College. A Spoonful of Sugar is her first book.

Facebook www.facebook.com/spoonfulofsugaramandaorr
Twitter @spoonfulasugar